BORN TO BE MAGIC

BORN TO BE MAGIC

JESSICA HOPKINS

Natural Ten Media

LISTEN TO THE OFFICIAL BORN
TO BE MAGIC PLAYLIST ON
SPOTIFY

*for my mom, who gave me the love of stories, and my dad, who has
always supported mine*

ONE

Do you have to pass a psych eval to join the circus? If so, I'd probably fail it.

Maybe I could go back to school, finish my degree. Or I'm pretty good with cars, I could be a mechanic. Some people think about this stuff when they've just graduated college, when they're stuck in a dead-end job, or maybe as part of a mid-life crisis.

Me? I generally think it when I'm getting shot at.

Debris rained down again and I threw up an arm to protect my eyes. Plaster dust filled the air, a musty, chalky cloud that made me cough. I adjusted my grip on my Sig and leaned to the left to take a look around the wall. The twang of a crossbow sounded and a rocket soared past my face. I jerked my head back just in time. A hulking, ruddy creature vaguely resembling a medieval knight lowered the bow and began to reload. Youthful laughter echoed around me.

"Dude, I think you played a bit too much D&D," I yelled around the wall as I loaded a new magazine. Light glinted off the sigils engraved on the bullets' casings. Some people carry armor-piercing rounds, I carry spell-piercing rounds. Because my life is fucked up. I was fighting a life-size chess piece in this kid's basement for Christ's sake.

"You're an insect, witch! No match for my power!"

I rolled my eyes. Grandiose statements and unsettling giggling from a barely legal corrupt witch drunk on demon magic, and a Lancelot-shaped golem shooting flaming arrows at my head. This day was climbing the ranks in my list of Least Awesome Days Ever.

Ethan, my partner, crouched on the other side of the doorway, loading the same spelled bullets into his own gun. I caught his eye and pointed to my chest, then jerked my thumb in the direction of Grand Master Evil in the other room. Ethan shook his head. Before I could move, he leapt up and began firing, diving into the room and looking for cover. I swore and followed him.

Claymation Lancelot loosed another bolt. I dodged to the right and the flaming arrow sailed past me. I emptied the magazine into the golem's head. Ozone and something sour, like decaying vegetables, tainted the air as white sparks of energy crackled over it. I'd blown its head clean off. Bits of clay crumbled to the ground as the golem staggered, lurching like a drunk zombie. It crashed to its knees and broke apart into a jumble of red rocks. I looked around for Ethan and reloaded my gun. This was my last magazine. Time to end this.

Ethan flattened himself beside a large vertical freezer, his shield active to fend off a barrage of corrupt spells. The kid tossed them without finesse or form. Our information said he was nineteen, but he looked twelve. Oily dirty blonde hair stuck to a forehead pockmarked with acne, flapping over eyes dark with power. Wearing a too-big t-shirt, stained jeans, and tennis shoes, he would have looked more at home at a gaming convention. Flabby, greasy power rolled off him, traces of the demon that rode him, but the red-eyed son of a bitch was nowhere to be seen. The demon had probably promised to make this kid's dreams come true and granted him power far beyond his control, all in a Billy Mays-like pitch--infinite power, kid, act now and it's yours for the bargain-basement price of your soul. It was a story I knew well, and I hated it. Now I'd have to kill this kid, barely out of childhood, because he'd become a corrupt witch.

"Hey, badass, why don't you share the love?" I prowled toward him, steps sure, breathing slow. The kid swung his gaze to me. He panted and his hands shook. He was running out of juice. A strangled scream left his mouth as he hurled a blob of magic at me. With a thought and a pulse of my will, I activated my shield. A sphere invisible to the naked eye but vibrating with magic hummed to life around me. The corrupt spell thwacked into it and splattered into rivulets of oily power. I ground my teeth, the tattoo on my shoulder that housed the shield heating up under the strain.

"Kid, you're outmatched. You got two seconds to give it up or I'm going to put a bullet between your eyes." I had no faith it would go that easy, but hey, can't blame a girl for trying.

"You can't touch me! I'm stronger than you!" His voice cracked with the notes of adolescence. Sometimes I really hated my job.

"One."

"Go to hell, bitch!" He flung another wad of magic at me. Splat, sizzle, burn.

"Two." The kid reached back, gathering power to him, and I fired two quick shots. The first one shattered his ward. The second nailed him on the left side of his chest. Despite my threat, I wanted to give this kid's parents the chance for an open-casket funeral. It was the least I could do.

A quarter-sized splotch of dark fluid stained his shirt and his jaw dropped. The madness drained from eyes that flew open wide and he scrabbled at his chest, as if he could pull the bullet out. Gunshot wounds aren't like the movies. For one thing, it takes longer to die.

I sank another round into his chest and he dropped to the floor.

I sighed heavily and jogged toward him, my gun trained on his head. The kid was dying, but he could still pull magic. His eyes found me and he made weak, mewling sounds that reminded me of a dying deer. He looked even younger now. Goddammit. I slumped him against the wall.

"How far?" Ethan asked softly.

I rested a hand on the boy's arm, dropped into the psychic realm and scanned his aura. Fetid shadows pulsed through him everywhere, burrowing like fat maggots through his soul. Full-blown journey into evil. I cursed.

"I'm sorry, I'm sorry, I'm so sorry." The kid was crying. A wet, phlegmy sound drowned his words and he gasped for breath. The bullet hole itself gurgled--it's called a sucking chest wound for a reason. Would have been kinder to put it in his heart, Rachel. "I j-just wanted...to be-be-be s-strong. To m-make people like me." I tried to shush him.

Bullshit. He wanted to cause pain, to make people fear him. Maybe he was bullied. Maybe he had a shitty home life. Maybe he'd just swan dived over the cliff of crazy. It didn't matter. The moment he made a deal with a demon and used that power to kill people, he made a choice. And now he had paid the price for it.

"I-it hurts," he sobbed.

"I know. It'll be over soon." I took his hand and he squeezed my fingers, gripping my hand like it could anchor him to life. His body jerked and twitched. His eyes, round with fear, darted around wildly as his blood pooled beneath him.

It took him twelve minutes to die. I closed his eyes.

"Were you seriously holding his hand?" Ethan's frown was far louder than his voice.

"Shut up." I pulled a flat grey disk, about the size of a quarter, out of my pocket and placed it on the kid's arm. It glowed bright blue for an instant, then swirled with black until it faded back to dull grey. I handed the disk to Ethan and stood, brushing crushed clay and plaster from my knees. A faint buzzing sound, like overhead power lines, filled the air, the sound of our super special bullets and their casings warping, rendering them useless to police forensics teams. The Council would take care of the rest. Andy Walker's death would go down as one more tragic victim of gun violence. Thank God we lived in America.

I pulled out my phone and tapped in a number.

"National Cleaning Services." That was a nice euphemism for hiding crime scene evidence from the vanilla cops.

"This is Deputy Rachel Collins. We're done here. Need a cleanup crew," I said.

"Text your location, deputy, and report to the local captain." The woman's voice was bland, professional, and efficient. It signified everything I hated about the Council.

"Aye-aye, Cap'n. Want me to pick up the dry cleaning too? Maybe a gallon of milk?"

"Just report in, Rachel."

Miss Manners hung up on me.

THE HIGH COUNCIL of Witches is a screwy group. It's been around since the plague and functions sort of like a magical government made up of born witches—people with innate magical ability. There are other kinds of witches. Low-level practitioners without enough magic to cause much trouble. And then there are the criminals: witches who get their power by making deals with demons. There aren't many born witches, a few thousand in the whole country, though not every born witch joins the Council. The ones that do get put to work, like at summer camp. Some witches are archivists, preserving our history and magical knowledge. Some are redactors, sneaky bastards that keep us out of the normal history books and newspapers. Some are teachers, showing young witches how to control their magic, and some eggheads manage the Council's investments. Those talented with bureaucracy work in the human government to ensure we stay hidden and get the cooperation we need when necessary.

Some very unlucky witches like myself end up in the Justice branch, which is like supernatural law enforcement. Deputies go out and track down corrupt witches, hopefully bringing them in alive. We also handle any unregulated super-natural creature that's gone off the rails. Captains dole out our cases using human law enforcement as a cover; weird shit goes down, and mysteriously the case ends up in Council deputies' hands. Only our perps never end up in the vanilla judicial system. No, we've got our own trials, our own judges, our own prisons--even our own executioners. Our entire purpose is to keep the most violent amongst our kind from wreaking havoc on the normals.

It's like *Law & Order*, but with witchcraft.

The Council doesn't like me much. Feeling's mutual. Born witches choose whether or not to join the Council at eigh-teen. It's a big commitment—lifetime of service or death. Guess the Council doesn't trust us not to blab its secrets if we bailed. I originally turned the Council down. I went to college, pre-med, until I got the mother of all wake-up calls my junior year. Then I came running back, and was put through the ringer for my trouble. Council witches have been up my ass since I was thirteen. But it's not exactly like I've got a lot of career options, so for the last six years, I've just kept my head down, done my job, and carried out orders to the best of my ability. The Council and I disagree over what *best of my ability* means, though. I'm not exactly a team player.

We'd done our jobs, and now the captain and cleanup crew would do theirs. When people died by magical means, there aren't good explanations, so, in the great tradition of secret organizations everywhere, the Council covered it up. Minutes ticked by. My nerves buzzed. I paced. I kept listening for the sound of sirens--the Council had fingers in all kinds of pies that generally kept my ass out of jail, but hanging around crime scenes didn't exactly instill a sense of calm. Exhaustion moved in as adrenaline fled and I rubbed at my right wrist. I felt like the dead kid was staring at me, accusing me. Maybe if we'd come sooner, if the local witches had been paying attention, he wouldn't have gone so far. Maybe we could have saved him. My temper flared. The Council made a lot of promises, but from where I stood, it seemed like all we ever were was too freaking late.

"Stop it, Rachel."

I ceased pacing and flicked my eyes to Ethan. He was giving me that lame-ass look that meant he was about to have a heart-to-heart moment with me.

"I'm not doing anything," I said.

"Yes, you are. You're second-guessing and getting pissed off and you know it's no use. We did our jobs."

"Yeah, right. Because killing teens was exactly what I signed up for."

"Rachel..."

"Yeah, yeah, I know."

The captain showed up about a hundred and fifty years later. She marched into the basement like she owned the place, flanked by two witches in black shirts and pants. I personally thought they should wear suits so I could call them J and K, but nobody appreciated my wit.

"Where's the usual captain?" I demanded.

"Busy." She smiled. I scowled and dug around in my memory for her name as she surveyed the carnage around us, Michelle Baycone. "Alright, so, what've we got?"

Ethan filled her in while I stood there feeling like a kid sent to the principal's office for blowing up the chemistry lab. Michelle was about my mom's age, her brown hair streaked with grey. She looked like a damn second-grade teacher in a pale pink blouse and Dockers, but if she was a captain, it meant she could kick some serious ass. I'd know.

"So the witch in question was a corrupted human, nineteen, Andrew Walker. You were unable to apprehend?" she asked. We nodded. "What measures did you take?"

Ethan answered before I could speak. "We tracked a series of hexes tied to suspicious deaths back to the practitioner. Magic signature was a match." He handed her the disk I'd used to sample Andy's aura, and two others just like it in plastic evidence bags. "He was using coins planted on the victims to target the spells. We then approached the subject at his home and informed him who we were. He conjured a golem and attacked us. We both confirmed demon involvement. Deputy Collins had no choice but to kill him, ma'am."

I gave him an annoyed sideways glance and he shrugged.

Michelle pulled an electronic device out of her pocket, roughly the size of an old graphing calculator, and slid the disks into it one by one. "Magic signature match confirmed. Soul analysis performed?"

"Yeah. Full-on corrupt," I said.

Michelle swung her eyes to Ethan. "Do you concur?"

"Yes, ma'am."

"Alright. Well, seems pretty cut-and-dried. Let's wrap this up, shall we?" She waved a hand at us and we both held out our right arms. Dimestore J and K took our right wrists and placed two fingers on the inside, as if checking for a pulse. A wave of magic rolled off them as they muttered an incantation and a brand swam to the surface of my skin. A sword. It rose in a brownish-red stain, as if burned there, but it wasn't anything so mundane. It was seared on my soul.

The sword glowed a bright white before fading back to

brown. The witch holding my arm gave me a curt nod, then looked at Michelle. "Both clean."

I rubbed at my wrist as the mark faded, doing my best impression of a drowned cat. Every fucking job they tested us. It got old.

"Good. Well, nice job," Michelle said. "We'll handle the rest. You two are free to go." The judgment on whether a boy's life had been worth taking was over in less than ten minutes. My stomach churned into a hard lump but I kept my face blank as we walked toward the door.

"Oh, Rachel?" Michelle said just as my foot was on the first step. "Victor wants a word. Give him a call, would you?"

Jesus Christ.

"Yeah, fine," I said, anxiety prickling up my spine. Ethan smirked and tried to put his hand on my back. I ducked it and jogged up the stairs. Victor freaking North. Awesome.

We left Fort Collins and headed to one of my favorite bars in Denver, even though I didn't feel much like celebrating and Ethan wouldn't shut up about a lot of shit I didn't want to talk about.

"All I'm saying is, it's not a bad thing for Victor to like you," he argued, wagging a fry at me.

I glared at my salad. "I don't think he likes me. I think he's waiting for me to screw up."

"Why do you say that?"

"I don't know. Just a feeling. You weren't there when I was sworn in." Victor had made it clear he didn't trust my judgment, coming back to the Council after three years of rejecting it. He hadn't said as much, but I got the message.

"Oh come on, Rachel."

"Whatever. I just feel like the fucking eye of Sauron is on me." I grimaced and took a drink of my beer. "It's just like with the scans."

Ethan sighed, giving me a look that said he'd rather be doing his taxes. "You know why they do it."

"Doesn't mean I don't think it's stupid."

"It's a failsafe."

"Still sucks."

"It's like that for every witch."

"No, it's not." My voice came out harsher than I intended and I hid behind another gulp of my beer. Most born witches are elementals—witches who command the power of nature. I'm something different: a ley witch, power that made me unpredictable, dangerous. A freak. I'd gotten that message too. Suspicion and distrust had followed me around ever since I was a kid.

Ethan didn't say anything for a long time. I'd been partnered with Ethan for about three months, and we were still feeling each other out. He had been born to a human family and carried baggage from that that made him practically worship the Council. It was nice to find a place to fit in. I wouldn't know, and it was possible I resented him for that.

My phone vibrated in my pocket. My brother. God bless his timing. "Hey, Danny. What's up?"

"Hey, sister. You still on the job?"

"Nah, we're done here. Just celebrating another one in the 'win' column."

"That bad, huh?"

"Kid was barely legal."

"I know." He sunk a lot of meaning into those two words and I picked at the withered corner of my placemat, wishing my big brother could just give me a hug. Sometimes I'm such a fucking child. "But hey, got something to take your mind off it. Feel like helping me with a case?"

"Sure. You joining the glamorous deputy life?"

He laughed. "No, just doing a favor for Elena. Meet me at Mom and Dad's tomorrow?"

I agreed, ended the call, and looked up to see Ethan staring at me. "What?"

"You just said you'd meet your brother in Dillon tomorrow."

"Yeah?"

"So we just got off a case."

"You know what they say, Ethan. Rolling stone gathers no moss." I flashed him my crazy smile and dropped a few bills on the table. I could physically feel the eye roll he gave me in response.

TWO

I picked Ethan up late the next morning and made the hour-long drive to Dillon. He ground his teeth, his hand clenching around the door handle as I careened my old hardtop Jeep through the mountains. It only made me drive faster.

My dad waited in the living room, the shirt of his uniform unbuttoned and his normally open and friendly face lined with exhaustion. He might have come across as a sleepy town sheriff, but his bright blue eyes still sparkled with intelligence. My dad never missed a thing. Our dog, Maya, a bear-sized black and tan Tibetan mastiff, barreled into my legs, knocking me back against the wall. I absently scratched her behind the ears and shuffled toward the couch.

"Y'all finally get outta bed?" My dad grew up in Texas and moved to Colorado forty years ago, but he'd never lost his drawl.

"Well, you know, need my beauty sleep. Speaking of getting out of bed, where were you yesterday?"

"When you get to my pay grade, you get a day off. Didn't they tell you that?"

"Yeah, right." My dad was a Council captain for the state

of Colorado. People expected me to be just like him. Didn't take them long to be sorely disappointed.

"You should ask her how fast she was driving on the way up here," Ethan said.

"What? It's summer. No snow." I disappeared into the kitchen, rummaging around for a beer. Returning to the couch, I took a swig as I folded a leg beneath me.

"Really, Rachel? It's not even noon." Ethan did a fantastic impression of an 1800s schoolmarm.

"I'm sorry, I thought *this* was my dad." I turned to face my father. "Anyway, do you know what this case is that Danny has?"

"Somethin' 'bout a missin' girl. Local pack petitioned the Council, but they denied it."

"Why?" Ethan asked. I made a face. Weres and vampires generally policed their own, but sometimes they worked with us on serious issues. It was beneficial for all of us to stay off the vanilla humans' radar.

"Not rightly sure. Council's been funny lately, y'know."

I snorted. Both men looked like they didn't get the joke. "Well, you know, it's the Council. I've always kind of thought they had their head up their ass."

"You do realize that the Council includes you?" Ethan asked.

"Only technically. Anyway--" I was interrupted by the sheer chaotic noise created only by hurricanes and nine-year-old boys. My nephew burst through the kitchen door, catapulted into the living room and flew into me with a tackle that would make Lawrence Taylor proud.

"Easy killer, you're going to squish me," I said, chuckling as I ruffled Jake's hair. Danny ambled in after his son, taking a seat beside me. A warm smile lit his face, although he sported some pretty spectacular bags under his eyes. Jake looked just like his dad--sandy blonde hair like Mom, Dad's summer sky eyes, looking like they should be on a freaking *GQ* cover or something. Me, though--Danny liked to joke I was the mailman's baby. No one knew where my dark red hair and honey brown eyes came from, and no one wanted to claim parentage for my mouth.

"Hey Aunt Rachel, guess what?" Jake crowed.

"What?"

"Chicken butt." He laughed hysterically and then took off again, bolting out the door into the backyard.

"Is that kid mainlining sugar?" I asked, punching my brother in the shoulder. He lashed out to sock me in the thigh. I yelped and jerked away, rubbing at it.

"I feed him a steady diet of amphetamines and chocolate milk," Danny drawled.

"So what's the scoop?" I asked.

My brother picked up a manila folder from the coffee table and passed it to me. The seal on the front said Summit County Sheriff's Office. So Dad had done some digging.

I flicked the folder open and scanned the contents. Police report for a missing person, Sadie Warren. Twenty-one, dark hair, dark eyes. Warm bronze skin. Kind smile.

"She a were?" I looked up at my brother.

"No."

"Thought you said this was a pack case?"

"It is. Sadie's connected to one of Elena's packmates. His girlfriend, I guess. She disappeared yesterday and I got the impression this was a time-sensitive matter. You know Elena."

I nodded, flipping through pages. Elena Rios was Alpha of the Platte River Pack and played things pretty close to the vest. The fact that she'd asked for Council help spoke volumes as to how serious she considered this case to be. Secretive and proud, Elena only barely tolerated witch involvement in pack affairs.

Ethan circled behind the couch to look over my shoulder. "What is she then?"

"Haven't gotten that far yet," Danny said.

"Since when does the pack care about outsiders?" Ethan crossed his arms, looking at the report like it was the one wrinkled corner on a perfectly made bed.

"You know Elena," Danny repeated darkly.

"Any reason to think this isn't just a regular case for Denver PD?" I shuffled through a few pages, chewing on my lip. Nothing jumped out at me. Despite creepifying stories about things with fangs and claws, sometimes the worst monsters are human.

"It could be," Danny said, "but Elena didn't seem to think so."

"Could it be hunters?" Ethan asked. Most humans lived in a state of ignorance regarding the supernatural. Others knew the truth.

"Maybe, but there's no body." I heard the unspoken *yet* in my brother's tone. Shit was apparently serious.

"And the Council doesn't think there's something here?" I asked. Without Council approval, we'd be working this case off the clock, which might ruffle some feathers. As a professional feather-ruffler, I didn't really care, but I was curious as to how my brother, Mr. Straight and Narrow, felt about it.

"'This case is not appropriate for Council involvement at this time,'" Danny said. Minute flickers of tense muscle played across his face. Freaking Council, man. "I owe Elena, and that's why I called you. Now that you've been trained up a bit, I thought you might be sort of useful."

I stuck out my tongue. "Says the guy who rides a desk for a living." I glanced at my dad. "If this is off the books, we won't have a cover with CBI." My particular day job was as an agent with the Colorado Bureau of Investigation Major Crimes Unit. Same for Ethan. It was official sounding and most people had no idea just what the hell the CBI did--the perfect cover. Council higher-ups made sure weird cases got passed to us through vanilla channels and ensured no one ever asked too many questions. It was all very CIA, and just like real CIA officers, I had to actually show up at my cover job, too.

"I'll get somethin' sent to your boss," my dad said. "Might not be an official Council case, but it's worth doin' to keep relations with the pack in good standin'."

"Works for me."

The smell of bacon and pancakes drifted into the room and my stomach growled. A few minutes later, my mom called from the kitchen. Excellent. Breakfast and supernatural crime fighting, these are a few of my favorite things.

THE SKY above the mountains looked like a freaking postcard as Danny, Ethan, and I left later that afternoon. The crisp air invigorated my senses, smelling clean and sharp. I climbed into my Jeep and followed my brother's Land Rover as we headed east on I-70.

Danny had left Jake in Dillon, and the plan was for us to divide and conquer: Ethan and Danny would tackle research, while I investigated Sadie. I wanted to stop by my house and get my shit together first. I spent a lot of time at my folks', but I actually lived in a small cabin closer to Denver.

I snaked up the winding dirt road that led to my property. I enjoyed its remoteness and the solitude of the trees, and the privacy both afforded. Nosy neighbors were not conducive to my witchy ways.

I made myself a cup of tea and spread the police report in front of me. I tried to make Sadie real, to imagine what kind of person she was. I didn't want her to just be a two-inch-square photo and some impersonal report.

Something about this girl was off. Weres didn't typically date outside the pack, and they sure as hell didn't run around with normals. Elena, the Alpha of Denver's werewolves, ran a tight ship. None of hers had ever harmed a human. To do so was an offense punishable by death, and I doubted she'd tolerate violence from an outsider either. If one had broken her rules and somehow escaped her justice, I would have known. I would have put him down.

So why did Elena want the Council's help? It didn't surprise me that she hadn't enumerated her reasons to Danny. Weres were notoriously tight-lipped. Back to Sadie, then. I needed to find out what she was, and if she had any skeletons in her closet. Victimology mattered. It told you more about the perp than almost anything else.

Like I had done a thousand times before, I organized and studied my evidence, looking for patterns. The police report included printouts from Sadie's email accounts, but nothing unusual stood out. I tacked a large map of the metro area to a wall in the third bedroom that served as my workspace, plotting out places she visited and trying to trace the connections. So far I was coming up with zip. Johnny Five needs more input.

I took a quick shower and downed another cup of tea before putting on my undercover gear: a pair of charcoal slacks, a dark green fitted blouse, a blazer, and a Colorado Bureau of Investigation badge.

The July sun streamed through my window as I drove toward the city, baking my pale skin and causing beads of sweat to gather between my shoulder blades and over my chest. I followed I-70 to 25, heading south as the highway hugged Denver's western edge. The gold peak of the Ritchie Center loomed to my right as I exited onto University. Sadie Warren lived only a few blocks from the University of Denver campus.

I knocked twice on her apartment door and received no answer. Well, then. Plan B. I pulled on a pair of nitrile gloves and gripped the doorknob, glancing over my shoulder to look for witnesses or security cameras, then sent out a small tendril of my will. My senses swam over the lock, finding the tumblers, and I pushed gently. The lock clicked, and I darted inside.

Breaking and entering and lying to people were unfortunate but sometimes necessary parts of my job. Thanks to my witchy abilities, I was also better at it than your average crook. Typically, the Council covered my ass, but I wasn't sure how generous they'd be with me moonlighting. I'd just have to activate my ninja mode.

Cheap Swedish furniture occupied the small but neat apartment, accompanied by pops of bright color and pictures of friends. I ran my hands over the knickknacks and books on the shelves, probing for traces of magic. Nothing. Freaking great. I searched under the couch cushions and in the kitchen cabinets. Just more run-of-the-mill crap. I snorted at a collection of dead plants on the windowsill. *You and me share the same black thumb, Sadie.*

My phone vibrated in my pocket, and my regular, human CBI captain's name flashed across the screen. Dammit. I'd need to turn up there soon. Deep cover life is hard, man.

I moved to one of the bedrooms, examining a few of the personal items to confirm it was my vic's. A twin bed dressed in pink and turquoise stood against one wall, next to a window, with a large bookcase and a desk on the opposite side of the room. I started with the desk. A number of pictures decorated a corkboard hanging above it, many showing Sadie displaying a hunter's prize. A regular hunter, not the supernatural kind—deer, elk, grouse. Outdoorsy chick. I could appreciate that.

I riffled through the papers spread out next to a laptop covered in *I Ride Breck* stickers. Homework assignments, a couple copies of her resume, some glossy flyers for events at DU. An expensive and well-used snowboard leaned against the corner. So far this girl was just a normal college kid.

I opened the drawers and sorted through pens and highlighters. In a row of hanging files, I found a collection of paystubs. I tilted my head as I read the company name: Hughes Corporation. That jived with the police report. Sweet. A lead. Judging from the amount, Sadie was only working there part-time. I shoved the drawer closed and turned to the bookshelf.

Books on management, accounting, and finance. Business major. I pulled out a few of the books, looking behind them for any hidden treasures. All I found was dust and cobwebs.

Some kind of powdery substance that smelled like refried ass was sprinkled across her windowsill. I fished out a small plastic bag and scooped up some of it. I had no freaking clue what it was, but that's what mass spectrometers are for.

I turned to her dresser, my gloved hands searching through her clothes. I probably should have felt like a giant creeper, but this job has a way of warping your perspective on things like riffling through someone's underwear.

Rows of stylish clothing hung in her closet, which was also filled with a big, fat, nothing. Maybe Sadie Warren really was just a regular, vanilla chick. Who happened to date a were-wolf. Right.

"Ugh, come on," I grumbled and flopped down on the bed. Something had to be here. I bounced my left foot and my heel struck something hard. Looking down, I saw an opaque plastic box sticking out from under the bedframe. Now we're cooking with gas.

I dropped down to my knees and opened the box, revealing a well-preserved swath of fur. It was too risky to do a full scan here, so I just skimmed the surface with my senses. The warm pulse of magic greeted me. Bingo.

I grabbed the box and double-checked that I'd erased all signs of my presence, then scurried from the apartment. A squad car waited outside the building, two uniformed cops looking grim as they passed me. I nodded at them and prayed they wouldn't ask me what I was doing here. Moonlighting meant I didn't have CBI cover, and that could make things sticky.

"Every Breath You Take" blared from my phone just as I was searching for an address for Hughes Corp. It was the ringtone I'd assigned to Ethan. I thought I was being ironic and clever. He wasn't amused.

"Hey, what've you got?" I asked.

"Well, according to everything I can find, Sadie Warren is a quiet, smart, boring girl from Arizona. Came here a couple years ago to go to DU. Danny's still checking on her bank accounts for anything suspicious."

"Okay. I got a couple leads here that I'm going to chase down."

"Like what?"

"Don't know yet. But I'll call you in a bit, okay? Oh, see if Danny can get us in for a chat with Elena."

"Will do."

I hung up, put the address for Hughes Corp into my phone's navigational system, and headed back out to I-25. Time to pay a visit to Sadie's employers.

THREE

Hughes Corporation dominated several floors of one of the high-rises downtown. I had no idea what they did there, but apparently it was important and made a shit ton of money. After cussing my way through circling the block four times, I finally found a parking space and walked up the sidewalk to the front door of the building. I paused to appreciate a glossy black crew-cab Ford F-350 parked at the curb, a late '80s model if I had to guess. Trucks weren't usually my thing, but it was in pristine condition. Whoever owned it took good care of it. That made me smile.

Pushing my way through the glass doors, I marched up to the receptionist's desk, flashing my badge. The barely-legal chick working the phones gave me a confused look.

"Agent Collins, CBI," I said. "I'd like to speak with whoever supervises Sadie Warren, please." The girl's eyes widened and she nodded, pushing a button on her phone. A few moments later, a guy in his thirties with watery brown eyes behind wire-rimmed glasses and wearing a rumpled suit exited the elevator. I was standing with my back to the lobby, examining some of the pictures of Colorado scenery, when he came up to the receptionist's desk, escorting two men. I glanced at them out of the corner of my eye. Both were tall, a few inches over six feet, and they looked a little like brothers, sharing the same dark brown hair and eyes the color of early summer grass.

They were also wearing suits that screamed cop.

I kept my back to them as they left the building, watching as they walked down the street out of my field of view. Well, this was going to be interesting. The dude with the wire-rimmed glasses skittered over to me, twitching like a sparrow with PTSD.

"Hi, uh, Agent Collins, is it? I'm Jason Wilkes, Sadie's supervisor. You, uh, with those FBI agents that were just here?" Shit, shit, shit.

"Pleasure, Mr. Wilkes. And no, I'm not. Must be an inter-agency oversight. I do apologize for the inconvenience." This was why working off the books sucked.

I sent a tendril of magic forward, creating a subtle glamour. Wilkes's eyes slid briefly out of focus and back again, then he smiled at me. He nodded and motioned for me to follow him to the elevators.

"I'm happy to talk to you, I'm just not sure what else I can tell you," he said as he pushed the button for the fifteenth floor.

"Well, let's just start with what you told those other detectives."

"Uh, okay. Well, Sadie started here a couple months ago. She's a summer intern in my department. Finance. Good kid."

"When did you see her last?"

"Two days ago. She didn't show up for work yesterday, and that just wasn't like her at all. Sadie's very responsible."

"Was anyone bothering her?"

"No, not that I knew about." The elevator dinged and Jason held out his arm, letting me walk out ahead of him. He led me through my personal version of hell—a cube farm with grey walls and striped corporate carpet. There were too many people, too many obstacles between me and the exit. I let out a breath I didn't know I was holding when we finally made it to his office. I slid into a seat across from his desk and removed a small notebook from my jacket pocket.

"Did Sadie ever miss work? Or seem ill often?"

"Uh, no," Wilkes said.

"Was there anything you would consider strange about her?"

"No," he said, drawing the word out. "Are you thinking she was on drugs or something?"

"We're just investigating every lead, Mr. Wilkes." I'll take Evasive Cop Talk for $100, Alex.

"I can show you to her desk--" Wilkes's eyes shot to the door. He froze, looking like a hen caught in the fox house. I turned around to see a dude that practically had *boardroom badass* tattooed on his forehead. Handsome streaks of silver at his temples exemplified the difference between old and experienced, but his eyes made me want to dig out my ski parka.

"Mr. Hughes," Jason said, standing. I got to my feet as well and turned around. Hughes raked his eyes over me, but it wasn't my body that interested him. I was being weighed and measured.

"Must be one of our boys in blue. Excuse me--lovely lady in blue. William Hughes," he said, extending his hand to me and ignoring Jason. I shook it, nodding.

"Agent Collins, Colorado Bureau of Investigation," I said. "I'm here about Sadie Warren's disappearance."

"I know. Nothing happens in my building without my knowledge, Agent."

"Well then, you wouldn't mind if I asked you a few questions?"

"Of course not. That's why I came down. I take matters concerning my employees very seriously." Hughes swaggered toward the desk, lounged back into Jason's chair and gestured for us to take our seats. What a jackass.

"I was just asking if there was anything unusual about Sadie."

"No. She was intelligent, to be sure, but that's very common among our interns. We only recruit the best and the brightest," Hughes said. Right. This guy really fancied himself as Denver's own Jeff Bezos.

"Were you aware of any problems she was having, maybe in her personal life?" I glanced between the two men, but Jason just averted his eyes. The deference he showed to Hughes made me grind my teeth. He reminded me of a kicked puppy. How in the hell had Sadie ever worked here? I would have set the building on fire before the end of my first day.

"Do you not have a first name?" Hughes asked, steepling his fingers.

"I'm sorry?"

"You introduced yourself just as 'Agent Collins.' I was wondering if you had a first name."

"Laura." I was superstitious about giving people my true name, but more than that, I just didn't want this guy to have anything personal about me. "Could you please answer the question?"

"Laura. Does the CBI not like you to use given names when interrogating witnesses?" Hughes thought himself an alpha fucking male and he was going to shove it in my face. Goddamn dominance games.

"Answer the question, Mr. Hughes."

"Sadie never said anything about any problems. She seemed happy," Jason said with the eagerness of a kid who wants Mom and Dad to stop fighting. Hughes tossed him a look and Jason squirmed in his chair. I had the strong urge to punch his boss in the face.

"Mr. Wilkes, would you please show me to Sadie's desk?" I asked, my eyes still on Hughes.

"S-sure. Mr. Hughes, is-is that alright?"

"Of course. Give Laura here whatever she needs," he purred. I barely restrained myself from rolling my eyes. Okay, Mr. Alpha Dick. My name isn't even Laura, so suck on that.

Jason led me through the cube maze to a workstation tucked somewhere in the middle of a sea of grey corporate monotony. Sadie might have only been a summer intern, but she'd made the cube her own, decorating it with pictures and colorful art prints—the same flashes of her personality that I'd seen in her apartment. I pressed my lips into a thin line as I sat down in her chair, taking in her bright smile and eyes that shone with a joy for life.

I needed to find this girl.

I picked up a framed photograph of Sadie and a guy a few years older than her. He had dark eyes and deep brown skin, his toned arms wrapped around her shoulders as they both grinned at the camera. Something tugged at my memory and I popped the photo out of its frame. *Me and Jeff, spring camping trip* was written on the back, and the connection solidified in my brain. This was Jeff Sharpe, her werewolf boyfriend. I knew I recognized him.

I poked around in her computer and desk drawers, but didn't find anything else useful. I slid the picture of her and Jeff into my pocket and thanked Wilkes, saying I'd show myself out. Walking back to my car, I chewed on my lip and fidgeted with the edge of my jacket. Was Elena wrong on this? Maybe it was just a vanilla kidnapping, in which case Sadie would be better served by the police department.

My phone rang as I unlocked my car door. "Elena will meet us tomorrow afternoon," Danny said without preamble.

"Awesome." I cradled the phone between my ear and shoulder as I peeled out of my suit jacket. It was way too hot for this shit.

"You find anything at Sadie's apartment?"

"Maybe. I'm going to check something, then I'll let you know."

"Alright. Keep digging, sis."

I heard the smile in his voice and one of my own spread across my face. "Bite me, bro."

~

BECAUSE SOMETIMES I make good decisions, I left Hughes Corp and headed west on 6th Ave. This was the best part about Denver: you could put the mountains in front of you and the city behind and somehow everything felt better. The CBI headquarters was closer to the foothills than downtown, which allowed me to live in my Unabomber cabin as far away from civilization as I could get and still have a pretty decent commute.

I reluctantly pulled the blazer back on and sprinted toward the sanctuary of air conditioning inside the building. The CBI office was a typical law enforcement hive of activity--phones ringing in the background, the muted hum of conversation, walkways cluttered with file boxes and evidence boards. My desk sat in the middle of this humming beehive of police work. It boasted a few pictures in expensive wooden frames--Danny and me; a family Christmas; my former partner and best friend, Pasha Devereaux, and me all dolled up during a trip to New Orleans; Jake's soccer photo--an overflowing inbox, and drab brown file folders stacked everywhere. My little slice of heaven.

Jamie Wallace, my CBI captain, was in his office, looking like he always did--shirtsleeves rolled up, tie loosened, half-empty mug of cold coffee on his desk. Jamie was former military and carried himself like he was still enlisted. Thinning brown hair and crows feet crowding around brown eyes were the only concessions he gave to middle age. His hair was rumpled today, which meant he was irritated, and I hoped to God it wasn't at me.

"Cap--you called?" I asked, knocking on his doorframe.

He looked up and there were dark circles under his eyes. Uh-oh. "Heard how it went down yesterday. You and Ethan okay?"

"Yeah, we're fine." I shrugged to cover for the knot in my stomach. "Just a dumb kid."

"I need your officer-involved shooting report today. DA is doing a review and he's not patient."

My eyes widened. "What? Why?"

Jamie sighed and leaned back in his chair. "We're seventeen percent over our average for suspect shootings and it's only July. Raises some red flags downtown."

I sighed. I'd bet my car that the majority of that seventeen percent was Ethan and me. Sure, the Council would protect its own, but what about Jamie and the rest of CBI? They were getting thrown under the bus while we merrily rode along on top of them.

"I'll do it right now," I said.

The report didn't take long—I just recounted everything that happened sans magical bits. It made Andy Walker out to be a sociopath instead of a kid who'd bitten off more than he could chew, but it wasn't like I could tell the truth. I dropped the report on Jamie's desk and stood in the middle of the office for a minute. Guilty conscience chewed on me. Moonlighting for Elena might irritate the Council, but it could cause real problems for Jamie. I needed a way to connect my two lives.

I called Ethan, informed him about the review of our department, and asked him to meet me at my cabin. An hour and change later and we sat in my workroom while I used a flat metal disk to take a spell sample off the coyote pelt I'd swiped from Sadie's apartment.

These disks, made of iron, analyzed magic signatures from people and spelled items. That particular metal absorbed magic, and with the help of some clever enchantments, it could absorb trace magic and analyze it against a registry of supernatural beings. Every magic user had her own unique ID, like magical DNA.

I slid the disk into the scanner. Its screen flared to life and ANALYZING blinked in green letters.

"It's uploading to SCID," I said. The Spell Coding Information Database stored magic signatures from all known supernatural offenders and Council witches. A line spiked across the screen and I studied its peaks and valleys. "Markers forty-two and twenty-six present."

"So shapeshifter," Ethan said. "Hopefully SCID will have better luck than I did with CODIS. Her DNA wasn't in the system, and the unis that responded to the missing persons report didn't find any at her apartment either."

I hummed my agreement and slid my chair out of the way, sitting down cross-legged in the middle of the room.

"I'm impatient. Want to hold a circle for me?"

Ethan snorted. "What are you doing?"

"Tracking spell. I swiped her hairbrush from her apartment. Besides, manual scans help me know the victim. The more we know about her, the sooner we can find her."

"I hate it when you get all logical. It scares me."

Around me, a six-foot-wide circle constructed of silver, copper, and tin decorated the hardwood floor. That thing was embarrassingly expensive, but it was worth it. You could do magic without a circle, in the same way you could perform surgery with your toes--possible, but not a good freaking idea. Without them, any outside influence could interfere, and that could cause some not fun things. Like having your mind fried by a spike of ley energy, or warping the outcome of a spell so that it melted your face off. The metal ring functioned like a conductor, making it easier for me to hold the circle myself when another witch wasn't around.

Ethan handed me several jars of herbs, a knife, and a copper bowl, then knelt just outside the rings. He closed his eyes and hair stood up along my arms as he gathered his will.

Ethan was an elemental witch, which meant he didn't rely on ley lines like me. Until such a time as we actually destroyed Mother Nature, he'd have a source of power. The air buzzed, crackling like a Tesla coil, and he touched two fingers to the ring in front of him. With a snap that reverberated deep in my chest, his circle closed around me. Nothing looked different to my eyes, but if I opened my second sight, I would see a perfect sphere, infused with the ocean-blue color of Ethan's aura.

Wrapped safely inside his power, I dumped iris root, mugwort, and cowslip into the bowl, along with a few strands of Sadie's hair. I didn't need a ley line for this, just my own natural power—which was the sucky part, as that power was contained in my blood. I pricked my thumb with the knife and massaged out a few drops, then closed my eyes and gathered my intent. When my magic felt solid and focused, I dropped a lit match into the bowl and let the smoke billow up into my face.

"Find," I said. My tracking spells operated off visuals. Landmarks, signs, buildings, that kind of thing. Two caveats: tracking spells could be warded against, and the target had to be alive. Didn't work in the netherworld. It was a useful tool but not one I employed much. Criminal witches know how to evade this kind of thing.

Normally, images flew at me in a dizzying flash, showing me where my target was with a gut-deep sense of certainty. This time, though, all I got was a massive black wall. It seemed like it was made of liquid darkness, shifting and moving. Every time I pushed at it, it pushed me back.

"That's weird," I said, my eyes still closed. "She's clearly warded, but, like... it's weird."

"How so?" Ethan asked.

"Like I'm not getting anything at all. It's just this giant wall blocking me."

"So our bad guy knows concealment magic."

"At least that solidifies that this is a Council case," I said. "Alright, hold on, let me get a feel for her magic."

I sank into the psychic realm and placed my right hand on the pelt, which I'd brought into the circle with me, and opened up my senses. Every witch could identify a supe through her second sight, but I could also detect energy left in objects used for spells. Lucky me.

My will wrapped around the pelt and strong magic slapped me in the face. The grit of sand rubbed against my hands and feet and I smelled the dry, crisp scent of the desert. Images of running wild beneath a brilliant moon flashed through my brain. The trace magic was so strong-- Sadie must have used this pelt frequently. I brought myself back into reality and opened my eyes. Ethan watched me, a small smile on his lips. I nodded and he dropped his circle.

"Well?"

"Desert. Definitely shifter, but not a were." I stood up, shaking off a head rush. Magic was like endurance running-- you could train yourself to go for miles, but at some point, you hit the wall and passed out. I could draw on ley lines, if they were available, for an extra boost, but it fricking hurt and I risked setting my brain on fire. And when it came to slinging around too much power, those were the least of my concerns.

I stared at my evidence map and plucked a Post-It from below Sadie's name. Who was this girl? I thought about the magic in the pelt. Desert and moon. Running. But she wasn't a werewolf--Elena knew every furry friend that came within fifty miles of the city, and the magic was wrong. I chewed on my lip, flapping the Post-It against my fingers. Desert and moon. Arizona. The hunting. The pelt.

I dashed from the room, the Post-It still stuck to my fingers.

"Rachel?" Ethan chased me into the living room, where I fired up my laptop. I Googled Sadie's hometown, a satisfied smirk curling my lips. With another click, I pulled up the Council database—a secure, private online directory of all our collective knowledge. We're high-tech witches. I typed in a few keywords and let it run.

Jenga.

"I think Sadie is a skinwalker," I said.

Ethan leaned over to examine the Post-It I'd stuck to the side of my screen. "How the hell do you get that from 'Tuba City,' 'hunter pics', and a magic scan?"

"Tuba City's where she's from—and it also happens to be the largest settlement of Navajo people in the country." I showed him the Wikipedia article I'd found and then clicked over to the database screen, where I'd searched coyote, moon, and Navajo. "Skinwalkers are a common Navajo myth—Sadic looks like she might be full or at least half-blood—and legend says they have to have the skin of the animal they want to turn into. I found several pictures of her hunting in her apartment, and that coyote pelt under her bed. Magic felt right." I shrugged, and Ethan nodded.

"Okay. Got a theory about what might have taken her?" Ethan asked as he walked into the kitchen, separated from my living room by a wide pass-through. I heard him shut a cabinet and turn on the faucet.

"Not in the slightest." The edges of a headache formed around my skull. What time was it? How long had I been awake? I slouched back against the sofa, rubbing my temples. Ethan handed me a glass of water. My head fell to the side, my mouth hanging slightly open as I gave him my best bitch face. "Water is weak sauce."

He gave me one right back. "You know that mixing booze and magic isn't exactly the best idea ever, right?"

"Hey, you do it your way, I do it mine. Now, are you going to get me a real drink?" Ethan rolled his eyes but trudged back into the kitchen. He opened another cabinet and returned with a tumbler of Downslope, my favorite whiskey.

His disapproval soaked into me as I sipped the amber liquid. I fought the urge to knock the whole glass back in one gulp, just to spite him. It was after six o'clock, it no longer qualified as day drinking.

"Okay, so what do we do now?" he asked.

"Now, I drink my whiskey. Tomorrow, we go see Elena and see if we can't talk to Jeff." I sighed, rolling the glass between my palms and stared around the room, mentally turning over all our evidence. So Sadie was a skinwalker. Dating a were-wolf. She worked at Hughes Corp. And for some reason, the pack thought this was important enough to deign to ask the Council for help. That added up to... I had no frigging idea. Lack of sleep dissolved my brain into oatmeal.

"I'm going to call Pash tomorrow, too. Make this case official," I said. Pasha Devereaux was my best friend and previous partner—until she'd ditched me due to a recent promotion up to captain. Her and her life goals.

"You want me to stay tonight?" Ethan asked as I knuckled my eyes.

"No, I'm fine. Go home." I managed to bustle him out the door with only a few protests. I listened to his truck rumble down my drive and turned the lock. The faint tingle of the wards surrounding my house brushed against me as I stripped and crawled into bed, passing out almost instantly.

FOUR

I t was a good night--I got close to six hours of sleep. That was a rare luxury for me. Even more rare, I didn't have one nightmare. Seeing horrible shit in your dreams was sort of an occupational hazard of mine.

Hauling myself out of bed, I rummaged around in my kitchen for breakfast, finding only whiskey and a pack of string cheese. Okay, so I sometimes fail at being a real adult.

Sticking one of the pieces of cheese in my mouth, I quickly dressed in jeans, a grey t-shirt, and my favorite dark purple leather jacket. Elena knew the truth about me, so there was no need for the cop routine today.

Heat assaulted me with a vengeance as soon as I stepped out of my cabin. Clearly, the universe had gotten confused and had relocated Colorado to the surface of the sun. My attire didn't help matters, but hey, better hot than cut up and bleeding. You never know what kind of shit is lurking in the bushes. Trust me.

Sticking a Bluetooth headset in my ear, I tapped Pasha's number in my phone.

"Rachel, we've been over this. No amount of begging is making me stay here," she said by way of greeting.

I grinned. "What if I bring you ice cream?"

"How about you get your shit together and get your own promotion?"

It'd been like this since day one. We had bonded over the fact we were both fluent in sass.

"Seriously though, I have a favor to ask," I said.

"Of course you do."

"I've got a case here. Elena Rios petitioned the Council under the Treaties, but they—"

"This is the missing girl?"

"Yeah," I said, surprised. "How'd you know?"

"I read it in the daily briefings," she said, a touch exasperated. Every day, Victor's staff sent out email digests of all things related to Council law enforcement. I might have filtered them into a folder I never checked. "What's changed?" she asked.

"I've got confirmation that the vic was a supe. Skinwalker. Doesn't fall under pack regulations, and last night Ethan and I confirmed the perp is magically skilled. Dude had a pretty impressive concealment ward up. Two plus two means it's squarely in our court."

"The Executive already denied the request."

"Yeah, but that was just when it was a missing girl. Now it's a missing supe girl and a practitioner is involved. And since you're all high and mighty now, you can assign the case under your own discretion," I said.

"And you want to remain lead investigator."

"I love how you, like, finish my sentences for me." I couldn't ask my dad, because that was nepotism or something, and I couldn't ask Michelle, because I had a reputation or something. Break a few dozen rules and everyone gets all angsty. "C'mon, do this for me before you blow town. For old time's sake. Please."

"Lord give me strength. Fine. I'm at regional, swing by and sign the paperwork."

"You're the best, Pash," I said.

"You owe me a bottle of Chateau Montelena and a spa day."

I grinned and hung up, navigating down 6th Avenue to Santa Fe, and into the parking lot of a nondescript office building on the south side of town. Built in the 1970s, the brick building looked like the kind of place you might find a dentist's office, or maybe a small legal firm. The Council's national headquarters was just a couple hours away, near Colorado Springs, but this was their regional office for the state.

They like to hide in plain sight.

The building housed a series of conference rooms and offices, and I found Pasha in one at the end of the hallway. It had no windows, only subdued blue carpet, wood-paneled walls, and rows of black folding chairs. Pasha sat behind a desk at the front of the room. Above her head, a navy banner with an emblem wrought in silver--an elder tree with a pentagram on its trunk, and a hare, a torch, and a key arrayed in a semi-circle below it--hung on the wall. The symbol of the High Council of Witches.

A man in his thirties stood in front of her. His shoulders shook with either silent sobs or terror, I couldn't tell. A witch I recognized from my basic training course stood beside him. Her name might have been Emily.

"Do you have any other evidence to present?" Pasha asked. She wore a blood red silk shirt, cut to look stylish rather than stodgy, that brought out the warm tones of her deep brown skin. She'd looked like that even when we were taking down ghouls in graveyards. I have no idea how she did it, but that was true witchcraft right there.

"I swear, I won't do it again, it was just a mistake, it went too far--"

"You bound a highly dangerous spirit to your will and used it to terrorize people whom you believed had done you harm.

At what point did you decide you'd crossed the line: when you bound the spirit, or when you had it flay someone alive?"

I hung back around the first row of chairs and arched an eyebrow. Jesus, Pasha wasn't screwing around here. This was the end of her probationary period as a captain, during which she'd supervised deputies, distributed cases, and judged trials like this one. In a week, she'd be back home in New Orleans, captaining away down in the grand old South. I tried not to think about that. I didn't have a lot of friends, especially ones like Pash.

The man hung his head. I didn't know this case, but I knew the look on Pasha's face, the way her mouth turned down at the corners and the hard glint in her dark eyes. She was pissed.

"Very well," she said after letting her question hang in the air unanswered. "You are hereby sentenced to fifteen years in the Lost Wilderness prison, after which, pending rehabilitation evaluations, you may be released."

"Rehabilitation?" he asked, and his face ashen. That was the Council's term for trying to turn corrupt witches back toward the light. I didn't have a lot of sympathy for him. Don't wanna deal with Council poking and prodding, don't sling forbidden magic. Pretty simple.

His trembling intensified as Emily took him away. She gave me a friendly nod as they walked past, but the man was giving the ground a thousand-yard stare. Spelled iron bound his wrists in front of him. I watched him go. I'd given the same escort to God knows how many corrupt witches. Talking about swimming against the tide.

"You do realize we have a dress code, right?" Pasha stood up from behind her desk and came around to meet me.

"I'm off duty."

"No, you're not."

"Jesus, one little promotion and all of a sudden you're

trying to change me. Did our friendship mean so little?" I gave her a fake pout and sniffled, and she rolled her eyes.

"You know, after I leave, you're going to have to actually play by the rules to get what you want," she said, handing me a manila folder. Inside was an incident report form for Sadie's disappearance. I sat down on one of the chairs and balanced it against my thigh as I filled it out.

"I'll make Ethan do it."

"Rachel," she said, and something in her voice made me look up, "for real. Victor's wanting to rein in the Lone Ranger stuff, keep his house in order. You might find your leash gets a bit shorter."

I frowned. "Is that why he wanted me to call him?"

"He wants you to call him?"

"That's what Michelle said yesterday. She came up to Fort Collins to judge our sanctioned kill." My sanctioned kill, really. God, it sounded so sanitary like that.

Pasha gave me a hard look. "But you didn't call."

"Not yet. Haven't had time."

"Rache, you know I love you like a sister, but you've got to grow up. Stop pissing off people in powerful positions."

"I'm not trying to piss him off," I said, and returned to filling out the form. "I just don't want to sit around playing bureaucratic patty-cake when a girl's in trouble. Isn't that my job?"

She didn't answer. We'd had this argument before.

"You caught up on your paperwork at CBI?" she asked. Accused, really.

I grimaced. "It's, like, mostly done."

Pasha groaned. "Rachel. You remember what happened last time."

"When you're in NOLA, are you going to call me and harass me about paperwork? 'Cause I'll sure miss it. Here," I said, handing her the form. "Look, I promise I'll be on my best behavior from now on. Smile nice and say 'please' and 'thank you' and keep all my files up-to-date and everything."

"I'd settle for you to just keep your mouth shut," she grumbled, signing the form and handing it back to me.

I was officially on the Council clock. Whee.

~

I WISHED I'd remembered to tie my hair up as I cranked down the windows of my Jeep and headed toward Denver to pick up my brother. Danny was one of the Council's money-makers, but he'd inherited a keen investigative sense from our father. It was thanks to witches like him, who worked in lucrative fields that were like freaking Greek to me, that the Council had the resources to run their shadow empire. He was some kind of investment analyst, and although he spent most of his time up in Dillon with our folks, he kept a house in a snooty suburb of Denver called Highlands Ranch. The place gave me the heebs. It was just so fucking beige.

I pulled up to the curb in front of an extremely normal-looking house with cheery brick siding and perfectly painted green shutters, surrounded by a manicured yard and nestled among the other neat, suburban dwellings. You would never have guessed it was a single dude's pad. Light purple columbines spilled out of stone pots on the porch and tasteful curtains peeked through the windows. Stark contrast to my place. Danny was only twenty-two when Jake was born, and he had raised his son almost entirely on his own. Jake's mom, Margaret, stuck around for a couple months until she decided a kid cramped her style. My brother never talked about it much, for which I didn't blame him. He'd wanted to marry Margaret, and apparently they had some big blowout fight. She'd bailed on my brother and nephew without a look back and I hated her for it.

I always found it funny that a powerful witch lived here—

my brother, cooking up potions and deriving spells in his kitchen while his neighbors baked apple pie, or whatever normal, suburban, yuppie people do. I walked across his lawn, smirking because I knew that Danny would lose his shit if he saw me tramping on his grass. As if summoned by my thoughts, my brother opened his door and treated me to one of his best scowls.

"Rachel, seriously. I have a damn walkway."

"This is a shortcut."

"You're a pain in my ass."

"That's my job, big bro. Are you going to keep bitching about your precious grass or can we, you know, get to work?" I waved the folded incident report. "Pasha's got me officially assigned to the case now."

Danny gave me the look that older brothers everywhere give their punk-ass little sisters as he locked his door, then reached out to pull me onto the walkway. I punched him in the arm and he swiped at my shoulders, trying to trap me in a headlock. We tussled like this all the way to my car.

I drove us into downtown Denver, once again cursing city parking. Luckily, I found a spot not too far from Full Moon Brewery, a pack-owned establishment where Elena was meeting us. I reminded my mouth to check with my brain before stirring shit. Dealing with were packs can be tricky business. As the official liaison to the pack, I even had some practice at it but still found it like navigating a field of land-mines. We approached the front door of the restaurant and I paused, frowning.

"What?" Danny asked, looking at me with mild concern.

"That truck. I saw it yesterday at Sadie's workplace," I said, pointing to the big black behemoth.

"So?"

"So it's probably thirty years old and look at it."

"Um... okay?"

"The paint's perfect. Rims and tires don't look like they

have a clue what mud is. It's a dually. And if I had to guess, I'd say it's a diesel V8."

"I have no idea what you just said to me."

"Trucks like that, they get used hard," I said, sighing. It was like having a conversation with an alien. "It's unusual to see one in such good shape. I just think it's weird. I saw it yesterday, and now it's here."

"Probably just a tourist. Dial down your paranoia."

I threw Danny a withering look and he shrugged his shoulders. I didn't really buy it, but I also had nothing more than a gut feeling to go on so I grudgingly followed him to the door.

We walked in and found Elena sitting at a booth near the back of the restaurant. It was an odd hour, caught between lunch and dinner, and not many other people were there. Thank God. Much easier to have conversations about crazy shit when you didn't have to worry about eavesdroppers.

"Hey, Elena," I said, sliding into the booth. Danny took a seat next to me, nodding at her. Elena Rios had been Alpha of the Platte River Pack for a decade, and had been a werewolf for much longer. She'd assumed control of the pack by succession rather than a fight, which was unusual. Her pack was exceedingly loyal, even for weres, and she kept any of them from stepping out of line. Proud and taciturn, her lack of words belied how much she cared for her people. That much was evident now in her appearance. Her dark hair, glossy with highlights, was pulled back into a low bun at the nape of her neck, and her round, open face lacked its usual perfect makeup. Her brown skin looked ashen, and dark circles sagged under her eyes. Balled fists, rigid shoulders. When she looked up at us, I almost flinched. Almost. Never good to show fear to a predator, especially one in this state.

"Hello, Rachel, Danny. How are you?" Elena asked, her tone tired but polite.

"Can't complain," I said with a small smile.

"Your parents are well, I hope?" I nodded, and she returned the smile. "Danny, how's your boy?"

"Jake's doing great."

Weres had strict codes of social behavior and the world would actually have to be ending before Elena violated them—and maybe not even then. Pleasantries out of the way, we settled down to business.

"I greatly appreciate your assistance with this matter," she said.

"Don't worry about it. The pack's been a friend to us, we're just trying to return the favor. Rachel's now the Council's lead investigator, so you're in good hands," Danny said.

Elena frowned. "I thought the Council was uninterested in this case."

"That was before my baby sister used her considerable charm." He flashed her a smile, which Elena couldn't resist. Danny had the kind of smile that doctors would kill for—he could deliver bad news and leave you feeling relaxed about it. He'd used it to talk me down off the ledge a time or twelve.

"What's up, Elena?" I asked gently. She didn't look relieved.

"You know. The missing girl."

"Yeah, but... no offense, but you look like you been up all night. I know Sadie was dating one of your packmates, but I can't see you getting that torn up over an outsider."

Elena met my eyes and I dropped my gaze to her chin. Her jaw clenched and her nostrils flared as she took an incredibly controlled breath. "It's not just the girl anymore. Jeff went missing yesterday."

Fuck me sideways.

Something had stirred up the pack enough that they petitioned the Council over a friend, and now one of their own was missing? I was surprised Elena hadn't sprouted fur.

"How's the pack holding up?" I asked.

"Not well. They're restless. It's hard to know he's in

danger and we're powerless to help." She flattened her palms on the table, the tips curled against the wood. I didn't have to work very hard to imagine claws at the end of her fingers. Her pupils dilated. The wolf was peeking out at us.

"What happened?" Danny sounded about how I felt—like our case had just gone from *serious* to *this is how Denver becomes a fricking crater*.

"Such concern. Where was it when we first asked for help?" She bit off each word like snapping a bone. Her body became unnaturally still, only her eyes moving between my brother and me. I would have preferred her to lash out and scream at us. This statue thing was fucking unnerving.

"We're here, Elena. We're working the case. We're not going to bail," I said. It wasn't actually proven that were-wolves could smell lies, but they could read body language so well it might as well be true. I forced myself not to fidget while the Alpha stared at me, and several eternities later, she nodded.

"Jeff was searching for Sadie. He didn't come home." Packs usually lived together, or at least near each other, and kept in almost constant contact. Jeff not coming home was the equivalent of a giant, flashing DANGER sign.

"We'll find him, but we need to get a handle on his life. His secrets. You understand?" I asked.

"Tell me what you want to know."

"Did he know Sadie was a shifter?"

"Yes."

"Skinwalker, right? Coyote?"

The corner of her mouth twitched into a ghost of a smile, and she inclined her head. "Clever girl."

Damn, I'm good.

"How did they meet?" Danny asked.

"She wandered onto pack hunting grounds." Sadie was lucky to be alive in that case. Elena caught my surprise and added, "Jeff defended her." The small smile grew and her face softened, giving me a rare glimpse of her emotions.

"Do you know if Jeff was having any trouble with anyone?"

"I would know if someone was bothering a member of my pack," she said. Her voice was almost literally a growl.

I swallowed a cringe as I prepared to ask my next question. "What about problems with someone inside the pack?" She gave me a stare that could melt glass and I held up my hands. "I have to ask, Elena."

"This was not done by one of ours," she snarled. "If it were, I would not need witches' help to deal with the matter." She closed her eyes, taking a calming breath through her nose. Weres who wanted to live in human society--those that didn't turn loup and run around like homicidal maniacs--did so only through extreme self-control, keeping their supernatural rage in check and finding safe places to roam during the full moons. As Alpha, Elena was the Hoover Dam holding back the Lake Mead of goddamn werewolf insanity. I normally had a hard time getting a read on weres, but right now Elena was letting all sorts of things bleed through.

"Speaking of... why did you call the Council?" I asked. Elena gave me that look again. I choked back a sigh. Yeah, I get it, secrecy is in your DNA, but I'm trying to frigging help here. Simmer down.

"Jeff went crazy when Sadie disappeared. We tried to help, but we found no trail. Same thing happened last night when we were looking for Jeff. The scent just died."

I frowned.

"What do you mean, the scent died?" Danny asked.

"I mean it was gone. We tracked him to her apartment and out onto Josephine, and then nothing. Like Jeff vanished into thin air." Elena licked her lips and forced her hands to relax. I caught Danny's eyes. They'd darkened to a stormy blue and he had a small wrinkle at the top of his nose. I knew what he was thinking. Werewolves were the best trackers out there. There was no way they just lost a trail.

"Both Sadie's apartment and the street smelled wrong. Apex predator," Elena continued. "They reeked of magic. That's your area, not ours."

"The Council knew this and still denied the initial request?" I asked, screwing up my face in disbelief.

"They didn't think it was enough," Danny said, his eyes on Elena. The Alpha had gone creepily still again, her eyes hard. I huffed out an annoyed breath and shook my head. We were all supposed to be on the same team here. It was no wonder the weres didn't trust us.

"We need to see Jeff's home," I said, not unkindly. She nodded and pushed herself out of the booth. We scrambled to follow her outside and drove to a posh neighborhood near Sloan's Lake. As we walked up to Jeff's house, I texted Ethan.

Me: Find anything on Sadie's phone records?

Ethan: Not yet. Elena have anything?

Me: Oh yeah. Jeff's gone missing too.

Ethan: ....You're fucking joking.

Me: Glad to see you appreciate the gravity of the situation. Danny & me are on our way to his place now. Compare notes later?

Ethan: K.

My fingers tapped out a staccato beat against my phone and I looked up at the stucco walls and Spanish tile roof of the house. Gardenias scented the air and I was careful not to stray from the stone path that led to the front door. Elena led us into a stylish foyer with dark slate flooring that bled into warm hardwoods. Both complimented the moss green walls of the living room, filled with a comfortable-looking umber sectional and a truly enormous flat-screen TV. This place took wolf den to a whole new level.

Danny and I spread out, searching through mail and cabinets and closets. My back itched where Elena stared at me. She was apparently channeling all her pent-up aggression into her laser vision because she didn't say anything. I focused on finding something. Invading pack property and coming up empty handed was not exactly how I wanted this to go.

We moved into Jeff's bedroom, which was just as neat and tasteful as the rest of the house. I needed to watch some HGTV or some shit—I felt like I should apologize for even thinking about my cabin in that place. Danny combed through Jeff's dresser while I pulled open his desk drawers. I found a paper datebook and snorted. In the age of iPhones, I didn't know they made these things anymore. Most of the pages were blank, but I paused over a note penciled in for yesterday.

"Know someone with the initials LC that Jeff might have been meeting with?" I asked. Elena said nothing for a moment, smoothing her bangs off her forehead. The gesture was casual, but too controlled. Every muscle in her body was rigid.

"Is he material to the case?" she finally asked.

"Would I be asking otherwise?" Brain, check the tone on the mouth, please. Elena slipped into what I thought of as her Alpha stare: strong, calm, protective. Like an idiot, I stared back. I was getting tired of dominance games. "Look, Elena, this LC might have been the last person to see Jeff. Do you want your pup back or not?"

Yeah, Rachel, awesome. Just keep poking the snarling wolf with a stick. That was bound to end well. I caught Danny smirking. Love you too, bro.

"LC stands for Leon Cartwright. He's a friend of the pack," Elena said, her voice clipped. I got the distinct impression she was evaluating me. "You must give me your word that you'll be delicate. He's had a hard life."

"We just want to ask him some questions, Elena," Danny said gently. "He could help us find Sadie and Jeff."

Elena sighed. "I won't give you his address, but I'll arrange a meeting."

"Thanks," I said. "We appreciate the help."

Elena gave me a hard look. "Why are you here, Rachel?"

"Why else? Something bad's out there, I'm going to stop it."

Her expression didn't change. Seriously, Elena could give Spock a run for his money when it came to being inscrutable. "Did you know there are hunters working this case?"

"What?" My eyes widened and Danny sucked in a sharp, short breath.

"They need to stay out of this." That was a nice way of saying she would have no problem snacking on their spines if they threatened her pack. Freaking hunters. They always complicate shit.

I may kill supernatural creatures that prey on the innocent, but I have a system of accountability. A system of justice. Regular human hunters have no such system. They saw the world in a stark contrast of human and not human, no ifs, ands, or buts. I had learned that lesson in a particularly painful way.

"Thanks for the head's up," Danny said, putting a hand on my shoulder.

Elena nodded and we finished searching the house. An unsettled feeling twisted my stomach as we left, like I was taking a test for a class I hadn't signed up for.

"Well, that's awesome. Now we've got to dodge hunters?" I said, unlocking the passenger door to my Jeep.

Danny smirked. "Thought you loved a challenge, baby sister."

"I hate you."

"Don't you like working with me?" he teased, knocking into my shoulder.

"About as much as a hole in the head." I poked him in the ribs. Ethan was fine, but nobody understood me quite like Danny.

I wanted to retrace Jeff's steps so we headed back to

Sadie's apartment. I thought about the cops I'd seen here yesterday and my shoulder blades itched again. Good thing we didn't need to go inside this time.

Danny followed me as I roamed around to the back of the building, through a narrow alley that emptied out onto Josephine Street. The pack lost the scent here. So what in the hell was I looking for?

I kicked a small stone, my eyes moving over the sidewalk, young trees supported by metal stakes, brightly colored flowers in large wooden planters. More apartments across the street, some brick, some 70s fabulous. Cars parked at the curb. The acrid, burning smell of asphalt. Big leafy trees provided some shade from the sun threatening to melt my skin off.

My eyes went back to the saplings. One was torn from the ground, its roots sticking up like twisted fingers. An ugly brown ring of dead grass surrounded it and the stakes holding it lay in a tangled mess nearby. Sadie's apartment building was new, upscale. The kind that chose trendy paint jobs and decorative mulch for drunk college kids to puke on. No way a place like that lets an ugly uprooted tree lie around for long.

"What've you got?" Danny asked, ambling up behind me as I crouched by the tree. A couple of the limbs were snapped off, the green flesh inside withering in the summer heat. I chewed on my lip.

I stood up and eyed my brother. He had almost a foot and about ninety pounds on me, and had the same combat training I did. Should work for this experiment. "Hey, try to grab me."

"What?"

"Make like a creep and act like you're going to kidnap me."

He tilted his head, arching an eyebrow. "Alright."

In a flash, my brother was on me. He grabbed my arm in an iron grip, wrenching it behind my back. I ducked my head and rammed my foot into his leg. His hand caught the ends of my hair but my boot connected just above his knee. Danny grunted and bent over. His fingers tightened in my hair. Several stands tore loose, my scalp stinging, as I slammed my elbow into his ear.

I tore away from him and tried to imagine what Jeff would have done. Now would be a great time to shift.

Danny caught me around the middle, driving me to the ground in a tackle much more painful than the one his son had given me. Lights popped in front of my eyes as my head collided with the earth. We landed on the toppled sapling.

"And what was the point of that?" my brother panted, rolling off me to sit on the soft grass. "Other than to give me a damn headache? Could have pulled your punches, baby sister."

"Not real that way," I wheezed. Jesus, the dude could hit. I heaved myself upright, flopping over to the side so that the tree wasn't jamming into my back anymore. "Say Jeff fought someone." I motioned to the sapling.

"Had to be a strong son of a bitch to take down a were, even in human form."

"Not just strong. Supernaturally strong." I crawled around on my hands and knees, fingers searching through the grass.

"Rache... what the hell are you doing?"

My fingers brushed over something powdery. I sniffed it and immediately jerked my head away. Positive for refried ass.

"This same stuff was inside Sadie's apartment," I said, scooping it inside a plastic evidence bag.

"What is it?"

"No idea. Smell."

I handed him the bag and he wrinkled his nose. "It reminds me of the time you set the kitchen on fire."

"Jesus Christ, Danny, I was thirteen."

"You tried to cook Hot Pockets with magic. Sorry, but you're never living that down."

I ignored him and took out a sample disk, dropping it into the bag with the powder. It glowed blue, then black, then dimmed, and I fished it out. Danny looked over my shoulder as I ran it through the analyzer. It errored out.

"What the hell?" I frowned and hit SCAN again. It whirred and blinked the uplink light that showed it was connected to SCID, but then the same error message flashed across the screen: SAMPLE CORRUPT.

"Have you ever seen that?" I asked.

Danny shook his head.

"I'll need the lab to take a look. Whatever this is, perp left it at both scenes, so it means something."

Other than the weird powder, we found precisely jack on the street. I dropped Danny back at home and returned to my cabin, stopping for groceries on the way. String cheese and whiskey will only get one so far. I made a simple dinner of shrimp tacos and plopped down on the couch, setting my plate and beer on the worn coffee table and digging out my phone.

"So guess who's in town?" I said as soon as Ethan answered.

"BTS."

"No--what?" I said, momentarily distracted before shaking my head. "Hunters."

"Shit. Seriously?"

"Yep. Elena said they're sniffing our case. So we got to be discreet."

He snorted. "You, discreet? If you could keep your mouth shut, that might happen."

"Die in a fire, Ethan. What'd you get off the phone records?"

"Lots of calls and texts between Sadie and Jeff. One a week to her folks. A few others to random places, and a couple to a burner cell."

"Huh. That's interesting." I remembered the pictures I'd

seen in her apartment and a pang went through my chest as I thought of her family back home in Tuba City.

"Yeah. For a shifter, she's pretty damn normal."

"Says the witch with a 401K."

"Hey, no harm in being prepared for retirement."

Now it was my turn to snort. Like we would live that long. Well, Ethan might. He eventually wanted to transfer to another branch, and I actually wasn't sure what kept him on the job. But not me. I was like those soldiers who keep reenlisting for duty in active war zones.

"Alright, well, I guess tomorrow we see what else we can dig up," I said.

"Gotcha. Sweet dreams."

Not likely.

I CRAWLED out of bed early the next morning after only a few hours' sleep and stumbled into my kitchen for some caffeine. My bullshit sleep habits made strong black tea necessary for survival. I was just pouring the hot water into a mug when my phone rang. I snarled at it. It stubbornly refused to explode.

"What?" I barked.

"Rache, good, you're up. We've got a problem," Danny said, ignoring my outburst. The tension in his voice made me straighten up. Irritation evaporated as my gut twisted.

"What?" I asked again, softer this time.

"We've got another missing person. A colleague of Sadie's. Went on an errand yesterday and never made it home."

FIVE

This dude--whoever he was--was getting way too grabby. Three people in three days. Ballsy. Also, terrifying. I didn't want to think about what he was doing to them. And we still had no clue who he was or how he was picking his vics.

I showered, but no matter how hot I made the water, I still felt cold.

Danny texted me the address and I donned my suit and headed out. One stop at CBI to alert Jamie that Ethan and I were on a new case and drop off the incident report form from Pasha, then I was back in Highlands Ranch. It unnerved me to discover that the most recent vic, Marcus Rodriguez, lived only a few miles from my brother. I drove down a quiet street, lined with towering trees and grass way too green for the current temperatures. The Rodriguez home, a sprawling two-story colonial, sat in the middle of the block, its pale yellow siding and rich mahogany front door warm and inviting.

A silver, late-model BMW sat in the driveway next to a flagstone path bordered by orange blazing stars and white rose bushes. I parked the Jeep a little ways down the street,

51

strolled up to the front door and rang the bell. An attractive, if harried-looking, woman in her forties answered. She wore tailored pants and a light cotton shirt, her auburn hair pulled back in a clip. Her eyes were red-rimmed and her skin had the papery, wan tint brought on by lack of sleep. My gut clenched. Most of my cases involved deaths-- corrupt witch murdering rivals, psycho beastie eating folks. This missing person shit was harder. There was still hope.

"Can I help you?" she asked courteously as she held open the screen door.

"Are you Catherine Rodriguez?"

"Yes, I am. Who are you?"

"My name is Agent Collins and I'm with the Colorado Bureau of Investigation. I'm here to ask you a few questions regarding your husband's disappearance." I held out my ID. She glanced at it, saw the picture matched my face, and accepted it.

"I thought the sheriff's office was handling the case?"

"Yes ma'am, but we think this might be connected to an open investigation. May I come in?" I didn't have to work very hard to convince her. Hope is a dangerous thing.

She escorted me to a charming living room appointed with rich dark woods and cream fabrics, and perched on the edge of a wingback chair. She reminded me of a bird about to take flight. Her fingers shook as she tapped them against the opposite wrist, her head twitching in small, jerky motions. I couldn't blame her. Sitting around waiting for the cops to call sounded like a special kind of torture to me.

"You think Marcus is involved with something?" she asked.

"We have a possible lead but I need some more information. I appreciate how difficult this must be for you, Mrs. Rodriguez."

"Please, call me Catherine. Anything I can do to help... I just want him home. The kids--" Her voice broke as she tried to choke back tears. I looked away. My eyes landed on pictures showing a happy family. Their older son looked to be about Jake's age. Fishing at the lake, baseball team portraits, birthday parties. If Rodriguez followed the pattern, then he was some kind of supe, but he led a pretty frigging Norman Rockwell life. A life that had been torn away from him. Just like Jeff and Sadie. A muffled cracking noise caught my attention and I looked down to see that I'd been gripping my pen so hard it nearly broke.

"We're doing everything we can, Catherine," I said. "I'm afraid I may have to ask you some uncomfortable questions."

She nodded, taking a tissue from a nearby table and dabbing her face with it. Her back straightened, her fidgeting stopped. She met my eyes, and though they were bloodshot, steel lurked there too. I smiled and leaned over to pat her hand. My gesture of comfort did double-duty as I sent out my will. It brushed against her aura--warm, bright, loving. Catherine had a big heart. She was also entirely human.

I kept my senses open, feeling for traces of deception. "I understand Marcus was married before?"

"Yes, twice." She didn't blink. Her gaze didn't falter. She answered like I'd asked her to solve a math problem. Was it possible that Marcus had managed three wives with no drama? This dude deserved a medal.

"May I ask what happened to his previous wives?"

"Nothing happened. They got divorced."

Calm. Factual. I scribbled on my notepad. "Any reason to feel that these women might bear your husband ill will?"

"I can't imagine why. They broke up on good terms. He even continued to pay for their medical expenses after they separated."

"Medical expenses?"

"Both of Marcus's ex-wives had pretty serious illnesses. He tries to make light of it now, saying he's bad luck, but you know. Bad things happen, sometimes for no reason."

"Do you know what kind of illnesses?"

"Marcus never said. I got the impression that it was something the doctors couldn't figure out. But both Helen and Irene eventually got better and are fine now, as far as I know." She cleared her throat and her eyes went to the pictures on the walls. I wanted to give her a hug.

"Have you ever been ill, Catherine?"

"No. I mean, not like that. What's this got to do with Marcus?"

"We're just gathering background information. Trying to explore every lead. So Marcus works at Hughes Corp?" She nodded. That company was starting to look like a kiss of death. "What does he do there?"

"He's a lawyer."

"Did he have any problems at his job?"

"Not that he talked about."

"Any other business dealings?"

"No, not really," she said, but she brought her hand to her face, covering her mouth. Cat was keeping a secret.

"Catherine, I really need to know everything. No matter how trivial or embarrassing." I let my voice grow stern and her eyes flew to me. She swallowed again, her hand still hiding her mouth.

"Well, he...he'd taken up a second job. I don't really understand why, it's not like we need the money." She shook her head and took a steadying breath. "But he said it was for the thrill of it, and he's such a good man, I didn't want to make him feel bad about it..."

"What was the job?"

"He was working nights for Bare Assets." She winced as she spoke and dropped her eyes to her lap, color rising in her cheeks. Her embarrassment hit me in a rush of heat and an uncomfortable twisting in my gut. Both sensations were once removed, like the diluted sense of pain you get when you slam your head into the door while drunk. Not that I've ever done that.

"And what do they do?"

"It's an all-male revue. You know...strippers," she mumbled. Huh.

"Believe me, that's not the worst thing I've ever heard." I gave her a reassuring smile but still made note of Marcus's moonlighting. "Can you tell me if there is anything that stands out to you about Marcus's behavior before he disappeared?"

"No. It was just a normal day. I asked him to stop by our designer's office to look at some granite samples. We're redoing the kitchen." She gave me a watery smile. "He never made it to her office."

I made some notes and then pulled out the picture of Sadie and Jeff that I'd swiped from her cube. "Do either of these people look familiar?"

Catherine examined the photo, pursing her lips. "Her, maybe. I think she worked with Marcus. Are these people involved in his case?"

"We're not sure yet." I needed to figure out what Marcus was. Catherine was either masterful at controlling her emotions or she had no clue her husband was not strictly human. I'd seen supes in front of cops. They were never this helpful. "Did Marcus ever take trips by himself?" She gave me a confused look and shook her head. "Special diet, allergies?"

"How does this help you find him?"

That glimpse of steel I'd seen earlier swam to the surface. Tiptoe, tiptoe. Goddammit. I'd never admit it, but Ethan was right--discretion was definitely not the better part of my valor. "Would you mind showing me where Marcus spent most of his time? Perhaps a few of his personal items?"

"I suppose." Her voice sank deeply into the hard consonants and she looked at me as if seeing me for the first time.

"But the police didn't want to see anything like that when I called them. They just told me to wait."

"I'm a specially trained investigator, Catherine. I pick up on things the uniforms miss. That's why I'm here." I was two seconds away from pushing a glamour onto her when she nodded. She blinked a little too rapidly, the lines in her face tense as she led me down the hall to the back of the house.

We entered a room with a massive mahogany desk, flanked by ornate bookshelves. Just like at Sadie's, I worked my way around the room, my fingers brushing over objects. Most of the stuff was mundane: documents, law texts, family photos. I stood behind the desk, seeing the room as Marcus might have. Drawers were filled with paper clips, pens, more papers. Catherine watched me with growing agitation. Each item of her husband's that I touched was an insult, a reminder.

A small clay pipe rested on the corner of the desk. It looked ancient, a solid band of gold wrapped around the mouthpiece and Celtic knotwork carved into the bowl and stem. I laid two fingers on it and sent out my senses. Wild energy flooded my hand, making my skin tingle.

"Would you mind if I took this? It may help us in the investigation." I smiled again, trying to look trustworthy, as I picked up the pipe. "I promise I'll return it."

"The pipe? You think it will help you?" Catherine stared at me, her eyes narrowed.

"Yes ma'am."

She smashed her lips together as if she were restraining herself from telling me to go to hell. I picked up on traces of confusion and suspicion wafting from her, but something stronger kept them at bay. Hope. She might have thought me a lunatic, but she was desperate to find her husband. After a long moment, she nodded. I dropped the pipe into a plastic evidence bag and slipped it into my pocket.

"Thank you, Catherine. I'll be going now, but if you think

of anything, please call me. I'll see myself out." I gave her a CBI business card with my cell number on it and walked to the door.

"Agent Collins," Catherine called, and I turned to face her. "Please... you'll find Marcus, won't you?" Tears welled in her eyes again and raw emotion socked into me like a frigging punch. I quickly shut down my senses, my head swimming. She looked older than she had when she'd answered the door, vulnerability and fear widening her eyes, making her jaw rigid.

I grimaced and laid my hand on her shoulder. "I'll do everything I can."

~

CBI OFFICE WAS BUZZING with activity when I walked in. Suits everywhere, and Jamie's door was closed while he talked to Pete Yates, the Colorado attorney general. Neither of them looked happy.

"What's going on?" I asked, my eyes on the captain while I pulled my laptop out of my bag.

"We're now under official internal investigation," Ethan said. His desk faced mine and mocked me with its consistently clear inbox. "You turn in your report?"

"Yeah, same day Jamie told me about the review. Yates didn't waste any time, did he?"

"Well, you know. There's national attention on police use of force. I'm sure he's taking political heat. But the Council will clear us."

"What about them?" I asked, tipping my chin toward the rest of the unit office. Our vanilla colleagues hunched over their desks, fists clenched, shirts rumpled, faces drawn. "They're paying for our crimes, Ethan."

"They're not crimes, Rache. We're doing our job. And the Council's not going to let the entire CBI get thrown under the bus."

I sat down at my desk and opened my laptop. "You have a lot of faith in them."

"Yeah. Don't you?"

I hesitated for a minute, then pulled my laptop lid low so I could look at him. "Council knew that a practitioner was involved in Sadie's disappearance and they still denied the request. We wreak havoc on local cops. They put us in the field and teach us how to kill with magic and then hold a frigging noose over our necks for doing just that. We put our lives on the line to protect the normals and then the Council hides it all. What kind of organization does that?"

"One that knows the world isn't ready to know the truth," he said, and there was something hard in his tone.

"It's been seven hundred years, man. When is the world ever going to be ready?"

"We're outnumbered, Rachel. We reveal ourselves..." He shook his head. "How'd that go for you and Ryan?"

"Don't," I snapped. "Don't bring that up." I regretted ever telling Ethan about him.

"I'm just saying. You of all people should trust the Council."

Trust the Council. Right. The same people that had covered me with suspicion and contempt since I was thirteen years old. Labeled me a hellbound waiting to happen. Left me, a frigging kid, on my own to figure out the powerful and dangerous magic of ley lines, and then made me prove on a weekly basis that I hadn't been corrupted. Yeah, that's a good foundation for trust.

Corrupted. The word made the think of the powder and I pulled out my phone.

Me: Hey dude got a question. What's it mean when SCID comes back with sample corrupt?

Pasha: It means you fucked up the sample.

Me: Haha. Seriously tho it happened twice now. Both on this weird powder I found at two crime scenes.

"Hey Rache?"

I looked up at Gina Perez, a fellow CBI agent, standing next to my desk. With her was a tall Black man built like he'd once been a linebacker. He wore a cheap grey suit with an expensive tie and had a gold shield clipped on his belt near a hip holster holding a police-issue Glock 22.

"This is Brad Green, homicide detective with Denver PD. He's here to see you," Gina said.

"Agent Collins," he said, extending his hand. He looked like he'd been on the job a while, even if I'd never seen him before. A few wrinkles lined his skin and his goatee had hints of grey.

I got to my feet and shook it. His hand all but swallowed mine. "Pleasure. This is my partner, Ethan Hale." I nodded toward Ethan. "What can we do for you?"

"Just got word CBI is handling the Warren, Sharpe, and Rodriguez cases. Was wondering if you wouldn't mind sharing some info."

I exchanged a look with Ethan. This was different. Usually, we were the ones bothering cops for information. "Sure, but there's no evidence our vics are dead. We're still pursuing this as a missing persons case."

"I know. That's why I want you to look at this. Case got handed down to me when the lead investigator retired." He held out a file folder. I took it and flipped it open, finding a report from a murder last year. Kenny Goodwin, fifty-six. Cause of death, blunt force trauma.

"Jesus, what happened to his house?" I asked, pulling out a photo of the crime scene. There wasn't one single piece of furniture that wasn't broken.

"Brutal fight, best we could tell. No prints, no DNA. Perp was careful," Green said. "No signs of forced entry."

"Anything missing?" Ethan asked.

"Funny you bring that up. Goodwin had about two thou-sand bucks in a safe and a bunch of electronics—hi-fi stereo system, multiple computers, expensive camera. None of it touched. Only thing that appeared to be missing was a bunch of books."

"Books?" I scrunched up my face. "And you think our missing persons are related to this? What's your theory?"

"You got a link between your vics?" Green's face was hard, like he was pissed off, and he avoided my question. It was a test.

"Warren and Rodriguez worked at Hughes Corp. Sharpe was Warren's boyfriend. He was looking for her, maybe got too close." That was as much as I could share with him. "Have we done something to offend you, Detective?"

He bent his head, hands on his hips, and huffed out a wry laugh. "You personally, no. But I don't trust this division. You have some discouraging numbers around here, and now with this investigation? Oh yeah, I know," he said when I looked surprised. "Frankly, I don't think these cases will have your full attention. I'm contesting the request for CBI assistance. If I get my way, Denver PD will handle this and every other case until you get your house in order."

"You're going to walk in here and ask us for help and then insult us?" Ethan snorted. "We're still doing our jobs, Green. Investigation or no."

"I'm not asking for anything. I'm the lead on the Goodwin case and if I connect it to yours, I'll be lead there, too. So consider this my formal request for your case notes." He collected his file and walked out of the unit office without a glance back.

"He came all the way down here to ask for our notes?" Ethan asked, and shook his head. "He didn't even stick around to get his answers."

"He didn't come here for our notes or for answers," I said, watching him get on the elevator. "He came here to size us up."

My phone vibrated on my desk and I picked up.

Wonderful.

～

I LAID on my brother's buttery leather couch, one arm over my eyes and half asleep. The smell of tomatoes and basil drifted from his kitchen, and occasionally I'd feel Jake looking at me. It was quiet, peaceful.

Which was completely shattered the moment my lummox of a brother decided to sprawl all over me.

"Sister, wake up," he called in a sing-song voice.

"Oh my God, get off me!" I shoved at him, but I was totally prone and he was nothing but dead weight.

He laughed and rolled to his feet, leaving me feeling like I'd just been steamrolled. "Dinner's ready," he said. "It must've been a hard day, you never let me cook for you."

I shuffled into the kitchen, yawning and rubbing my eyes. "Yeah. CBI is under investigation, and had a lovely detective from DPD come in for a dic--" I spied Jake and swiftly cleaned up my vocabulary-- "jurisdictional tug-of-war. Real fun."

Danny set a platter of caprese on the table and heaped spaghetti and meatballs onto my plate. He wasn't exactly the foodie that I was, but he did alright, especially for being a single dad.

"Beer?" he asked, and I nodded. He popped the cap on a bottle of Great Divide and handed it to me. I took a long drink and held the bottle to my forehead, the frigid glass soothing against my skin.

"You okay, Rache?" Danny asked, then added almost absent-mindedly, "Elbows off the table, Jake."

"Aunt Rachel has her elbows on the table," Jake said sourly.

"Aunt Rachel failed her Emily Post classes. Listen to your dad," I said, and gave my nephew a tired smile before looking back to my brother. "Yeah, I guess. Just... All this stuff that's going on. Ethan always thinks the Council's going to fix everything--"

"And Pasha didn't. You're back to feeling like the outsider."

I poked at my meatballs. Pasha had her own qualms with the Council, mostly stemming from the way they'd totally freaking abandoned the hoodoo community in Louisiana after Hurricane Katrina. Her mission in life was to change the system from inside it, but we'd shared not only a skepticism about the Council but also the feeling of being its unwanted children. Ethan was a true believer.

"Yeah, I guess. Just stirs up a lot of crap, you know?"

"I can imagine." His face twisted in a pained expression. "I should have stood up for you more. You were a kid, you didn't deserve all that."

I waved his apology away. "You were a kid too, Danny. Not your fault."

"All what?" Jake asked.

"Well, buddy, you know how we talked about not judging people on their skin or what they believe or if they're a boy or a girl?" Jake nodded and Danny continued, "It's sort of like that. Your Aunt Rachel has a really special power, and some witches were mean to her when she was growing up."

"Why?"

"Because they were scared of it. People do bad things out of fear. They made her feel really crummy."

Jake looked at me with wide blue eyes that were so like his father's and frowned. "Are you okay now?"

I smiled. "Yeah, Jake, I'm okay."

Lying to a nine-year-old wasn't exactly going to win me any awards, but there was no way I was going to expose him to the Council's bullshit any sooner than necessary. There was still a chance he wouldn't be a witch at all, and if he were, he'd probably be an elemental witch like his father. A wild genetic occurrence made me a ley witch, a fact that asshole witch kids had used to bully me for being a freak. The Council never did anything to put a stop to it, instead perpetuating the line that ley witches were more likely to be corrupted. Kids and adults alike used that to fuel their bigotry. I had turned my hurt into aggression, which my parents tried to channel into judo, but that had only made me better at fighting.

After dinner, I helped Danny clean up and then put Jake to bed, at his insistance. Since Danny had told him the truth about our family last year, my nephew had been demanding more and more time with me. I hated that I could give him so little. My work was my life, and I moved from case to case like it could keep my ghosts from haunting me. It never really worked, but sometimes, on nights like this one, I felt a little bit of peace.

"Aunt Rachel?" Jake looked up at me from where he was curled against my side. I lay on his bed with him, my back propped against the headboard, as I read him a book.

"What's up?"

"Were witches mean to my dad too?"

"No, buddy," I said, and gave him a small smile. "Your dad was the most popular guy in school. Everyone liked him, just like they do now."

"Dad said you have a special power."

That was one way of looking at it, but I decided to spare Jake my cynicism. "I'm a pretty rare kind of witch."

He smiled. "That's so cool. I hope my magic is just like yours."

"No," I said sharply, and then grimaced when Jake looked taken aback. "My magic isn't nearly as amazing as your dad's. He can control fire and water and all sorts of stuff."

"But he never does it. He never does any magic at all," he said plaintively and twisted his comforter around his fingers.

"He doesn't need to. Your dad is much smarter than me and has a way better job."

Jake sighed. "I just wish he did awesome stuff like you."

"Come on, now. Your dad has raised you entirely by himself. That's pretty awesome, right?" I nudged him with my shoulder.

"Yeah, it is," he admitted after some thought. "And he never misses my soccer games."

"See? I miss them all the time, because my job sucks." I closed the book and kissed his head. "I think it's about time you go to sleep."

"Will you come read to me tomorrow night?"

Christ, just twist a knife in me. "I'm sorry, Jake, I can't. I'm working a case. There's a bad guy out there hurting people and I have to stop him."

He gave me a serious look. "Are you good at your job, Aunt Rachel?"

"Depends on who you ask." Confusion crossed his face, and I gave him a lopsided grin. "Yes, I am good at it."

Jake perked up, and smiled contentedly as he snuggled down under his covers. "Then those people will be okay. You'll help them for sure."

I turned out the light and closed his door, and then wandered out to the deck where my brother sat in an Adirondack chair. He passed me a beer as I dropped down into the chair next to his. We didn't talk for a while, but it was a comfortable silence.

"You make these chairs?" I asked, running my hand over the cherry red paint. He nodded, and I grinned. "Turning into an old man, making furniture."

"Hey, you do your engine thing, I do my woodworking thing. Don't get all judgy with me."

I smirked, but I recalled my conversation with Jake, and

the expression faded. "You need to talk to your kid. He told me he wants to be a ley witch."

"And?"

"And I never want Jake to be like me, in any way," I said heatedly, and then looked away and took a pull from my beer.

Danny eyed me and warmth spread across my cheeks. "I know a lot of things have happened to you to make you think that. But Rachel, you're not some bad, awful thing." He leaned forward and rested his elbows on his knees. "What else did Ethan say?"

"What do you mean?"

"I know you. Council's been giving you shit since your magic came in. That doesn't drag you down like this. So what else did he say?"

I picked at the label on my bottle. "He just... he brought up Ryan. Said I should know why the Council keeps everything secret." The name burned the back of my throat and I instinctually covered the scar on my side. It'd been six years and that scar still ached like new.

Danny shook his head. "He shouldn't have said that."

"I shouldn't have told him in the first place."

"Rachel, that's not the solution here." He smiled, but there was something sad in it. "I know you're scared to let anyone close to you. I know I didn't help that, bailing on you the way I did. But you don't have to go through life alone."

"Sure. How much've you been dating since Margaret left? Because I remember, Danny. You shut down too."

"And I'm telling you to learn from my mistakes. For once in your life, let me be your big brother and look out for you, okay?"

"You always look out for me. Think how screwed up I'd be without you."

He laughed, but he was shaking his head again like I was hopeless. We finished our beers and I stood up, stretching.

Danny walked me to the front door, where I yawned again and knuckled my eyes.

"Why don't you stay here tonight? I've got to take Jake up to Mom and Dad's in the morning but you could crash out here, actually get some sleep. I'll even read to you if you want."

A slow smile curved my mouth. "I'm not a kid anymore."

"Fine, whatever. Too grown up to accept my love." He mock pouted and I shoved him in the shoulder, which he deftly pivoted into a hug. He held me for a long time. "Be good to yourself, Rache. I don't want to see you burn out."

"Better to burn out than fade away."

"Said by a guy who committed suicide. Yeah, not comforting." Danny released me and gave me a worried look. "Get some sleep. Work the case. Everything will be fine, I promise."

I gave him a kiss on the cheek and left, making sure to follow his walkway out to my car.

THE NEXT MORNING, I sat at my desk at CBI, staring at my laptop and twirling a pen in my fingers. Using magic of an entirely different sort, Ethan had hacked Marcus's emails and sent me the files. We could've used CBI techs, but this was faster. For two hours, I'd trawled through a bunch of mundane, boring shit—crap in Latin I assumed was legalese. Languages have never been my thing. My gut nagged me about the fact that both Marcus and Sadie were supes who worked for Hughes Corp. It could be a coincidence, but damn if the coincidences weren't stacking up. Call me crazy, but that shit seemed suspicious. Maybe someone was trying to hurt William Hughes. The guy was such a colossal dick, I wouldn't be surprised.

Of course, maybe Hughes was involved.

"Take a freaking nap, Don Quixote," I muttered, setting my computer aside and grabbing a bottle of iced tea from my desk. I clicked over to another window showing an email from Danny. I'd asked him to take a look at our vics' bank records, and he discovered that all three missing people had transferred large sums of money to this Leon Cartwright. I had no idea what the hell that meant, but it seemed like it should be important.

I stared at the numbers until my eyes blurred. It was definitely time for a break, and to call in someone who actually did financial shit for a living. Sighing, I pulled out my phone and tapped my brother's number, idly surfing a website while I waited for him to pick up.

It rang to voicemail. I was ten seconds past the beep, my brain stuck like a broken record player, when I finally processed that he hadn't answered.

"Hey, uh, it's me. Give me a call when you get this." I tapped the end button and stared at my phone as if it were an alien device. Danny always answered my calls. I tried him one more time with the same result. He said he was going up to Dillon this morning. Maybe he left his phone in the car.

I needed to look at something else for a while. Maybe there was something I'd missed in one of the reports. I shoved files around, trying to find Marcus Rodriguez's case notes from the Douglas County Sheriff's Office, and ended up knocking over a stack of books. Spitz and Fisher's *Medicolegal Investigation of Death* sprawled on the floor, its pages askew, and I sighed as I bent over to pick it up. I froze as I straightened my back, looking between the blue hardback cover and the other books on my desk. Books. Green had said that the only thing missing from Kenny Goodwin's house was books.

I logged into the joint law enforcement database that CBI shared with every local jurisdiction and looked up the case, clicking over to crime scene photos. The splintered furniture made it hard to see anything else, but I was looking for something very specific.

"Son of a bitch," I breathed. There, above Goodwin's door, was a gold charm bag: a witch's spell to protect his home from evil energy. Born witches used inlaid wards, but low-level practitioners had to rely on fetishes like charm bags.

"What?" Ethan asked, looking over at me.

"Goodwin was a witch, but not Council. Look." I turned my laptop around for him to see.

His eyebrows lifted. "But Goodwin wasn't kidnapped. He was killed in his home."

"I think this was the perp's dry run. He didn't anticipate the fight he'd get from even a lowbie like Goodwin. Had to perfect his method before going after bigger fish. And then there's the stolen books."

Ethan sat back in his chair. "Perp needed a way to learn about supernatural weaknesses. Goodwin probably had a well-stocked library."

"We need to take another run at the evidence."

We packed up and headed to my cabin. We often worked out of my house, telling Jamie that we were interviewing witnesses. Our evidence would look strange on the boards at CBI. The framework of a theory had been itching at my brain since I woke up, but I just couldn't quite put it together. Three supes. Four now, including Goodwin. All different kinds. Jeff was connected to Hughes Corp tangentially, so maybe that was the perp's hunting grounds. But why? He hadn't killed them, he'd *taken* them. That distinction kept sticking in my mind. And he had a hell of a lot of power to do it, too. I still had no clue what Marcus Rodriguez was, but the magic in that pipe was nothing to dick around with.

And how had the kidnapper known what they were? I'd spent three days turning my victims' lives inside out. They all carefully concealed their true natures. Blended in. A witch could have known, but there was no way a witch could snag a werewolf. I'd tangled with loups. The only reason I wasn't puppy chow was that I carried silver bullets and was a damn good shot.

Maybe it was just a strong witch. A really strong witch. With no fear of death.

Maybe it was Voldemort.

Assuming He Who Must Not Be Named was not, in fact, my bad guy, I still couldn't figure out why someone would want to start a living X-Men collection. Werewolves had preternatural strength. Skinwalkers could look like anything. Marcus could... lawyer your way out of jail. That seemed like a legit superpower to me.

I groaned and ground my palms into my eyes. I was getting nowhere. Ethan mulled over the evidence map on my wall, hands on his hips. He straightened one of the pictures and I gave him a massive side-eye. Ethan was the kind of guy who ironed his t-shirts. I was lucky if my jeans didn't have holes in them.

"Except for Jeff, it could be some kind of corporate attack thing," he mused, trailing in the wake of my thoughts from this morning.

"Yeah. I hear Wall Street is real big on using monsters for white-collar crime." Sarcasm didn't so much drip from my voice as gush from it. Frustration sent my snark factor to Tony Stark levels.

"Okay, so we've got two known supes and a—you figure out what Marcus is?"

"Some kind of fae. SCID had nothing, but the magic I'm getting off that pipe is wild and powerful."

"Okay, so three known supes go missing. Two work at the same company. Dry run on the local witch. Could still be the hunters Elena mentioned, but why would they go after vics that are so... normal? And why kill Goodwin?" He rubbed at his chin, dark eyes following my mess of arrows and lines.

"This doesn't feel like hunters. It's too methodical." I

chewed on my lip. "What if Hughes Corp isn't the target but the perp?"

"What?"

"Well, I mean, William Hughes more specifically. What if he's, I don't know, using these people for something?"

"You got evidence I'm not seeing here? Hughes Corp has probably five hundred employees, and that's just here in Denver. What are the chances he knew two random people?"

"Oh, he made it very clear to me that he knew everything about his company." My shoulders bunched and I forced them to relax. Even remembering Hughes made me want to punch something. "But anyway, it's just a feeling."

"Stretching a bit, aren't you?"

"You didn't meet this guy. He was one of those alpha male douchebags."

"Just because you didn't like him doesn't mean he's involved, Rache." Even though I wanted to kick him, I had to admit he had a point. Actually, that just made me want to kick him more.

"I know," I said, shrugging. "The guy just gave me the heebs."

"You said the same thing about Victor, and he's the vice chair of the Executive. I think your heeb meter is broken."

"Bite me." I puffed out my cheeks and snatched my phone off the table. Maybe Danny had gleaned some insight from their financials. I was a little annoyed that he hadn't called me back. Unlike me, my brother generally enjoyed full nights of sleep and rose early. Also unlike me, he always returned phone calls. I'm the younger sibling. It's my job to be irresponsible.

The phone rolled to voicemail. Again.

"Have you heard from my brother?" I asked.

He frowned. "Not since yesterday afternoon."

A bad feeling turned my insides to ice. He was probably just busy, or left his phone in the car. Right. Of course. In the middle of a case where supes were disappearing left and right.

Fuck.

I called him three more times, with the same result.

I called my parents.

"Is Danny up there?" I asked when my mom answered.

"I thought he was with you?"

"I can't get a hold of him. You haven't heard from him?"

"No," she said slowly, her voice pitching higher. "He dropped off Jake this morning and said he was headed back to Denver."

It was possible I was having a heart attack.

I hung up the phone and snatched my jacket off the chair, then bolted out to my Jeep, Ethan on my heels. He barely shut the door before I peeled out of the driveway, gravel flying as my tires spun. My expression was blank, my body steady, but inside I was coming apart. Danny had to be okay, he just had to be. I couldn't take it if he wasn't.

I hurtled down C-470 at a truly alarming speed, but for once, Ethan didn't say anything. He wasn't that stupid.

Danny's house sat there, prim and proper and completely at odds with the chaos erupting in my head. His car was in his garage, keys on the table by the front door. I swept through the empty house, fruitlessly calling my brother's name. Buttery leather furniture and cheery curtains and pictures of Jake on the wall--the best thing I could say was that it didn't look like there were signs of a struggle. I should've stayed. If I had stayed, I could've protected him.

An iron fist squeezed my heart when I found that same burnt-smelling powder by his back door. Danny's house was warded--not as heavily as my parents, but well enough. He should have been safe.

I sprinted back out to my Jeep and drove around the city in a panic. CBI, Douglas County Sheriff, Denver PD--I talked to every cop I knew, checked out every supernatural bar, shop, and hidey-hole. Called the other local witches Danny sometimes hung out with. I knew it was stupid, but I just couldn't sit there. This wasn't happening. Danny was the good one, the smart one, the responsible one. He had a son. He took care of me, despite my best efforts to shove him away. He made everyone feel better with his smile.

I was supposed to be the one that bit it in some bloody mess. Not Danny. My brother was supposed to grow old and have grandkids and teach them to play catch and volunteer at a museum and build furniture as a hobby in his garage.

I thought of Catherine Rodriguez, the dark circles under her eyes, the fragile shell that held her together. I had a fucking keen sense of sympathy for her.

Each hour that passed squeezed my heart harder.

We returned to my cabin late that night--or, rather, early the next morning. I was physically and emotionally drained, my body sluggish and my mind worse. As we stumbled inside, I turned right down the hallway and headed back toward my workroom.

"Feel up to holding a circle for me?" I asked.

Ethan stared at me in disbelief. "Rachel, are you serious? You're beat, I can see it on your face."

"I'm fine."

Ethan often treated me like a fragile flower. He cared about me and I appreciated that, but lately it had been grating on my nerves. I knew my limits. I knew the dangers. I didn't need him bitching at me. I stalked off to my work-room, grabbed a copper bowl, and began shoving around jars of herbs. Ethan stood in the doorway and watched me unhappily.

"What are you doing?"

"Tracking spell."

"Rachel--"

"Don't 'Rachel' me," I snapped. "Something has my brother, Ethan. I'm going to fucking find him."

"Do you even have a focusing object?" he asked.

"Got some of Danny's hair in my safe." He kept some of mine too. It was our version of life insurance. Jars of iris root, mugwort, and cowslip slammed down next to a short knife and I dug into the small fire-safe I kept in the closet before sitting cross-legged inside the circle. I clutched the small bundle of sandy blonde hair like a lifeline and gave Ethan a mulish look.

He sighed and shuffled over to the circle, dropping down to his haunches. Once again, he gathered energy to himself and touched two fingers to the metal ring, sending up a sphere of protection around me.

I took a deep breath, centering myself, and dumped the herbs into the bowl, using the knife to prick my thumb and squeeze out several drops of blood. I pulled my will into a tight ball, expanded it, packed it tightly with my intent, then struck a match and set the herbs on fire.

"Find," I whispered, pushing my will into the word. Smoke curled up from the bowl, tickling my nose in a familiar way. I inhaled deeply and closed my eyes. The spell wrapped around my mind, and images flew by at warp speed. I recognized the skyline of Denver. I-25. A sign, Exit 235, CO-52 Dacono/Fort Lupton. I pushed harder, sending more energy into the spell. A thick column of impenetrable darkness loomed ahead, just like it had when I tried to find Sadie. The spell circled it, looking for a way in, but it was as if a magical wall enclosed the town. The spell tugged and fought, trying to show me Danny's location, but the barricade rebuffed it again and again.

Ethan raised an eyebrow as I reached for another jar. Dragon's blood—a bullshit new-agey name given to an old-age compound resin—acted like a nitro booster for an engine, juicing up any spell. It was also flammable as all hell. I dropped a small pinch onto the smoldering herbs. It bloomed into flame, smoke roiling over me. I poured my will into it, but it was like ramming into a brick wall with a shopping cart.

"Alright, goddammit," I muttered. I reached for the ley line, pushing its power into the spell. I hammered at the smoky black wall, trying to bludgeon my way through it. Slick, hot power bowed for a moment and then slammed outward, throwing me back. The line inside me spit and hissed, burning against my skull.

With a thunderous crack, the copper bowl exploded.

"Holy shit!" I yelped, scrambling backwards and throwing my arms up to protect my face. Ethan dropped his circle and leapt toward me. I jumped up and began stomping out the embers searing my floor. The acrid smell of burning wood lingered in the air as Ethan and I stared at the shattered remains of the bowl.

"What in God's name caused that?" He looked seriously unnerved. Join the frigging club, buddy.

"I don't know. Something was blocking the spell. So I drew on the line and tried to break it down. Then boom."

"Did you get anything?"

"Just the city. Fort Lupton."

"Well, that tells us something." Ethan grimaced. "Wherever Danny is, he's heavily warded."

"And more importantly, he's alive." Tracking spells wouldn't work if the subject were dead. I stared down at my charred floor and the remains of my spell bowl.

"You know of anything strong enough to do that?" I asked, a cold feeling in my chest, and motioned to the ruins of my bowl.

"No," Ethan said quietly.

Fan-freaking-tastic.

SIX

I didn't sleep--at all. Every time I drifted off, nightmares set in. I saw the kid I'd killed in Fort Collins. When I looked down at his face, Danny's dead eyes stared back at me.

Around six, I stalked out of my bedroom. It was like I'd stuck my finger in a socket--an uncomfortable buzzing pulsed along my limbs. My stomach churned. My head throbbed. I opened my refrigerator and stared at the contents, wanting to cook.

Danny usually ate my leftovers.

I took another run at our evidence, rubbing one of the plastic bags containing our foul-smelling powder between my fingers. I needed to get this shit analyzed, now. I was missing something, I could feel it--like working a jigsaw puzzle when the dog has chewed up one vital piece.

A pounding at my door nearly made me come out of my skin. My gun was in my hand and the line singing through my brain before I even realized I was standing. Jesus, Rachel. Chill. The person knocked again. I took a minute to clear my head, because I always hated to start the day by shooting someone.

"Hi, uh, delivery?"

I peered out at a dude in khaki shorts and a green polo with some logo embroidered on the chest. He carried a large bouquet of flowers, white lilies and carnations and other stuff I didn't recognize.

"Delivery? For the Collins funeral?" the guy said, slowing his words like maybe I didn't understand English.

"What did you say?" It came out like a threat and the look on my face must have been freaking terrifying, because he actually took a step back.

"The, uh, uh, this is for the--" He dug a rumpled piece of paper out of his pocket, eyes flicking back to me like I was a wild dog about to chew his face off. "The Daniel Collins funeral."

The guy dropped the flowers as I grabbed his wrist. My fingers dug into his flesh and I knew it'd leave a bruise, but I was having trouble giving a fuck about that at the moment.

"Who sent these?" I demanded.

"I-I don't know! We just got a call, placed an order for the--for the flowers. Look, I'm sorry, okay. I'll take them back if you don't like them."

I snatched the paper out of his hand and shoved him away. "Get the fuck out of here."

He didn't need telling twice, his Toyota chewing up gravel as he sped out of my driveway. Choking down bile, I picked up the flowers and carried them inside. I sat them on the pass-through, where they looked suffocating, sucking all the air out of my cabin. I plucked out the card with trembling hands.

You should know I did everything I could, it was just too late. How does the shoe fit now?

I don't know what I'd expected, but it wasn't that. What was too late? Was I supposed to know what this was referencing? I braced myself against the counter, licking my lips and taking several long, slow breaths. Danny was a witch. I'd thought he'd been taken for the same reason that Sadie, Jeff, and Marcus were snatched, thought it was random bad luck. I looked back at the flowers, doing my damnedest to keep breathing. Somebody clearly had an axe to grind.

Somebody that knew my brother. Knew where I lived. Somebody arrogant enough to taunt me. That's what set me off. It wasn't enough to hurt these people, their families-- innocent, good people. It wasn't enough to take my brother. Now this asshole was rubbing my face in it. Playing a goddamn game. Anger surged, clawing its way up my chest and devouring my fear. Send me flowers for my brother's funeral? What a fucking cheesy move. I shoved down all my worry, all the helplessness I felt. I grabbed on to that anger and fucking rode it.

Fine, Darth Douchebag. Let's play.

I snatched my phone up from the counter and turned the card from the flowers over to see the back. I tapped the number into my phone and tried to breathe through the tachycardia consuming my heart.

A cheery woman answered the phone. "Petal Passions, how can I help you?"

"My name is Agent Collins with the Colorado Bureau of Investigation. I need the credit card information for an order that was delivered today."

"Um, credit card information? I'm afraid I can't give that out over the phone."

"Lady, I'm a cop," I said, exasperation leaking into my voice. "I can get a warrant, but do you really want that hassle? Police all over your business?"

"I'm sorry, but I need some sort of proof you are who you say you are." She sounded genuinely apologetic. "Could you come by the shop?"

I ground my teeth. I didn't like the delay in getting what I wanted, but I also couldn't terrorize innocent florists. "Fine. I'll be there in half an hour."

Besides, I could always glamour her if we met in person.

I forced myself to sit for a moment, my fingers drumming against my thigh so rapidly they were basically vibrating. Okay, so Danny was missing and I was getting sent bouquets of doom from a bad guy we couldn't identify. Supes were disappearing without a trace. And let's not forget that some crazy fucking magic that could block ley spells was wrapped up in all this, along with some weird-smelling powder. I could figure this out. Just work the damn case, Rachel.

I called Ethan.

"Someone just sent me flowers," I said.

"Generally, that's a good thing, Rache."

"They were for the Daniel Collins funeral, with a note saying, *You should know I did everything I could, it was just too late. How does the shoe fit now?*"

Ethan was silent for a long time. "But the tracking spell--"

"I know. I don't think he's dead." Please, God, don't let him be dead. "I think it's somebody fucking with me."

"What the hell? Why?"

"For kicks. I don't know," I snarled, rubbing at my face.

"He's clearly focused on you," Ethan said. "Your brother. Asking you how does it feel to be a vic."

"I'm not a vic," I snapped.

"He's putting you in that position, though. He wants you emotional. Any other time and deputies would be interviewing you."

I ignored that thought. "We need to get a handle on this shit, and fast."

"Rachel, I know you don't want to hear this, but you should really turn this over to another deputy."

"Over my dead body." Bitterness colored my words. "They'll sit around having a goddamn strategy meeting and wonder about how to cover it up."

"Rachel, you can't do this alone."

"Fine. You call the Council. I'm going to work." I hung up on him, catapulting across the room and grabbing my jacket.

The Police blared again from my pocket. I let it roll to voice-mail. I jerked open the front door and darted out to my Jeep, my chest heaving. Adrenaline sent tremors through my hands. I clenched my jaw and exhaled a shaky breath.

Work the damn case, Rachel.

I had holes in my evidence. I needed to get that goddamned card trace on the flowers. I needed to know what Marcus Rodriguez was. I needed to retrace his steps, look for witnesses. Get my mystery powder analyzed. Figure out the pattern with the victims.

"Dad, I need a sample run," I said, my phone in one hand as the other turned the key in my ignition.

"Somethin' with Danny?" He sounded both hopeful and tired, and I hated that sound in a voice I knew so well.

"Maybe. I don't know. It's a powder I found at his house."

"What's stopping you from sending it?"

I hesitated. "I haven't called the Council. Can't you just put it in the CBI system and I'll run it over?"

"Why haven't you called in? You got resources there to help you."

I hesitated. "I don't want them to take me off it." Ethan wasn't wrong—my head was all over the place. I was the Council's redheaded stepchild, almost literally, and I knew they'd tell me I was too close to the case. That it was too personal, that my judgment was clouded. Poor judgment in witches, especially ley witches, led to bad places, and I hadn't exactly done a lot to instill trust. I moonlighted on off-book cases, I experimented with magic without another witch's protection, I mouthed off to my superiors and was surly and broke rules when it was convenient. Whatever the Council told me to do, I habitually did the opposite. It was my way of exerting control with an organization that had been brow-beating me for over a decade. Unfortunately, that did not help the Council viewing me as a risk.

"I'll put the order in, but you gotta promise you'll report," he said after a long minute. As a captain of the Council and in his cover job as a sheriff's deputy, he could submit evidence to the CBI lab without raising eyebrows, but each word sounded precise, measured, despite his drawl and gentle tone. He knew I was treading dangerous ground going around protocol like this.

"Yes, sir."

Alright, step one: drop off samples at CBI lab, so I could hopefully get the results back today. Then I'd hit up the florist, Marcus's office, and do a little research on Rodriguez.

I'd get around to calling the Council at some point. Honest.

IT's amazing how many wheels the correct paperwork greases. The CBI lab never questioned me, as long as they had their evidence submission form on file. Sample testing took weeks for vanilla cases, the result of too many crimes and not enough resources. We bypassed that--every Council-doctored case came with a rush order. The tech told me he'd have my results by that evening. I gave him my card and a tight-lipped smile.

My badge made the florist more cooperative, but she still didn't give me much. Order placed by phone that morning, paid for same-day delivery. She gave me a credit card number and a name, Bonnie Turner, that was almost certainly fake. I'd run it through the police databases just to be sure, but I didn't have a lot of hope. No way this guy was going to make it that easy on me.

I flashed my badge at the receptionist at Hughes Corp again and obtained the location of Marcus's office. I drummed my fingers against my thigh, wishing the elevator moved faster. My mind kept chewing on the evidence, trying to see where it was leading me. I walked through the cube farm on the nineteenth floor—which looked almost exactly like the cube farm on the fifteenth floor, where Sadie had worked—without really seeing it, finding an office with a gold placard engraved with Marcus's name.

I snuck inside, still distracted by the tornado in my head, and shut the door behind me. When I turned around, I had to swallow a shriek. A vaguely familiar guy blinked at me from behind Marcus's desk, his mouth hanging open.

"You lost, sugar?" His eyes dipped from my head to my toes and my mouth twisted into an expression that I'm sure was less than encouraging. He dressed like a cop, in a dark blue off-the-rack suit, crisp white shirt, and striped tie, but something about him seemed wrong. He exuded the same kind of belligerence I recognized in myself. Dark brown hair stuck up in a jaunty, mussed look, and stubble in the same shade covered a strong, well-defined jaw. The five o'clock shadow at midday, the messy hair, the mouth that seemed a half-second away from a smirk—all subtle acts of defiance. A look of amusement glimmered in eyes green like summer grass. I pegged him at a few inches over six feet, built like someone who actually worked for a living as opposed to riding a desk.

"I'm Agent Collins, with, uh—" Shit. I finally realized where I'd seen him. It was the eyes that did it. This was one of the cops that I'd seen in the lobby the day I'd talked to Wilkes. What the hell was he doing here?

I collected myself and flipped open my badge. "With the Colorado Bureau of Investigation. Who are you?"

The corner of his mouth twitched.

"Name's Callahan. I'm with the Denver field office." He handed me credentials of his own, but it wasn't an FBI badge. It was an ID of some sort that read Sean Callahan, special investigator. It looked legit, but that didn't mean anything. I still didn't fully buy what this guy was selling. Why was the FBI even involved? I handed his ID back, studying him again.

"Why are you here?" I asked, narrowing my eyes.

"I'm afraid I have jurisdiction here."

My ass. "I'm investigating a disappearance. Feds don't have this case. And what does that even mean, special investigator? You're not an agent." I fought the urge to fidget, my heart hammering in my throat. I needed this guy out of here, and I definitely didn't need the fibbies to jump in the jurisdictional catfight already underway with DPD.

The twitch bloomed into a full smirk. "It means I'm an expert that consults with the FBI on occasion. And no offense, sweetheart, but federal trumps state."

"How about we call your SAC and see about that?" I said casually, pulling out my phone. I knew I looked like Civvie Jane, with my faded black tank top, torn jeans, and purple leather jacket. What I lacked in decorum I made up for with a hell of a lot of attitude. I could have pushed a glamour on him, but some instinct made me stop. Glamours are subtle magic, and exceptionally strong-willed people could throw them off. Callahan looked like a stubborn son of a bitch.

He came around from behind the desk, closing the distance between us. I held my ground. "Aw, c'mon. We're on the same side, aren't we? I just want to find these people."

"People?" I studied his face. The trace of amusement was still there, but so was something else: concern. Huh. Investigator Badass had a heart.

"Jeffrey Sharpe, Sadie Warren, Marcus Rodriguez. Same case you're chasing, I'm guessing?"

"It would appear so."

"What have you found so far?" he asked.

"Nothing much." This was going to be tricky. I had to give him just enough information to get him to get the hell out of here without actually giving anything away; if the feds pulled jurisdiction, the Council would definitely take the case away from me and give it to a deputy on FBI payroll. In times like these, I wished I had better people skills. Something in his expression said he didn't believe me and I upgraded my estimation of Callahan. This guy had a pretty decent bullshit detector.

"Collins, huh? You got family in the area, sweetheart?" He watched me the way cats watch a fish tank.

"Why do you ask?"

"We got wind of another possible case connected to these folks. A Daniel Collins. Some kind of hedge fund manager."

"Investment analyst."

Callahan smirked and I wanted to bang my head against the wall. He'd baited me on purpose, and like an idiot, I gobbled it up. I exhaled a controlled breath and pushed past him to start looking through Marcus's desk.

"Let's see... no wedding ring, so he's not your husband, too young to be your dad, but you're worked up enough it's got to be someone close. I'll bet he's your brother."

"What makes you think he's connected?" I struggled to keep my voice even, my eyes on the papers in front of me but not really focusing on them.

"When did you see him last?"

Goddammit, Ken Doll, answering questions with questions is my trick. Stop using it against me. "Day before yesterday. How'd you know he was missing? Fibbies never move this fast."

"Extremely good investigative skills."

I rolled my eyes. "What've you got on the other vics?"

"Sorry, sweetheart, I can't share those details."

"Can we drop the cutesy names?" I snapped. "And what happened to us being on the same team?"

"Help me out with your brother and maybe I'll share." Callahan's eyes twinkled again. I wanted to punch him in the nose.

"Fine. What do you want to know?" I sat down in Marcus's chair and began looking through his computer files. Between Danny's disappearance and Callahan's prodding, my concentration was shot. I kept staring at the same lines, but none of it penetrated.

"Was your brother acting strange recently? Did he have any weird stuff in his home, unusual symbols, old relics, things like that?"

My conversational thin ice just cracked a little. "The weirdest things I ever saw in Danny's possession were the *Twilight* books." I desperately wanted to get rid of this guy and get to work. My left foot bounced as I tried to focus my thoughts. Callahan flipped open a notebook and gave me a smug look. I threw him one that said I wanted to wipe it off his face with my fist. He noticed and smirked.

"I see," he said. "Did he know any of the other vics?"

I shook my head. His eyes had turned sharp and focused, and he radiated intensity. I wondered if this was how I looked when I was investigating. I seriously fucking hated the tables being turned.

"Any enemies?"

I shook my head again. None that I could discuss, anyway. Callahan turned and started looking through Marcus's filing cabinets. I waited thirty whole seconds before I blurted out, "How'd you connect Danny?"

"Brother of the lead CBI investigator goes missing in the middle of a case? Not exactly a stretch." He grinned at me over his shoulder and I wanted to strangle him. The ways in which I wanted to maim this man were racking up, and I took a moment to get my shit under control. Eyes closed, I exhaled a long breath. It was pure, childish instinct. Hurt and scared, I lashed out like a wounded bear, and Callahan kept poking me with his stick-like questions.

The investigator paused, and when I looked at him, I caught a flash of honesty. It was like his mask slipped and he appeared on the verge of saying something else, but then he plastered a bland smile on his face. "C'mon. Let's finish up with ol' Marcus."

I wanted to strap him to a chair and grill him until he told me everything he knew, but the way I understood it, the FBI frowned on that kind of behavior. So I gritted my teeth and returned to searching Marcus's computer.

A little over an hour later, Callahan walked with me through the lobby. We'd found jack squat in Marcus's office, which did nothing for my rapidly fraying nerves. My back itched and I couldn't stop fidgeting. I dealt with all manner of dangerous, crazy crap for a living, and it never shook me up. Monsters and corrupt witches I got, but this—my brother missing, maybe dying, it was beyond my (admittedly severely limited) coping skills. Callahan shot me furtive looks, like he was studying me. It didn't help. He stuck with me until we drew up next to the well-kept Ford F-350 I'd seen around town.

Callahan pulled out his keys and grinned. "Give me a call if you find anything else, alright, sugar?"

"This your ride?" I jerked my chin in the direction of the truck. His smile broadened, edged with pride. I knew the expression well. "That don't look like it's government-issued."

"Well, you know, cutbacks." He winked at me and climbed in the driver's side.

"Yeah, 'cause that wasn't shady at all," I said, watching him pull into traffic. Just what the hell was going on here?

I didn't have long to ponder it. My phone vibrated in my pocket and I pulled it out to see an extremely unwelcome number splashed across the screen.

"Yeah," I answered, scrubbing my free hand over my face.

"Deputy Collins. You are hereby ordered to report to the Denver office." Miss Manners, the receptionist at Council regional HQ, sounding exactly as displeased with me as she always did.

I winced. "I'm kind of in the middle of something here. Rain check?"

"Now, Deputy Collins."

And the hits just keep ooooon comin'.

~

I HEADED down Santa Fe to the unassuming maybe-dentist's-office building that was regional HQ and parked at the back of the lot. Inside, I found Ethan sitting on a bank of chairs near the wall. He'd dressed up, but I said fuck that. My job was not to look pretty, and I had limits to my agreeableness. It was simply too goddamned hot for my purple leather jacket, no matter how much I loved it, so it stayed in the car, leaving the tattoos on my shoulders, chest, and arms exposed. My hair was falling out of its ponytail and sticking to my face, my cowboy boots worn and scuffed, and deep bags hung below my eyes. With his dark blue suit, starched white shirt, and tasteful red tie, Ethan looked like a cop bringing in a hooligan.

I slouched into a seat next to him. "They yank your leash too, huh?"

He nodded, giving me a small smile. "You have any luck today?"

"Not really. Ran into a fibbie at Marcus's office. They're apparently hot to our case."

"Wonderful." Ethan sighed, pursing his lips. "Hey Rachel, I just wanted to say--"

A crisp voice cut him off. "Deputy Collins, Deputy Hale?" Miss Manners, we meet again. She frowned when she looked at me. Yeah, yeah, I know. Hooligan. "This way, please."

We followed her from the bland, professional, and efficient office lobby into a large conference room at the back. A long, dark table surrounded by comfortable leather chairs dominated the middle of the room. Miss Manners motioned for us to have a seat.

I sulked in my chair and swiveled back and forth. Minutes ticked by, each one reminding me that my brother was out there, a lunatic was on the loose, and I was stuck in here. Let me name the million other things I'd rather be doing. The door opened and I turned to say something snarky, but the words died in my throat.

Victor North walked in, followed by my dad and Michelle Baycone. My mouth was suddenly the texture and moisture of sandpaper.

Victor moved like an aging lion--perhaps not as spry as he once was, but still not something you wanted to encounter in the dark. As vice chair of the Executive, he was head of the Justice branch, and he'd put in his time as both a deputy and captain. He was young to be in that job--about my dad's age, his dark brown hair receding but not yet grey. Crow's feet gathered around eyes that glittered like saw blades. I didn't have to deal with him often, but our first encounter, when I'd taken my oath, had set the stage for our relationship.

Frankly, he scared the shit out of me.

"Thank you both for arriving so quickly," Victor said as he took a seat, my dad and Michelle on either side of him. He flashed me a charming smile. I ground out something that attempted to be a smile, careened off that path, and crashed into a grimace. I remembered that I'd said I'd call him and didn't. Oops.

"Ethan notified us that Danny had gone missing and we thought it best to get this thing under control as soon as possible," Victor continued. I shot Ethan a look, but he wouldn't meet my eyes.

"We're going to do everything to bring Danny back," Michelle said. I stared at the table. "Local law enforcement has been brought in to cover the mundane ground."

"What, couldn't be bothered when it was just a missing girl?" I snapped.

"Rachel." With a single word, and without even raising his voice, my dad shut me up.

"Hindsight's always twenty-twenty. The point is we need

you to tell us what you've found." Victor's tone left no room for argument. That was a direct order from my boss--my boss's boss, actually.

"Four vics in four days. No bodies yet. Don't know what Marcus Rodriguez is, but he had a pretty powerful magical artifact in his home, and SCID markers indicated fae. Some kind of powder was found at three scenes, sent it to CBI for analysis. SCID identified it as corrupt magic. Other than Danny, the only connection is Hughes Corp. May have been an earlier vic last year, Kenny Goodwin." My words were clipped, tone flat. I should be out there looking for my brother, not dealing with Council wrist-slapping.

"And someone sent a threat to Rachel this morning," Ethan said.

"What kind of threat?" Victor leaned forward, his palms flat on the table.

I glared at Ethan. "Flowers. They, uh, the delivery guy, he said it was for the Daniel Collins funeral." I focused on a spot just over Victor's left shoulder, swallowing hard. "The note said something about it being too late, and asking how the shoe fit."

"Any signs Danny is...gone?" The minuscule tremor in my father's voice, the way his fingers curled tightly over the armrests--my composure almost disintegrated.

"No," I said hoarsely. "I did a tracking spell. Something blocked it. But it got me as far as the town. But it, I mean, it worked, so we're pretty sure that Danny, he's--"

"Alive," Michelle said. She traded a glance with Victor. My father was too busy looking at me. "But what's that mean, the message?"

"No idea. Creepy bullshit from some psycho trying to yank my chain." I sighed and shook my head. "The best I've got is that it sounds like something a vic's family would hear."

"Any of your collars recently paroled?" Victor asked.

"No. None of my recent cases have been hostile, either."

Michelle looked between Victor and my dad. "The shifter girl and the were—it's not impossible for the perp to know Rachel has connections in the city." It grated on me in a nonspecific way that she didn't use their names.

Victor grimaced. "The shifter disappeared before we took the case, but the moment Rachel was made lead investigator it would've been on CBI record."

"Wait," I said, lifting up a hand. "Are you saying this is my fault?"

Michelle shook her head, but Victor just looked maddeningly inscrutable. "Not your fault," he said evenly. "But I think you know this isn't a regular case, either."

"Listen, I've worked serials before. Guys like this, they want to insert themselves into the investigation, taunt us with how much smarter they are." A pit started forming in my stomach. "Any deputy could've been given this case." But that wasn't true. My brother had come to me because of my relationship with the pack and the favor he owed Elena. How could the perp have known that when he took Sadie, though?

"Any other deputy would've left it alone when the Council denied the case," Victor said. "And you think I was wrong?" I said hotly, leaning forward with my palms on the table. "Look what's happened! The Council fumbled this."

Victor started to say something, but my dad cut across him. "Did you trace the order for the flowers?" he asked. He had relaxed his hands, and his expression had smoothed into a practiced calm. He'd stowed away the panicked father and brought out the lethal, calculating captain.

"'Course. Didn't go anywhere though. I'm still working on it."

"What blocked your spell?" Victor asked. His quiet tone was a little breath of cold crawling up my spine. I stared at him stupidly, and he added, "The tracking spell. The one for Danny."

"Don't know." I looked at Ethan, who chewed on his lip.

Jesus Christ. Better get it out there before he opened his big fat mouth again. "But it was strong. I dumped a shit-ton of ley energy into it and couldn't even dent the ward. Blew up my bowl and knocked me on my ass. Same thing blocked a tracking spell on Sadie."

A long silence filled with the kind of tension that made me want to punch the table followed. "Rachel... we're going to take care of this. We'll find your brother and bring the person responsible to justice. But you're off this case," Victor said. I finally met his eyes, and he looked just like he had six years ago when I'd taken my oath. Compassionate, but unyielding. It wasn't comforting. Instead, it made my stomach twist and pinpricks erupt along my skin.

"No. You can't. Elena--"

"You will continue to act as liaison to the Denver pack, but other deputies will handle this."

"Like who? This is my turf. Who you going to get, Masterson? It'd take him two days to get here and we'd be waiting 'til goddamn Christmas because that man is a functioning moron. You can't take me off this!" I slammed my palm onto the table and shot to my feet. I knew it. I fucking knew they'd pull this shit.

"Look at you. You're not thinking clearly. It's too personal, Rachel," Michelle said. She was playing good cop, with her gentle tone and sympathetic eyes.

My hands balled into fists. "All my cases are personal."

"You failed to report in when asked. You kept the Council out of the loop. You leaned on a personal relationship with Captain Devereaux to take control of the case. You asked your captain to circumvent Council procedure to run evidence for you. Dangerous, powerful magic is involved and you're crashing up against it in ways that could do worse than kill you. You're angry, emotional, and out of control. The situation is delicate, and your track record--"

"What track record?" I snapped. "I close more cases than the next two deputies combined."

"That's not the record I mean." Victor's tone matched mine, and his eyes were like bits of granite as he glared at me. "You refuse orders. You moonlight without regard for the attention it draws from both the supernatural community and human law enforcement. You break rules when it suits you and you've been fighting the Council since the day your magic came in. Not to mention, regardless of whether it's connected to your old cases, the perp is clearly fixating on you. You will stand down," Victor said. His voice hit me like a slap in the face.

"This is my case." I sounded like I was chewing glass, my words coming out all sharp edges. "This is my *brother*."

"You will stand down, Deputy Collins, or face consequences."

I looked at my father, silently begging him. "Dad..."

His eyes flicked to Victor, then back to me. "Rachel, Victor's right. We need--"

I didn't stay to hear what else he had to say.

Ethan caught up to me in the parking lot, grabbing my arm. "Hey, hey, wait a second!"

"I can't fucking believe you, Ethan! Really? Going behind my back, ratting me out to the goddamn Executive--"

"Hey, I didn't know Victor was going to be here, okay? I just called it in to Michelle. And I'm not sorry for that." He gave me a bullheaded look and I spun away in disgust. "We can't do this alone."

"Right, and now I'm just supposed to sit on my ass while someone else does my job? While my brother's in trouble?" I shouted. I wasn't doing a great job at proving Victor wrong about my state of mind.

"The Council will handle it. They're not going to let Danny get hurt. Rache, come on, you've got to trust them."

He put his hands on my arms and I ripped away. "Trust them? Like I trusted you to have my back?"

"I did what was right. That magic that blocked your spell, the number of vics--you're in over your head." He put his hand on my shoulder and I snapped, shoving him hard in the chest.

"Fuck you!"

Ethan caught my wrist and pulled me to him. I fought against him, not wanting his comfort, not wanting him anywhere near me right now. "We'll find him, Rachel. We will. He'll be okay."

I ducked out from under his arms, leaned against my Jeep and ran my hands back through my hair. My heart hammered in my chest and my hands twitched. Somewhere in the still-logical part of my brain, I knew this was fear. I was fucking terrified, but fear made me feel weak. So I hid behind anger instead. I never said I was rational.

"You have more faith than I do. And I can't sit here doing nothing. I just can't." My phone chirped and I pulled it out to see a text message from my dad.

Dad: Good guess--Masterson will be here in two days at the earliest. You are absolutely not to do anything in the meantime.

Dad: Definitely do not keep looking for Danny.

Dad: That's an order.

I could hear his tone as if he were speaking to me instead of texting, and I heard the subtext too. My dad was awesome.

"Where're you going?" Ethan asked as I pushed off my Jeep and walked around to the driver's side.

"Off to drink my feelings. Why don't you report that?" I knew I was being petty, but partners were supposed to back your play, not rat you out.

Ethan just watched me drive away, his hands on his hips.

～

I swung by my cabin and picked up the pipe I'd taken from Marcus's house. I made myself eat something, although I wasn't sure if a handful of grapes and a piece of toast really counted as a meal, then headed north to Boulder. I'd forgotten more weird shit than most normals ever knew, but lore was never my strong suit. Whatever Marcus was, it wasn't any of the usual flavors, and when it came to obscure crap, no one was better than Dr. Peter Gilman.

A professor of occult literature and mythology at University of Colorado, he'd helped Danny and me a few times before with research. He was a plain old vanilla human, but he knew a truly obscene amount of folklore, and he was a believer in the supernatural. Even better, he wasn't connected to the Council. He was a weird guy, though, even by my standards.

I navigated my Jeep along the picturesque streets of the CU campus, looking for Gilman's building. I found him in his office, looking every inch the mad professor. Stark white hair stood out in an unruly halo around a balding head. Small, beady eyes peered from behind wire-rimmed glasses at an ancient-looking book on his desk. Wrinkles creased his face, and his skin had the pallor of those who spent their time in libraries. His rumpled shirt was several decades out of style, and chalk stains marred his brown corduroy pants.

Mugs of stale coffee jockeyed with stacks of paper and towers of books on a desk with no visible spare space. Bookshelves lined the walls of the office, containing many volumes with names in strange languages and others that looked older than Moses. They were crammed two- and three-deep into the shelves, stone figures, rolled parchments, and other strange relics jammed into every nook and cranny. I knocked on the open door and Gilman jumped out of his seat as if he'd received an electric shock.

"Dr. Gilman? Sorry if I startled you. Do you remember me? I'm Rachel," I said, offering a hand.

"Of course, of course. Three—no four—years ago, the art museum. Particularly nasty spirit. Orange pekoe," he said, hurriedly shaking my hand and waving me into a nearby chair. Like the desk, it was covered in stacks of paper.

I carefully moved the documents to the floor. "Orange pekoe? I'm sorry, I don't follow."

"Your tea."

"What?"

"The tea, the tea. You drank orange pekoe at the museum. When we met to discuss the spirit. Although last year, the library, *tavara* in Monument, you chose sparkling water. Do you still drink tea?"

"Er, yes. But Dr. Gil—"

"Lady Grey?"

"I'm sorry?"

"All I have is Lady Grey," Gilman said, blinking at me like I was exceptionally slow. I'd forgotten how utterly batshit conversations with him were and I felt a keen pity for his students.

"That's fine, Dr. Gilman. I'm here about my brother, Danny," I rushed out. He stood and turned to face his window, where he kept an electric kettle on the sill.

"Danny, yes, yes. Particular interest in arcane legends. Coffee, black. Very smart," Gilman prattled, putting bags of tea into two mugs that I sincerely hoped were clean.

"He's disappeared, Dr. Gilman. I'm trying to find him, and I was hoping you might help me identify what might have owned this. Whatever he was, he's missing, too." I pulled the pipe out of my pocket and held it out to him. He seized it like Orphan Annie at Christmas.

"Ah, oh my, this is very interesting, very interesting indeed." Gilman's eyes swarmed over the pipe as he rotated it in his hands. "Male or female?"

"The owner? Male."

"Accent?"

"I don't know. He's missing, remember?"

"How many women?"

"What?"

"How many women were with him?"

I fought the urge to rub my forehead in frustration. Talking to this man was like talking to a manic pixie hopped up on an unfortunate combination of caffeine and speed. "Dr. Gilman, I found this in the home of a man named Marcus Rodriguez. He has a wife--"

"Alive?" His eyebrows made like snowy caterpillars trying to bounce into butterflies. His hands trembled, but it wasn't in fear. Gilman loved the weird shit--the weirder, the better.

"Yes."

"Hrm. Very interesting." He was silent for so long I wanted to poke him. "What is the magic like?"

"Wild. Ocean and flowers."

"It could be a *gancanagh*, but very strange. They always kill." He began flipping through papers on his desk.

"Gan-kuh-what?"

"*Gancanagh*." Gilman fixed me with that look again, as if I were a dim-witted pupil. The electric kettle clicked off and he poured water into my mug.

"What's a *gancanagh*, and why does it always kill?"

Gilman sighed at my apparent stupidity and set my mug before me. I checked nothing was floating in it before taking a cautious sip. He marched over to one of his crowded bookshelves.

"*Gancanagh* are fae, the Little People. But a very particular kind, oh yes." His fingers flew over the books like spiders, coming to rest on a thick volume bound in battered leather. He thumbed through the pages until he found what he was looking for, then tossed the book into my lap. I barely had time to catch it and somehow managed to not dump hot tea all over myself.

I chewed on my lip as I studied the book. The paper felt

several centuries old and showed an inked drawing of a nude man. He was beautiful--long hair, toned muscles, bewitching smile. At his feet lay several swooning women. In his hand was a pipe not unlike Marcus's.

"Um..." The naked love guru was about all I got from that book, because the rest of it was in a language that had a really sick obsession with long strings of consonants and accent marks.

Gilman gave me an eye roll that would make teenage girls proud. "Translated to mean love talker. Seduces human women, you see. Body actually secretes a pheromone that makes the human women literally addicted to him. He feeds off their love and adoration. Eventually, the women succumb to their desire and die."

"They die...from desire?"

"They die from an inability to focus on anything *but* their desire. They waste away. The *gancanagh* can't help it, it's just the natural outcome."

My face puckered in confusion. "Could it be possible for one to live without killing? This man has two ex-wives, both still alive."

"Lots of women!" Gilman exclaimed, slapping his hand down on his desk.

"What?"

"If he had lots of women, it may be possible. He has several wives, yes? And a pipe. It fits the bill, but none of the women ever died. It would be so unusual!" Gilman's voice rose in pitch, and he actually laughed a bit. I took a deep breath and counted to ten.

"If a *gancanagh* left a woman before she died, would she recover?" I asked.

"Possibly, but they never leave. They savor the sweet succor of life and desire."

A light clicked on in my mind. If *gancanaghs* fed off desire, perhaps Marcus had found a way to satiate his hunger without hurting humans through his nighttime stripping activities. Marcus didn't have a trail of bodies on him, but his wives did have a history of sickness. Sometimes things didn't always match with the knowledge in Gilman's books. I'd learned that firsthand when a *baykok* nearly ate my best friend. Pasha claims I fucked up the spell. I say I was fed faulty intel.

"That man has disappeared, along with two other people. And now Danny. Danny is missing, Dr. Gilman." I kept my voice sharp, hoping to keep his attention.

"But a *gancanagh* wouldn't have taken him. They're strictly heterosexual."

"Good to know," I said, more than a little exasperated. "The other people who disappeared are all supes too. Why do you think someone might kidnap them?"

"Oh, I have no idea, my dear." Gilman smiled sweetly at me and I reminded myself that it would be terribly impolite to throw something at him.

"Give me your best guess."

"Butterflies." I was holding on to my patience by a thread. Apparently, Gilman read the frustration on my face because he quickly added, "It's like a butterfly collection. A gathering of different specimens."

"Different specimens? Like different kinds of supernatural creatures?"

"Precisely."

"Why would someone do that? *How* would someone do that?" I was clearly unfamiliar with a *gancanagh's* power, but subduing two shifters and a witch like Danny took serious skill.

"Why—for myriad reasons. Study, experimentation, collection. How—with traps and nets. Like any biological researcher." Gilman smiled happily up at me, as if we were discussing insects rather than my brother and three other innocent people. A wave of anger pushed through me. My jaw clenched. I drained the rest of my tea and stood, my motions twitchy and tense.

"Thanks for your help, Dr. Gilman. If you think of anything else, please call me." I gave him a card with my cell number, then abruptly left. If the professor was right, some lunatic was collecting supes like his own little science project and I saw no way that could possibly end well.

SEVEN

We sat in my workroom, staring at the evidence and trying to make sense of it. I had two days before Masterson took over as lead and I was going to make the most of them. Ethan had called me repeatedly, and once I'd finally given in and answered, he was all apologies. I still was pissed at him, but my dad was right. I needed help, and Ethan was a skilled witch.

"I still don't see a pattern," Ethan said. Tension lined the air between us and we spoke with careful words, tones nothing but polite.

"Gilman said something about a collection."

He snorted. "Like with baseball cards?"

"His analogy was butterflies, but yeah." Scrubbing my face, I glared at the map as if I could force it to give me answers just by the power of my stare. "A seriously heavy magic user could trap them, maybe. If they knew their weaknesses."

"I could see that for the were, skinwalker, and fae. But who knows about us?" Ethan looked like he'd just suffered an attack of bad Mexican food. I could relate.

"Maybe the same person who knows how to block a ley spell." His eyes were on me and I looked everywhere but him.

"So, are we just not going to talk about it?" he asked finally and turned to more fully face me.

"That was my general plan, yeah."

"I'm sorry you felt betrayed, Rachel. I want to find Danny and catch this guy and I thought having all hands on deck was a good thing."

"You said that before." The room felt too small. "Just forget it, okay? I'm riled up. Not thinking straight. I was mad at Victor and mad at you and let it go to my head."

"You've been on edge for a while now. You think I don't notice, but I do. You're not as much of a mystery as you think."

For some reason, that made me think of Inspector Callahan and the way he'd seemed to see right through me. I busied myself straightening the jars of herbs. "What, is that like a pickup line or something?"

Ethan sighed and walked over to stand close to me. "I know it's not easy for you as a ley witch. But you make problems for yourself, too, Rachel. You're arrogant, and—"

"Excuse me?" I shot him a look.

He lifted his hands. "You always want to go it alone. Like nobody else can do this job but you. At some point you have to trust people."

"So they can sell me out, like you did? You're my *partner*, Ethan."

"That doesn't mean I have to follow you over a cliff. But I am someone you can trust, I'm going to prove that to you."

I jutted out my jaw. "Little late for that."

"I'm going to stick with you through this. Regardless of what the Council says. I'm going to show you that you can have faith in people, especially me."

My fingers tapped out a frenetic rhythm against my thigh

and I tried to dispel the nest of angry hornets swarming through my guts. Hard rock music blared from my pocket, sending a jolt up my spine and saving me from having to make a response.

"Yeah?" I answered cautiously. I didn't recognize the number.

"Agent Collins? This is Kyle Davis, with the lab. I'm calling with your sample results."

Sweet. I shoved things around on my desk until I found a paper and pen. "Go ahead."

"It's a compound mixture. Sulfur, silica, carbon, and chlorine trifluoride."

"Um, okay. Any idea where it came from?"

"Honestly, I'm not sure. Silica and carbon are common enough, but chlorine trifluoride is mostly used in semiconductor plants and for rocket fuel."

United Launch Alliance was headquartered in Greenwood Village, and Rocky Flats, near Golden, made nuclear fuel. Maybe our perp used one of their old buildings as a workshop. "Alright. Anything else you can tell me?"

He hesitated. "It, um, it's a little weird, actually."

Story of my life, dude. "How so?"

"Well, all these components, they were bonded together. Like they were one chemical unit. That's just... weird."

I scribbled out *trifluoride* to the best of my spelling ability, a giddy feeling in my stomach. I had a lead. To what, I had no frigging clue, but it was information I didn't have five minutes ago, and that was enough to give me hope.

"Yeah, I have no idea what any of that means," Ethan said after I relayed to him our discovery.

"Me neither. But it gives us something to search at least." My stomach lurched, like missing a step going down stairs, and I grabbed my laptop, intent on looking up every possible place this combination of chemicals could be found in

Denver. I'd done maybe thirty seconds of research when a call came across the police scanner. I'd set up the device, letting its quiet chatter fill the room while we worked, to keep my finger on the pulse of local cops. Council wasn't going to be calling me with any updates.

A dispatcher crackled over the line, directing units to Union Station. She requested detectives from Major Crimes and a forensic crew. Shit must be bad.

"Masterson's still not here. Council might not have anyone there," I mused, my eyes on the scanner. Ethan didn't even answer. He just grabbed his jacket and headed out to my Jeep.

We didn't talk during the entire drive downtown. It wasn't as if murders didn't happen in Denver. It had its share of violence, just like every other major American city. But there had been something in the dispatcher's voice, the slight tremor, the clipped nature of her words, that sent hairs prickling along the back of my neck. I hoped I was wrong. I hoped this wasn't our case.

I hoped it wasn't my brother.

Union Station, home to Denver's light rail and commuter buses, held court near the touristy part of downtown. I parked my Jeep a couple blocks away and we walked up to a knot of people milling around behind two black-and-whites blocking the sidewalk. Police had set up a perimeter beyond the two patrol cars, but a crowd still gathered at the edges of the yellow tape, like goddamn vultures circling road kill. Someone had made a spectacle of this poor person, and these assholes were feeding right into it. The crowd made my skin itch. All those people, it was hard to keep an eye on everything.

I'd give this perp one thing—he certainly had a flair for the dramatic. The girl was tied to the flagpole right in front of the station's entrance. She was nude, slumped down on the ground with her wrists bound to the pole above her head. Her face was a pulpy ruin, and dried blood matted her dark hair. Bruises and cuts mottled ashen brown skin. I knelt down in front of her body, pulling on a pair of nitrile gloves.

"Surprised you had time to turn up." Our friendly Detective Green. He held a paper cup of coffee and wore a look I'd seen before--forced calm, cavalier. The mark of a man trying hard not to care.

"Think what you want about CBI, but we're good at our jobs. And this girl was innocent," I snapped. Something must've hit home because Green only grunted in response.

"It's Sadie Warren," he said after a long moment. "Poor kid."

I closed my eyes. Goddammit. I thought back to the pictures I'd seen in her apartment, of the happy girl who was an avid hunter. She had a sister. She was twenty-one.

Too fucking late. Again.

"Who leaves a body tied to a flagpole in the middle of downtown, anyway?" Green said, hiding his fury behind a sip of his coffee.

"Who knows with these guys," Ethan said, his lip curling.

"Bastard really worked her over. Fifteen years in Baltimore, Murder Capitol USA, and I never saw anything like this."

"Still want to have a jurisdictional pissing match?" I asked quietly.

Green gave me a hard look. It was like someone had tasered him--every line in his face went rigid. "No. Somebody's got to catch this asshole. I don't care who."

Good cop. I stole a glance at him, trying to read his emotions. He kept his expression detached, clinical, but his dark eyes were hard, and he was throwing off waves of rage and violence.

"How'd you ID her?" I ran my hands down the flagpole and around its base. I couldn't screw too heavily with the forensics, but I had my own kind of investigation to do. No sigils or talismans.

"Still got to confirm it with the ME, but she had a driver's license laying on her leg. Already bagged it for evidence."

"Anyone see who brought her here?" My fingers slid over her arms, down her legs, across the soles of her feet. I tried to see past the patchwork of bruises. No signs of spell work. No blood on the cement.

"No, and something's jacked up with the security footage too. About twenty minutes of it is just static," Green said.

"Something wrong with the tape?"

"Heh, that's the thing. No tape. It's a digital system. Supposed to be stable. Our techies are taking a run at it, but would you rather have your guys do it?"

Yes, of course. Just let me take it back to my witchy Batcave.

"Just let us know what you find," I said. I eased her hair over her shoulder. Dozens of jagged cuts ripped her neck to ribbons. They were too shallow to be fatal. This was done to inflict pain. The ragged edges suggested a dull instrument, something that tore rather than cut.

"Hey, you know, CSU has already been here," Green said. A hint of suspicion floated in his voice.

"Just like to be thorough. They find anything in these cuts?"

"Think so, yeah." His eyes lingered on Sadie's face, and that tightness pulled at his features again. "We're fighting for a rush order. Something like this... Doesn't seem human."

Deep gouges split her chest. It took me a minute to piece them together. I sucked in a sharp breath as comprehension hit me.

"Sick shit, isn't it?" Green said, his eyes flashing. "*We're next*. What's that even supposed to mean?"

"Hard to say." A cluster of little red dots marked the

inside of her elbow. Puncture wounds, and they didn't look like fangs. I caught Ethan's eyes and jerked my head.

"Hey, Brad, could you give me a rundown of what you know so far?" he asked, flashing a friendly smile. Green gave me an appraising look, but turned to follow him. The two men moved away and I pressed a sample disk against her skin. A human body should never be that cold. Skin shouldn't sag when you touch it, lacking the firmness supplied by blood flow and cell regrowth. I swallowed my distaste and stared at the disk. Nothing. Either magic hadn't been used on her, or it had long since dissipated.

I hadn't really expected to find anything, but I had to try. An item used over and over, like Sadie's pelt, would store trace magic, but one-off spells evaporated within a couple hours. I stood and trudged over to Ethan and Brad, pulling off my gloves.

"Let us know what when the reports come in, will you?" I gave Green one of my cards.

"Sure. Listen, about before..." He cleared his throat and put his hands on his hips. "I just don't like bad cops. Got me kind of fired up."

"We're good," I said with a tight smile.

Ethan and I left, me looking back over my shoulder as the crime scene techs began to load up Sadie's body. I'm sorry I wasn't fast enough to save you, kid.

"You really think our killer is grammatically challenged or-_"

"Was that a threat against Jeff?" I interjected, ice surging through my guts. "Those cuts in her chest were done when she couldn't heal, and given all the supernatural angles, yeah, I think our guy is sending us a message in a big way."

"You think maybe it's the hunters?" He raised his hands in surrender. "I'm just saying. All the vics are supes, and now we've got a body."

"Hunters may be violent psychopaths, but they avoid the cops. They wouldn't put Sadie out like that."

"What *is* the purpose of putting her on display?"

"Threaten us. Taunt us. Get his rocks off," I seethed. My jaw clenched and I tried to pull my temper back under control. Beating the shit out of something might have felt satisfying right then, but it wasn't going to help me catch Sadie's killer.

As we turned the corner, I caught sight of two men walking toward us. Curses--the non-magical kind--spilled from my lips and I pushed Ethan into the nearest store.

"What the hell?" he asked, giving me a look that plainly said he thought I'd lost my damn mind as I dragged him behind a rack of Broncos sweatshirts.

"Feds. Or something. Those are the guys I saw at Hughes Corp," I said, tipping my chin toward the window as the two men walked past. I really didn't want to talk to them. Callahan was making violent slashing motions with his hands and the other one looked like he wanted to shove his partner into traffic.

"One problem at a time, Rachel. We just stay out of their way and work the case," Ethan said, putting a hand on my shoulder. He was right--I just didn't like it. I had a bad feeling about those guys. My bad feelings could probably build a bridge to China by now.

SUNLIGHT RUDELY SMACKED me in the face. I let out an inhuman noise and buried my head deeper into the pillows. I could hear Ethan moving around in the kitchen. The asshole was a morning person and obnoxiously cheerful about it. We'd stayed up late discussing theories and going over the evidence about eleven million times, and I'd let him crash in my guest room rather than drive all the way home to Denver. I spent the night tossing and turning, tormented by images of Sadie's broken and bloody face turning into Danny's. The lack of sleep was starting to take its toll through a series of nonspecific aches and itchy eyes. I knew I needed to clock some serious rack time, or else my muzzy brain and slow reactions were going to get me killed. I just didn't know how to actually achieve that--laying there willing myself to sleep hadn't worked well so far.

Ethan flipped on the television, because he was a cruel soul and wanted me to suffer needlessly. I groaned and dragged myself from the bed.

"Welcome to the land of the living," he teased as I shuffled into the kitchen. I wasn't sure, but I may have been bordering on zombieism at that point--I had a distinct urge to kill him.

"Braaaaiins," I growled quietly.

"What was that?"

"Nothing. Caffeine. No talking." I filled my electric kettle with water and dug a box of tea out of the cabinet. Waiting for the water to heat, I snagged a container of yogurt and slouched against the counter while I ate.

"You get any great ideas during the night?" I asked, tossing the empty yogurt container into the recycling.

"No. You?"

"Nope." I poured the water into a mug and added honey and almond milk. I sipped it slowly, inhaling the nutty aroma. "I want to go back to Danny's today. Maybe we'll find something there that we missed before."

"Whatever you say, boss."

A couple hours and several shots of caffeine later, we rolled up in front of Danny's house. I'd thrown the coyote pelt and clay pipe into the car, keeping them on hand, just in case. For what, I had no idea, but experience had taught me to be prepared. I shoved down the knot in my stomach as we walked up to Danny's front door, taking care to stay off the grass.

I slid the key into the door and stopped. An uneasy feeling gripped me.

"It's unlocked," I murmured. Ethan nodded and reached inside his blazer for his gun, holding it low in front of him. I felt for one of the tendrils from the massive ley line that ran through Denver and pulled its energy to me. Drawing my Sig, I eased the door open. Voices emanated from the back of the house.

"I still say we bust it down," a deep male voice said. It sounded familiar.

"Yeah, because that won't mess with the cops' investigation. This still could be just a non-supernatural kidnapping, you know," another man argued back.

"This guy fits the pattern, I'm telling you. And I'm betting answers are down in his basement," the first said. Anger curdled in my chest. I didn't know who these guys were, but I wanted them the hell out of my brother's house. Their presence scraped along my brain like a jarring note in a well-loved song.

I crept through the living room and circled to the back of the house toward the kitchen. A wall hid us from sight, and with any luck, we'd catch them off guard. Ethan stayed on my six. I rounded the corner and shouted, "Police, don't move!"

The two men whipped around with speed gained only from years of combat training and I found myself looking at the barrels of their own guns. Mexican standoff. Awesome. The man closest to me had chestnut hair and warm green eyes that I'd seen before. Had he not been pointing the business end of a stainless steel CZ 9mm at me, I would have described his face as friendly and good looking. My eyes flicked to the man behind him.

"Well, Investigator Callahan, fancy seeing you here, breaking into my brother's house," I said.

Callahan tried for a smile that I'm sure other people found charming. "Hey, Agent Collins. I, uh, might've been a little misleading when we met before."

"What, you mean you're not actually with the FBI? You don't say."

"That part is true. Just we're kind of... on the downlow. This is my brother, Luke. We're brought in on very particular cases."

"What kinds of cases?" I asked.

"Why don't you put down your guns and we'll tell you," Sean said. The hint of a smirk played around his lips. He wasn't scared of me at all.

"Tell us and we'll put down our guns," Ethan said. The four of us stood there for a long, tense moment.

"Okay, okay. You win," Luke said, bending over to place his weapon on the ground, moving at about the speed you'd expect when someone has a gun on you.

Sean looked like the dog had just peed on his shoes, but he also put his pistol on the floor. "We're trying to help. We're trying to find whoever killed that girl and took those other

people," Luke said.

"You're hunters," Ethan spat. Muscles twitched along his jaw and his entire body was rigid. How the hell had he known that? I looked the two men over again and noticed a tattoo on Luke's forearm. A wolf totem.

Just my goddamn luck.

"Uh, what?" Sean asked.

"Don't be cute. We're playing on the same team," I said. Well, sort of. I holstered my gun. Now it was Ethan's turn to look like his slippers had done duty as a canine urinal, but he could suck it up. I had no time for pissing matches with these two.

"Are you guys hunters?" Luke looked surprised.

"No, we're cops. But we handle the weird cases. Are you really on FBI payroll?"

Luke nodded. "We've got a friend in the field office here. He brings us in when stuff looks...unusual. What're your names?"

"I'm Rachel. This is Ethan."

"Nice to meet you. Right, Sean?" Luke said pointedly, and Sean smirked and waved a sarcastic little wave. Ethan continued attempting to develop laser vision.

"Okay, our turn for some truth. What's the deal with your brother? You'll save us a lot of time if you just tell us," Sean said. His demeanor changed from when he played the part of the FBI investigator; now he was gruff and efficient. The spark of amusement had vanished from his eyes. Apparently, I was less entertaining when I had him cornered.

"Listen, I know you think you're helping, but you guys should clear out. You're way out of your league here, and this is our turf. We've got this one," Ethan said.

"No offense, hoss, but you have no idea what our league is," Sean countered.

"Oh, I think I know, pal. It's somewhere between pee-wee and junior." The two men swaggered closer to each other, both radiating the threat of imminent violence.

"Alright, guys, that's enough. Put the rulers away. We've still got three missing people, including my brother. In case you forgot," I snapped, separating them.

"Then let us help you," Luke said quickly. "Surely four minds are better than two."

Ethan shook his head and stalked off. I heard the front door slam.

"What's his problem?" Sean chewed the words and spat them out.

"He doesn't like people stepping on his toes, and he thinks you're amateurs," I said bluntly.

"We've seen a lot of heavy shit," Luke said. "We can hold

our own. And if it were me, with my brother missing, I'd want all the help I could get. The more people who are looking, the better the chances of finding him." Jesus, this guy knew how to push emotional buttons. He was like a freaking Sally Struthers commercial.

"Look, I appreciate it, really, but it's better if you just leave. We're better suited to handle this one." I tried to push past them toward the basement door. Sean blocked my path.

"You figured out the connection between the missing people yet?" He crossed his arms and I considered his usefulness as a punching bag. He had that intense look on his face again, the one he'd given me as Special Investigator Callahan. I couldn't read anything off him except stubbornness and spite. Dude was probably a hell of a poker player.

"Have you?" I shot back.

"Oh yeah."

My jaw ached from clenching it so hard. He had me, and he knew it. For the second time in two days, I wanted to sock him in the nose. "Are you offering to trade information?"

"Sure. I get your whole solo thing. Hell, we're like that most times ourselves. But we're tracking something here, and it's gotten thirty-one flavors of crazy. Was supposed to be a simple hunt, but it turns out, at least one of the vics was a monster. Did you know that?"

Monster. I thought of Jeff defending Sadie from his pack, of happy faces in pictures. Of Marcus Rodriguez's family. Freaking hunters. They saw the world only one way: us versus them.

"How you figure?" I asked coolly.

"Simple. That Jeff dude had to take off every month, right around the full moon. And he was a little too cozy with a group of people totally not related to him, plus not one piece of silver in his house. Sound like normal non-furry behavior to you?"

These guys had been on pack property. Elena was going to eat them. "Maybe a hunter got him."

"Doubt it. We got here first, and until you two, didn't hear of anybody else working the case. Nah, something else is going on here. So, c'mon, honey. Share."

I was going to take that *honey* and shove it up his ass. Council had strict rules about mixing it up with hunters, which generally began and ended with *don't*. It was too dangerous, both to them and to us. It was a rule I'd only broken once, not out of any loyalty to the Council, but because witches didn't deserve a war with human vigilantes. But if these dudes had information we didn't, and that intel could help Danny, I couldn't refuse, no matter what the costs.

"Fine," I snarled. "But you two get yourselves killed, don't say we didn't warn you. So, spill."

"You first."

"Is everything always this difficult with you?"

"Right back at you, sweetheart."

Well, this was awesome. The corner of Luke's mouth twitched at our hissing and spitting, but I failed to see what was so damn amusing.

"What do you want to know?" I hurled the words at Sean like weapons, but the jackass just smirked.

"Your brother. How's he involved?"

"Danny's like me. He actually called me in on this case." I wasn't about to tell him that we were also witches. With the way he talked about Jeff, he'd probably try to burn me at the stake.

"Do you know how he's tied to the other vics?" Sean asked.

"Not yet. I've got a name for a lead, that's it."

"And?"

"Nope, your turn."

Sean looked at me as if I'd just asked him for his first-born son. I dazzled him with my crazy smile. "What do you know about demons?"

I think my jaw actually dropped. "Uh, what?"

"The case we're tracking, it's a demon. We followed it here, and we think it's involved with these disappearances. We just don't know how."

"How do you know?" I asked, fear turning my tone more hostile than I intended. Demons were so above my pay grade, it wasn't even funny. Despite years of taking down corrupt witches, I'd never actually faced a demon directly.

"It's what we do, honey," Sean said with a humorless smile.

"So, what, you think a demon is taking these people?" That didn't make any kind of sense. Best I knew, demons wanted souls, or minions. Hostages weren't their style.

"We think that whenever a demon is involved, it's never something good and we need to stop it as soon as possible," Luke said. "We're just trying to help."

"So what's your lead?" Sean asked. He barked the question the way generals bark orders. My shoulders bunched as I rocked my head back.

"Local contact. Knew one of the vics." I congratulated myself on not spouting off some snarky response. I can play well with others. Sometimes.

"You getting a meet set up?"

"Yeah."

"Awesome. You'll bring us along."

"Sorry, homeslice, I don't take orders from you."

"Thought we were working together, cupcake."

"Not on this." Elena had been so protective of Leon, if I brought hunters around him she'd completely lose her shit, and that would just end in a lot of pain and paperwork for me. Sean snorted and opened his mouth to respond, but Luke cut him off, darting in front of his brother.

"Sean, c'mon, just leave it," he said.

Sean glowered at me from around Luke's shoulder. "Fine. For now. You got a key for this door or what?"

I prayed for patience. Another alpha male asshole. I had definitely reached my quota for the next year.

"If you'll get out of my way, I'll gladly open it." My voice dripped with sarcasm, but the brothers moved aside anyway. Key was a loose term--really, I had to drop the wards. I mimed unlocking the door while I laid a palm against the smooth stained wood, murmuring the counter-phrase. The door grew hot beneath my hand for a moment, then the heat dissipated--the exothermic reaction of magic being withdrawn. Physics still applied, even to the supernatural.

The Callahans followed me down the stairs. I fumbled on the wall for the switch and bathed the basement in harsh fluorescent light. My brother's workroom looked a lot less ordinary than the rest of the house. A long counter ran against the wall to my left, bookended by an industrial stainless steel sink and a gas-burning stove. Heavy shelves lined two sides of the basement, boasting an array of precisely labeled containers and a wide assortment of books. At the opposite end of the room, several handguns, a pump-action tactical shotgun, a modern crossbow, and other dangerous instruments--Danny's arsenal--hung on the concrete wall. Even though he worked in the Council's finance department, he stayed ready for anything. Probably the result of growing up with our dad as a deputy. Above the counter was a map very similar to the one I had at home, decorated with Post-Its covered in Danny's neat handwriting.

"Damn," Sean murmured appreciatively, examining Danny's weapons.

"Looks like your brother was pretty thorough." Luke pointed to the map.

"Yeah. He's like that." My stomach twisted and I fought to keep my face from following suit. Luke caught it and gave me a small, sympathetic smile.

"What's all this crap?" Sean lifted up one of the jars from a shelf and sniffed it, jerking his head back in disgust.

"Tools of the trade. What's your storeroom look like? Or the back of your truck?"

Sean replaced the jar with a shrug. "It looks a lot like your brother was into some witchcraft."

I forced out a laugh. "Yeah, right. Danny just believes in being well prepared and knowing what you're up against."

"Good," Sean said with an exaggerated shiver. "I hate witches. Freaking creepy sons of bitches."

That I refrained from punching him was a goddamned miracle.

EIGHT

Ethan finally came back inside and helped us turn the place upside down, but we didn't find much that we didn't already know. My brother would kill me when he saw the mess. I texted Elena to check about meeting with Leon, appropriately relaying my urgency with liberal use of the f-bomb. She responded that we should meet her in a few hours downtown.

I leaned against my brother's kitchen counter, tapping my thumb against the granite. That weird-ass powder was here, so good chance Danny had been snatched from home. But why hadn't he fought back? How had the perp even gotten inside? I thought about what Sean had said, that a demon was involved, and my gut churned into an anxious slushie. Council had specialists--secretive, mega-powerful witches--to deal with demons. Regular witches like us were absolutely forbidden from tangling with hell's frat boys. The risk wasn't that we'd get killed. It was much worse than that.

But if I called them now, I'd just get my ass chewed. Worse, there was no guarantee they'd bring Danny back alive. I still had some time. I could still do this my way.

I locked the front door behind me out of habit as we

walked outside, always keeping my eye on the brothers. No matter what kind of sappy looks Luke gave me, I didn't trust them.

"You'll call when you got a meet with your contact setup," Sean said.

"You have got to stop with the frigging commands," I snapped.

Sean chuckled and climbed into that big, gleaming F350, and Ethan and I watched them drive away.

"I can't believe you agreed to work with them," Ethan said hotly.

"It's not like I had much choice. And besides, you heard them. If a demon's involved, we need help." The glacier in my guts still hadn't melted and fear gurgled in my throat, threatening to choke me. If a demon had Danny... I couldn't bear to complete the thought.

"So we call the Council."

"Fuck the Council."

"Rachel, seriously? You'd rather trust these random hunters than your own people?"

"No. But I'm not abandoning my brother to a fucking demon while the Council tries to figure out how to deal with it politically, or nukes the block and chalks him up to collateral damage."

"Alright, fine." He sounded anything but. "Then we do it ourselves. We don't need two goddamn hunters."

"You're right. I only asked them to team up because I think they're cute," I drawled.

"Dammit, Rachel! Are you that fucking stupid?" he yelled, slamming his fist against the hood of my car.

"Where the hell do you get off? I don't care if I have to make a deal with the devil himself, I will do what I have to do to get Danny back. He's my brother, Ethan, and some freak psycho has him!"

"I just thought you learned your lesson."

I flinched as if he'd struck me.

"You got no right to say that to me." I couldn't believe he'd throw Ryan in my face again. I'd told him about my last run-in with a hunter one night in a fit of alcohol-fueled trust, wanting to bond with my new partner because I ached from losing Pasha. It had been a mistake. Ethan glared at me, then silently climbed into the Jeep, slamming the door like it had done him personal injury. I followed suit. I drove out of Highlands Ranch, the air thick between us as we both seethed.

"I'm sorry," he said as I merged onto I-70.

"Don't worry about it."

"It's just... you're not the only one who's been burned by hunters."

"What do you mean?" I asked.

"Never mind." A strange look crossed Ethan's face.

"Really? Just going to clam up on me?" I tried to analyze that look, reaching out with my senses, but it vanished behind a smooth wall of ha-nice-try. Witches knew how to hide their feelings from each other.

"Look, I said I'd stick with you, and I'm not backing out, but this is one of those times when you're creating problems for yourself. There's no way working with hunters ends well."

There was something about the way he said it, and I remembered how he'd reacted when I told him about Ryan. Ethan had looked at me with pity, which I fucking hated, but there had been understanding there, too. For him, it had been a moment of camaraderie with his new partner. For me, it had been an embarrassing mistake.

Thoughts of the hunters and Danny and poor dead Sadie and now a goddamn demon tumbled through my brain. I kept returning to Sean and Luke, wondering if they were on the level. Most hunters had good reason for their hatred of anything supernatural. They were typically normal humans that got the mother of all wake-up calls. A vampire kills a girlfriend, loup werewolves kill a brother, a demon kills a sister. It was a brutal way to be introduced to the reality of our world. I thought about the wolf tattoo I'd seen on Luke's arm and my hand drifted to my left side, subconsciously rubbing the old wound there.

"You know they don't see us as human. Doesn't matter what we do. For them, the only good supe is a dead one," Ethan said quietly. Sympathy lurked in his eyes and I jerked my hand away from my side. He didn't need to remind me. "Rachel?"

"What?"

"If you grip your wheel any harder, it's going to break."

I relaxed my hands. "I get it, okay."

Ethan smiled and laid a hand on my shoulder. It was too heavy, and I had the kind of tight-chest, squirmy reaction people get when they're trapped in an elevator. I shrugged it off.

I followed I-25 north into the city, heading to a joint called My Brother's Bar, where we were supposed to meet Elena. She sat in the very back booth, a few members of her pack spread out in a perimeter. They sprawled in chairs, smiling and talking and looking totally casual, but their bodies were just a little too tense, their eyes a little too sharp. They were definitely on duty, and I was doubly glad I'd shaken the Callahans. I really didn't need Sean trying to kill the local were Alpha.

"Rachel, Ethan," Elena said, inclining her head as we slid into the booth. Beside her was a man with precisely combed salt-and-pepper hair, who looked like he'd gone ten rounds with life and lost. His whole face seemed to sag, as if he had been deflated, and his eyes darted everywhere like nervous birds, alighting in one place only to take off a moment later.

"This is Leon," she said, gesturing to the man. "Rachel and Ethan are here to help, my friend."

Leon looked at us like someone confronted with sushi for

the first time--convinced we were going to make him puke. "What do you want to know?" he asked, words popping in little anxious bursts.

"Sadie Warren, Jeff Sharpe, Marcus Rodriguez. They all paid you money. Why?" I asked, trying to sound friendly.

Leon looked to Elena and she nodded. "I helped them. Reinvent themselves."

"What do you mean?" Ethan asked.

"They-they wanted to start over. Somewhere new. Where no one knew about who--what--they were. So that's what I do."

"What, like witness protection for supes?" I asked.

Leon gave me a level look and something flickered behind his eyes. Old hurt. Regret. "I set them up with new documents, IDs, whatever they need. So they can have a new life."

"So our three vics were all clients of yours?"

"That's, ah, actually how Jeff knew Sadie."

Well, that explained a lot.

"It looks like someone is hunting off your Rolodex, dude," I said, fixing him with my Detective Benson stare. The guy crumpled like a gas station receipt and made me feel like a colossal dick.

"I don't know, okay? I know I'm their connection, but I don't know why. It's--it's just a coincidence." His pupils dilated and his hands clenched on the table. Dude was so rattled he couldn't have lied to me even if I wasn't a witch. He was the polar opposite of Elena, but Leon still had to have some control since his wolf wasn't slipping loose. Finding that tipping point was going to be interesting.

"You can help us find these people. Catch Sadie's killer," I said, sharpening the edge in my voice. He squirmed.

"Look, I don't know, okay? Not anything for sure..."

"Leon."

He looked deeply uncomfortable, shifting his weight in

his seat, but his eyes remained a solid deep brown. Elena leaned forward, her lip curling and a gold sheen rolling over her pupils. Tough, wolfie. I needed info.

"There was a guy. He contacted me a couple weeks ago, acted like he wanted my services. But he seemed strange. And I couldn't find anything that said he was a supe. So I told him no."

"What was his name?" Ethan asked.

"Walter Brown, but it's fake. That's not unusual. Most of my clients use aliases."

"What'd he look like?"

"We only dealt over the phone and email."

"You still have the emails?" I asked.

Leon looked at me like I'd just asked if the earth was round. "Of course."

God bless paranoid people. "We need everything. Any way of knowing who might be next on the hit list, and anything that could help us find this guy," I said.

"Okay. I'll get it together and call you."

"Thanks. Oh, by the way," I said, turning to Elena, "we ran into the hunters you mentioned. One's a real piece of work, so you might want to tell your folks to keep a low profile while they're in town." I hesitated. "They, uh, they've been to Jeff's. Do me a solid and don't actually murder them, okay?"

Her jaw clenched and that gold light flared again in her eyes. Leon went paper white.

"Hunters?" he whispered.

"Yeah, two. The Callahan brothers. They're working this case apparently." I played it off like I was talking about a shoelace that wouldn't stay tied, but Leon looked like a rabbit sighted by a wolf—which was a pretty ironic image. I might have laughed if I hadn't felt so bad for the guy.

"Hey, buddy, you alright?" Ethan asked.

"I've got to go," Leon said. He shoved himself out of the booth so hard the table slid a couple inches, and then he bolted from the bar.

"Something I said?" I looked back at Elena. Her hands balled into fists. Shoulders raised like hackles, arms rigid, every inch the Alpha defending her pack. I was mildly afraid she was going to launch across the table at me.

"Hunters killed his mate. He lost control and killed one of them. They chased him for years, until he was ready to just lie down and die. I found him first." She smiled tightly, teeth looking more like fangs as she struggled to keep the wolf inside.

Damn. No wonder he'd looked so worn.

"I helped hide him and brought him to Denver. Now he helps others do the same." Elena forced her fingers to relax, brushing them over the table. "Now you tell me hunters are circling my pack, breaking into our property. And where is your Council?"

She never raised her voice. She didn't have to. People who know true dominance don't shove it in your face. It's quiet and pleasant and ties you down like silk.

"Um... yeah, about that. I'm, um, technically off the case. Council's picked it up and other deputies will--"

"What?" A punch in the face would have been softer than that word. "So a girl was not enough? What is the point of the treaties if my requests will only be denied?"

"Elena, look you have every right to be pissed. But I got the Council on it and they'll find who did this." I wasn't actually begging her, but I was close. "It's--my brother, he's been taken."

For a brief moment, she met my eyes. For all the ways Elena could be fucking terrifying, she was a good person, and she'd never wished me ill. "I'm sorry, Rachel. Can we help?"

That just made me want to shrivel up into a little ball of

shame. The Council had ignored her when the tables were turned, and here she was offering assistance. Jesus, we were a bunch of assholes. "Uh, not right now. Thanks, though."

"Anything else I should be aware of?"

"Sadie's dead." I stared at the table and heat crawled up my neck. The Council pretended like we were all created equal--witches, humans, weres, vamps. Like the only line that mattered was good versus evil. I'd bought into the Rainbow Nation crap, put my life on the line for it. Imagine my surprise when reality didn't live up to the ideal. "I'm not giving up, Elena. I'm going to find Jeff, and Danny, and make sure this guy goes down for what he did."

"I'm sure you will. But Sadie is still dead, and the Council has made their priorities very clear." Have you ever been stared down by a predator? It's not fun. "We'll protect our own. I don't care about hunters or police or anything else. I care about Jeff. Consider this my notice that we will be taking this matter into our own hands."

Elena marched out of the bar, her pack falling in behind her with military precision. She would rip the city apart looking for Jeff and not leave any witnesses to complain about the mess. My head thunked against the back of the booth and I ground the heels of my hands against my eyes. Whoever decided I should be a liaison to anything was fucking insane.

We drove back to my cabin in silence. I took the exit for Lookout Mountain, winding my way up into thick forest. Up here the air was crisp and cool, and the silence of the trees wrapped around my overheated brain like a soothing balm. Denver lay in the distance, a fuzzy, yellow glow against the night sky, as I steered the Jeep onto the gravel road that served as my driveway. I pulled in next to Ethan's truck, cut the engine, and sat there for a moment.

"You okay?" Ethan asked.

"Not really." I worried at my lower lip. "Does it bother

you that the Council denied Elena? I mean, if we'd tried harder, maybe Sadie would be alive."

"You can't think like that, Rache. Council's not perfect, but think about all the things they're juggling. They probably just thought it was a matter for the regular cops."

"Yeah." My voice was void of conviction. My head hurt and I felt lost. A week ago things made sense. People committed supernaturally flavored crimes, I arrested them, justice was served. A week ago my brother had been safe. It was surreal to think only several days had passed since then. It felt like decades. I sighed and tiredly climbed out of my Jeep.

"Hey, what do you--"

A shadow crashed into my left side, cutting me off mid-sentence. It hammered me to the ground, slamming my head against the earth. Ethan shouted, voice muffled like he was underwater. Little white lights exploded and the world greyed at the edges.

Sharp pops. Cordite. Gunshots. The dump truck on my chest lifted as the shadow peeled away. I sucked in a strangled breath. Sheer spite and instinct alone drove me to my feet.

"Where is it? Where'd it go?" Ethan sounded so far away. My eyes wouldn't focus. I shook my head, grunting. The pounding in my skull made it fucking hard to think.

I shut my eyes and brought up my second sight. When I looked out at the trees, I saw a pulse of green, flitters of pale blue that were birds, threads of gold weaving it all together. In the middle, a dark stain hunched on a branch--malformed, oily, wrong. This thing violated nature in a way that made me retch. Gagging, I clawed onto the line. Its energy flooded into me, pine and earth and wood smoke covering my tongue.

"Third tree back, eleven o'clock," I groaned, leaning against my Jeep. Ethan fired. If he hit the creature, I had no idea, because it slithered through the trees and barreled straight for me again.

I crouched and let it hit me, rolling with the momentum, and jammed my hand into what I imagined to be the middle of its body. It was moving too fast for me to really get a fix on proportions.

"Release," I snarled, drawing the electric strength of the line through me and into Shadowfang here. Fire swam through my veins, the line burning against my psyche.

Shadowfang dug its claws into my shoulders. Skin tore and hot saliva dripped onto my neck. I was sure pointy teeth weren't far behind. I braced my arm against it, feeling like I was shoving against a fucking bear.

It lunged at my neck again, and I grabbed onto whatever body part I could reach. My leg hooked around something solid and I bucked my hips. Shadowfang couldn't fight physics and I rolled with it.

Being on top was only marginally better than being underneath it. Claws raked at my arms. Desperate, I yanked harder on the line, shoving energy into the beast. White-hot strands snaked through my body, fighting to take over my mind. Electricity crackled. My hair began to float.

Shadowfang thrashed and snarled, a sound somewhere between a dog's yelp and the screech of a dull spike being shoved through sheet metal. It seized up for a moment and then grabbed my shoulders, flinging me away so hard that I lost my grip on the line.

For the second time that night, my head exploded in pain as I collided with my Jeep. Ethan fired two more rounds. He might as well have been shooting with a Nerf gun. It squatted before me, two coal-bright red eyes brimming with hatred puncturing the darkness. Either I'd taken one too many hits to the head, or Shadowfang was made from ever-moving, amorphous shapes. Like smoke made solid. Its distorted face looked like a wolf molded from clay, if the artist had only the faintest idea of what a wolf actually looked like. The arms were muscular and overlong, like a gorilla's. I couldn't even tell if it had skin, fur, scales, or reinforced tank armor for its hide.

"*It'sss youuu*," it hissed. Well, that was unsettling. I stared back at those solid red pits, fear burning in my throat. I tapped the line again and it seared my veins, scorching and slippery in my grasp. Sparks of ley energy spit from my fingertips and I dropped the line. Fuck. I was too exhausted and beaten up to control it.

I pulled out my gun, for all the good it would do me. Ethan bellowed a curse--the magical kind--and a bag of something exploded at Shadowfang's feet. It shrieked again, the noise grating on my ears, and recoiled.

With one last venomous glare, it doubled back on itself in a way that bones don't bend and melted into the trees.

Ethan squeezed off two more rounds. For a moment, the only things I heard were our panting and the echoing ring of gunfire. I used the Jeep for balance and staggered to my feet. Ethan jogged over, his gun still trained on the tree line, and slid an arm around my waist.

"What the hell was that?" he said. I leaned against him, trembling--the after effects of adrenaline and throwing around a ridiculous amount of power.

"No idea. What was in the bag?" I wheezed, letting him half carry me toward my front door. I hoped my wards were Shadowfang-proof.

"Powdered silver and wolfsbane. It was still in my coat from that loup we hunted last month."

"What made you think of that?" I sounded like a fricking chain smoker.

"Desperation." Ethan navigated me onto the couch. My legs quaked, the beginnings of a concussion-induced headache scraping along my skull. He brought me a glass of orange juice, then collapsed onto the recliner, his face pale.

"I thought it was going to kill you, Rachel."

"That makes two of us." I gulped down some of the juice,

leaning back and closing my eyes. It wasn't enough that I had a werewolf pack about to go postal, a dead co-ed, hunters stirring up shit with my case, three missing people--including my brother--and my ass in the ringer with the Council. Now I had a monster-movie-mash-up trying to turn me into dog food.

NINE

I t was easier to name the places that didn't hurt: the top of
my right ear, a couple toes, and a two-inch patch of skin
on my back. Someone was using my head as a bass drum and
nausea hit me in rolling waves. At least I'd slept.

Shadowfang left us alone the rest of the night, and I'd
been too concussed to argue with Ethan about standing
guard. I stumbled into my bathroom for a shower, convincing
myself that it would make me feel better.

Jesus Christ, I was a hot mess. Dirt, twigs, and leaves
tangled together in my hair, which was sticky and matted. A
giant, dark purple bruise decorated my left ribcage. Dozens
of small cuts crisscrossed my arms. My right shoulder sported
a lovely spot of road rash, bits of gravel embedded in the skin.
I definitely wasn't winning any beauty pageants soon.

I let the water heat up to almost scalding and gingerly
began to wash the crap off me. Even the soap hurt. I worked
my fingers through my hair and found two goose eggs on my
scalp. Awesome.

"Here, you need to eat," Ethan said, pushing a plate of
bacon and eggs toward me when I shuffled into the kitchen.
"How you feeling?"

"I'll live. Sore, mostly. That thing hit like a ton of bricks." I picked up a fork and was immediately distracted by Ethan shining a penlight in my eyes. "Dammit, stop!"

"You should be at the hospital. You probably have a concussion." He tried to shine that goddamned light in my eyeball again and I swatted it away.

"You make me go to the hospital, I'm telling them you did this to me." I snatched my fork back up. He left me alone and I shoveled food into my mouth. Manipulating that much ley energy was like bench-pressing a semi, not to mention the strain of my supernatural wrestling match.

"You need to put up a perimeter ward, especially since you like to live out here in the middle of nowhere."

"Yes, Mother."

Ethan gave me a bitchface that would make teenage girls jealous. "What do you think it meant, 'it's you'?" he asked, changing tracks. I shrugged, but his question nagged at me. I didn't even like being singled out on my birthday, let alone by some freaky creature. I finished wolfing down my breakfast and stood up to make a cup of tea. My heel bounced and I spun my phone around between my fingers as I waited for the water to boil. A wild hare crawled up my ass, and I scrolled through the numbers, hesitating before finally tapping one.

"You're not seriously calling them?" The exasperation in Ethan's voice threatened to reach out and strangle me.

"I am. Maybe they found something." I held up my hand for silence as Sean picked up. "Sean? It's Rachel."

"Oh, well, fancy that. I figured you'd stiff us and then I'd have to track you down." Please. If I wanted to, I could cast a ward so heavy that he couldn't find me with two hands, a Sherpa, an iPhone, Google Maps, and a flashlight.

"I'm just full of surprises. What are you doing?"

"Research, but we're not finding much. You got a meet with your contact?"

"Not yet." Lying was so much easier over the phone.

"Right." Maybe not. He didn't sound like he was buying it.

"Listen, I really don't think it's a good idea for you to be there. This guy is...delicate."

"I'll play nice, I promise. I'm good with delicate."

Yeah, I bet. Delicate like a Howitzer. "Why don't we meet up afterward and compare notes?"

"Yeah, how about not. You'll want us there when you question him. We're good with this kind of thing."

"Are you implying that we aren't?"

"Not at all. Just trying to give you the best chance of finding your brother in one piece, sweetheart."

"Don't call me sweetheart." Ethan gave me an I-told-you-so look and I flipped him off.

"Whatever you say, honey," Sean said.

"You're an ass, you know that?"

"So I've been told. Now, when's the meet?"

Jesus Christ, you are not fucking Patton. Pacify thy mammaries. "You should take another run at Hughes," I said. "Marcus worked there too, and something about the guy seemed off to me."

"We already did."

"And?"

"What'd you find at the crime scene for the Warren girl? That was you there, wasn't it?"

"What did Hughes say?"

"Nope. I can play the evasive game too, baby."

I hung up on him and threw my phone onto the table. It skittered across the wood and bounced onto the floor. This guy was fucking infuriating.

"That sounded extremely productive," Ethan drawled, tossing my phone back to me.

"No one asked for your opinion." I rubbed my temples, my head reminding me that I'd just gotten my ass kicked last night. My phone rang and I tapped the screen with unnecessary force.

"What?" I snapped, not looking to see who it was.

"Um, Rachel? It's Leon."

"Oh." Shit. "Sorry. Bad day. What've you got?"

"I think I've worked something out that might help you."

"Great." I waited, but he said nothing. "That's your cue, dude."

"Can you come to my house? I'd much rather discuss this in person."

"Leon, just tell me now."

"Cell phones aren't safe, Rachel. Please. Just come to my house."

"Alright, fine." What time was it? Was it too early for a drink?

"Two o'clock, okay?" he asked. I agreed and hung up.

I poured hot water into a mug and no sooner had I brought it to my lips than my phone rang again, and this time I looked at the screen. Sean. I almost threw the cup across the room.

"You through throwing your hissy fit?" he asked aggressively, not bothering with a greeting.

"You through being an insufferable dick?"

"Just trying to do my job, sweetheart. I'm good at this."

"So am I. I don't need your help."

"And yet you called me."

"Temporary insanity. I thought maybe you'd share info instead of just demanding it."

"You ain't exactly been forthcoming. It's give and take, honey."

"Stop calling me that!" I smacked my free hand against the counter. He was silent for a long moment, and then I heard a muffled conversation with who I presumed to be Luke.

"Couldn't find anything on Hughes," Sean said to me. "You're right, he's a dick, but so far clean. Can't connect him to your brother." His voice was clipped and harsh, but he sounded truthful.

"Sadie was worked over pretty bad. Chest carved up. Threat said *we're next*, best we can figure. Cops pulled trace evidence, waiting for report. Video surveillance screwed up." My voice matched his and he grunted in acknowledgment. I felt Ethan's eyes on me, but I didn't look at him.

"So we still have precisely shit," Sean said.

"Pretty much."

"Call me when you're meeting your contact."

"Whatever." I hung up and sincerely considered turning off my phone.

My nerves were shot. I paced. Pounded at my laptop. Splashed a few fingers of whiskey into a glass but didn't drink it. I wanted to do anything just to feel like I was doing *something*--as evidenced by my calling that jackass Sean. Ethan watched me prowling around. His stare made me itch.

Fuck this.

I disappeared back into my bedroom and jerked on my cop suit. Stalking back into the living room, I slid my Sig into its holster and grabbed my keys.

"Do me a favor. Go see what you can dig up on Hughes," I said. It was possible I didn't trust Sean's investigative skills, but really I just wanted Ethan gone.

He took in my change of clothes and lifted a brow. "Where're you going?"

"To speed things along."

~

THE DENVER COUNTY MORGUE occupied a five-story building, all brick and mirrored glass, across from the city's largest hospital. I'd been here often and knew the routine, flashing my badge and winding my way back to the autopsy suite. The medical examiner wasn't there, but I didn't need her to rifle through files.

"Looking for this?"

I may or may not have squeaked. Bastard caught me flat footed. I turned around to see Detective Green standing there holding a manila folder. He wore the same clothes as yesterday, his jacket rumpled, his tie loosened. None of that diminished the sharp look in his eye. I had the unsettling feeling that my ass was about to get nailed.

"Warren girl's autopsy report. That's what you're after, right?" He waved the folder and I wisely kept my mouth shut. "You know, you could have had this sent over. Evidence request from your office to mine, would have been all yours."

"I like the hands-on approach."

He snorted, putting a hand on his hip and pacing a few feet while he talked. "You sure do. I saw that at the crime scene. Real involved." He stopped pacing and fixed me with a stare I was sure had brought down many a suspect. "But for someone so involved, you're pretty shitty at your job."

"Excuse me?"

"I checked up on you. Pulled your jacket. Five years at CBI, but you're only twenty-six."

"I'm a prodigy."

He snorted, sticking out his bottom lip. "Could be, could be. But you know what's funny? In five years, you haven't made one arrest. Your case closure rate is a big, fat zero. And no work history before that either. It's like you just dropped out of the sky."

The corner of my mouth twitched. "Maybe I'm Denver's fairy godmother."

He smiled, but there was no warmth in it. He prowled toward me, invading my space so that I was pinned against the metal counter. "Keep cracking jokes. I'm going to find out what the deal is with you, and so help me, if you're mixed up in this case, I will hogtie your pretty little ass and drag you down to holding myself." He slapped the folder down onto the counter and lumbered toward the door.

"Hey, wait a second." I should have just let him go. Sometimes, I'm an idiot. "Listen, I know this looks shady as hell, but you got to believe me. We're on the same team here. I want to catch this guy every bit as much as you do."

The cop looked at me like he could see straight down to my bones. I tried not to blink. "You want me to believe that? Prove it. What the fuck is going on here?"

I hesitated. "You know. Murder."

"Right. I got a vic that, for all intents and purposes, didn't exist before a couple years ago. I got her friends telling me about a boyfriend, except I can't find him either. I got people saying that feds are working this case, but the local field office doesn't have any idea what I'm talking about. I got death by anaphylaxis and a body missing so much blood I'm two steps away from putting out a BOLO for a goddamn vampire."

"It's not a vampire," I said, almost absently. Green looked at me like he didn't think I was very funny. Thank God he took it as me being a smartass.

"You know what killed this girl."

"A lunatic." Lie by telling the truth. My best strategy. The small muscles around Green's mouth tightened. I'd been right about him--he was an excellent cop. Smart, tenacious, passionate, good instincts. Unfortunately, what I really needed right now was dumb, lazy, and bored.

"Maybe you're not a perp, but something's not right with you. You're lying and keeping secrets, and in my experience, that's not what the good guys do."

I rolled my lips inward and looked up at the ceiling. If I'd played by the damned rules, this never would have happened. The witches at CBI would have gotten me the report through regular channels, and no one would have been the wiser. If Green poked around too far, they'd find a way to quietly and firmly shut him down. But since I was playing Lone Ranger, I had to handle this on my own.

"Look, you're new here, right?" I asked.

"To Denver. Been on the job for fifteen years."

"You ever see something you can't explain? I don't mean like normal human depravity. But legit something you cannot explain." I opened my senses, feeling him out, but Green was bunkered down behind a brick wall of suspicion and anger. He gave me a grudging tip of his head. "That's the stuff I work on. And I can't tell you any more than that, so you're just going to have to trust me. I am one of the good guys, Green."

If I'd been in his hotbox, I would've been fidgeting and asking for a lawyer. As it was, I shoved my hands in my pockets and tried to look calm. I was asking him to believe one truth and a whole basket of lies, and I didn't think he was buying it. He stared at me for about seven thousand years, then turned and walked away.

Nice job, Rachel.

I snatched the manila folder off the counter and hauled ass out of there.

Later, I poked at a box of Chinese takeout, sitting cross-legged on my couch while I read the autopsy report. Sadie's file confirmed what I already knew—cause of death was extreme allergic reaction. Medical examiners often classified deaths of supes like that. When you have only one real weakness, the body tends to reject it in a big way. Her throat and eyes were swollen, and blood tests showed elevated levels of white blood cells, C-reactive protein, and sedimentation rate--all signs of inflammation. The ME used this to confirm that Sadie died from anaphylaxis, although she noted the cause was unknown. Oh, doc. You had the answer in the white ash wood fragments pulled from the wounds on her neck.

Multiple contusions, blunt force trauma likely caused by a long, thin object. Dozens of shallow cuts. Ligature marks around the wrists, ankles, and throat. Fractured skull, cheek-bones, nose, femur, radius. Every finger was broken. This much overkill and torture--our perp had lots of rage. The best thing I could say about it all was that the carving on her chest had been done postmortem. Thank God for small favors. A microscopic smirk tugged at my lips at the ME's baffled remarks about accelerated bone remodeling. See, Green? Shit you can't explain.

Sadie was missing thirty percent of her total blood volume. None of the cuts were deep or large enough to cause her to bleed out. Every word, every injury marked on the diagram built a picture in my mind. Sadie tied up, alone, scared. Tears in her eyes as she was tortured. The faint hope that someone would save her. Her face shifted to Danny's, and I buried my face in my hands, tasting bile in my throat. Maybe Ethan was right. Maybe I was in over my head and should just leave this to the Council.

I'd worked murders before, whether it was at the hands of a corrupt witch or a supe gone off the rails. Death was never pretty. It was sticky and gelatinous, flesh that felt like cold rubber and eyes gone filmy and vacant. It was rib shards poking up like dead trees, the gaping, ragged edges of torn arteries. It was mottled stains on ashen skin and the unique stench of copper, shit, and decay. But it was never like this.

Corrupt witches killed for revenge, money, power, sex, amusement. Supes gone primal killed because they were apex predators. I could understand that. But none of Sadie's injuries were designed to kill. This girl had done nothing, *nothing* to anyone, and she'd been beaten so badly the son of bitch had to leave us her driver's license to identify the body. Which he did to taunt us. And for what? At least my other cases made some kind of sense. What was the fucking point of all this?

My mind returned to the blood loss. I flipped back to the page where the ME discussed the puncture wounds on Sadie's arm. Her guess was an IV. No drugs in the tox screen, so something was going out, not coming in. Why the hell would someone drain three liters of blood out of her? Some illegal magic spells required a blood sacrifice, but in my experience, that was a slit throat over a bowl, not extraction by medical device.

I looked at my phone, considering calling Sean. I wondered if he read this report, saw the damage done to Sadie, if he'd still think she was the monster in this equation. I knew Ethan thought I was an idiot. Hell, I thought I was an idiot. But some desperate, childish part of me wanted to show Sean I was good. That supernatural didn't equate to evil. That I wasn't some ticking time bomb. I rubbed at my right wrist, my favorite nervous tick, and stared at my phone. I knew why I wanted his approval, but I didn't want to poke that particular hornet's nest. Introspection just ain't my thing.

My head still pounded, my body ached, and I'd thrown up twice since getting home from the morgue. I knew the drill. It wasn't my first concussion. But crises don't stop for a sick day. I needed to get all my cylinders firing, so I strapped on my running shoes.

Running was my refuge. Sure, it helped with my job—I lived by a strict code of "if you can't catch me, you can't eat me"—but it was also the only time when my thoughts slid into place. When I was beating my head against evidence that just didn't stack up, when I wanted to shove Ethan into a closet, or when I was just pissed off and had no convenient outlet to punch, I went running. It and fixing cars were the two things that actually kept me sane. It's cheaper than therapy—and doesn't get me thrown in the nuthouse for telling folks monsters are real.

A nice, secluded trail wound up the mountain not far from my cabin, and I attacked it without mercy. I kept a good pace, working my way higher in elevation, until I crested the summit. It wasn't really right to call where I stood a mountain, not with the towering 14,000-foot peaks behind me, but it was a respectable foothill at least. I only stopped a few times, dry heaving behind a tree, and a hot buzzing still circled my head like a halo from brain injury hell, but the run did its job. By the time I returned to my cabin, I was sweaty, tired, and ready to tackle the world.

I still didn't have a clue about solving this case, but I had my spirit back. I could do this. Witches wobble but they don't fall down.

I glanced at my phone as I stripped down for a shower. Seven missed calls. Three from my dad, two from Ethan, one from a number I didn't recognize, and one from Elena. I called my dad back first.

"Rachel, where've you been?" His twang didn't hide the tension in his voice, and my optimism vanished like a goddamn virgin on prom night.

"Out on a run. What happened?"

"Turn on the news."

I jammed the power button on my TV, sinking down onto my couch. A reporter was at Washington Park in Denver, a popular place for runners and dog walkers. She wore that expression unique to the media--sincerity mingled with just a hint of sensationalism-- as she stood in front of yellow police tape. The crawler along the bottom of the screen read "Body found in Wash Park, police believe connected to Union Station victim."

"Shit," I breathed. "Is it--"

"Not Danny. Think it's Jeff--Elena sent notice to the Council that the pack will be handlin' this, and she don't appreciate our interference, 'specially since we denied her initial request."

"She's right. It was a huge mistake to ignore her."

"You an' me might think that, but the Executive's got a

different view on things. But I wanted t'give you a head's up. Pack's likely on the warpath."

"Yeah, no joke." I was surprised they hadn't torn the city apart, actually. My insides felt like they were going to fly apart and I took a minute just to breathe. "Council actually looking for Danny?"

"Yes." He sounded grim. "An' we tried a trackin' spell last night, me and your mom and Joe. Same thing you got."

At least he was still alive. "I'm trying, Dad. I swear I'll find him."

"You just be careful, Rachel. Why don't you come up here? We'll work it together."

God, wouldn't that be nice. Hide behind my parents and uncle, suffer this fucked up situation together. But I couldn't. I'd never been good at sitting still, and was even worse about letting people help me. "I've got to go see Elena, Dad. She loses it, we're going to have bigger problems."

"Just... watch yourself, girl." A hitch in his voice again, and for the first time I considered what this was like for my parents. One child missing, the other throwing herself in the line of fire. I hated myself for it, but if one of us had to go, it sure as hell wasn't going to be Danny. "I'm talkin' to Michelle, gettin' some feelers out. Your mom's talkin' to local small-time witches. Somebody's gotta know somethin'."

"Sounds good." I cleared my throat and jammed my thumb and forefinger against my eyes, fighting the sting. "I've got to go, Dad. I'll call you later."

I returned Elena's call next, and was greeted with a voice that was more animal than human.

"Stay out of our way, Rachel. We will have vengeance, hunters and Council be damned."

"Elena--"

"No."

I took a step back, and she wasn't even in the goddamn room.

"You had your chance. We're done." She hung up without another word. Well, okay then. Glad we were all keeping cool heads about ourselves.

I made it downtown in record time. Ethan was already there when I got out of my Jeep, my still-wet hair wound into a bun at the nape of my neck. His hands were on his hips, a grimace carved into his face as he put a hand on my back, guiding me toward a knot of cops about twenty feet away. I shrugged off his touch as we got closer. Once again, a crowd had gathered. An itchy, prickly sensation crawled up my spine, my stomach feeling more and more like a cement mixer with every step.

Jeff's body was sprawled right in the middle of the running trail, naked and worked over. Just like Sadie. His body bore so many bruises that his dark skin looked like one purple mass. Jeff was a were. It took some serious muscle to lay a beat down on someone like him. I swore quietly, running a hand over my face. The pack was already about to lose their shit. Once they saw the state of Jeff's body, we'd have full-on war.

"Happy now?" Detective Green glared down at me. He looked like he hadn't slept. At least he'd changed clothes. "If you'd have been straight with me, maybe we could have saved this guy."

"You don't know what you're stepping in here," I said. God, I was tired. The spark I'd felt after my run was a distant memory. The scraped skin on my shoulder burned, my head felt like Superman was trying to crush it, and I thought I might throw up again.

"That's exactly the goddamn point, isn't it? I don't know, and that means I can't do my goddamn job," he hissed.

Ethan raised a hand. "Detective, we have shared jurisdiction here. Please don't harass my partner."

"Jurisdiction?" Green's face folded in on itself and he took a step closer. "This is a DPD case. CBI assists us. You really want to get bureaucratic, boy?"

"Feel free. But we'll be here, trying to solve the murder."

That seemed to slow Green down. He looked at Jeff, then at me, his mouth puckered and eyes narrowed. I pulled on a pair of gloves and got to work.

"Check the inside of his right elbow," Green said gruffly, squatting down beside me. I picked up Jeff's arm and found three small puncture wounds, just like the ones on Sadie. I'd bet my car that he was missing blood too, but I didn't need an autopsy report to tell me what had killed Jeff--the only thing that could. Silver.

I avoided looking at his chest. I didn't want to see more words carved there. Maybe on some instinctual level, I knew what they'd say. Finally, I forced myself to look. The urge to vomit intensified.

"We've got company," Ethan said, tipping his chin toward the police tape. It took me a moment to process what he said, panic rushing through me in hot, deafening streams. Pulling together the tattered remains of my composure, I tore my eyes away from Jeff and looked where Ethan pointed.

Nuclear rage erupted in my chest. I shot to my feet, storming over to where Sean and Luke were trying to talk their way past the uniforms. I had no time for this bullshit.

"Well, look who's here, Miss Marple and her faithful side-kick," Sean said, smirking.

"Get out of here, I mean it." I stopped just outside arm's reach. It was for his safety, not mine.

He rocked his head back, eyeing me. "What happened to working together?"

"Leave." He took a step forward, invading my space, and I tapped a line, so angry that I didn't care we were standing in the middle of a huge crowd of people. Ethan grabbed my arm and jerked me backward.

"Rachel, get a grip," he said, glancing at the hunters. I was still staring at Sean.

"We're just trying to help," Luke said, raising his hands. Where his brother was all piss and vinegar, Luke was calm and soothing. It didn't work on me, and I yanked my arm out of Ethan's grasp.

"Go. We'll call you," Ethan said. He moved in front of me, but his eyes were on Luke.

"I'm tired of waiting on you," Sean snarled. "No more bullshit."

"You're the one that keeps making demands. Sorry we won't do your job for you," I said. My tone could have etched metal, there was so much acid in it.

"That's rich, coming from the chick keeping all the secrets."

"Because you piss me off!"

"Whatever, honey. Keep hiding behind your boy toy there."

"Both of you need to knock it off," Ethan said, looking between Sean and me. "We've got two dead bodies, and this isn't helping." The four of us stood there for a few moments, Luke and Ethan looking like referees.

"She better call," Sean said, his eyes still burning into mine.

"Stop ordering me around."

The corner of his mouth lifted in a wry grin, and if Ethan hadn't been in the way, I would have decked the son of a bitch. Everything about him sent a fire burning through me. Luke nodded and put a hand on his brother's arm, pulling him backwards. Sean and I continued to glare at each other until he finally turned away, his shoulders hunched.

"Are you crazy, tapping a line here?" Ethan hissed, gripping my arm again as he steered me back toward the crime scene. I jerked away from him.

"I'm not in the mood." My voice vibrated with anger,

barely drowning the fear that clawed at my throat. "You saw what was on Jeff's chest."

Ethan's expression softened and he tried to reach for me again. I knocked his hand away.

The gaping slashes of the words in Jeff's chest burned behind my eyes every time I closed them. *Witch next*.

TEN

Ethan put Leon's address into his phone's navigation system and we headed north. I swerved in and out of lanes on I-25, fear turning to recklessness as I practically dared a cop to pull me over.

We soon left the city behind, buildings giving way to the farmlands of Adams County. My Jeep kicked up a storm of dust as we rattled down a gravel road, but not enough to disguise the big, black truck following us. Swearing, I slammed on the brakes, cutting the wheel so that my Jeep blocked the road.

"What the hell, Rachel?" Ethan demanded. I didn't say anything, but shoved the car into park and jumped out, slamming my door closed. I stood in the middle of the road with my arms crossed and anger radiating from me.

The truck slowed, rumbling to a stop a few feet back, and Sean got out.

"What the hell are you doing?"

"Think that's pretty clear. Figured you wouldn't call." He wasn't even slightly ashamed of following me.

"I'm not fucking around here."

"I'm not either, babe."

I closed my eyes and prayed for patience. If I killed him, that might cause some problems. "Look--"

"You can skip the speech. Here's how this goes. We're not backing off this case, so you might as well learn to work with us." He set his jaw and gave me a level look. Stubborn ass.

"Why?" I demanded, throwing my arms out. "Why are you so goddamn hung up on this?"

"Because. It's our jobs."

"So this is some kind of territorial pissing match?"

"We told you. We tracked a demon here. Is it really so bad to work together?" Luke asked. He stood between Sean and me, as if expecting us to go for each other's throats. I tipped my head back toward the sky. Green, the Callahans... What the hell had I done in a past life to be cursed with these tenacious bastards?

"There's stuff you don't understand," I said.

"Then explain it." Sean raised his eyebrows, as if daring me to tell the truth for once. I really, really wanted him to just go away.

"Later. Just go and we'll call you later."

"Right, because you've been so great at that so far."

"Leave her alone," Ethan said. Sean swung his gaze to him.

"I'm sorry, did it look like I was talking to you?"

"I mean it, man. Back off."

"She don't need you to fight her battles. Do you, baby?" Sean gave me a sly look and it caught me off guard. It was less taunting, more playful. I wondered if he just really enjoyed baiting me. I wondered if they were serious about helping. I didn't know how to fight demons, and I'd need help to get Danny back. And there it was, that feeling again--wanting just once to be trusted, to not be looked at with suspicion. The Council could blame themselves for that shit. I fiddled with the zipper on my jacket, looking at Sean and contemplating just how badly this whole situation was going to blow up in my face.

"Let it go, Ethan," I said, chewing on my lip. "We'll go together. But we run this show."

"Whatever you want, sweetheart."

"I'm serious. Leon doesn't like hunters and I don't need you busting in there like some Dirty Harry wannabe and scaring the hell out of him. Deal?"

"Deal." He gave me half a grin. I rolled my eyes, but I was smiling.

We got back in the Jeep and Ethan looked at me like I'd just invited Lucifer over for tea. "You're seriously taking them to Leon's after what Elena said?"

"What choice do we have? They're already following us out here. At least this way we can keep an eye on them."

"That's not what this is about," he said, his lip curling. "This is about you wanting to stick it to the Council. This is about Ryan."

I shot Ethan a look and he actually flinched. This was so not the fucking time.

Leon lived in the middle of nowhere, on several acres of flat, grassy fields. Whereas I liked the hidden aspect of the mountains, Leon apparently wanted to see who was coming at him for miles in any direction. No car sat in front of the modest rancher. I killed the ignition and climbed out of the Jeep just as Sean pulled in beside me.

"Is he home?" Luke asked.

"Should be. Meet was for two," I said, frowning. We filed up the steps and I banged my fist against the door. No answer. No sounds inside the house. I knocked again.

"Maybe he's running late," Ethan said, shrugging a shoulder.

"Maybe he skipped town," Sean said, surveying the house. I knocked once more and then tried the knob. It was unlocked. I pushed the door open and edged inside.

"Holy shit," I breathed. Every square inch of the walls and ceiling was inscribed. Runes for protection, glyphs for concealment, wards against demons, angels, corrupt witches, fae. The inscriptions ran across multiple mythologies. Leon had certainly covered his bases. I moved farther into the living room, sparsely furnished with a threadbare rug and a worn and mismatched sofa and recliner. Several towers of books filled one corner, but there was no television, no pictures, no personal items of any kind.

"Holy hell, this guy is fruit loops," Sean said.

"He isn't crazy. He's scared," I snapped. "See that?" I pointed to an inscription above the door and windows, a sort of stylized S with sharp angles. "*Eihwaz*. For protection. And that one?" I pointed at a rune that resembled a C with extra marks at the ends. "*Perthro*. It helps hide the subject."

"Rachel's right. All these sigils are defensive," Ethan said. Sean looked at me with a strange expression on his face.

"How do you guys know all this?" he asked.

"Because we can read. You should try it sometime." I turned back to the books. They looked like old magical texts. I caught Ethan's eye and nodded toward them. While he examined the books, I prowled back into the kitchen. Clean and sparse, it would have looked like a bachelor pad except for the magical graffiti. A battered kettle sat on the stove and an old farm table was pushed against the far wall. Copper bowl, knife, jars of herbs and sigils drawn in blood--Leon had done his homework.

"Ugh, freaking witches, man. Why do they always have to smear their bodily fluids everywhere? That shit's a biohazard," Sean said, coming up behind me as I looked over Leon's workspace.

"What the fuck is the matter with you?" I rounded on him, heat prickling over my skin.

"What? What are you talking about?"

"You hate anything that's not just like you."

"Rachel, chill. I was just joking." He looked confused, and that just inflamed me further.

"Do you even know what you're looking at here? Do you know the hell this man has been through?"

"Yeah, he's some shady dude and probably a witch. Excuse me while my heart breaks for him."

"He is not a witch!" I roared. My temper, bubbling close to the surface ever since seeing Jeff's body, erupted and drove all reason from my brain. "He's a man who was chased down by hunters like you!"

"Hunters like us? What the hell is that supposed to mean?"

"You have no idea about how the world really is. Leon has lost everything and he's terrified, but he still helps people. He gives them the safety he's never had. But you don't see that. You just see a werewolf and you'd kill him on sight." Ethan and Luke had frozen in the entryway to the kitchen, watching us.

"A werewolf?" Sean cocked his head, blinking, and then his eyes narrowed and his expression turned stony. "You're saying Leon is a were? Good to know. I'll add him to the list."

"You won't touch him." My hands clenched into fists and magic called to me, begging to be let off the chain. The rational voice I'd shoved into a box in my brain peeked out to remind me that no matter how good it might feel, I didn't want to accidentally fry his ass.

"Rachel, what the hell? He's a monster. Why would you protect that?" His words scratched at an old wound. My hurt and fear and anger from our earlier argument slammed together like a chain reaction and I fucking lost it. I launched a right cross at his face. His arm flew up, the move too fast to be anything but instinctual, and blocked my punch. He used my momentum to spin me around and clamped his arms around mine, pinning me with my back against his chest.

"Calm down, dammit! What's your problem?"

"You are my problem! Hunters like you see things only one way, and you play God, killing anything you think deserves it. Don't you have a soul?" I struggled against him and landed an elbow into his solar plexus. Sean gasped for air and released me. I whipped away to face him. "It was a mistake to work with you on this. These people aren't monsters, and you're not interested in rescuing them. You're only interested in the next kill."

"Okay, okay, that's enough," Ethan said, moving between Sean and me. "We still have a job to do here." Sean stepped back and rubbed his abdomen where I'd hit him. I got some satisfaction from that.

"We'll take a look around," Luke said, pulling Sean backward. I dimly registered that Ethan had a protective arm around my shoulders and I shoved it off, turning around and bracing my arms against the kitchen table.

"You okay?" Ethan asked after a moment. I shuffled through the papers without really looking at them, my heart pounding.

"Fine." I made a frustrated noise. "Don't know why that dick gets to me so much."

"Yes you do."

I ignored him.

"Hey guys? You should see this," Luke called from the back of the house. We walked down the hallway to a small bedroom that apparently served as Leon's office. Several computers and a homebrewed router covered a simple wooden desk. Grey filing cabinets stood next to the door and I caught a glimpse of fake birth certificates lying in a stack.

Leon was slumped over a chair in the middle of the room. His eyes were glassy and unfocused, his skin pale. Dried blood caked his face from the single gunshot wound to his forehead. Leon was a were, and he hadn't even put up a fight. Fear still twisted his features, but I thought I saw resignation there too. I grimaced, a hard knot forming in my stomach.

"Why didn't he wolf out?" Sean asked quietly, and I realized he was standing beside me.

"You pitying him? I thought he was a monster and you were going to kill him."

He glanced at me. "Just doesn't make sense. I mean, werewolves... it looks like he didn't even stand up." His mouth twitched, like he was wrestling with the image in his head and the reality in front of him.

"I think he hated what he was. I think he wanted to die." Elena was going to tear someone apart. Muscles clenched along Sean's jaw, and an unreadable expression crossed his face.

"Well, at least we know we're on the right track. Somebody didn't want us talking to him," he said, a forced gruffness in his voice. Looking at his brother, he added, "Think you can crack the computer?"

"I'll give it a shot." Luke bent over the keyboard and began typing away, looking up at the dual monitors as lines of code flew across the screen. My eyes kept going back to Leon.

"Leon had quite a talent for security," Luke said after a while. "He certainly didn't want anyone getting in without him knowing about it."

"So what'd you find?" Sean asked. I jumped. I'd forgotten he was there.

"Looks like Leon was in the business of fake identities. Guy was thorough--new birth certificates, social security cards, even school transcripts. He's got accounting records too. Different amounts, almost like he worked on a sliding scale."

"Okay, but why? Were these people on the run from the law or something?" Sean asked. I traded a glance with Ethan. The Callahans were discovering what we already knew, but if they realized all our missing people were supernatural, that could cause some problems. Especially for Danny and me.

"Not that I can find. Just seems like they wanted to start over," Luke said.

"You got names?" I asked.

"Uh, yeah, give me a minute." He banged out a few more keystrokes. "Looks like our killer is working off a hit list." We crowded around Luke, looking at one of the monitors.

"Marcus Rodriguez, Sadie Warren, Jeff Sharpe—bingo," Sean said. "So our bad guy has a problem with Leon's clients."

My eyes skimmed over the names. "There's so many, and no order. How do we tell who's next?"

"Guess we split up and start trying to contact them," Sean said. I was spared trying to invent a reason why that was a terrible idea by Luke.

"Leon has a lot of info here about William Hughes, too."

Now my interest was definitely piqued. Leon had wanted to tell me something. Maybe that was it. "Like what?"

"There's a whole file here with notes on conversations and movements, like Leon was watching him," Luke said. "And man, this Hughes has his fingers in all kinds of pies. Real estate, government, rare art and antiquities..." Made sense. Rare artifact dealings usually covered someone buying up magical items. "It looks like Hughes may have tried to contact Leon about making connections between him and various people. Can't tell for what, though."

"Butterflies," I mumbled. Sean shot me a quizzical look, but I just shook my head.

"Can you print the list of business dealings for Hughes?" Ethan asked.

"Sure thing." Luke turned back to the computer and hit a keystroke, and the printer hummed to life.

"I'll take the list and see what I can dig up," Ethan said as Luke passed him the papers. We searched the rest of Leon's office but didn't turn up much. I found a series of news clippings about a missing kid, Thomas Springer. He'd disappeared a week or so before Sadie. His name hadn't been on the list on Leon's computer, but I slipped one of the clippings into my pocket anyway. I wasn't passing up anything that might even remotely help find my brother. The more we looked, the more pity I felt for Leon. Elena was right: life had been cruel to him. I hoped he was finally at peace.

We wrapped up and I walked outside, toying with my phone. I knew I needed to call Elena, but I didn't relish giving her such bad news on the same day that Jeff had been discovered. I was standing by my Jeep, staring out into space and putting off the call, when Luke ambled over.

"Hey," he said. "Um, sorry about my brother back there. He's pretty black and white, and we've been going through some stuff. Sarcasm and hostility are pretty much his basic defenses."

"Don't worry about it. I shouldn't have lost my temper. His attitude's common among hunters."

"You say 'hunters' like you're not one."

My eyes lingered on the tattoo on his arm. "I'm complicated."

We watched the late afternoon sun play over the fields for a few minutes. "So what happened to you?" he asked.

"What do you mean?"

"To get you into the life."

"Oh, um. It's just something we do. My family."

"Nobody died?" He didn't seem to understand. "So you just... hunt monsters for fun?"

"Something like that." I sighed. All this walking on eggshells was exhausting. "What about you?"

"Vamp came to our town when I was fourteen. Killed my sister."

"I'm sorry." I meant it. I couldn't imagine that kind of heartache. I thought about Danny and slammed the brakes on that frigging train of thought before it sent me careening off a cliff.

"Thanks. My brother and me, we were part of the local search party when she went missing. Thought it was like, a regular kidnapping, you know? We just wanted to find her, either way. Anyway, we met this guy. Mysterious, had a kind of weird rep, but always seemed to turn up when something happened."

"A hunter."

"Yeah. Vamp was preying on our town and Elliot, he just was there, you know? Me and Sean, we stuck by him, he started coming by the house. My dad, well, he went nuts when Julia died. Elliot... he told us the truth. Got hooked up with some people and went to work."

"And the FBI role-play?"

Luke gave me a crooked grin. "Let's just say we've got friends in high places. We're on contract for the weird ones."

Huh, so the Council wasn't the only one with law enforcement cover. "What about your dad?"

"He sticks around Cheyenne, trying to protect the town. Sean... well, at least he's here." He sounded bitter. I didn't know what to say, so we just stood there in growing silence, me still playing with my phone.

"What did you mean that these people aren't monsters?" he asked.

Shit. I hadn't realized I'd let that slip during my temper tantrum earlier.

"Nothing. Just a figure of speech," I said, a little too defensively.

Luke gave me a long look. "I'm not like my brother, Rachel," he said sharply, taking me aback.

I studied my boots. Maybe he wasn't, but that still didn't mean I could trust him. I heard how Sean referred to witches, and that wolf totem on Luke's arm told me everything I needed to know.

"You know, those people on Leon's list—they might not want to be found," I said. "People don't get fake identities if they're cool with strangers rolling up at their homes."

"Yeah, but what else are we going to do? Something's after them."

"Maybe we just find it first."

Luke smiled. "Gotta say, I like how you think." He cleared his throat, eyes flitting between everything else and me. "What's happening with your brother--we really do want to help, Rachel. Sean might be a dick sometimes, but we've been in your shoes. I never wanted anyone else to go through that. That's why I became a hunter."

I didn't doubt his good intentions. But I knew what happened when those intentions crashed up against reality. Ethan was right--we weren't human to them. I had to remember that. "Did you ever catch the vamp?" I asked quietly.

"Yeah. Last year. It came at a heavy price."

"Things like that usually do."

A couple minutes later, Sean and Ethan emerged from the house and I gave Luke a tight smile as he walked over to the truck. He seemed like a good guy, compassionate. I'd been wrong before, though.

The Callahans left, Ethan rode with me to my house and then took off to start investigating Hughes, and I dragged my exhausted, beaten ass onto my couch. I felt like this day had gone on for about seven hundred years, and I planned on a glass of whiskey, some bad TV, and an early evening. I was simply burnt out, and even though fear still itched at my brain, I knew I needed to recharge. I'd just dropped down onto the couch when my phone rang in my pocket. I really hoped it wasn't Sean. I didn't have the energy for another fight.

"Hey girl." Relief washed through me at the sound of my dad's voice. Part of me wanted to drive up to Dillon like he'd offered and just dissolve against him. I was so scared I wouldn't be able to save Danny, and the childish side of me still saw my dad as a superhero. I wanted him to fix this.

"Hey," I said wearily. "Any word?"

"Not yet. Local cops are lookin'. I been watchin' the stuff

come through police channels. Douglas County's gettin' a search party together, for all the good it'll do. Masterson's here."

"Wonderful."

"He took a team to Danny's, found it quite a mess." A microscopic trace of amusement lined my dad's voice and I smiled a little. "Wouldn't know anything about that, wouldja?"

"Nope."

"Good girl." He sighed. "The whole thing's a mess, Rachel. Nothin' can break the concealment ward around Danny."

"They bring in a Genesis team?"

He hesitated for just a moment. "Should they?"

"Not yet." Genesis teams, the Council's demon-hunting commandos, were like nuclear strikes, and I wasn't ready to launch one.

"Alright. How you holdin' up?"

"Fine." Automatic response, automatic lie. I just couldn't muster the courage to tell him about what had been carved in Jeff's chest. My beleaguered mind fumbled for something else to say and I blurted out the first thing it landed on. "The other day, this... thing attacked me. I'm thinking there's no way this isn't related to our case, but I just can't figure out how."

"What?" His voice was sharp. "What was it?"

"No idea."

"Dammit, Rachel, why didn't you say anything?"

"Because we got enough on our plate, and I'm alive, and I just—it was right after Danny disappeared and I just didn't think about it." I sounded pathetic. Welcome to my bad habit—keeping shit from people who care about me.

"Tell me about it."

"Big, fucking strong. Red eyes. Weird shifting skin and bones, claws. I honestly have no idea what the hell it was. I flooded it with enough ley energy to kill, and it just got pissed off at me."

"You check the database?"

"Not yet."

"I'd start there. It don't sound like nothin' I've seen before. You sure you're alright?"

"Yeah." I brushed it off by changing the subject. "How's Jake?"

"Scared, askin' lots of questions. Y'know how he is."

My heart twinged. His mom had bailed. The kid didn't deserve to be left all alone. "Anythin' else happen?" I heard the tightness in his voice, and an iron fist seized my

stomach. It should have been me that was missing. Danny was too good for this.

"Dad... Leon Cartwright is dead."

His silence told me he knew who that was and why this was a Very Bad Thing. "I'll talk to Elena and handle the pack. You just work the case. Council said Masterson is runnin' around Denver, so keep your head down. We're comin' down there tomorrow to talk to some folks who mighta seen Danny." He sounded so worn that I wanted to cry. I wanted to say I was sorry, that I'd find my brother, that I'd bring this lunatic to justice.

"Yes, sir," was all I said instead.

That phone call obliterated my plans to get some rest. I pulled my laptop over to me, logging into the Council's database. Twenty minutes later I'd searched every version of "shadow", "smoke", "reaction to wolfsbane and silver", "immune to gunshot" and "creepy bastard" I could think of, and had precisely jack squat. Something heavy and hot had taken up residence in my gut, clawing at my insides. The longer I sat still, the more it hurt.

~

I CHECKED THE TIME--JUST AFTER SEVEN. Still early enough for a house call.

Exhaustion and a blinding pain behind my eyes told me driving anymore today was out of the question, so I called a Lyft—always fun when I made them come out here to East Jesus Nowhere. I downed far more than the prescribed dosage of NoDoz while I waited, so that by the time the driver arrived, I was vibrating. I'm fairly sure that caffeine overdose is not an accepted medical treatment for head injury, but I could be wrong.

I scrolled my phone and ignored the driver's attempts to talk as we headed east on I-70. I'd found Hughes's address on DMV records. The Council hadn't revoked my privileges to state databases.

Sometimes the Council isn't too bright.

We wound our way into the posh neighborhood of Cherry Creek and I finally spoke up to direct us a few streets over. It was bad enough that there would be a record of my ride; I didn't want to be dropped off right on Hughes's frigging doorstep. I stood in the shadows until the Lyft was well out of sight and after a couple steadying breaths, I shoved my hands in my pockets and walked over to Hughes's street. I'd just turned the corner when I saw a hulking shape in the shadow of a large maple. Sean's truck. I huffed out a laugh. Stubborn ass.

I marched over to the truck and climbed in the backseat as way of announcing myself. "We need to talk."

Sean and Luke looked over their shoulders at me with mild expressions of surprise. Sean recovered first.

"No offense, but you look like shit," he said.

"You're so suave," I drawled. "Why didn't you tell me you were taking another run at Hughes?"

"Why didn't you tell us you were doing the same?"

"Spur of the moment decision." That was about as far as

my plan took me, and I rubbed my hands together for a minute looking for words. "How's your solar plexus?"

Sean touched his abdominal muscles while Luke ducked his head in a small grin. "You're little, but you got some heat," he said, but he didn't sound angry. He sounded impressed.

I smiled a little. "Thirteen years of judo, seven of Krav Maga. I'm not built like you two, I had to learn to defend myself somehow."

It was like we'd arrived at some unspoken truce. Despite me slugging him earlier, something had shifted in Sean. Maybe it was seeing Leon. Whatever it was, the tension had started to ease, and I had to admit I was relieved. I needed their help.

"Not sure what we're going to get out of this," Luke said. "We turned up nothing the first time we questioned him."

"Yeah, I was thinking less question and more threaten the hell out of him." The brothers traded a look. "You don't have to come in. I'll handle it."

"What, think we're afraid of some smarmy boardroom douchebag?" Sean asked, glancing at me in the rearview mirror. He almost sounded playful.

"No, just--it's my mess. I'll clean it up."

"Look, just saying, you don't have to go it alone." Huh. He wasn't ordering me around. It was more like... a suggestion. Fucking weird.

The lights were dark inside Hughes's house. We sat in the truck, parked a little ways down from the sprawling McMansion that Hughes called home. The three of us, in our jeans and skulking in an old Ford, were several million dollars out of our element. I had to give it to the Callahans, though--they knew their shit. Sean had removed the plates from the truck before he parked, and the black truck blended nicely into the shadows on the street. No bitching, no fidgeting, nothing but sharp eyes and casual conversation. They were practically professionals at stalking--or, as we in the biz call it, surveilling.

"You guys work with many other hunters?" I asked, leaning forward to rest my arms on the back of the front seat.

"Sometimes. Mostly we just trade information, help out if we're needed. Why you ask?" Sean said, his eyes still on Hughes's house.

I looked at Luke. "Your tattoo. I've seen it before."

"Ah." He ran a hand over the black wolf totem. "Yeah. Went a little gung-ho."

Sean snorted. "That's an understatement."

"Don't listen to my brother. No one likes him very much. You know the Network?" Luke asked.

My shoulder twitched in a shrug that did a reasonable impression of nonchalant. "Sort of. I never really liked group adventures though." The Network, as it was known, was the closest thing hunters had to organization. It had another name, but not one I knew. They were big on secrecy. They were also big on killing anything that wasn't pure human.

Luke's expression darkened and he rubbed the tattoo the way I rubbed the spot where my soul brand was. "You're not missing much. I thought they were trying to do something good, but they're really extremist bastards. We had disagreements."

"By which he means he punched one of the leaders in the nose," Sean said, flashing a lopsided smile at his brother and something like pride flickering in his eyes. I chuckled, but my heart twisted. Their banter reminded me of conversations with Danny. Something must have shown in my face, because Sean reached back to lay a hand on my arm.

"Hey, I know we got off to a rough start, but we'll find him, Rache."

I met his eyes, hiding my rapid blinking with a forced smirk. "I don't think you know me well enough to use nicknames."

"Would you prefer 'sweetheart'?" He grinned at me, his eyes twinkling again.

I just rolled my eyes, but the edges of my smirk transformed into something genuine.

"Guys, head's up," Luke said suddenly, sitting forward and pointing. A black Town Car pulled into Hughes's drive, headlights washing over the house before it disappeared into the garage. We slid out of the truck and stole along the sidewalk. Sean led the way around the house to a back gate. I balked.

"What's the problem?" he asked.

"This is just... I feel like a creeper."

"Hey, this was your idea. I'm just getting you inside the house."

"Yeah, but I figured we could just knock on the front door."

"That usually work for you?" Sean gave me a skeptical look.

"All the time," I said, winking. I jogged across the yard toward the door, the Callahans in my wake. A woman in a maid's uniform answered, looking confused. It was close to ten o'clock, and none of us looked like anything remotely resembling a cop. It didn't matter. That's why God gave me magic.

"Can I help you?" she asked.

I summoned my will and sent out a moderate glamour. The Council wouldn't like it, but it would be the least of my worries if they found out about this little excursion. "We're here to see Mr. Hughes. He's expecting us."

The woman's pupils slid out of focus and back again, then she offered a warm smile. "Of course. Right this way." She stepped back and let us into the house.

Sean shot me a shrewd look and I lifted a shoulder, trying to play it off as just me being that damn smooth. I wasn't sure he bought it.

The maid led us back through marble hallways decorated

with expensive art. At least I assumed it was expensive. I'm better with Ramblers than Renoir. Hughes's personality was everywhere, from the heavy, overbearing drapes to the arrogant, douchebag hardwood floors. She showed us to an office and Hughes looked up from behind an ornate desk, eyes wide. Recognition dawned as I stalked forward and he stood, a smooth smile curling his lips.

"Ah, Laura. How unexpected. Although if you were so impatient to see me, I'm sure arrangements could have been made."

"Yeah, that's so not why I'm here." I crossed my arms as Luke shut the door, the brothers coming to flank me. Hughes regarded them like they were something stuck to his shoe.

"Really, Laura? You didn't need your attack dogs here. I thought we got on rather well just the two of us."

"Listen, douchebag. I'm done messing around with you. You're going to tell me what you know about Sadie and the others, no bullshit."

Hughes chuckled and returned to his chair, leaning back and steepling his fingers in front of his chest. Cold amusement glittered in his eyes.

"I told you what I know. But I do enjoy your... passion." He raked his eyes over me in a way that would have made me blush if it hadn't pissed me off so badly. I really wanted to set this guy on fire.

"We know you're involved. We know you talked to Leon Cartwright. 'Fess up or this is going to get real ugly, pal," Sean said. I fleetingly wondered if it hurt his throat to growl that low.

Hughes threw him a bored look. "I don't believe I was speaking to you." Those hungry eyes swung back to me and he smirked. "No, Laura here asks the questions. But now I'm getting the feeling that's not even your name, is it?"

"Tell me about Cartwright. How did you know him?" I demanded.

"What's your name?"

"You like these stupid games? People are dying, you dick."

"I'm aware. And yes, I do like these games very much. Give me your name."

Sean started forward, but I held up a hand. I really didn't need an Alpha Male Showdown, and I was having enough trouble controlling my own temper.

Hughes chuckled again. "Sit. Stay. Such an obedient dog."

For fuck's sake. I glared at him, hating to give in but not seeing another choice. "Rachel. Now what was your deal with Cartwright?"

"Rachel. Lovely. I don't know anyone named Cartwright."

"Really? Because we've got a lot of evidence that says you do," Luke said, his expression deadly calm.

Hughes ignored him, keeping his eyes on mine as a smile played around his lips. "You know, I know what you are." Heavy, writhing fingers squeezed my stomach and Hughes's smile turned wolfish. "Oh, but they don't, do they?"

"I have no idea what you're talking about."

"Oh, yes you do. Rachel." The way he said my name was almost obscene. Hughes prowled around his desk, coming so close to me that I could feel the heat from his skin. The smell of his cologne, which I'm sure was expensive and tasteful, soured my stomach, but I refused to back up. I caught Sean moving out of the corner of my eye. He looked livid.

"If you mean I'm the chick who's about to kick your ass if you don't start giving us some answers, then yeah, you got it."

"No," he purred. "But there's that fire again. I knew when you came to my office. Do you really think a man in my position isn't aware of everything that happens in his city?"

"What the hell are you talking about?"

He leaned so close that his lips brushed against my ear when he spoke. "Do you really want me to say it? In front of these two hunters?" he whispered, reaching up to curl a strand of my hair around his finger. My heart skipped a beat and Hughes smiled.

"You need to stop touching me." Hughes didn't know me well enough to know that when I got quiet like that, shit was about to explode.

"You'd be a valuable resource. I could make it worth your while. You and your brother both. Assuming he's still alive."

I fucking lost it.

I shoved Hughes hard in the chest and tapped a line so fast that my vision blurred. He stumbled backward, colliding with his desk. I lunged forward, but strong arms caught me around the waist.

"My brother is in this mess because he was trying to help people, and you're playing fucking games!" The smell of something clean, soap and gun oil, rolled over me. It was strangely comforting. I ripped at the arms holding me, half turning to shove the person away. I realized it was Sean.

"Calm yourself, Rachel. You don't want to make an enemy out of me," Hughes said. He leaned back against his desk as if he'd intended to end up there all along.

"You need to start talking. Now," Sean barked and pulled me behind him. His body was tense but not rigid, and one hand drifted to his back.

"I don't answer to the help," Hughes spat.

Moving with coordination that would make synchronized swimmers jealous, Luke and Sean pounced. Luke snatched Hughes's arm, pinning it behind his back, while locking the suit-clad dick in a chokehold. Sean drew his pistol with measured calm and pressed it flush against the dude's forehead.

"Talk," Sean said.

I wasn't sure if it was out of sheer terror or if the guy was really that much of an arrogant ass, but Hughes laughed. "You think you can hurt me? Do you know who I am?"

"Do you know who we are?"

"Oh, I do. Sergeant Sean Michael Callahan. Terrible business what happened in Syria. What you did." Sean's expression went blank and Hughes smirked. "Rachel's not the only one keeping secrets, is she?"

For a split second, I thought Sean might actually fire a bullet in his skull. But then Luke jerked the guy away, putting himself between his brother and Hughes. It wasn't for Hughes's sake. People think it's only the older sibling that gets protective, but that's not true. Luke's fist slammed into Hughes's nose, the small bones of his face crunching and popping. The younger Callahan didn't storm and rage like Sean. He moved with methodical grace, clocking Hughes again. He looked like the goddamn Terminator, his face was so still and blank. Luke could make one hell of a were.

"Let him go, man." Sean struggled with his brother, hauling him backward. Hughes sagged against the desk, his hand touching his face and coming away bloody.

"You morons. You don't even know what you're involved in. You think this is about a few missing creatures?" He jerked a handkerchief out of his pocket and held it to his nose.

"What do you mean?" I asked, a bad feeling slithering through my guts.

"No. My moment of helpfulness is over. Pity for your brother. If you're this far behind, I don't think you'll find him in time."

The stupid son of a bitch hadn't learned the first time that I respond extremely poorly to jabs about my brother. The line still burned through me and I mimicked his actions from earlier, putting my mouth against his ear.

"You say you know what I am. Then you know what I can do. And I swear to God if you don't tell me what you know, I will burn you from the inside out," I hissed.

"Ask me nicely."

"Tell me what you know!" I screamed, and shoved a hand against his chest, feeding a small taste of the ley line into him.

Hughes yelped, his body spasming as the energy sizzled across his nerves. His eyes went wide with fear, but also lust. It made me sick. It took everything I had to pull the power back and not dump the entire line straight into his skull.

"It's a spell! To make an army!" he yelped.

"Who? How?"

"I don't know, I swear!"

"Who told you about the victims?"

"Wilkes, it was Wilkes. He knew a lot, I paid him for information on the supernatural."

"Sadie's boss guy?" I asked, remembering the timid dude with the glasses.

Hughes nodded and I opened my senses. He wasn't lying, but my anger was spiraling out of control, fed by my utter revulsion for him and fear for my brother. Magic stirred around me, crawling over my skin in hot little sparks. A malicious voice whispered inside my head, telling me to punish him, to make him pay for toying with me. He trembled, and I smirked. Not so fucking alpha now, are you? I clenched my jaw, the rage and fear churning in my chest threatening to overwhelm me. I needed answers. I needed to save my brother. I needed to not feel so fucking useless.

"Rache..." A hand on my arm and I snapped my head to the side. Sean stared at me, a strange look on his face. "Let him go."

I looked back at Hughes.

"No." I didn't recognize the sound of my own voice, and I couldn't seem to relax my grip on Hughes's shirt.

"C'mon. We got work to do." He pulled gently on my arm and I swung my eyes to him, holding his gaze for a long moment. Suddenly, I realized what I was doing. Jesus Christ, I'd just attacked a human. I jerked away from Hughes as if shocked and stumbled backward, Sean's hand still gripping my arm. I licked my lips, my cheeks burning as I sucked in air. I wanted not just to kill him, but hurt Hughes. Make him suffer. What the hell was wrong with me?

"Not a fucking word of this or we'll be back," Sean said, glaring at Hughes. The man stood up, straightening his suit. He said nothing, but gave me a long, calculating look. I couldn't believe I'd lost control like that. Swallowing hard, I spun around on my heel and ran from the house. I sprinted down the street toward the truck. Sean caught up to me.

"Hey, you okay?" he called. I leaned against his Ford, hunched over, my hands on my thighs. I'd attacked a human. I'd been one step shy of killing him. I gagged, falling down to my knees.

"Rachel... hey, it's alright," Sean said, wrapping an arm around my shoulders.

"No. It is anything but alright, Sean!" I tried to push him away, but didn't have the strength.

"Dude's a dick. He was pushing your buttons about your brother. I get it."

"Do you?" I asked savagely. "Because I was about to torture him. Because I was pissed. Because I lost control."

"We all do, Rache."

"Yeah," I scoffed. "But it's different for me." I realized my hands were shaking. I'd never gone off like that before, especially not against an innocent person—and no matter how much of a dick Hughes was, he was innocent. I thought about all those scans, all the warnings about how pulling power could corrupt the soul, how it started with small actions. Did corrupt witches know when they started going down the path to hell? And I could try to justify it all I wanted by saying it was to save my brother, but wasn't that path paved with good intentions?

Sean brushed the hair out of my eyes and I stared down at the pavement. I wanted him to trust me, to believe that I was good. Problem was, I wasn't sure I trusted myself.

I WAS RUNNING ON FUMES. My body was itchy and felt strangely out of sync, my head pounded, and my eyelids drooped. Sean kept glancing at me in the rearview mirror during the drive across town to Jason Wilkes's modest home. I'd called my CBI office to get his address off of motor vehicle records, and while I should've felt good that we had a lead, I mostly just wanted to throw up. Something was fucking terrorizing my city, my family, and I had no idea how to stop it. I needed to find a way. I needed to get Danny back.

We parked in front of Wilkes's house. Neighborhoods like this, everyone had street parking, so we didn't stand out nearly as much as in Hughes's one-percenter area. I followed Sean and Luke up the steps and stood behind them as Sean banged his fist against the door. No one answered. I was having déjà vu from Cartwright's house and I started to fidget. Sean nodded at Luke, who knelt down before the door and removed a slim case from his pocket. He slid thin metal instruments into the lock and a few moments later, it clicked open.

We slipped inside and the thundering in my brain intensified. I gasped and curled my arm over my stomach, my expression twisting.

"Rachel?" Luke asked in alarm, putting an arm around me.

I swallowed down bile and took a shuddering breath. "I'm okay. Just... concussion bullshit." That was a convenient excuse. Magic, strong magic, was hitting me, seemingly from everywhere, but it was also muted. The mother of all trace magic.

Sean watched me as if I might collapse and I struggled upright. I'd never admit it, but I was glad they were with me. I was having a hard enough time staying vertical, let alone do any real investigating. Chewing on my lip, I plodded farther into the house. Luke searched upstairs while Sean prowled out back. I meandered into Wilkes's kitchen, searching for a clue as to what he was.

Utter chaos greeted me. Splintered cabinet doors dangled from their hinges, dishes lay shattered on the floor. The window above the sink was cracked and an ugly brown stain marred the beige tile.

I made the idiotic decision to bend over and examine the stain, and the world suddenly slid sideways. My limbs turned watery and my stomach lurched. I started to fall face-first into the puddle of dried blood, but Sean caught me around the shoulders.

"You alright?" he asked, and helped me to my feet.

"I'll live," I wheezed. "Think we're too late, though."

"There's a car out back." His eyes darted over the scene, taking in everything in an instant. Luke came down the stairs and joined us, and Sean passed me over to him. "Watch her."

"Nothing upstairs. Bed's still made," Luke said.

I pulled away and stood on my own two feet, but Luke still kept a hand on my back.

Sean picked his way across the kitchen, carefully avoiding the blood and anything else that looked like it might be evidence. He stopped in front of the sink and examined a collection of potted plants in the windowsill. One was knocked over, another's pot was cracked. All were dead, brown leaves lying atop the spilled dirt like gravestones.

He swiped his fingers along the sill. They came back powdery, and he sniffed the substance once before jerking his head back in disgust. "Think it's pretty safe to say Wilkes is our newest vic."

Dammit.

ELEVEN

It was a sign of just how far my ass had been kicked that I let Sean carry me into my cabin. He was surprisingly gentle as he settled me onto my bed. I remembered that he'd had a little sister and tried to give his hand a squeeze. I missed and only caught the blanket instead.

I'd apparently reached the point where physical damage overruled all my mental shit, and I slept solidly for a good four hours. No dreams, nothing. Freaking fantastic. It was still dark outside when I woke up, stumbling into the kitchen in search of some Advil to evict the large marching band that had taken up residence inside my head. I rummaged in a cabinet, pulling down a bottle of pills, and then froze. I turned my head to look across the pass-through into my living room. Sean was sitting on my couch, drinking a beer and leafing through one of my books.

"Um... what the hell are you doing here?"

"Keeping watch. Luke's in your guest room, hope you don't mind." He didn't look up. "You read a lot?"

"Yeah, actually, I do mind. And don't change the subject." I knocked back four pills with a glass of water and leaned forward with my elbows on the pass-through.

"You were in rough shape. Didn't seem right to leave you. How you feeling?"

"Better. You didn't think I could take care of myself?"

"Honey, you couldn't walk, let alone defend yourself. Can't you just accept someone doing something nice for you?"

I made a noise that said, no, I really can't, but I smiled anyway as I dropped down onto the couch beside him. "You go through my stuff or what?"

"Sorry, got bored. You have a lot of books. Never would have pegged you as a nerdy chick." The corner of his mouth tugged into a grin. "Nice comic book collection."

"Hey, do I go through your shit and pass judgment on your hobbies?"

"It's actually kind of cute. I mean, the sword-and-sorcery stuff. I can just see you, all princess in a tower, waiting for your knight in shining armor."

I laughed. "Yeah, have you met me? I'm clearly not the princess type." I toyed with my glass while he took a pull from his beer, the silence stretching. I thought about what Luke said about the Network, about the careful way Sean had laid me in my bed. "You think Wilkes is alive?"

He shrugged. "Could be. Blood looked bad, but there wasn't enough to think he died there."

I lifted my eyebrows. "You know forensics."

He smirked. "A bit."

I remembered the powder on Wilkes's windowsill. People were in danger. I needed to get over myself. "There was, um, some powder left at the other crime scenes too. Lab said it's some kind of compound of sulfur, silica, carbon and--"

"Chlorine trifluoride."

"Yeah. How'd you know?" I asked, surprised.

Sean licked his lips, rolling his beer bottle between his palms. "Seen it before. It's otherwise known as brimstone. Demons leave it behind."

"Brimstone? As in, hellfire and?" He nodded and I rubbed at my eyes. "Freaking great."

"Plants dead, too?"

"Yeah."

"Definitely demon then. Those are their calling cards."

"That's how you knew Wilkes was a vic. So chances are it's probably that demon you were tracking, right?" I asked.

"More than likely. We caught wind of it in Fort Collins and followed it down here. I don't know what it's doing though. Demons don't usually snatch people."

"Wait a second—Fort Collins? When?" I sat up a little straighter, my chest tightening.

"About a week or so before we met. Why?" Sean studied me, picking up on my unease.

I thought about what he'd said—demons don't usually snatch people. They tempt, they corrupt. They turn regular people into agents of violence.

"My case," I muttered, seeing Andy Walker's pockmarked face. I cleared my throat and tried again where Sean could hear me. "I worked a case up there. Kid made a deal, had to take him down."

"You think it's related to this mess?"

"I think it's too big of a coincidence not to be." I rubbed at my wrist, trying to puzzle it out. Hughes had said someone was working on a spell to build an army. A demon was involved. Two people were dead. My brain felt like it was stuck in a vat of Jell-O, and I was kicking myself for not stopping it.

"You okay?" Sean asked. I realized he was staring at me, and my face warmed.

"Yeah, just..." Just what? That I blamed myself for not somehow magically figuring out this thing back in Fort Collins? That even the thought of demons made my chest seize up, and now one had my brother? That I felt responsible for the death of two innocent people, and I was going out of my mind trying to stop the murderer? That I was paralyzed by the fear of losing my brother?

"Tired," I said.

Sean eyed me, sharp and keen. "Bullshit."

I huffed. "Maybe, but what is this--a therapy session?"

"I'm asking you how you're doing," he said, and there was a hint of kindness to his voice. He laid his arm across the back of the couch and shifted around so that he faced me. "Luke said he told you about Julia. So consider for a moment that I know how you're feeling."

I pulled my knees to my chest and my mouth was suddenly very dry. My eyes stung. "Doesn't matter how I feel."

A warm, comforting weight covered my shoulder and I glanced down, surprised to see Sean's hand there. "It does, Rache. Keep shoving it down and at some point you're going to explode."

God help me, but I leaned closer to him. I laid my hand on top of his as if I was desperate for some kind of human contact. For comfort. "Maybe, but what makes you think I'm just going to open up to you? Not like we're friends."

"Try me."

That frigging stare was going to be the death of me. He was such a stubborn ass. I chewed on my lip as his thumb rubbed soothing circles on my back. "I hate it," I whispered. "He's out there, Sean. Maybe hurt, and I just--I can't--"

"You feel powerless." His tone was flat, but his eyes burned like a summer sunset, all green grass and heat. "Angry. Violent and desperate."

I looked him over like I was seeing him for the first time. I tried to imagine him at sixteen, not quite a man, marching along with a search party. It made it hard to remember that he was a hunter, and that I needed to be careful around him. "Something like that."

A small, sad smile pushed at one corner of his mouth, and suddenly his arm wrapped around my shoulders. I curled against his side, drawn in by his warmth, his strength. "I know we got off on the wrong foot, but what you're going through, it's hell. You need to take a minute and cry, I won't tell no one."

I smirked and lightly smacked his chest. "Who said I'm going to cry?"

His arm tightened around me and somehow I ended up with my arms around his neck, my face buried against his shoulder. There was that smell again, gun oil and soap. Sean didn't say anything, just continued rubbing my back. It was like he didn't care what I said--like he could see right through the front I put up and was going to give me what I needed whether I wanted it or not.

Somehow, my face ended up wet.

"We'll find him, Rache," he murmured, voice low and rough and his breath hot against my ear. "I'm not going to let you go through that, sweetheart."

"Stop calling me that." I lacked conviction and he apparently knew it, because he chuckled.

I didn't want to move, but I had to. I couldn't do this right now--any of it. For a million reasons, only about half of which were Danny. I exhaled a ragged sigh and pulled back, wiping at my cheeks. I didn't move far though, and his arm remained draped around my shoulders.

"Sooo... are we just not going to talk about what Hughes said?" he asked after a while, staring at my coffee table like it was something far more interesting than a battered old piece of second-hand furniture. "About the secrets."

"I'm okay letting that sleeping dog lie if you are," I said. I knew he'd have questions. I just wasn't up to facing the answers.

He smiled, leaning back against the couch. "'Suppose I could live with that. For tonight at least."

"What happened to the take-no-bullshit guy that wouldn't give me an inch?"

"That was before you got hurt. What can I say, I'm a sucker for a damsel in distress." He winked and I laughed. "Hey, one thing though... what'd you do to Hughes? I mean, I had a forty-five to his head and dude didn't even blink. How'd you get him to squeal?"

For about two seconds, I considered telling him the truth. It would make everything so much easier, and I could put down this weight I'd been carrying ever since I ran into him at Marcus's office. Of course, he'd probably turn that forty-five on me, but at least I wouldn't have to keep lying to him.

"Pressure point," I said. "Under the arm. Hurts like hell."

I slept for another six hours, and woke up ready to find Shadowfang and his master and punch them both in the nose. I bounded into the kitchen, the smell of bacon and eggs hitting me hard. I was freaking starving.

"Hey, she lives," Luke said, looking up from his laptop. He'd taken up residence at my kitchen table, while Sean folded up blankets and stacked them neatly on my couch. At least they were good houseguests.

"Sleep forgives a multitude of sins." I grinned and sauntered over to the stove. "You guys cooked?"

"I did. Couldn't find your coffee though, so I made a Starbucks run. Just why in the hell do you live so far from civilization?" Sean came up behind me, his hand resting lightly on my back as he passed me a plate. I didn't have the heart to tell him I didn't drink coffee, so I just smiled as I loaded up food.

I checked my messages as I ate and found four texts and three voice mails from Ethan. Checking in, checking in, update that he'd found nothing yet, urgently checking in, panic, panic, panic. Jesus Christ, Ethan. Chill.

"Why don't you guys see if you can figure out who might be next on the hit list?" I said, rifling through my stacks of evidence for the printout from Leon's house and passing it to Luke. My gut twinged, evil whispers in my brain, but the fact was I couldn't tackle all the angles by myself, and I didn't want more people to suffer. "Ethan's working on property holdings for Hughes. We can catch up later."

"Where're you going?" Sean asked as I shrugged on my jacket, but it wasn't General Patton barking orders this time. He sounded merely curious.

"To see if I can't figure out this spell thing Hughes mentioned. Call you later?"

"Guess we're actually working together now, huh?"

"Yeah, yeah. Don't let it go to your head." I grinned and pushed my sunglasses on, locking the door behind us.

Sean smirked, giving me a teasing brush of his fingers. "Whatever you say, sweetheart."

I FOUND Dr. Gilman exactly where he'd been before--shut away in his office, avoiding sunlight, his nose buried in some book that was written when God was a boy. I couldn't be sure, but I thought he was wearing the same clothes. At least, they had the same chalk stains.

"Rachel, I'm so glad you're here!" He waved me in, blinking rapidly behind his smudged glasses. "I have just discovered something most interesting. Crocodile dung."

"I'm sorry?"

"Crocodile dung. It was the first known contraceptive, used by ancient Egyptians. I postulate this is related to Sobek's alignment with creation and fertility." His head wobbled, as if he could barely contain his excitement.

"Um... fascinating. Dr. Gilman, I need your help," I said. "Um, again."

"Is it the *guntanagh?* Did you find him? Ouh, perhaps I could explore how he has adjusted his feeding habits--"

"Hey, I really need you to focus, alright? Remember how we talked about butterflies last time?" He stopped short, almost as if I'd struck him, and I actually felt kind of bad. It wasn't his fault he was so goddamn loony. "Do you know about some kind of spell that would... use them or something?"

"A sea cucumber is in fact an echinoderm, not a vegetable."

And there went any lingering guilt. "Listen, prof, I don't have time for our usual merry-go-round-on-acid convo, okay? Just what do you know about spells that would use a blood sacrifice from a shifter, were, witch, and fae?"

Gilman shot up from his seat and scurried out of the room. I exhaled all my frustration and tried to breathe in some patience. It didn't work.

He came back a moment later carrying a thick three-ring binder. Papers of varying shades of yellow threatened to spill all over the floor and the guy almost shoved me out of the way to lay it on his desk. "Some things look like other things, or are called other things, but they are something different entirely. It's a problem of language, too constrictive, yes, yes. Need to name things, English especially." He tutted. "So unfortunate."

I watched him flick through pages covered in chicken scratch running in all directions, drawings, and diagrams. It looked like a serial killer's sketchbook—or a witch's grimoire. Sometimes it was a fine line. He stopped at a rumpled piece of notebook paper, running his fingers over it like it was a precious gem. I leaned forward and saw a passable sketch of Shadowfang.

"*Bakemono*. Japanese. It means 'thing that transforms'. Much more accurate terminology." Gilman rubbed his hands together in glee. For him, this was all academic. A fucking research experiment. I didn't think he could actually connect to the fact that one of these creatures had tried to rip my face off, and that two people had died to create it.

"How many of these could someone make?" I asked, skimming over the paper. My guts turned to ice. This whole thing was such a level of fucked up, it wasn't even funny.

"No conservation of mass. Metaphysics dictated only by energy consumption."

"So... as many as he can juice up. Fantastic." I popped open the rings on the binder and pulled out the paper. Gilman's face dropped like I was taking away a favorite toy, but I just couldn't find a fuck to give. If this spell was for real, we were about to have a serious frigging problem on our hands.

I stalked out of Gilman's office, intending to go home and get to work on something that could hurt these bastards. My phone rang as I was climbing into my car.

"Way to answer your phone," Ethan snapped. "I've been worried sick about you."

"I'm fine. Find something for Danny?"

"Working on it. Hughes's got so many shell companies and subsidiaries, it's taking some time."

My foot pressed harder on the gas pedal. "I've got a line on our mystery monster. But we're going to need some help." I ground my teeth. "Tell the Council to start looking into *bakemono*, and to check out the other people on the list we got from Leon's. Especially Wilkes—Hughes said he was clued in, so I've got to wonder if he's a supe too. We'll handle Danny."

He was silent for a moment. "I know you don't want to let this go, but it doesn't feel right betraying our own people."

"Betraying? If you feel like that, why are you even helping me? Just go tell the Council and let me take the consequences."

"Because," he said, sighing, "I know what it's like to be

alone. I want to show you it's okay to trust again. You just have to trust the right people."

I didn't know what to say to that. "Let me know if you find a place that could be holding the vics."

I made record time back to my cabin and immediately began to deconstruct the spell. I'm not the smartest witch out there, or the best trained, but spells and sigils were pretty much my bitch. I'd learned them at my uncle's knee, and he was a freaking genius at it.

It wasn't a true *bakemono*. Those were creatures of Japanese folklore. This was a goddamn illegal magic spell anchored to the spirit. God knows where Gilman had turned this up. I felt like I needed a shower just reading the thing.

The spell required blood sacrifice to power it. Perp already had his living Energizers, so we couldn't disrupt it that way. It also needed a binding agent and a ritual, which required us to know where his spell was set up. Strike two.

I poured myself a glass of whiskey, rethought my poor life choices, and traded it for a glass of water, sipping it as I twirled a pen around in my fingers. All spells had the same basic theory. Sympathetic ingredients--herbs, minerals, whatever, stuff that had certain metaphysical properties-- combined with a focusing object and a catalyst. Put the lime in the coconut and mix it all up with intent, and boom, magic. In this case, the sympathetic ingredients were blood from the donor species, pushed through the spell to create Shadowfang.

Maybe the whole was no greater than the sum of its parts.

I scribbled out some thoughts on my notebook, the back of my mind always on Danny. I figured we had a day, maybe two before he ended up as the next body with a message carved on his chest. I'd passed the point of panic and was careening dangerously toward desperate anger. We were close, so close. All we needed was a weapon, and then we could save my brother.

I clung to that the way a drowning man clings to air.

Darkness climbed through my windows, finding me surrounded by notes and books and my laptop. My eyes itched and while I was in better shape than yesterday, I knew I was running out of steam. Sleep first. Loins could be girded in the morning. I shoved my laptop onto the coffee table and flicked on the television, trying to lull my brain into a false sense of security. I sipped my whiskey while I restlessly channel surfed. None of the programs held my attention. My eyelids drooped.

Someone pounded at my door and I came up off the couch like I'd been goosed by a cattle prod. I snatched my Sig off the table, too worn out to handle magic at the moment, and crept toward the door.

"Hey, something wrong?" I asked, finding Sean and Luke on my front step. Luke reminded me of when you're about to watch someone get punched. Sean looked like the one doing the punching.

"We need to talk," Sean said gruffly, shoving past me. I stumbled backwards, gaping at him. Gone was the playful, friendly nature from this morning. Patton was back, and he was looking to tear someone a new one.

"Um, okay. Come right in." I shut the door behind them and crossed my arms, shoulders bunching.

Sean faced me, hands on his hips and his eyes boring into mine. "Rachel," he said, with that throat-shredding growl. "We know."

TWELVE

I was so fucked.

"Know what?" I swallowed and tried to ignore my heart beating a tattoo against my ribs. Shit. I should have told him. I should have told him last night when we were on the couch. Now he'd found out what I was some other way and I looked like a shady bitch. I *was* a shady bitch.

"Did you think you could keep it from us?" Sean barked.

"Sean, listen, I can explain--"

"Well, you better fucking start. When did you first know?"

Okay, weird question. "What? Why does that matter?"

"Because I want to know how much time we've wasted chasing our tails."

Maybe it was the head trauma, but I was rapidly losing my grip on the conversation. "Woah, slow your roll. What exactly are you so pissed about?"

"Cute, Rachel. You want to play coy, fine. The vics. They ain't exactly what they appear, are they?" His eyes turned hard and he took a step toward me.

I blinked. The vics?

"What? What about them?" I asked. I felt like I'd

stripped the gears in my brain--nothing was making sense. I didn't look away though. Staring might be a challenge to Elena, but I got the feeling that if I dropped my eyes for an instant, Sean would take it as a sign of guilt.

"The guy, Jeff. We knew he was a goddamn werewolf. The girl, some kind of shifter, right? And the lawyer had an unnaturally long life span," Sean snarled.

It finally clicked into place what he was on about and I almost laughed. Jesus Christ. "What's your point?"

"So they're fucking monsters, Rachel!"

Heat erupted in my chest. "Like Leon?" Sean's mouth twitched and he had the good sense to look a little ashamed. "The guy who killed them, he's a monster. Get some fucking perspective."

"You should have told us from the beginning. This changes things."

"How?"

"Because now we're hunting something that hunts monsters."

"And maybe you should just let it finish the job, is that it?" My nostrils flared and I hated to admit it, but hurt crept into my voice. I thought maybe Sean and I had reached an understanding.

"No, dammit, listen--"

"No, you listen." I'd had it with his fucking bigotry. It was possible it hit a little close to home, but I didn't care. He wanted on this case, he was going to open his goddamn eyes. "This guy, this monster, has managed to tag a whole group of powerful supes. He's murdered two. And he has my brother. Did you forget that, or do you just not care?"

"Rachel, that's different. Your brother is--"

"Human? So that means more. Of course." If I'd ever developed pyrokinesis, he would have been on fire. "Jeff and Sadie had families, Sean. Parents. Siblings. They were *innocent*."

He stared at me for a long moment and then turned away, scowling.

"Look, Rachel, we just feel like we've been working without all the info. It could have changed how we approached the case if we'd known," Luke said, using a voice much like one adopts when speaking to violent children and enraged dogs.

I studied him. "So you still want to find this thing?"

"Yes, of course. Please, just talk to us."

My mistrust of them warred with my desperation to find my brother and the hope that maybe the Callahans could help me. "How did you find out?"

"Thomas Springer," Luke said. He smiled at my surprise. "You weren't the only one that noticed those news clippings."

"So what about him?"

"He's a psychic," Sean said. Some of the tension in his face was gone, although his voice still snapped like a bowstring. "That made us take a look at the other vics. We were doing what you asked, trying to figure out who might be next."

"We still want to find your brother and stop this guy from hurting more people," Luke said.

"But you have got to stop with the secrets, okay? We can't do this with one arm tied behind our backs."

Oh, Sean. How I wished I could. But Luke was right. I needed to put everything on the table--or at least as much as I could afford to. "I'm pretty sure Marcus is a *gancanagh*, some kind of fae love-talker. Seduces women, drains them. Except there's no evidence Marcus ever killed anyone."

"Just like the other vics," Luke said, with a hint of vindication.

"I'm still not convinced. When have we ever met a friendly monster?" Sean demanded.

"First time for everything. These people, they never hurt anyone," I said, working to keep my tone even. I tried to remember where Sean was coming from. His perspective was different than mine.

"How do you know that?" Sean asked. "Ever think they just covered their tracks really well?"

"If they'd killed, there'd be a trail and you know it."

"These things live on humans. They can't just not eat."

"They find ways around it," I said, sinking down on the couch. "Marcus worked a second job as a stripper. Sort of spread out the damage of his hunger. He left his ex-wives rather than let them die. Jeff, Thomas, and Sadie had no need to harm humans."

"Sharpe and Warren are shifters. They treat people like Scooby snacks and wear the skin of the dead. That sounds pretty harmful to me," Sean said.

"Loups eat people, and only skinwalkers that want to impersonate humans wear their skins. Supes come in different flavors."

Sean chewed that over and finally bowed his head. "I didn't know that."

"Hey, at least you can be taught," I said, the corner of my mouth twitching.

"I still don't think—" Sean cut off as his face twisted and he pressed a hand to his chest.

"You alright?" Luke asked. Sean looked for a moment like maybe he was suffering from bad heartburn, but then he let out a strangled groan and doubled over. His knees buckled and he gagged. Blood poured from his mouth.

"Sean!" Luke caught his brother as he crumpled to the ground. I leapt up to help, but a wall of noxious magic hit me. My stomach roiled and I staggered, bracing myself against the wall.

"What's happening to him?" Luke's panicked voice filled my ear.

"I don't know," I ground out, my head swimming from the magic attacking the hunter. Shit. Luke frantically scrabbled at his brother's chest, jerky, useless gestures, as if all he needed was his airway cleared. I stared at Sean, rooted to the spot. It was a spell. I could probably break it. But fear short-circuited my brain. I didn't know if I could face this again.

"Help him!" Luke yelled, snapping me out of it. Sean writhed on the floor in front of my coffee table, his body curled up in agony. Blood dripped from his mouth and nose. A powerful energy surrounded him, tearing at my psyche.

Who was I kidding? There was no choice here. I ran to the kitchen, grabbing a knife. I sliced my palm and slammed my hand against a sigil carved into the wood beside my door. Magic bloomed around me as my strongest wards went up. I watched Sean for some sign of relief, but the spell still had a hold of him. Double shit. I dropped to my knees beside him.

"You have to trust me," I said.

Spasms wracked his body, but he nodded. I took a deep breath and laid my hand on his chest. The awful magic slammed into my senses, making me gag as an invisible thickness climbed into my nose and throat. I closed my eyes and reached for the line.

Alright, you son of a bitch. You want to play games? See how you like this.

Pine and earth rolled over my tongue as I pulled as hard as I dared, energy washing through me and into Sean. The spell recoiled for a moment, then surged back at us in a raging storm. An unnatural wind stirred my hair, static electricity crawling across my skin as I pulled harder on the line.

"Release," I commanded. The ley energy flowed around Sean, creating a bubble of protection against the evil power. He gasped, sagging against the floor. The spell was still active, but I'd pushed it out of him. I smothered it with my will, backed by the ley energy.

It hurt so bad I was almost numb from the pain. Every nerve was on fire and my consciousness greyed at the edges.

Just a few more minutes. Keep it together, Rachel.

I crushed the vicious spell with the electric energy of the ley line, grinding it into nearly nothing. Finally, it broke. It evaporated with a hot pulse of air, and I dropped the line. Panting, I looked down at Sean. His breathing matched mine, but his face was no longer contorted in pain. I took my hand off his chest and rocked back onto my butt, leaning against the coffee table. Standing was definitely out of the question right now.

"Are you alright?" Luke asked, reaching down to help his brother up off the floor. I blinked, and the next moment I was looking down the barrel of Sean's Colt. He leaned over me, one hand jamming me back against the table.

"What the hell was that?" he shouted.

"Jesus, Sean, take it easy!" Luke tried to pull him away, but he shoved his brother off and kept his gun trained on me. I closed my eyes, too tired to fight with him. I'd been here before. I knew how this dance went.

"I have been jerked around since the get-go and I'm fucking sick of the secrets and lies, Rachel. You better start talking." Sean didn't relax an inch.

"You know what it was. A spell." I scrubbed a hand over my face, trying to stop the world from doing its best impression of an overzealous Tilt-A-Whirl. "I'm not your enemy, Sean. Get that freaking gun out of my face and I'll answer your questions."

"Oh, now you want to play nice? I don't think so. Why should I believe a single word you say?"

"Look, I know I haven't been honest--"

"Yeah, no shit."

"--with you, but this, right here? This is exactly why. I know what hunters think about people like me."

"People like you? What's that mean?" Luke stood behind his brother, the compassion evaporating from his eyes. They turned a glacial green just like Sean's, and he crossed his arms.

I'd escaped from a hunter once. Didn't look like I'd be lucky a second time.

"She's a goddamn witch," Sean spat. "I felt it, she did... something."

"What I did was save your ass," I croaked, barely holding on to consciousness. "So if we're going to have a problem here, I think that buys me at least ten minutes to rest."

"You made a deal with a demon," he accused. "You're playing us."

"No, I didn't. And I'm not playing you."

"Bullshit. I know how this works, sugar."

"Witches without natural power deal with demons. I'm a born witch, Sean." I hated how I sounded. I hated that I wanted him to believe me.

He stared at me and his gun lowered a fraction of an inch. "What's that mean?"

"What does it sound like?" I shot back. He lifted the Colt again and I checked my annoyance. "Magic's in my blood. I don't deal with demons and I'm not evil."

"Are you human?"

"What?" I was having trouble focusing.

"Are you human?" he shouted again.

"Yes, dammit!"

Sean removed a silver knife from his pocket. I tensed. "Arm."

"What?"

"Give me your goddamned arm!"

I stared at him. "Seriously?"

He just motioned toward me with the knife. I let out a frustrated groan and thrust out my arm. He swiped the blade across my skin and I winced, but other than the bite of steel and a thin line of red, nothing happened. Luke disappeared into the kitchen and returned with a bunch of paper towels, which I pressed against the cut, glaring at Sean. He produced a metal flask and shoved it at me. I was fairly certain it contained holy water.

"Drink."

"I'm not a fucking demon, Sean!"

"Then drink!"

I snatched the flask from his hand and took a long pull. Tepid water ran down my throat and I threw the flask back at him. "Happy now? Want to try trapping me in a salt circle next?"

"How do we know you aren't working with a demon?"

"Because I just nearly killed myself saving your stubborn ass!" I yelled, and immediately regretted it. The throbbing in my head intensified as my vision swam. Muscles twitched along Sean's jaw as he considered me. I reached out for the line, just in case. It ripped into me, a blowtorch on my soul, and I dropped it. I was fucked if he didn't listen.

"Yeah... maybe." He straightened up and lowered his weapon but didn't holster it. "That spell that hit me, where'd it come from?"

I shook my head. "I didn't have time to trace it. But it beat my wards, which means it had some sort of link to you."

"Why me? You're the witch."

I let out a tired little laugh. "You're chasing a demon. You're sniffing a case that's wreaking havoc on the supernatural community. Why *not* you?" His question stirred something in my thoughts, and the exhausted smile faded from my face. "You're chasing a demon. Why don't you have protections?"

"We do," Luke said, and Sean shot him a sharp look. "But they're pretty specific to demons. We don't deal much with witches."

"So it didn't come from a demon," I said, thinking about the brimstone and dead plants. "That doesn't mean one's not powering a witch. There's some serious magic wrapped up in all this and a corrupt witch could quite possibly get through your defenses."

"So find out who sent it," Sean said gruffly.

"I can't. I fully evaporated the spell to keep it from killing you."

"So what do we do? I'm not going to be some fucking sitting duck," he said.

"If the witch has a link to you, there's not much we can do. Just find them first." He didn't like that answer. I started to tell him that we could set a magical trap-and-trace in case it happened again, but before I could speak he put his gun away and jerked his head toward his brother.

"You saved my life? Consider us even. We're done." It wasn't his anger that surprised me. It was the look he gave me as he walked out the door, the tiny flash in his eyes as he glanced over his shoulder. It wasn't rage, or fear, or disgust.

It was hurt.

"Wait!" I crashed into the doorframe as I chased after them. I half ran, half fell down the steps, clinging to the railing as my last hope to stay on my feet. "Please, I need your help!"

Sean slammed his door closed and stalked toward me. "No. You had your chance to ask for help and all you did was lie. It's not enough that the vics are a freaking who's-who list of the supernatural, but now you're a witch? Just no."

"Look, I'm sorry, okay? But would you have trusted me if I—"

"Trust? Honey, you don't know the meaning of the word."

"You're one to talk. How did Hughes know who you were? Why are you really here, Sean?"

"I'm doing my damn job!" He stopped about two inches from my face, forcing me to tip my head back to look at him.

"Right. Helping people. So help me. My brother is still out there." My cheeks flushed at the vulnerability in my voice. "I don't know how to fight demons. You do. I know spell work. You don't. So please, help me. I'm begging you."

He glared at me, jutting out his jaw. "Why do you think I care?"

"Because. You lost a sister." My eyes burned in a way that made my cheeks burn.

Sean swore and turned away. He paced beside his truck, gravel skittering under his feet. "That's fucking manipulative and you know it."

"It's the truth."

"You get that hiding it makes you look guilty, right?" Luke asked.

"What was I supposed to do?" I sagged against the railing. "I'm sorry. Everyone has secrets. Doesn't make them evil."

"You could have told the truth." Sean halted, his hands on his hips. I thought about what Hughes had called him-- sergeant. I didn't know the military, but I was a cop. I figured trust played a similar role with soldiers. I'd told Sean I'd watch his six and then lied to his face. I knew I'd fucked up in a big way, but I had good reason to play things close to the vest.

"Was I wrong? I heard what you said about witches, Sean. I made that mistake once. Sue me for being careful."

"What happened?" Luke's expression softened.

I gave him a humorless smile. "Trusted the wrong person. But none of that matters. What matters is that a murderer has my brother. He's planning something big and I can't do this alone."

A loaded silence surrounded us. Even the damn woods had gone quiet, as if the squirrels and the birds and freaking Bambi were all deeply interested in our little soap opera. Luke kept his eyes on me but turned his head toward Sean. "Did your--"

"Shut up, Luke," Sean snapped. He looked down, spinning the ring he wore on his right hand around and around. He stared at that ring like he thought it was a Magic 8 Ball, as if it could tell him whether or not he should trust me.

"Sean..." Luke said. The brothers exchanged a conversation consisting entirely of head tilts and eyebrow twitches. Sean looked at me, still fiddling with his ring. Finally, he heaved a sigh and ran a hand back over his hair.

"Dammit. Fine. We'll help you with your brother, but then we're done. And you come clean about everything, you understand?" Sean marched toward me, wagging his finger. "I get one whiff, and I mean if I even think you're lying to me again, we're gone, got it?"

"Fair enough," I said, unable to keep the relief out of my voice. That was a big promise, and one I'd probably have to break—being a witch was really the least of the skeletons in my closet. But if it got him to come back inside and help me save Danny, I'd agree to pretty much anything. I could always deal with the fallout later.

I trudged back inside, collapsing down onto my couch. Sean took up position on the recliner, his hands resting on the arms and looking like the goddamn Godfather. Luke sprawled beside me. I might as well have been facing a firing squad.

"Anybody else feel like this conversation requires alcohol?" I asked, trying to inject some humor. Sean grunted and hauled himself out of the chair, walking into my kitchen. "Left corner cabinet. There's, um, some protein bars on the counter. Bring me one, would you?" The adrenaline fled my system, leaving behind a bone-deep exhaustion and shaking limbs. Sean returned a moment later, handing me a glass of booze and a Luna Bar. He watched me carefully, an inscrutable look on his face. I couldn't tell if he was worried I'd pass out or suddenly set him on fire.

"So what're we looking at?" he asked. He sounded marginally less likely to shoot me.

"What do you guys know about *bakemono*?"

"Japanese spirits, folklore. That's about it," Luke said, shrugging.

"Normally, yeah. But they can also be used as a base for building your own custom monster. There's a spell, it takes a *bakemono* and sort of grafts in pieces of other supernatural creatures. Taking on their strengths." I took another drink of my whiskey, wanting it to calm the queasiness in my stomach.

"So, what, they combine into Voltron from hell?" Sean asked.

"Basically. The spell uses a human psychic as a supernatural joystick to control the *bakemono*." I pulled out the page I'd taken from Gilman, twitched it around so Sean could see it, and opened the protein bar. "It requires a blood sacrifice to catalyze the spell."

"The girl and that dude in the park," Sean said, looking up at me for confirmation.

"Yeah, that's what I'm thinking. It's a bitch of a spell, and takes a lot of energy to maintain. Seems like it only lasts for two, maybe three days before a new sacrifice is required. Does this look like something a demon would do?"

"Not that we've seen," Luke said. "And it definitely wouldn't call attention to itself by leaving bodies in public places. Could a witch pull this off?"

"No way. Not without a boost."

"You sure about that?" Sean eyed me like he was hoping to catch me in a lie.

"Corrupt witches are kind of my area of expertise. The amount of juice this spell needs, a single person couldn't do it. Storms, a coven, or a demon. And since we've got the brimstone..."

"Survey says demon." He scrubbed a hand over his face. "Awesome."

"So if the spell smashes them all together, it's got a were's strength, a fae's ability to make people their bitch and walk between worlds, and a skinwalker's thousand different disguises?" Luke asked.

"And a witch's magic. My brother."

"Jesus. And you're sure a witch can pull this off?"

"I'm pretty sure one attacked me the other night." I took another drink. "I flooded it with enough ley energy that it should have been dead, and nothing. I think I just pissed it off."

"Wait, you did what now?" Sean squinted as if I'd just started speaking German.

"Ley energy. I'm a ley witch."

"Yeah... I have no idea what that means."

"It's--there're two types of born witches, elemental and ley. Elemental witches get their power from nature. Ley witches--me--use ley lines, which are like... these currents of power running through the earth." I left out the part where ley witches were rare, and generally treated like the magical versions of Bruce Banner. Everyone was just waiting for us to go off the rails.

"Explain this to me like I'm a six-year-old. What do ley lines do?" he asked.

I stifled a sigh. I should be glad he wasn't trying to shoot me. "It's life energy. The magical bits and pieces that make life what it is."

"Wow, thanks, Rainbow Songwater," Sean drawled. "That new age crap means nothing to me."

"Dude, I'm trying, okay?" It was hard to describe when witches themselves didn't have a good handle on it. Learning to control it as a kid had been a very painful game of trial-and-error. I grabbed my notebook and started drawing a very poor sketch while I talked. "You've seen *Star Wars*?"

"Yeah. What's that got to do with anything?" The brothers exchanged a glance, Sean looking suspicious. Man, he wasn't going to trust me an inch now.

"Ley lines are like the Force, and I don't mean that

retconned midi-chlorian crap." I showed him my drawing, which was a rough outline of the US with lines drawn across it.

"That looks like a highway map," Luke said, and I nodded.

"Very close. For reasons no one really knows, ley lines roughly run along the same routes as the Interstates--or rather, the Interstates follow the ley lines, since they came first. So it's like if the Force was divided up into big rivers, instead of just blanketing everything. Some witches can feel it and manipulate it."

"So what does that make you, a Jedi?" Sean asked, snorting.

"Yeah, kind of, I guess. I had to learn how to control it, and it's stronger than other kinds of magic."

"Are there Sith?"

I grimaced. The Cursed were not something one discussed in polite company. "Power like that, it's not inherently good or evil. It's about intent. What you use it for."

"So what do you use it for?" Luke asked.

"My job. I use it to make spells--tracking spells, one-off spells when I need something, attacks when I'm in a fight. I use it for my shield, to defend myself. I can use the lines to travel. Break hexes, like I did on your brother."

"So if you can just track your brother, why haven't you done that?" Sean asked.

"I did. Something's blocking the spell." Heat spread through my chest again as I remembered that impenetrable wall.

"You can't break it?"

"No. You know how Luke Skywalker couldn't really beat Darth Vadar at first? It's like that. Just because ley lines are powerful magic, doesn't mean I can use all that power." At least not right now. With time and practice, I'd get stronger. I could teach myself to channel more power. Of course, that also upped my risk of going corrupt.

"The other kind of witches--elements, you called them," Luke said.

"Elemental," I corrected.

"They can do the same things?"

"Some of it, yeah. All born witches can make spells on the fly. It's--it's like we're chefs. We know what ingredients to combine, and our blood is what makes it magic. But they can't use the ley lines, can't walk them. Their power comes from nature."

"Hence elementals." Luke nodded. "What kind of spells can you do?"

"Pretty much anything I want. Physical force, blow shit up. Magic is a tool, guys. I shape it. And ley energy is... it's not well understood. So a lot of what I do is making it up as I go."

"Alright, whatever. Magic lesson later--how do we kill this thing?" Sean slipped into the focused, efficient manner I'd seen at Danny's house, and I thought maybe the soldier in him was coming through.

"I'm working on that. I think we can sort of attack its joints, so to speak. Make a weapon out of all the things the donors are vulnerable to." I stuffed the rest of the protein bar in my mouth and flipped through my notebook to show them what I'd been working on earlier.

"Iron, silver, white ash... what the hell is an *ofuda*?" Luke asked.

"Japanese ward. Banishes the *bakemono*. But guys, it's bigger than just one creature. Way I understand that spell, what I fought was like a prototype. Our mystery bad guy finishes the ritual and he can create an army. Plus, then the *bakemono* loses all weaknesses."

"So it becomes an unstoppable death machine. Freaking great." Sean pursed his lips. "What's he need to finish the ritual?"

"He's got it. It's just a timing issue. Spell has to be done on the full moon."

"When's that?" Luke asked.

"Three days," I said, my voice far steadier than I felt.

"What, you got some kind of freaky connection to the lunar cycle?" Sean scoffed. I gave him a withering look.

"Yeah, it's an old witchy secret known as a goddamn calendar app." I waved my phone in his face. Luke looked like he was fighting a smile and losing.

"Smartass. Any idea on who's doing this?" Sean asked.

"Not since we eliminated Hughes," I admitted grudgingly. "But priority number one is Danny. Get him back, maybe we'll get more clues."

"You got a location on your brother?" Luke asked.

"Ethan's close to one."

"And let me guess," Sean said. "Demon, bad guy, and probably a bunch of these Frankenstein things guarding him?"

"I think we should probably plan for that as a worst-case scenario." I knuckled my eyes and slouched lower on the couch.

"You need sleep," Sean said.

"Not going to argue that one." I stood up and walked toward the door.

Sean didn't move. "We'll stay here."

I blinked stupidly at him. "What?"

"That *bakemono* could come back, and clearly this guy can reach out and touch us with his magic. It's safer to stay together."

"Really? I mean..." I shrugged, mildly afraid he'd lost his mind. Not an hour ago he'd held a gun to my head. I had figured he couldn't wait to get away from the creepy, bodily-fluid-spewing witch.

"Don't read too much into this, honey. It's a tactical decision."

Right. Of course. Stupid me for hoping he might be different.

THIRTEEN

I woke up at an ungodly hour the next morning. Despite it being the asscrack of early, I felt pretty damn good and decided to whip up a big breakfast. I loved to cook, and I figured that if we were going to tackle Team Evil and save my brother, we needed to eat our Wheaties.

It was sort of like that moment when you say goodbye to someone, only to follow them because you're going in the same direction and it's just fucking awkward. Luke was polite enough, but Sean only spoke to me in clipped responses using as few words as possible. Although, he apparently wasn't pissed enough at me to refuse pancakes, and I hid a small grin at the way he shoveled them into his mouth. There's a reason food has been a peace offering for millennia. While the guys finished eating, I slipped into my bedroom and called Ethan.

"Hive mind. Was just about to call you," he said. He sounded cheerful, energetic. My heart lurched.

"Tell me it was with good news?"

"Think so. Found a warehouse in Fort Lupton. As long as he hasn't moved Danny, that's our best bet."

"Thank you, Ethan," I gushed. "And, uh, there's no bad news to go along with that, is there?"

"Not that I can tell. Stuff seems quiet."

"Yeah. Maybe too quiet. You pass the word on about *bake-mono* to the Council?"

"Yep. And they want you to report in." Of course they did. Well, they could just sit and spin. I had crap to do. "How's a *bakemono* tie into all this, anyway?"

I filled him in on Gilman's spell. He swore on a level that impressed even me. Good to know he understood the situation. "And hey, listen. The Callahans are here. I kind of came out of the broom closet to them."

He was silent for so long I wondered if the call had dropped. "Rachel, you're not dumb, but sometimes you are so goddamn stupid."

"It's okay, honestly. It's fine. They're going to help with Danny." It was possible I doth protested too much, since Ethan merely groaned.

"So when it blows up in your face, you're not going to freak out and run again?"

"Can you cut the freaking attitude?" My cheeks burned and my free hand clenched and unclenched. "I didn't have much choice, okay? Spell hit Sean and I had to break it."

"Spell? From who?"

"I'm guessing the same Dr. Doom that sent the *bakemono* after me."

"But... how?" Ethan asked, bewildered. "Long-distance spell like that, he needed a focusing object." He was right. Flinging magic at someone in a fight was a lot like horseshoes and hand grenades--close definitely counted. But the hex that hit Sean was targeted. Spells like that were directed either through DNA or a curse object, like a coin or hex bag. Since Sean was clean for anything magical, Dr. Doom had somehow gotten a piece of him—blood, hair, or even saliva. It's one reason I'm so freaking paranoid about leaving my blood anywhere.

"Maybe it was a message to me, like the flowers. We've got to stop this guy," I said, pinching the bridge of my nose.

"One problem at a time." He paused. "You sure you don't want to have Council back up going after your brother? If you told them you had a location, they'd go with you."

"I'd love back up. But I'm two steps shy of the Council throwing me in a cell. You said you'd help, and the Callahans are here. All I'm asking is to save my brother. Then the Council can do whatever the hell it wants and I'll be a good girl."

Ethan's disapproval practically oozed through the phone. I almost checked for goo. "Sometimes I think you do things just because you're told not to."

"My need for an attitude adjustment aside, you know any Shinto priests?" I thought I had everything else for the weapon, but I was a little short on *ofuda*.

"Actually, yes." He gave a long-suffering sigh. "You know I have your best intentions at heart, right? So when I say I think we should leave this to the Council, it's not because I don't care about Danny."

"We're prepping now. Can you meet your priest pal and tell him we need five or six *ofuda*?"

"You're changing the subject."

"Look, Ethan, I know, okay? But right now I've got a million problems and none of them are going to get solved by talking about my precious feelings. Just get the *ofuda* and meet me here." I hung up and ran a hand through my hair. I just wanted to get my brother back and get this over with.

Given that we knew what species Dr. Doom had used like living Legos to build his creatures, putting together a weapon was actually pretty easy. I rummaged through my supplies until I found white ash shavings and an iron spike, which I engraved with the symbols necessary to enchant it against a witch's power. That made me feel really dirty. Sort of like fashioning your own hangman's noose. Sean melted down some silver bullets I had on hand, and we stirred in the white ash before coating the iron spike with the mixture.

"One going to be enough?" Sean asked.

"Probably not, but I only had one iron spike," I said.

"Hold on." He went out the front door to his truck and returned a moment later brandishing a crowbar. "Here. Pure iron."

"Thanks." I gave him a small smile and thought I saw the corner of his mouth twitch. We repeated the procedure with the crowbar, and by the time we were finished, Ethan was parking in front of my house. He walked in without knocking.

"We've got step one done," I said, showing him the spike and crowbar. "Now we just need the *ofuda* from your priest."

"Can I talk to you for a minute?" His voice was unnaturally controlled. "Alone."

My face flushed and I followed him into my workroom. Ethan paced for a few moments, one hand rubbing the back of his neck. "There are a lot of variables here, Rachel. You don't know what kind of protections this guy's going to have around Danny, you don't know if this weapon is going to work, you just don't know a lot. So I'm going to ask one more time. You sure you want to introduce more unknowns into this situation?"

"What are you talking about?" I asked, even though I was pretty sure I knew.

"How'd they react when they found out you were a witch?" My mouth puckered and I suddenly found the wood grain on my floor very interesting. "Yeah. That's what I thought. But you really trust them to help you?"

"They're here, aren't they?"

"But why? You know better than most that hunters can't wait to put witches down. So what's their angle here?"

"Maybe just sympathy. They lost a sister. They know what it's like."

"Maybe. Maybe they're using you, and as soon as it's convenient, they'll kill you, me, Danny, and the vics you're trying so hard to save."

"Using me?" I screwed up my face in confusion. "What the hell for?"

"I don't know. But I don't think they're here out of the goodness of their hearts."

"Jesus, Ethan. And you call me paranoid. If they'd wanted to kill me, they could've easily punched my ticket last night."

He swallowed like he was chewing on something bitter. "So maybe it's something else then. Something more intimate."

I stared at him, my jaw hanging open. "Are you suggesting I slept with one of them?"

Ethan just glared back at me, jutting his chin out in defiance. "Wouldn't be the first time, would it?"

I let out a bark of harsh, disbelieving laughter. "I can't fucking believe you. We've got a psycho leaving bodies all over the city, my brother hanging in the balance, and you're grilling me about my sex life?"

"I'm just trying to protect you, Rachel," he snapped. "Since you so clearly have no interest in protecting yourself."

"Super. You know what I really need? To get Danny back. So either stow your crap and help, or get the hell out of my way."

Ethan's mouth twitched like words were physically trying to crawl out of it. He took several steps toward the door, stopped, turned around, and marched back to me. He jammed his hand in his pocket and pulled out a long strip of white paper, decorated with black squiggles.

"The *ofuda*," he said.

"Thanks." I hesitated for a moment. "Ethan, what's going on, man? You been acting like you want to kill Sean and Luke since we met them."

He pressed his lips into a thin line and I thought he might

walk out on me, but then he said, "You don't know what it's like."

"What?"

"The real world. You grew up in a Council family. You knew about the supernatural since birth. I didn't." His eyes met mine and I tried to figure out what he meant. Ethan was born to vanilla parents in western Colorado. He was fourteen when he came to live with a witch family in Durango. He'd never talked about the circumstances that brought him there, and I never asked.

"I don't follow."

"Rachel, for most people, you show them the supernatural and they try to put you in a mental institution. It doesn't matter if it's real. To them, out there," he gestured to the front of my cabin, "it doesn't compute. They fear it. They hate it. And they will try to destroy it."

"Ethan, that's not true," I said, frowning. "Supes live among humans all the time."

"By hiding what they are. How many regular humans do you spend time with outside of CBI? Ones that know you're a witch?"

I mulled that over. There was Dr. Gilman, but I didn't exactly hang out with him. I thought of my friends, the people I trusted. They were all supes.

"What happened to you?" I asked quietly.

He dropped his eyes to the floor. "There were no witches where I grew up. When my magic came in, no one knew what was happening to me. My parents were evangelicals. They took me to the church. They thought I was possessed, and their methods weren't kind." He turned around and pulled up his shirt. Ragged white scars crisscrossed his back. I sucked in a gasp.

"When that didn't work," he continued, "they committed me. Eighteen hours a day I was so drugged up I could barely get out of bed. Whole thing made me think I was crazy. Tainted."

"So when the Council found you..."

He tucked his shirt back in and gave me a tight smile. "I found a place where I belonged. You belong with us too, you just fight it so hard. Why do you want to be a part of a world that hates you?"

Now it was my turn to look away. "You don't know what it's like being a ley witch. My whole life everyone's just been waiting for me to lose it. Even my family. So when I met Ryan, I just thought..."

"You thought you could be normal."

"Yeah, something like that. I never wanted to join the Council. I just did as a matter of last resort."

"You've got a good heart, Rache," Ethan said, and looked down at me sadly. "But you think we're all on the same side and we're not. I just don't want see you taken advantage of. Promise me you'll be careful."

I stared at the floor and shifted my weight. "I'm not a kid, Ethan. I know, alright?"

He didn't say anything, just squeezed my shoulder and gave me a skeptical look. The moment evidently over, he turned away and left my workroom. I stood there feeling off-kilter and confused, doubt hollowing out my chest. I shook my head. Ethan's baggage was his own. One freaking problem at a time, and right now I needed to focus on saving my brother.

I returned to the living room and started checking my gear. Luke and Sean looked between Ethan and me, but neither said anything.

I strapped on my holster and checked the magazine in my Sig, then slid two additional magazines into my pocket. Wolfsbane, silver, rosemary, and a couple vials of holy water joined a few hex bags on my belt. I stuffed a wicked-looking butterfly knife and a large bag of rock salt into my jacket pockets, then looked around to see if I'd forgotten anything.

"Damn," Sean said.

"What?"

"You armor up well."

"Thanks, I think," I said with a small laugh.

"What's with the gun?" When I looked confused, he added, "I mean, you're a witch. Can't you just zap shit?"

"Dude, it doesn't work like that. Big spells, the kind you use in a fight, they're expensive."

"So's ammo." Sean followed me outside, fiddling with his keys.

"You saw me after I pulled that hex off you. That took a ton of power. The more I use, the greater the risk, and it knocks me on my ass. I eventually run out of juice, and sometimes I can't get a refill."

"Thought you said you use ley lines or whatever?"

"I do. But they're not everywhere, Sean. If I can't connect to a line, I've got to get creative, just like you." I shrugged. "Downside to being a ley witch. I've got more raw power than elementals, but only if the geography's right."

"Hmph." It was like his eyebrows were being thoughtful without his permission, because a second later he remembered he was supposed to hate me, and pulled them back down into a scowl.

"Are we still going with the theory that your brother is at Hughes's property, even though the dude clearly isn't involved with this?" Luke asked, giving his brother a look that plainly said he thought he was trying too hard.

"Someone was using Hughes's name to get into all kinds of stuff. It's the best lead we've got," Ethan said.

I nodded. "At this point, I'm willing to grasp at straws. I don't know how else to find him." More emotion than I would have liked leaked into my voice, and heat flooded my cheeks.

"If he's not there, we just keep looking," Sean said after a moment. I glanced up and gave him a small smile of thanks. I was surprised to see him return the expression.

Ethan passed out the *ofuda*--one for each of us, and he gave me an extra one.

"These are from a real Shinto priest, right?" Sean said, squinting at the paper. His expression harbored deep lines of doubt, like we were about to attack Godzilla with a Pez dispenser.

"Yeah, but we need to be careful. The *ofuda* should work, but Hideo said they're not always effective."

"What do you mean, not always effective?" Luke asked, raising an eyebrow.

"Magic isn't an exact science, guys," I said. "What degree of confidence are we talking about here, Ethan?"

He lifted a shoulder. "About a sixty percent chance it will work, according to Hideo."

"Sixty percent. Awesome," Sean said.

"Better than nothing," I said.

"Alright, we've got six pieces of magic paper, two makeshift weapons made by cobbling together totally unrelated bits of lore, and a strategy that is based on little more than guesses. Yeah, this is going to go great," Sean grumbled as we walked to our cars.

"It's not the absolute worst plan we've ever had," Luke said.

"It's more than we had this morning," I added, flashing him my half-crazy smile. Sean snorted, but his mouth curved into a grin. "The idea is to stick the *ofuda* to the *bakemono's* head and then drive the iron through its heart."

"And this needs to be a team effort." Ethan gave the brothers a level look.

"Yeah," Sean said, his brow knitting as he looked at my partner. "What else would it be?"

FOURTEEN

The sun dipped behind the mountains as we headed north, setting the sky ablaze. I felt the ley line drifting farther away as we drove. Before it totally disappeared, I pulled some of the energy, bundling it in inside me. I couldn't hold much, but it was better than going in there empty handed.

The land flattened out as we left the city behind, farms and cattle emerging on both sides of the highway. By the time we reached Fort Lupton, twilight fully grasped the sky. I drove slowly through the small town, following the directions on my phone to the warehouse. Fields surrounded us, punctuated with the occasional house.

The warehouse was on the outskirts of town, squatting there like a broken down Chevy. Decrepit loading bays sat vacant, and broken windows gaped from the battered walls. I scanned the area as I slowly pulled into a rundown parking lot, weeds bursting through the asphalt, parking next to Ethan's truck. Luke and Sean parked beside me as I got out. Windows empty. Nothing in the fields around us. No imminent signs of danger.

Way too fricking easy.

Ethan got out of his truck and ambled over to stand between the Callahans and me. He didn't look at me, but rather watched the brothers. I pulled my gun out of its holster and crept to a side door near the loading bays. Locked.

"Can't you just *alohomora* it?" Sean asked.

"Why yes, Harry, I could, but that might give us away," I said dryly, but it was the truth. If Dr. Doom was expecting company, he could have laid traps that would be triggered by magic.

"I got it," Luke said, elbowing his brother out of the way. He pulled a lock pick set from his pocket and knelt down, working the lock with practiced motions. I backed up next to Ethan. He met my eyes once, then looked away.

Luke got the tumblers to click into place and slipped inside. I followed suit, Sean behind me, and Ethan on our six. No light penetrated the darkness of the warehouse. We switched on small penlights. Better that than stumbling around blind.

We stole along corridors lined with decrepit metal shelving. Animal nests and trash littered the floor. A break in the shelves opened up onto a cavernous room with a round space about fifteen feet across cleared out in the middle, lit by a solitary utility light. Chained to a support beam in the center of the lighted circle, bloody and beat up, was my brother.

"Danny," I breathed, and made to run to him. Sean grabbed my arm.

"Wait," he whispered, his eyes scanning the shadows. All four of us clicked our flashlights off. The hairs stood up on the back of my neck, but nothing happened.

"It's waiting for us," I murmured. I holstered my gun. "I'm going to go for Danny. Cover me."

"No," Ethan hissed. "Let one of us go."

"He's my brother, Ethan. I'm going."

"Go. We've got your back," Sean said, nodding at me.

I took a deep breath. I didn't even bother spending the energy on a personal ward, given how useless my magic had been against the *bakemono*. I licked my lips, then burst out of the shadows at a full sprint. Danny looked up as I entered the light. Horror crossed his face.

"Rachel, no! It's a trap!" he shouted hoarsely. No sooner had the words left his mouth than a piece of the inky darkness peeled off behind him. Hateful, coal-bright eyes stared at me as a nightmare on paws barreled forward with preternatural speed. I crouched, preparing to dodge. Gunshots echoed behind me.

"That's right, big boy. Over here!" Sean yelled, firing at the *bakemono* again. It hesitated, its claws gouging the concrete floor as it pivoted toward him. I catapulted back into action. Digging out a handful of the powdered wolfsbane on my belt, I tossed the herb into the monster's face. It let out an eerie, high-pitched wail as it flailed to a halt.

I dove forward, snatching the *ofuda* out of my pocket. Shadowfang Mark 2 clawed frantically at its face, the herb sizzling against its skin. It saw me at the last moment and swatted at me. I slipped inside its reach, but I wasn't quick enough. Fire erupted down my back as its talons ripped through my leather jacket and flesh.

I gritted my teeth, swallowing the pain, and slammed the *ofuda* against its face. Shadowfang's head snapped back, a tortured yelp escaping its lips. It collapsed to the ground, limp, and I rammed the iron spike into its chest. I was a little rusty on Make-O-Monster anatomy, so I prayed I got the location of its heart right.

The *bakemono* looked up at me with its burning red eyes, its mouth drooping and its legs slack. It wailed once more, and then, like the remnants of a long-dead fire, it began to flake away. In a few moments nothing remained of it but a trail of ashes.

I rushed to Danny.

"Rachel, get out of here. This was all a set up to get you," he breathed, weakly trying to push me away.

"Shut up, Danny. We're getting you out of here." Someone had worked him over pretty good. Deep cuts lined his arms, but he was still breathing and talking. That was good enough for me. I looked down at the heavy metal cuffs on his wrists and the bottom dropped out of my stomach. Spelled iron. Shit.

"Luke!" I called, looking back over my shoulder. The Callahans and Ethan were scouting the perimeter, looking for more *bakemono*. I gestured wildly and Luke jogged over to me.

"I can't break these. Can you pick the lock?" I asked.

"I'll try." He pulled the kit out again and set to work on the cuffs. I stood up and looked around. Only one monster? No magical traps? Something wasn't right. As if on cue, someone called out my name.

"Rachel, Rachel, Rachel." A man's voice, echoing around the room so that I couldn't tell where it came from. I peered into the darkness, but the utility light blinded me.

"Ooh, threatening voices from the shadows. That's very B-movie villain of you." My voice sounded calm and steady against the emptiness of the warehouse, but my heart was trying to do its best impression of a chestburster. Sean and Ethan edged closer to us, their eyes flitting around the room. I glanced down at Luke. He was still working on the cuffs.

A man stepped out of the shadows directly across from me. He didn't just walk--he fucking *strolled*. Except for the fact that he was acting like frigging Professor Moriarty, he was totally unremarkable. Brown hair, brown beard, brown eyes. I had no idea who he was.

"Rachel! He's a demon!" Sean yelled. He sprinted toward me, and the dude raised his hand in a lazy gesture, as if shooing a fly. I braced for the impact of magic, but he wasn't aiming at me. Ethan and Sean flew backwards, colliding with one of the sets of metal shelves. They hung there as if pinned.

The guy looked back at me and smirked. His eyes flooded red--the entire sclera punctuated only by bright, burning white irises.

Fuck.

"Ah. Choir boys. You guys are like clingy girlfriends. Just can't shake you," the demon said.

"Yeah, we're annoying like that." Luke pulled my brother, free of the cuffs, to his feet. Danny sagged against the support beam and Luke pulled out a wicked looking knife.

A look of interest crossed the demon's face. "Not your normal little pig sticker, is it?" Luke lunged forward and the demon closed his fist. The younger Callahan dropped to the ground, his face contorted in agony. "Rude. I'm trying to have a conversation here." He looked back up at me and smiled.

"Who are you?" I asked.

"Call me Finn." He stepped over Luke and stood a few feet in front of me. My eyes flicked to Danny and Finn chuckled. "By all means, Danny boy here is free to go. It's you I want to chat with."

"Sure. Just let me break out the tea set." I moved in front of Danny and spent an inordinate amount of energy on breathing. I'd never faced a demon head on before. I didn't even know how.

"Out of curiosity, how'd you find us? Got to say, I was really disappointed you couldn't break my concealment ward. Wondered if you'd been oversold."

"Well, you know what they say. If at first you don't succeed." I had no fucking idea how we were getting out of this. I had limited magic. Danny was hurt. Sean, Luke, and Ethan were apparently Finn's meat puppets. If I could get a shot off, that might do something. Maybe. Or he might go all Neo on me.

"Did it hurt, watching two people die and just failing over and over?" Finn pouted, clucking his tongue. "It was pretty amusing though, how you latched on to Hughes so quickly."

"Since when do demons set up high rollers for murder?"

Finn snorted. "Try again."

"Your super special monster league here? What, running short on hell hounds?"

He actually laughed at that. "I couldn't care less about his plans for the city or his grudge match."

"Who's he? What plans?"

"Ah-ah-ah. Sorry. Got a non-disclosure agreement. Red tape, you know how it is."

"So what, you're just his bitch?"

"I'm keeping up my end of the bargain. You know how deals work. Or ask your demon-hunting pals here if you need a crash course." Finn's eyes glittered as he took another step toward me. If I could lay a hand on him, I could blast him with the ley energy I had stored up. I didn't know if that would be any more effective than shooting him, but hey, options were always good. Especially when you're way out of your fucking league. My pulse thundered in my ears and little tremors shook my hands. One other rule of the Council's that I'd always followed--don't mess with demons. Until now.

"So what'd you get out of this deal?" I was just rambling off questions, trying to keep him talking until I figured something out.

"Isn't that obvious? You."

That got my attention. "Then why take my brother? Why not just take me?"

"We had to take you for a test drive first. The kid up north. The concealment ward. The hex on Teen Scene over here."

"That was you? Cute. You realized I crushed that spell in about two minutes, right?" I shoved bravado into my voice to compensate for the pain fogging my brain. Blood trickled down my arm, and my shirt stuck to my back.

"That was my human friend. I'm much more... virile." He clenched his fist again, and Sean bellowed.

"Stop punching below your weight, you dick." I drew my gun, but Finn only laughed.

"I don't think you can take me, Rachel. Especially not this far from a line."

"Yeah, well, you don't really expect me not to try, do you?"

"Oh, I'm counting on it."

I fired.

Finn held up a palm and my spelled bullet dropped to the ground. A hungry smile spread across his face, and then he swished two fingers.

Invisible hands grabbed me around the throat and slammed me backward onto the concrete floor. I managed to turn so that my shoulder took the brunt of the fall rather than my head, but that only made my back erupt in a fresh wave of agony. Danny called my name, but the demon must have pinned him in place too, because no one came to my rescue.

"C'mon, Rachel. I know you can do better than that." Finn prowled forward and jerked me to my feet, lifting me with a seriously unfair amount of strength. He opened his mouth again and I slapped my palm against his head, unloading all the ley energy I had inside me. It wasn't slick, but it was powerful, and I was tired of hearing the douchebag talk.

Finn dropped me and stumbled backwards, shaking his head like a wet dog. "Nice. That tickled. Maybe you are worth all this trouble."

"If you're going to kill me, kill me. Let them go," I rasped, struggling up onto a knee.

"Yeah, that's not really the plan. But I'll tell you what. Come with me and I will let your friends scamper away. Your brother too."

I looked at Luke panting on the floor, my brother on his hands and knees beside him. Ethan and Sean still stuck to the wall like Velcro dolls. Bullets didn't work. Ley energy didn't work--and even if it did, I'd spent my load.

"Make me a deal," I said.

"No!" Danny shouted, something wounded in his voice.

"You make a deal, you have to keep it, right? That's how it works?" I struggled to my feet, my eyes roaming over all of them again. Ethan knew about the *bakemono*. He could warn the Council. This would get them all to safety. Sean was staring at me, his mouth working like a dying fish. "I'll go with you. You leave them alone."

Finn smirked. "Look at you. All martyr-like. Alright, we can do business. But it takes an act of intention."

"What the hell does that mean?"

"A kiss, a handshake, a signature. You've got to do something to show you're willingly signing up for this deal."

"Fine. Whatever. Let them go first." Fear curdled in my stomach, but I just didn't see another way out of this. It was my fault. I shouldn't have been so stubborn. If we'd come with Council backup... it didn't matter. Spilled milk and all that shit. Finn waved his hand again and Ethan and Sean dropped to the ground. I jerked my head toward the exit. Luke helped Danny to his feet and the four of them crowded around me.

Finn stuck out his hand. "Unless you'd rather get intimate," he said, leering. I swallowed, finding my mouth had gone suddenly dry. Witches that made deals with demons ended up only one way. Even if I had the best of intentions, we all knew where I was headed. But Danny would be safe. Jake would have his dad back. Small price to pay.

I took a step forward. My hand was inches from Finn's when someone grabbed me from behind. Danny flung me backward into Sean, power stirring around him.

"Get her out of here!" he yelled, then let loose with a spell. A tornado with laser-focused intensity wrapped around one of the metal shelves, bringing it down with a scream of steel. It toppled right onto Finn.

Sean dragged me toward the door. I fought against him, looking back for my brother. Danny followed close on our heels, and for one heartbeat, I thought we might actually make it.

Greasy, hot magic billowed over me. It felt a little like what we got off corrupt witches, but a thousand times stronger. It choked me, roiling my stomach. Danny faltered, crashing sideways into the wall.

Finn just fucking materialized behind him. His features were twisted into a snarl of rage, and he lifted a hand. Danny whirled, staggering. He was hurt and hurling a lot of power. He wouldn't last much longer.

Sean didn't slow, even though I squirmed violently. I watched my brother like he was in slow motion, raising a hand. He looked straight at me, a sad smile on his face. "Go!" he yelled, and another spell burst from him.

"Danny!" I screamed. The curse plowed into the ceiling above us, shattering support beams and cement. A rumble that I felt in my chest rolled through the air just as Sean hauled me out the door, and a whole section of the second floor caved in behind us.

I was still fighting and screaming my brother's name as Sean shoved me into the passenger side of his truck. "Keys," he said. I didn't respond, staring at the plume of dust emerging from the warehouse. "Rachel! Keys!"

"We have to go back. We can't leave him." I choked on the words.

"He wanted you out. We'll get him, but not right now. I swear we'll get him." I couldn't take my eyes off the building as Sean stuffed his hand in my jacket pocket. Pain and fear burned at the edges of my mind. I felt totally disconnected from my body. We'd been right there. We almost had him.

"Rachel, I need you to focus, okay?" Sean said, and tossed

my keys to Luke, who climbed into my Jeep. Sean jumped into the driver's seat of his truck and tore out of the parking lot. I smelled burnt rubber. Why the hell was I thinking about that? A demon had my brother. Oh God, a demon that I'd pissed off. Danny, no, no, no.

"Rachel!" I mechanically turned my head to Sean. My lungs didn't want to work. He caught my eye, his hands tightening on the steering wheel. "Stay awake, alright? We need to get you patched up, regroup. Where's the safest place you know?"

I chewed over his words, trying to make sense of them. Slowly, thoughts congealed into words. "My-my parents' house. Strong wards." It washed over me then. I'd failed. Danny was likely dead. Jesus Christ, I'd failed.

I buried my face in my hands, hot tears sliding down my cheeks.

FIFTEEN

Night swallowed us, the ruddy glow of light pollution giving way to stars as we headed farther west, the big V8 hurtling us away from Denver. Sean stole glances at me every couple of minutes. I'd stopped crying. Now I just sat there like a goddamn zombie.

"How's your back?" he asked as we passed Idaho Springs.

"Okay. Hurts." I shifted in my seat. "Hope it missed my tattoos."

"You have such great priorities."

I gave him a microscopic smile. I kept staring at the side-view mirror, half expecting to see a *bakemono* loping along beside us. "Why isn't he coming after us?" I asked hoarsely.

"Who? The demon?" I nodded and Sean tapped the roof. "Truck's got protective sigils. Besides, they know you'll come back."

"I left him, Sean. I just—what if he's—"

"Don't, Rachel." His voice was firm but kind. "Don't go there. That whole thing was engineered to bite you in the ass. They're not going to give up their best piece of bait."

"You're sure of that, are you?"

"Totally."

"You know witches can tell when you're lying, right?" Didn't always work, but he didn't need to know that.

"Then you should know I'm telling the truth when I say we'll get him back." His words reverberated along my skull, warm and comforting like a favorite blanket. Honesty. Sean believed what he was saying, but that didn't make it true.

"Not your problem anymore," I said, squinting at his dash.

"Hey, I said we'd help. I keep my promises." He cleared his throat. "How'd you hit that demon anyway? I heard him say you couldn't reach a line or something."

"It's like a reserve tank. You sort of bore out a part of you, then you pull the energy in and hold it there." I shifted in my seat again, trying to find a position that didn't make my back feel like sadistic nymphs were chopping at it with thousands of tiny swords.

"Sounds painful."

"It is. Using ley magic is like grabbing a live wire."

"Hence the collapsing and asking for a candy bar." The corner of his mouth pulled into a grin and I couldn't help but return it.

"Are you ever going to let that go?" I asked.

"Nope. I've got to have some way to repair my dignity after having a chick save my ass."

The ghost of a laugh escaped my throat. "Does it help that I'm a magical chick?"

"A little."

The conversation died and I rubbed at my right wrist, struggling to stay awake. I was pretty sure I was about to go into shock—either from the physical trauma or blood loss or emotional strain. I had ninety-nine problems, and this goddamn case was a hundred and five of them.

"What's your Jeep, a CJ7?" Sean asked. "Your dad fix it up for you?"

I snorted. "I fixed it up for me."

"Huh. You know your way around an engine?"

I couldn't tell if he was actually interested or just trying to keep me from passing out. Either way, I appreciated it. "Yeah. Dad taught me. Your girlfriend fix up your truck?" My words slurred a little and my breathing was labored, but I made myself focus on his face.

"Cute. I keep her running alright. Got a '70 Gran Torino I'm working on though."

"Cobra-Jet engine?"

He shot me a look like I'd just started juggling fire. "Yeah." He chuckled. "Funny, the things we got in common. My dad's a mechanic. Grew up in engine grease."

"Where..." I swallowed, shook my head, and tried again. "Where's home?"

"Dad's in Cheyenne. But I spend most of my time around Denver."

"Look at that. Personal info." I thought I was smirking, but judging by the concern on Sean's face, it was probably more like a grimace.

"Just trying to keep you conscious, sweetheart."

"Thought I was a creepy monster."

"Yeah, about that." Now it was his turn to fidget in his seat. "I'm still trying to get my head around it. Just... give me some time."

"Guess I owe you that." I chewed on my lip, stealing a sideways glance at him. "I'm sorry I lit into you."

"Don't worry about it." Another small smile, followed by more awkward silence. I picked at my cuticles, only looking up when Sean said, "So tell me about this hunter who did you wrong."

"What do you mean?"

"I'm not the only one with prejudices, sugar."

"Not much to tell. Met a guy. Was with him for a while. Ended bad."

"That's how you recognized Luke's tattoo."

I nodded. Ryan had a very similar one. Hunters that did the job full-time usually ended up in the Network. The tattoos were how they recognized each other. Sean looked at me like he was waiting for me to say more, and I wondered how long I could put him off. I sniffed, rubbing at the seam on my jeans.

"He didn't like that I was a witch," I said.

"He break it off?"

"Well, he didn't say as much, but I sort of took him stabbing me in the chest as a Dear John." I shrugged a shoulder, but it was too jerky to be casual. I hadn't seen Ryan in six years, and no matter how much I hated him, my chest still ached when I thought about him. I wished it were because of the injury.

"Damn. That's rough." He sounded like he meant it. "Sorry."

"Yeah, well. That's why I'm kind of touchy about the whole monster-human thing."

"I'm getting that. But you've got to look at it from our perspective. We don't cross paths with many Glindas." He tapped his thumb against the steering wheel. "Speaking of, how come we've never run into you before?"

"We try to stay clear of hunters. For obvious reasons."

We lapsed into silence again. I directed him onto the Silverthorne exit, circling around the Dillon Reservoir and winding up Swan Mountain Road. The Ford bounced along the old dirt road leading to my parents' ranch, pulling up in front of a simple two-story house with a wide front porch. The security light was on, and as our vehicles crunched to a stop, my mom and dad burst out the front door.

"She's hurt," Sean said, helping me out of the truck. My dad's expression was stony and my mom looked like she was about to pass out. Her short blonde hair was pushed back with a headband, and dark circles encased warm honey eyes so like mine. She looked like she'd aged ten years in just a few days.

"I'm sorry," I mumbled. "Danny... He... I'm sorry."

"Get 'er inside," my dad commanded. Sean helped me up the steps, but I tore away from him at the door and bolted inside toward the kitchen. Jars clattered to the counter as I pulled down ingredients before dropping to my knees in the middle of a set of metal rings embedded in the tile floor.

"Rachel, what are you doing?" my mom cried. I ignored her, haphazardly dumping herbs and a lock of hair into a bowl. I didn't have the energy to hold a circle. I didn't care.

"Find," I commanded, dropping a match onto the spell. Uncontained magic pulsed through the kitchen, crackling in the air. My head swam as images of Denver flashed before my eyes. I barely registered them, buildings and signs melding together before I hit a now-familiar black wall. I didn't have a location, but I had something better: confirmation. I broke the connection and crumpled in on myself.

Something wet slid up my face, and fur tickled my nose. Maya, our bear-sized Tibetan mastiff, whined and butted her massive head against mine. I circled my arms around her neck, burying my face against her shoulder.

"C'mon, girl." Strong hands slid under my arms. "That's enough." The dry, earthy scent of wood and the tang of scotch washed over me, and I hid my face in my dad's chest as he lifted me up.

"He's alive," I choked out. "I'm so sorry, Dad. I tried. I was right there... I just..."

"It's alright," he murmured. I clung to his voice like I was five-years old again. He guided me into a spare bedroom on the first floor, situating me on the bed. I stared at the wall. Danny was alive. The demon blocked my tracking spell, but Danny was alive. He'd survived the building collapse. He'd survived the demon. Maybe Sean was right.

The full moon. The spell. They needed him for the spell,

and they needed him for bait. I still had time. It wasn't over, not by a long shot, but at least Danny was alive. Fear and anger and fucking self-pity waged war inside me. My mom came into the room, bending down and tugging at my shirt.

Anger won.

I caught her arm and pushed her away. "I'm okay."

"Rachel, you're covered in blood. Let us just--"

"Mom, stop." The words were tight and sharp, and she blinked at me. Guilt added to the cornucopia of unpleasant emotions souring my gut. My mom and I had fought ever since I was little. I knew she loved me, and I loved her, but it was always like she wished I were different. More like Danny. Wished I were someone else. This was something else though. Every scrape, every bruise I'd ever had, no one but Danny could get near me. It'd been the same when I was a kid. I don't know if it was some deep-seated fear of weakness or if I was just a stubborn brat, but I was a royal bitch when hurt. Try to help me, and I'd rip your head off. My mom moved toward me again, but my dad stopped her. They had a hushed argument, which probably consisted of my mother very reasonably pointing out that I could be bleeding to death. Whatever my dad said, it got her to leave me alone, and he pulled her out of the room.

I leaned my elbows on my knees, itching, burning pain carving into my back, and covered my face in my hands. I didn't even bother to turn on the light. I swam through a hurricane of rage. I couldn't think about anything else--if I did, I'd fall apart. Somehow my palms became wet. It couldn't be because I was crying. If I was crying, that meant I wasn't focusing on revenge. I didn't have fucking time to get all weepy.

"Hey," Sean said softly, and I jumped, pissing my back off even more.

"Quit sneaking up on me like that." I swiped at my face, my cheeks warming.

"Are you okay?" he asked.

I laughed bitterly. "Oh, I'm great. I'm awesome, really." The scene from the warehouse replayed in my mind. My brother, his body broken, using his last ounce of energy to help me escape. Goddammit.

Sean put a hand on my shoulder. "Rache, you need to be patched up."

"You telling me what to do?" I wanted to lash out at something, beat it into submission.

"Nope. Just making a friendly suggestion." He smiled and gently pulled me to my feet. It was only then I noticed he held his left arm tight against his ribs.

"You hurt?"

"Got a little banged up when that son of a bitch knocked me into the wall. Your dad got me sorted out."

"Shouldn't be carrying me around then," I said as we walked out of the bedroom, his arm around my waist.

"Now who's telling who what to do?"

Sean steered me into the kitchen, which was surprisingly empty aside from Luke. He sat at the island bar, eating what looked like leftover pot roast. No one can set foot in her house without my mother feeding them. Maya followed the smell of cooked meat and lumbered into the kitchen, sitting expectantly beside Luke. He fed her a bit of food and she favored him with a doggy grin.

"Where is everyone?" I asked.

"Ethan left, and we told your parents we'd take care of you, said they should get some rest. They looked dead on their feet," Luke said, sympathy in his voice.

"Let's see your back," Sean said. I sat down on a stool across from Luke and gingerly removed my jacket. The leather was shredded to ribbons. Dammit. That was my favorite jacket. Sean picked up the med kit and made an upward motion with his hand.

"What?"

"Your shirt. It needs to come off."

"I'm not that easy," I said, narrowing my eyes.

"You want me to get your dad?"

I shook my head. What I wanted was to fall into bed and sleep for a week. Luke peeled off his outer shirt and handed it to me. How chivalrous. I crossed my arms and tugged the shirt over my head. The fabric stuck to my back, heavy with blood. I used Luke's shirt to preserve some degree of dignity, dropping my shredded clothing to the floor. Water drummed against the sink, followed by a cloth gently dabbing at my back. I hissed as it hit one of the cuts.

Maya watched with keen interest, her dark eyes following Sean's movements. "Since when do people keep bears as pets?" Sean asked.

I grinned. "Don't let her size fool you. She's sweet."

"I feel like she's going to eat me."

"Only if you piss her off."

He chuckled and continued doctoring my back. Maya padded closer, sniffing Sean's leg before plopping down beside me. I stroked her head absently, taking comfort from her warmth.

"Well, it missed your tattoos, but the middle of your back is a hot mess," Sean said. "The tree's a little creepy. What's with the cowboy boots and bird?"

"Jesus, you're nosey," I grumbled, although there wasn't any real heat in my voice. "They're for my parents."

"Your family's real tight, huh?" Luke asked. "I've got to say, they seem pretty damn calm despite everything."

"It's an act. Or, rather, triage. Get through the crisis, fall apart later."

We didn't talk for a while as Sean cleaned my wounds. He had to fetch a second washcloth. The cuts must have been worse than I thought. Luke pulled a container out of the fridge and set about fixing a plate for me just as Sean passed a bottle of whiskey over my shoulder.

"I'm about to start stitching," he explained.

"Uh, not that I'll pass up the drink, but there's lidocaine in the med kit." The brothers exchanged a look that told me, yes, they absolutely used alcohol as an anesthetic. Probably as a disinfectant, too. Jesus Christ. Sean removed a small glass vial and a hypodermic needle from the med kit. A few pricks where he injected the drug into my skin, then my back went blissfully numb.

"Why do you think that demon wants you so bad?" Sean asked as he began to sew the wounds closed. Luke passed me the plate of pot roast and a glass of water and I gratefully started to eat, my hunger overruling my discomfort.

"I don't know," I said in between bites. "I don't get what he meant about testing me either. I'm not that special."

"How do you mean?"

"Ley witches are kind of rare, but I'm not the only one in the country. Seems like a lot of trouble for..." I trailed off, the gears in my mind spinning furiously. That was a good point. I was a deputy for the Council. Going after me meant lots of attention and pissing off a whole host of witches. Plus, if Finn did manage to corrupt me, the Council would rain holy fire down on my ass before I could put two spells together. It didn't make any sense.

"Rachel? Hey, you still with us?" Luke asked, waving at me.

"Yeah... Finn has a partner, right? Some guy that's doing this spell. But he could have picked any city—hell, any country. Why Denver? Why call attention to himself by staging the bodies?"

"Because he's a nutjob?" Sean said.

"Maybe, but everything he's done has been methodical. He's sending messages. Like the flowers."

"What flowers?"

"The day Danny went missing, someone sent me flowers

for his funeral. There was a note with a cryptic message and the whole nine. Ran a card trace, but got nothing useful."

A sharp burst of anger exploded out of Sean like sparks from a welding torch. Considering how much he usually controlled his emotions, this must have really set him off. "What'd the message say?"

"It said, 'You should know I did everything I could, it was just too late. How does the shoe fit now.'"

"That mean anything to you?" Luke asked.

"Not really. I mean it sounds like the standard stuff cops say to victims' families, and he obviously wants me to feel something. But I couldn't place it."

"Great. So he's going all Glenn Close on you," Sean said.

"Yeah, but the question is why? Why tip me off at all? Why take my brother, when there are tons of witches in the city? Danny's tough, there're much easier targets. He wanted my attention. He wanted me twisting, suffering." *You should know I did everything I could, it was just too late.* That sounded like something I would say. He asked how the shoe fit now. He wanted me to walk in his shoes, to know how he felt. "Luke, can I use your laptop?"

He set it up for me on the counter while Sean continued to stitch me up. He sewed with confidence, like he had done this many times before. I considered the Callahans' situation. Working off of information pieced together by other hunters, chasing demons from town to town, few friends. For better or for worse, I had the Council. I had resources. I wasn't always smart enough to use them, but I had them. I logged into one now--the Council database. We didn't just keep lore here. Like all law enforcement organizations, we kept case files.

"What are you doing?" Sean asked.

I hesitated. "You didn't want me to lie to you. So I won't. I'm looking up my past cases, but I can't tell you how. There's some stuff I just can't talk about." I sighed, folding under Sean's look. "C'mon, please. Cut me some slack."

He grunted in what I assumed was Army-ese for okay and I turned back to the database. I put in my name as the deputy on record and hit search. Son of a bitch. I'd worked a lot of cases in five years. Careful not to move too much, I tugged the ribbons of leather that had once been my jacket toward me and rummaged in the pocket. I pulled out a rumpled piece of paper from when I'd questioned the florist. The order sheet for my artfully arranged threat, with the fake credit card registered to Bonnie Turner. I added the name to my search.

Nothing.

"For fuck's sake," I hissed, frustration creeping into my voice. "No match on the name from the florist."

"Try leaving off the last name," Luke suggested. I took his advice and ran the search again. Hit.

"I'll be damned." I opened the file and skimmed through the notes. Council caught wind of a series of unexplained deaths in Pueblo. I'd been assigned the case with Pasha. "I remember this case. Particularly frigging nuts corrupt witch, killed five people."

"You think the witch is back?" Sean asked.

"No. He's dead. But the name on the flowers..." I clicked through the victim profiles. Holy shit. "Bonnie Wilkes. I'll bet you anything Turner was her maiden name."

"Wilkes? Like that jumpy dude from Hughes Corp? What was his name—Jason?" Luke pushed himself upright from where he'd been leaning against the counter and looked at me.

"Yeah, Jason Wilkes. His wife was the last vic on that case," I said, a strange combination of excitement and terror pumping through me. "We had a hell of a time finding the witch. We knew he'd targeted Bonnie Wilkes." I swallowed, the message on the flowers taking on a whole new meaning. "We were too late." By which I meant we'd used her as bait and failed.

"Jason Wilkes knew Sadie, Jeff, and Marcus. He had access to Hughes," Luke said, comprehension flashing in his eyes.

"Makes it pretty easy to buy up shit in his boss's name, plant a false trail," Sean said. "And he has a hell of an axe to grind against you, Rache. Means, motive, and opportunity."

"I been thinking Jason Wilkes was a victim. He's our goddamn perp." I was almost certain that's what Leon had wanted to tell me--the information that got him killed. He'd left as many clues as he could in his computer. I was just a little slow piecing it together. "This whole thing is my goddamn fault."

"How the hell do you figure that?" Sean asked, bewildered. He tore off a few pieces of tape and stuck them to the counter. "Because you didn't save his wife?"

"Because I was frigging hot and bothered about Hughes. I should have gone straight to Wilkes. He's connected to the vics, I should have known." Guilt squirmed in my stomach. If I'd done things differently, maybe we could have caught him before he took Danny.

"Rache, you were working the case. It's not your fault." Luke looked so sincere I almost said what I was thinking-- that I should have called in the Council--but I caught myself at the last minute. My bosses weren't super keen on the spilling of state secrets. Loose lips got your ass sunk in a deep, dark hole. So instead I just shut my trap. Shoulda, coulda, woulda. It didn't change the situation at hand anyway. I still needed to get my brother back.

"Alright, done," Sean said, taping gauze onto my back. "You've got three deep ones that'll probably add to your scar collection, but the other two should heal okay."

"Thanks." I stood, clutching the shirt to my chest. "There's a guest bedroom upstairs and there should be some clean clothes in the closet. Don't know if they'll fit, but anyway. They're there."

"Your folks are prepared," Luke said as we crept up the stairs.

"They're used to situations like this."

Luke disappeared into the bedroom, but Sean lingered in the hallway with me.

"Watch your ribs while you sleep. I think we might have a splint if you need it."

"Be careful of those stitches," he said, a smile playing around his lips. We stood there quietly, looking at each other.

"Thank you," I said haltingly. "For you know. Not bailing."

"Yeah, well. Still our case too." It was like he tried to sound gruff, but just couldn't quite get there. "I'll put up some demon-proofing, make sure you're safe through the night."

"Why'd you do it?"

"Do what?"

"Help me." I picked at my cuticles, watching my toes curl against the carpet as I shifted my weight. "I mean, you were ready to split. What changed your mind?"

I felt him looking at me, but I couldn't raise my eyes. "Like you said. I lost my sister. Maybe I'm not on board the witch train, but no one deserves that shit," he said. I nodded. "Why'd you save me? With the hex. You knew it wouldn't go over well."

I looked up in confusion. "Because you were going to die. I couldn't just let that happen."

"My stunning good looks, huh?" Sean grinned and I laughed. He gave my arm a squeeze, his fingers trailing down my skin.

"Get some sleep," I murmured, unsure of what to do. Spells I know. I suck at human interaction.

"You too. Remember, I'll keep you safe." He winked at me, then headed back down the stairs. I walked slowly down the hallway to my old bedroom, shaking my head. Jesus Christ. Roller coasters had fewer ups and downs than this hunter and me.

SLEEP CAME in fits and spurts, and I eventually crept downstairs in search of Ambien or something to help me sleep. Finding nothing stronger than tea, I dropped in a bit of valerian root and settled down on the couch, sipping the steaming liquid.

"You should be sleeping."

I jumped, tea sloshing onto my hand. "Jesus Christ, Sean! How do you do that?" I had good senses, both magical and otherwise, and an obscene amount of paranoia that meant almost nothing got the drop on me. Except this frigging ex-Army dude. He chuckled and sat down beside me while I sullenly sucked tea from my skin.

"Skills, sugar. What's got you up?"

I shrugged, rubbing my thumb against the side of the mug. "Stress. This'll take care of it though."

"What is that--some kind of hocus-pocus?" Sean eyed the mug like he expected it to bite him.

"Oh yeah. Very old potion, very powerful. Called chamomile tea," I said dryly.

He flicked his eyes to me, one eyebrow arched like he didn't believe me, but then cracked a smile. "Alright, guess I deserved the sass."

"Not everything I do is magic, Sean."

That smile turned boyish. "That's debatable."

"Oh shut up." I hid my stupid grin behind a sip of tea. "Don't you ever sleep? Every time I wake up you're prowling around."

Sean settled back against the couch, his arm draped over the back like it had been at my cabin. I wished he wouldn't do that--it made it way too easy to lean against him. "Habit, I guess. On deployments you don't exactly get a solid eight every night. And I just can't relax when there's a threat."

I snorted. "You're a hunter. Isn't there always a threat?"

"Guess that's why I drink a lot of Red Bull."

Rough, calloused fingers brushed almost absently over my bare shoulder. His touch was soft, comforting.

I stared at my mug. "Can I ask you a question?"

"Go for it."

"How many witches have you killed?" My voice was so quiet it was almost inaudible.

Sean inhaled a deep breath, held it for a moment, then let it out in a rush. "I know why you're asking. But the answer's none, Rache." I shot him a skeptical look. "Honest. Luke and me, we stick pretty exclusively to demons these days."

"Why?"

"Because there's no grey area with them."

"You really think they'll keep Danny alive?" Christ, I sounded pathetic.

"I do. That demon son of a bitch--this isn't just about that ritual. You've got to be careful."

The valerian was doing its job. Warmth spread through my chest and my face was pleasantly fuzzy. I snuggled a little closer, my head resting on his shoulder. "That's funny. You were ready to shoot me and now you're telling me to be careful."

"Should have figured you were the kind of girl to hold grudges." Sean glanced down at me, grimacing, but the twinkle in his eyes said it wasn't entirely serious.

"Redhead." I drained the last of my tea and reached across him to set the mug on the end table. My hand didn't make it back the whole way and mysteriously settled on his chest. "I'm so tired, Sean."

"Go to sleep, sweetheart."

"No, I don't mean--I'm tired of all this. Of failing. Being scared. I just... How am I supposed to do this?" I stared at the folds of his shirt, ashamed of the tremor in my voice. "Save Danny, stop Wilkes, keep the cops off my ass. I'm not some kind of superhero. I barely keep myself alive. Shouldn't be responsible for other people." Awesome, I was rambling in an herbal narcotic-induced haze.

Sean didn't say anything, but his arm closed around me and he kissed my forehead. "Don't expect me to have the answers, sugar. But you don't need to do this alone."

I tipped my head back, studied his face. "Don't mess with me."

He cupped my cheek, fingers sliding down over my jaw and onto my neck in a way that made me sigh in a totally embarrassing way. "You said you could tell if I was lying. So--am I?"

I don't even know how it happened, if he made the move or I did, but the next thing I knew his mouth was on mine. Slightly chapped lips, his mouth tasting a little salty from the pot roast, one hand still resting on my neck and the other warm on my back, careful to avoid my injuries--it was like my brain just shut down. I loved how Sean pushed me, how he could wind me up without even trying. I shifted so that I straddled his lap, and I couldn't even spare a thought for how unlike me this was. I wasn't a prude, but being that vulnerable made my scar itch and my brain reel.

Sean somehow slipped under my radar.

Even with his orders and his bullheadedness and his attitude--he also had kindness and compassion and God help me, I felt good with him.

Sean groaned and his teeth grazed over my bottom lip, making me shiver. His tongue invaded my mouth, hot and demanding this time, his arms pulling me close against him.

His fingers slid into my hair and I sighed again, my cheeks immediately flaming.

"I'm sorry," he said, breaking away. "I know you're not in the mood, and it's not a good time." He totally contradicted that by kissing my neck just below my jaw and I sucked in a ragged breath.

"Waiting for me to deck you?" I tipped my head to the

side and Sean took full advantage, laying a series of kisses so soft against my skin that it somehow made me think he was holding himself back.

"Pretty much." He worked his way back up, across my cheek. "I like the fight in you."

His skin radiated heat through his t-shirt as my hands slid over his shoulders, feeling the muscles bunch and tense beneath the thin fabric. I kissed him again, desperately, hungry for something that made me feel safe. It felt so good to give in, to let slip loose the iron bands of control I kept wound around myself at all times. It felt good to be wanted.

"Wait, wait," I said, breathless. I squeezed my eyes shut, my forehead resting against his, and tried to pull together my frayed thoughts. This was insane. I couldn't do this. It only ended one way. "I'm sorry, I just... I can't."

"No, I'm sorry. This is all fucked up--your brother's out there, and here I am putting moves on you."

I shook my head, but slid off his lap and back onto the sofa. "It's okay. I mean, I didn't punch you, right?"

He snorted and gave me a lopsided grin, and then the awkward cloud descended and we sat there in silence. I kept telling myself this was for the best. And Christ, how I hated it.

SIXTEEN

I awoke late the next morning. To say my back was sore was so much of a goddamn understatement I should have punched myself for even thinking it. I remained in bed for a while, watching the sunlight filter through the curtains of my old room. Not much had changed since I moved out. Sports trophies and medals lined a shelf along with pictures from high school. A large black poster of the band Disturbed decorated one wall. My mom hated that poster. She said the guys looked like a biker gang.

I knew I needed to get up. The clock was ticking. But there was safety here, comfort. This room was from a time when I didn't have to be responsible for other people's lives. When things were easier.

Boo freaking hoo, Rachel. Get your whiny ass up.

Stitches tugged at the skin on my back and I grunted as I dug through the drawers. I pulled on a pair of grey compression pants, the kind runners wear, and a black tank top, then bound my hair up into a ponytail. A pit stop in my parents' bedroom yielded half a bottle of Vicodin--prescribed to Maya for a non-existent injury. My uncle Joe was a large-animal vet by day, which meant he also often treated the bumps and bruises that came along with my job. I've been told there's not much difference between a horse and me.

Jake sat at the dining room table, listlessly playing cards with my mom. He gave me a subdued greeting, lacking all of his usual frenetic energy. I kissed the top of his head, barely keeping my shit together.

"How you doing, kiddo?" I asked, swiping a pear from the fruit bowl on the counter.

Jake just shrugged.

My brow pinched and I rested my hand on his shoulder. "Hey, Jake, it'll be okay. This will all be over soon."

Again, he didn't say anything, and I slid my hand off his shoulder as I started to turn away.

"Aunt Rachel?" I turned to look back at Jake, who was chewing on his lips like he was dying to ask something but afraid to. Blue eyes so like Danny's locked onto mine and I swallowed hard against the lump in my throat.

"Did you mean it?" he asked.

"Did I mean what?"

"When you said you are good at your job."

I gave him a half-hearted smile. "Yeah, I did. What about it?"

"So you'll get him back, right? You'll save my dad?" The way he looked at me, my chest felt hollow. It wasn't just about justice. If I failed, a little boy was going to be orphaned.

"Absolutely," I said with confidence I didn't feel. "I promise." I glanced at my mom. "Callahan boys up yet?"

"Yep," my mom answered. "Your dad wanted to let you sleep so he took them out to the range." Oh Jesus. Dad only took guys out to the shooting range on our property for one reason: to put the fear of God into them. He'd done it to more than one boyfriend over the years. "Joe's here too. Brought these for you." She tossed me a pill bottle. Amoxicillin.

I downed the morning dose along with the Vicodin as my

mom's smile faded and she tipped her head toward the kitchen. I followed her out of Jake's earshot.

"Rachel, we called the Council last night. A team went to the warehouse, but..." Tears made her eyes over-bright and she blinked too fast.

"Nothing was there," I guessed. She nodded and I drew her into a hug, her shoulders trembling. "He's alive, Mom. Somewhere. You guys find anything yet?"

"Your dad's working all the regular law enforcement angles--put a missing person report out on him. I talked to the low-level witches in Denver, but they didn't know anything. Council's using all the usual channels--the Denver Camarilla and pack and even got CBI checking into Hughes."

"Tell them to look at Jason Wilkes. Don't know how much good it'll do, but he's our perp." I stepped back, leaning against the counter.

"We can try to get a cell phone trace. But Rachel, the Council will want a briefing," she said, wiping at her eyes. Right. Because it wasn't as if we were under a deadline here--a confab was just what we needed.

I stormed out the back door.

I needed to think, to get a plan together. Maybe I could convince the Council to back me for once instead of sitting me on the bench. My brain always seemed to work better when I was moving, so I jogged down a dirt trail leading to a large, weathered red barn. Well-oiled hinges made little noise as I pushed the door open and flipped on the light. While my parents owned ranch property, they didn't raise livestock, so the barn served more as a training space and repair shop. On the far left, my Trans-Am sat on blocks, awaiting my attention. The middle and right side hosted a variety of gym equipment, from a weight bench and dumbbells to a makeshift boxing ring. A heavy bag hung in the center of the room. Just what I needed.

I plugged my phone into a radio sitting on the shelf,

cranked the volume up on my favorite playlist, and rolled my shoulders. Crouched in a fighter's stance, my fists gathered before my chin, I worked a series of slow punches against the bag. The narcotics I'd taken kicked in, making my head a little fuzzy but lessening the ache in my back. Besides, I was used to playing through pain.

I picked up the pace.

I could get a hair sample from Wilkes's house—no. If his demon bro blocked my tracking spell on Danny, he'd certainly block it against himself.

I slammed my fist against the bag with all the force I could muster, then spun on my left foot to land a side kick against it.

We could use property records to look for any place Wilkes owned. That was assuming he was hiding out in a place that had his name on the deed and not an alias—or just some random location. It also assumed we had time to play hide-and-go-seek.

Whipping around, I smacked the bag with a backhand. Punches and kicks flowed from my body, made graceful by many years of training.

I'd gotten Finn's attention with the ley energy, and that was just with my emergency stash. Maybe with enough power from the line, I could break his ward. That scared the hell out of me. If it worked, I didn't really want to consider the implications.

I wondered if Wilkes was stupid enough to use a cell phone like my mom suggested. Council could use GPS to track him. What I needed was some kind of magic trace, but without a hex bag from Wilkes, that was a no-go.

Sweat broke out across my forehead. Every time I punched the bag, I saw the demon's cold eyes. Another kick and I saw my brother lying broken on a dirty concrete floor. Jeff and Sadie's tormented bodies. Marcus Rodriguez's face flashed before me and I attacked in a near frenzy. I vented my anger on the bag, punishing it with all the rage I wanted to unleash on Wilkes and Finn.

"You're going to tear your stitches out," Sean said, sidling up beside me.

A jolt went through me and I spun on instinct, lashing out with a backhand. Sean caught it in a practiced deflection and the motion carried me to rest against him. My face warmed as I remembered how his lips felt against mine and I backed up a step.

"Nah. I have faith in your skills," I said, and return to the bag, whacking it with a left cross.

He still kept his left arm close to his body, but he looked clean and refreshed. I spun again, this time on my right, planting another kick against the bag. I felt Sean's eyes on me.

"I see you survived shooting with my dad," I said, pausing to catch my breath and grab a towel from a stack against the wall. I buried my face in it under the pretense of wiping sweat away.

"Yeah. Does he threaten all visitors, or are we just special?" Sean smirked.

"He's a dad. And a cop. Threatening is what he does best." I opened a small refrigerator and snagged a bottle of water. "How're your ribs?"

"Not bad. How's your back?"

"Sore, but I've been through worse." I took a drink from the bottle and leaned against the wall. Sean joined me.

"One thing I don't get. Your brother's a witch, right? So why didn't he just ice the guy earlier? I mean, he had enough juice to collapse the building."

Dangerous ground. The Council had worked long and hard to protect the secret of our vulnerabilities. I wanted to trust Sean. I wanted to believe he was a friend.

"He couldn't," I said. I struggled to make up my mind about what to tell him as he reached behind me and peeled back one corner of the gauze, checking my wounds. "Remember what I said last night about not being able to tell you some stuff?"

"Yeah." He drew out the word, suspicion soaking every syllable.

"That's one of them. Sean, I'm sorry, I just can't," I said, turning to face him when he opened his mouth to protest. "It's... it's, like, classified."

"Rachel..." He sighed. "How am I supposed to trust you when you won't trust me?"

"I'm not trying to be shady, I swear. But this, I could get in trouble. Serious trouble. And it could totally bite me in the ass."

"You think I'd sell you out? If I were going to kill you, honey, I'd already have done it. But I need to know what we're looking at in order to fight it."

I gnawed on my lip. He had a point--several points, actually. The Council would be pissed if they ever found out. But then, the cat was already out of the bag if Finn and his BFF knew about it. "There are two ways to disrupt magic. Running water and spelled iron."

"Okay, water I knew, but what's spelled iron?"

"Iron that's been inscribed with enchantments. Slap a pair of spelled iron cuffs on a witch and she's cut off entirely from her power. That's what they had Danny in." Iron itself absorbed magic--it was one of the properties that made it so useful as a talisman. The whole idea skeeved me right out. It was like thinking about cutting your own arm off with a dull knife.

"And that works on your flavor of witch as well as the other kind?"

"Yeah. It works on all born witches."

"Huh. Why haven't we heard of that in the lore?"

"Told you, it's classified. So be careful who you share it with."

"My lips are sealed." Sean meandered over to the Trans-Am, hands on his hips as he sized it up. "This yours?"

"Yep, that's my baby. I've got the bodywork done, now I'm rebuilding the engine. I finally found a 455 last month, but I've got to replace the camshafts and cylinder heads." Pride crept into my voice and my grin stretched into a full-blown beaming smile.

"You restoring it to original specs?"

"Oh, yeah, definitely. I don't see a reason to mess with perfection."

Sean walked around to the front and lifted the hood. "I totally agree," he said, leaning over to examine the engine. The sleeves of his dark T-shirt hugged his biceps as he supported his weight. Thin white scars marred his skin in places, the brand of a dude who'd seen his fair share.

"Is that a cross?" I asked, tipping my head toward a bracelet on his left wrist.

"Rosary." Sean straightened up, running his fingers over the small wooden beads. He caught the what-the-fuck expression on my face and laughed. "I know--I'm no saint." He sobered, his thumb rubbing over the bracelet. "That's kind of why--you know. Bible's pretty specific about witches."

"Yeah, let's judge people based on bigoted crap written by dudes wearing bed sheets a million years ago and twisted throughout history. Not like wars have started that way or anything."

"Hey, easy. Church does a lot of good too, and not all of it is crap. What, you don't have religion?"

"I got thrown out of Sunday school when I was six for punching a boy who said girls should stay home with the kids. That count?" Sean chuckled and I ducked my head, grinning. "Anyway, that why you do this? Make like Jesus and save humanity?"

"I don't exactly figure myself as the Son of God, but yeah, something like that."

He ran a hand back through his hair and I caught sight of his own tattoo, some kind of shield or a coat of arms. Memories of last night, his fingers trailing over my skin, played in my mind and heat flared in my face. Stop it, Rachel. For fuck's sake.

"That's military, right?" I asked, pointing to the tattoo.

"Seventy-fifth Airborne." When I looked at him blankly, he added, "Rangers."

"You were an Army Ranger?" I had to admit, I was impressed. "Where did you serve?"

"Wherever they sent me." It was like a switch flipped on his expression—where he'd been friendly and even maybe flirtatious a moment before, now he was stony and cold. Touchy subject.

"Is that what Hughes meant when he was talking about stuff you'd done?" I couldn't help it, I was damn curious.

Sean gave me a level look. "There are things I can't talk about either, Rache."

Oh. Right. Stuff that was probably legit classified, and I was poking at him. The flush deepened and I rubbed at the inside of my wrist.

"Listen, about last night..." Sean began, and I cut him off by shaking my head.

"Yeah, me too. I put valerian in my tea and it was making me all weird. No worries. Never happened."

Sean fixed me with a look that I imagined was akin to him catching someone in his crosshairs. "That wasn't what I was going to say."

My gut twisted, and my heart pounded so hard I was afraid he could see it hammering through my skin. "What, um, what were you going to say then?"

He stepped closer, reached out to brush the hair behind my ear. "I shouldn't have taken advantage. But that don't mean I regret it."

"Sean, I, um..." I forced myself to swallow, my whole body

prickly and full of adrenaline. I fucking panicked. It was like goddamn history repeating itself and my brother was out there and I had work to do and last night might've been nice but I wasn't thinking clearly and I couldn't do this. I just couldn't do this. "I don't--there's so much going on right now and it's not you, but last night was just a moment of weakness."

A wry grin curved his mouth. "It was just a kiss, Rachel. Not a marriage proposal. But I'm not a douche. I won't do it again unless you want me to."

I began backing toward the door. "I'm, ah, going to go get cleaned up." I felt his eyes on me as I turned my back and made a beeline toward the house, looking back once to see Sean following me. I was a goddamn idiot with the worst timing in the world.

I walked through the front door only to be immediately intercepted by my dad. He pulled me into the kitchen, keeping his eye on Sean as he went to join Luke in the living room. My dad directed us toward the kitchen door, still looking toward the living room to make sure the Callahans were out of earshot.

"Michelle just called and Ethan's on his way," he said in hushed, urgent tones. "Victor's on his way here now. Council wants to know everything that happened last night, and then they want you to go down to Denver and meet Masterson. He's assigned to this case now and you are to bring him up to speed." His mouth pressed into a tight line. "Rachel, this is serious. If you don't cooperate, they're gonna write you up."

I gave him a sharp look. Written up was a gentle euphemism for putting me on trial. The Council would tolerate some level of defiance and rebellion, but push it too far and they started to question where your loyalties lay, and as an organization full of people that risked turning into unhinged magic-slinging death dealers, loyalty was pretty damn important. It was the thin layer keeping us all civilized.

"Alright," I said, and shot a quick glance toward the living room. "When and where for Masterson?"

"Two o'clock. CBI."

I groaned. "I should probably check in there anyway." Several neglected voicemails let me know the Council was definitely leaning on my cover job to keep me out of trouble. My vanilla boss was asking if I was dead and telling me I had reports to file. There is a surprising amount of paperwork in law enforcement, both magical and mundane.

I walked back out into the living room. "Hey, uh, I've got to take care of some stuff."

"What's up?" Sean asked.

I gave him that tight smile that was coming to mean I'm-sorry-I-can't-tell-you. "Just a few things to prep."

Luke looked at his brother. "We got a name now for that demon and some intel. Could see what we could dig up and regroup."

Sean nodded, his lower lip pushed out in a thoughtful expression. "Hell, why not. Not like we got much else to go on." Those summer green eyes turned to me. "Meet back at your cabin later?"

"Sounds good."

I watched them pull out of my parents' driveway, my arms huddled across my middle and my stomach feeling like it was coated in lead. Whatever Victor wanted to say to me, it wasn't going to be good. I'd taken my lumps before though. I was good at my job, but not good at the politics—hence why I was still a deputy when Pasha had moved on. Ethan, though, surprised me. He was smart and played ball. He should've been doing something much less shitty than running around with me.

I didn't have to stew for long. Victor showed up about twenty minutes later, his silver Escalade gliding across the gravel as if it couldn't be bothered by such paltry things as dust and paint dings.

Victor strolled up the walk with a kind of rangy grace, wearing jeans and a striped seersucker shirt with the sleeves rolled up. My heart made like a frightened bird, but I let him in and sank down onto the sofa in what I hoped was a cool and calm manner.

"Hello, Rachel," he said. He smiled kindly, but his eyes missed the memo and remained sharp, predatory.

"Am I in trouble?" I asked. No use beating around the bush.

Victor sat down in the recliner, leaned forward to rest his elbows on his knees and braided his fingers. My family converged around me, a subtle statement. Ethan stayed in the middle.

"Let me ask you. Do you think you should be? I'm serious, Rachel." Victor pinned me with his weaponized glare. "Ignoring the fact you blatantly defied a direct order to stand down, you definitely should have told us a demon was involved. I want to understand why you felt the need to keep this from us. We're your allies."

"I wasn't sure until last night." It wasn't a complete lie.

"Did it really say that it wanted you for something?"

"Yeah. He said they'd used Danny as bait."

"I see. When the first *bakemono* attacked you, did you use ley energy to fight it?" he asked.

"Yeah. I tapped the line and gave the release command. Though I had to really pump energy into it. Why? What's it matter?"

Victor glanced at my father. A prickly sensation crawled up my neck and my foot began to bounce as I rubbed at my wrist. We were at DEFCON 2 levels of alarm here and my fidgeting was going into overdrive.

"He must know," my dad said. "I just don't get why the elaborate set up."

"Know what?" Ethan asked.

"That you are a ley witch," Victor said. I wished like hell I could read him, but he seemed equally likely to either put a bullet in my skull or bring me a cookie.

"What? Why?" I felt like an enormous, scalding spotlight was trained on me.

"Your blood," Victor said simply. "Theoretically, it could allow a sufficiently strong enough practitioner to tap into ley magic."

"No. That's not possible."

"It could be. For the right demon." Maybe I imagined it, but I thought Victor recoiled slightly from me. Like I was dangerous. Tainted.

"But... they're demons! Isn't that like trading an Uzi for a squirt gun?" Every bad thought and anxious feeling I'd ever had about myself and my place in the world tumbled through my head. If a demon thought it could corrupt me... Hell, what did I mean *if*? I'd offered myself up to Finn on a fucking silver platter.

"Ley lines, in their purest form, trump everything, Rachel. They are the highest power we know. It's why witches like yourself are at such risk," Victor said. "With your power, they could break out of circles, collapse wards, anything." He gave me a hard look. "You need to stay out of this."

"It's my brother!"

"You defied this order once. This time I mean it, Rachel. You're not to go near Wilkes or that demon."

"Yes, sir," I snarled. "I know how important this is to you. Clearly. Since the fucking vice chair of the Executive is now making house calls about a case that the Council couldn't be bothered to take in the first place."

"Rachel." His voice snapped against me like steel and I actually came up short. "I'm here because your involvement in this case has brought you to the attention of a madman who could hurt you. You must be careful. For your own sake."

"So how do we protect her?" my dad asked, his blue eyes stormy as he looked at Victor.

"We need to keep her out of this," he said. "She's already pushed herself too far."

"How do you figure?" My dad puffed himself up, glaring at Victor like he'd just said something very rude about me.

"All the magic she's been pulling. We have... concerns."

"You think I'm unstable," I said flatly. Victor tilted his head, as if to say if it walks like a duck. I shoved myself to my feet, pacing beside the coffee table. "I can't fucking believe you guys. I'm fine." I glared at Victor, but something nagged at me. I thought about the way I'd acted with Hughes, how easily I'd lost control. I thought about how easy it was to pull more and more power. How arrogant I was to think I could command it.

There it was.

That slippery fricking slope I'd been warned about my whole life. My parents exchanged a pained look and my stomach twisted. We weren't done with the bad news yet.

"It's why you've been watched so closely, Rachel. The last ley witch that was corrupted, she... it wasn't good." My dad looked like his heart was breaking as he talked, and that's what finally did me in. They'd already written me off.

"I know. Believe me, I know. That's all I've fucking heard since the day I could first feel the lines. Well, newsflash—I'm not her. But, you know, thanks for the trust." I thought about when I'd taken my oath, Victor's behavior then. All the whispers, the mistrust, the suspicion from Council witches.

"We had to take certain measures." Victor didn't seem the least bit troubled about how his measures had affected me.

"So you think I'm on some kind of one-way ticket to evil." I backed toward the door. "Fuck this. I don't want it."

My parents and Ethan got to their feet and walked toward me, in what I was sure was meant as a show of solidarity, but had the effect of making me feel pinned down.

"Rachel, honey," my mom said, laying her hand on my arm. I jerked away from her. Electric fingers ran through my skin, making me jumpy. A wounded look crossed her face as she reached for me again. I forced myself to stay still.

"Hey, Rache, it'll be okay," Ethan said, putting a hand on my shoulder.

"Don't fucking say that. It's not your head on the chopping block." I felt caged, trapped. This plucked at every insecurity I'd ever had. No wonder the Council didn't trust me.

"Rachel..." My dad moved to my left, but didn't try to touch me. They were hemming me in, and adrenaline flooded my body. Fight or flight—either way, if they kept pushing into my personal space, I was going to freak.

"It's alright, no reason to be upset," Victor said, and I'm sure he thought he sounded soothing, but his voice just made me want to punch a wall. "We'll handle this. But you need to be careful, Rachel. No stupid stunts until we sort this out."

"But my brother—"

"The Council will send a Genesis team to deal with this Wilkes situation." Victor prowled toward me and I instinctually backed up. Before I knew what was happening, he grabbed my arm and pulled it toward him. He wasn't rough, but I panicked anyway, jerking against his hold. "Rachel, please. I just need to check. You'll be okay."

He pressed his fingers to the inside of my right wrist and cool magic reminiscent of cave pools and forest gloom swam over me. The brand bloomed onto my skin. I stared down at the sword, my heart thundering in my chest. It began to glow.

It failed to flare to a bright white. It remained a stubborn, terrifying light grey.

SEVENTEEN

I couldn't breathe. I needed to be outside. I turned to make a run for it, but Victor tightened his grip. For a half second, I considered decking him and bolting. But what would that get me? My brother was still out there and I needed less Council up my ass, not more. My eyes closed and I struggled for breath. Control. Control kept me sane, and I desperately needed it now.

"You think I'm a time bomb. Fine. But until the point at which I actually explode, I'm going to keep doing my damn job." I spoke to Victor, and Victor alone.

He almost looked sad. "I can't let you do that, Rachel. You won't know what's happened to you until it's over."

"So what are you going to do?" my mom demanded. She nearly shoved Victor back, putting herself between him and me. My mom was five-foot-nothing, but she didn't back down an inch from the vice chair. It was like someone gave a silent command—my dad and uncle took up positions on either side of her, forming a wall between Victor and me. It meant the fucking world.

"I'm trying to protect her," Victor said, looking at each of them in turn. "You have to know that."

I sucked in a steadying breath and gently pushed a hole through the Collins Family Blockade. "So like she said--how do you plan to do that?"

Victor grimaced and glanced down at my wrist. "It's the best way. Just until this whole thing is over and we can get you properly tested."

I swallowed thickly.

"Wait just a--"

"Dad, it's okay." I gave my father a tight smile. "This way I can't give into temptation, right?" I rolled my lips inward and stuck my arm out toward Victor. "Go ahead."

The vice chair watched me like he expected a trick and cautiously took my arm. He pulled a slim bracelet out of his pocket. Dull grey with twisted bars ending in a bulbous lock and sigils etched into the surface. He grimaced just from touching it, but that didn't stop him from locking it around my wrist. Magic drained out of me, leaving me hollow and empty. I wondered if this was how amputees felt--aware of something only through its absence.

"Just until this case is over," he said. He squeezed my shoulder and gave me what I'm sure he thought was a fatherly smile, but it just unnerved the shit out of me. I had a father and he was beside me, looking horrified.

Victor nodded to my parents and uncle. "We've got a few leads on Danny. I'll keep you all informed. Try to get some rest, Rachel."

The door had barely shut behind him before my family erupted into protests.

"This just isn't right. I'm gonna call Bill and talk to him. Victor's got no cause for this," my dad said, voice sharp and eyes hard.

"Dad, don't. Just let it go." I understood their shock--it wasn't like me to just roll over. "Right now Victor thinks I'm locked down. Buys me some breathing room."

"Breathing room? Rachel, you can't use magic and we

can't break that bracelet." My mom looked like she feared for my sanity. "What's wrong with you?"

"We can't break the bracelet, but I know someone who can." I rubbed at the alien thing, its weight far heavier than it should be. "Trust me. You guys keep working on finding Danny. I need a shower." My family stared after me in a mixture of excitement and fear that echoed the squirming in my gut. I was blatantly defying the vice chair of the Executive. It was sure to land me in suspension at best, but I didn't really see another option. At least Victor hadn't dropped my ass in a detention cell.

In the upstairs bathroom, I stripped off my sweaty clothing. The gauze still stuck to my skin and I peeled back a corner to examine the wounds. Three deep gouges sliced diagonally across my back. Two shallower cuts ran on either side of them. A few more for the collection.

Rows of precise stitches knitted the wounds together. Sean sutured like a surgeon. I wondered if he'd learned that in the Army, or as a hunter.

The shower wasn't quite orgasmic, but it was close. I scrubbed my body and hair, the hot water pounding into my sore muscles. I tipped my head back and let the water deafen me to the world. I remembered the flecks of gold in Sean's eyes, the sharp arch of the Cupid's bow on his mouth. The scent of something bright and clean mingled with gun oil. Like spring and violence mated.

A furtive smile crossed my lips and was immediately drowned by reality. The spelled iron bracelet banged against my wrist as I showered. I traced the etchings, coldness spreading through my gut. Who was I kidding? I was in such deep shit, I'd be lucky to get through this with my hide intact, and I was daydreaming about Sean? Our lives were not conducive to long-term relationships--and even if they were, what kind of relationship could we have? Keeping secrets from each other, walking on eggshells because of our jobs. He was a hunter. I was a witch. Forget oil and water—it was like fire and nitroglycerine. We just didn't work, and it would only end in pain and a massive frigging explosion. The key was to keep it casual.

Right.

I rinsed the conditioner out of my hair and turned the water off, wrapping myself in a fluffy white towel. I padded down the hall to my old bedroom to rummage for clothes, finding a grey t-shirt and jeans, and a brown leather jacket. Not as cool as my purple one, but it'd have to do. I snatched the Vicodin from my parents' medicine cabinet and the antibiotics Joe gave me, and pulled on my boots.

"What are you going to do?" Ethan asked.

"What they want. Meet with Masterson, keep my head down."

He huffed. "Rachel, I'd like to think we're friends. Don't bullshit me."

"Ethan, look—I don't want to drag you into this. You could get in trouble, and I mean serious trouble. Look at me, man. I don't want your head in a noose, too."

He shook his head. "We're partners. And you're not the only one that cares about Danny. I'm in."

I gave him a grateful smile. "Thanks, Ethan. You're an idiot, but thanks. I'll call you, okay?"

I shouted that I was leaving, my usual method of bidding farewell, and Ethan and I walked outside. He followed me onto I-70 until I exited on to 6th Avenue. Jamie Wallace, my CBI boss, wasn't in when I arrived, so I dropped a time-off request on his desk and sat down to file backlogged case reports. I would've felt guilty about the several-inches thick stack on my desk, except it didn't really matter. Not like my cases ever ended up in Colorado courts anyway. It was an easy way to kill time waiting for Masterson to show, and dull enough that it let my subconscious chew on a way to find Wilkes.

I had my headphones in, cranking along on my reports with a nervous tension squirming in my belly, when my cell phone rang. A name flashed on the screen and I stared at the device in suspicion.

"Hey Reed," I answered. "What's up?"

Reed Nazari--which I seriously doubted was his real name--was the local vampire Master. Old and powerful and scary as hell, he liked me for some reason, but that didn't mean he made social calls. I really didn't need vamps mixing it up on top of all this other shit.

"Just a head's up--you may want to take a drive to Five Points," he said, voice sliding through the phone in a way that was downright unfair. Reed preferred charm to violence, and was annoyingly good at both.

"Why, what's going on?"

"Elena's furballs are throwing a fit. Apparently, it's quite messy."

I frowned. "Why do you care what they do?"

"I don't, generally, but I heard about your case. Bad for business, the mongrels violating the treaties like that."

"Yeah, I'm sure diplomatic accords are real important to you." Reed had made it clear to me before that vampires followed the code of conduct set forward by the Walsenburg Treaties not because of anything the Council did, because it was in their favor to do so. I often wondered what would happen when that changed. "Still don't see why you're taking a break from fancy-pants artsy shit to call me."

"Consider me interested enough that I don't want more problems for you, and they're harassing humans." He sounded amused. The more I sassed him, the more he seemed to like me. I suspected Reed might be a closet masochist.

"How do you know?"

"Because I know."

"One day you're going to tell me how you seem to know everything about everyone," I said, cradling my phone between my shoulder and ear while I shoved paperwork back into a folder.

Reed chuckled. "Maybe. If you're good. But you better hurry, Rache. We don't want humans finding a wolf using a gangbanger as a chew toy, now do we?"

No, we definitely do not. I hung up and grabbed my jacket off the back of my chair, vaguely waving to my fellow agents telling me to enjoy my vacation. Man, what must it be like to actually get a day off?

~

FIVE POINTS WAS the closest thing Denver had to a rough neighborhood. Most of the city's violent crime occurred here, gangs and drugs and murder among century-old houses and abandoned businesses. The city poured money into revitalizing the area to varying degrees of success. It might've helped if they knew that supernatural forces were at work to keep Five Points shady and decrepit. Things that preferred the dark didn't like shiny new apartment buildings and rustic French restaurants.

If the Council was the magic police, then the Shadowland was the other side of that coin. It sounds much more organized than what it is, which is really the supernatural crime world. Every city has one, and Shadowland was Denver's, crouching like a fat spider with Five Points swallowed in its web. The details might vary a bit, but gangs and drugs and murder weren't restricted to humans. Pretty much any sentient being is capable of being a dickbag.

It didn't surprise me that the weres were here. I knew they'd be on a rampage after Jeff's death, and starting with the scum of our world was the most logical place. Vanilla humans didn't go up against weres and live.

I navigated streets scarred with so many potholes it was almost like the road wasn't paved at all. Little blooms of gentrification in the form of coffee shops and renovated mansions broke up the vista of peeling wood and boarded windows. Three white dudes wearing baggy jeans and backwards baseball caps leered at me from a battered porch as I turned a corner, but I paid them no mind. I headed to Welton Street, the very heart of Shadowland.

I suppose I could've called Ethan, or someone else in the Council, but Elena was so pissed, I was afraid shoving more witches at her was just going to make the situation worse. At least the pack knew me, and knew I was busting my ass on this case. My plan consisted of finding the enraged werewolves, somehow talking them down without using magic, and then finding my brother. How exactly I was going to do all that was a bit hazy, but I'd always been good at improvising.

Part of my brain screamed that I shouldn't be here, that this wasn't my problem and I should be focusing on Danny, but until I got that damned spelled iron off, I didn't know what else to do. Saving the city from psycho werewolves seemed a noble cause.

Of course, another part of my brain, one that sounded like Victor, wondered if this wasn't part of my corruption. I was losing the ability to prioritize. I craved violence. Anger and vengeance and lust for power ruled me. I rubbed at my wrist, beneath the spelled iron bracelet that seemed cold no matter how long I wore it. Could I really judge what was noble anymore?

Stow it, Rachel. Self-doubt will only get you killed in this game. I parked my Jeep and climbed out, intending to ask around until I located my errant weres. Turned out, I didn't have to.

Snarls, grunts, and the unmistakable meaty sound of flesh hitting flesh echoed from a nearby alley. I sprinted down Welton, turning into a brick alcove marred with graffiti and overflowing Dumpsters.

Two weres in a half-changed state faced off with a dude and a chick. Saliva dripped from the weres' mutated mouths, elongated and full of teeth that looked more like fangs. A mane of fur rippled down their necks, disappearing under torn and dirty shirts. Their hands were too big and ended in razor-sharp claws.

The dude and the chick looked completely normal except for two things. One, they weren't the least bit scared by facing werewolves. Wary, definitely, but not scared. Two, their eyes rippled with a metallic shine, the way a cat's eyes light up in the dark.

Shapeshifters.

The girl held a knife and bled from a cut above her eye. The dude gripped an aluminum baseball bat, an ugly, purple bruise forming on his cheek. Blood stained his shirt—whose, I didn't know.

"Back the fuck off," the girl snarled.

"You know something. That smell, the predator, you reek of it," one of the weres growled back. The words came out mangled by jaws that were meant for breaking bones, not talking.

"Hey!" I shouted, then did perhaps the dumbest thing I've ever done in a lifetime of dumb decisions. I ran right into the middle of four of them. "Knock it off!"

The were who spoke eyed me. "Leave, Rachel."

I tried to see past the lupine features and thought I recognized him. I took a chance. "Will, c'mon. You're in broad fucking daylight, man. This isn't smart."

"Leave!" he roared. "You witches don't care. Our pack-mate is dead and you don't care."

"I do care. I'm close to finding him, Will, and I will get justice for Jeff. But I can't have you wolfing out in the middle of the goddamn city."

"These vermin smell like that creature," he spat, jabbing a

clawed finger at the shifters. I glanced at them. "Magic, twisted and wrong."

"Go to hell, mutt," the male shifter said. "We told you, we don't know anything about your fucking boyfriend."

"He was our packmate," Will growled and lunged forward. I intercepted him, thus proving that my legacy of making dumb frigging decisions was well intact.

Will collided with me, two hundred pounds of supernatural strength and rage, and swiped at the shifter. A snarl of pain told me he'd found his mark. Will knocked me backward into the shifter girl, who shoved me forward into the other were, and for a moment I thought I might die in stabbing-bludgeoning-werewolf-mauling incident. I managed to keep my feet and nailed the were with my shoulder, driving him back a couple inches. Before another spat could break out, I snatched my gun from its holster and leveled it at each of them in turn.

"I said, knock it off." I was panting, my heart hammering. I didn't have magic. If they got the bright idea to team up and kill me, there really wasn't much I could do about it. "Look, this dude's an asshole and he shouldn't have said that, but shifters didn't kill Jeff. It's a demon and a corrupt witch. And if you would calm the fuck down, I could go back to hunting them."

The weres froze, their eyes on my gun. "You wouldn't," Will said.

"I won't kill you, sure. But I will definitely pop you in the kneecap and drag you down to Council holding." I looked at the shifters. "Clear out of here. And stop dealing with fucking demons or I'm coming after you next."

The chick smirked and the dude gave a little wave of his baseball bat. "Don't know what you're talking about, deputy. We're law-abiding citizens," he said. They glared at the weres as they stalked out of the alley. I watched them while keeping my gun trained on the wolves, their yellow eyes flicking between the weapon and my face.

"Now. Shift back to people-form before someone sees you," I said.

"You give a lot of orders for someone here alone," Will said. He stepped back a half foot and jerked his head at his companion. I let out a breath I didn't know I was holding when bones snapped and skin slurped back into place, leaving two human-looking but still pissed off guys in front of me.

I holstered my Sig. "Thanks. Tell Elena I've got the guy, I just have to find him."

Will gave me a level look. "How do we know you're not lying?"

My face screwed up in confusion. "Why the hell would I lie?"

"Because," he said, invading my space. I held my ground, not dropping my gaze, and thought big, scary, intimidating thoughts. "You have the stench of those hunters all over you."

My eyes widened. Shit, I'd forgotten about that. Sean and Luke broke into Jeff's house. It was amazing the pack hadn't killed them already.

"They're helping me," I said. "I'm not lying. I got no reason to—this lunatic has my brother."

Will stared at me for a long moment, then finally turned away. "You better hope for your sake that you keep your promise."

The wolves prowled out of the alley and I sagged back against the brick wall, running a hand through my hair. Jesus Christ, that was close. If the Council brought in a Genesis team, I wondered if they'd notify Elena of the outcome or if they'd just consider it case closed and move on. How the hell did I end up the one trying to negotiate inter-supernatural-nation diplomacy?

Intuition prickled the hairs on my neck and I sprang forward, facing the mouth of the alley with my gun drawn.

A man with a frigging Yosemite Sam mustache strolled toward me. He wasn't concerned at all by the Sig pointing at him. "I knew you were never going to play ball."

"Masterson, Jesus," I spat. "Sneaking up on me like that is a bad fucking idea."

"I wouldn't have to if you were where you were supposed to be." He gave me a smug look, his bushy mustache twitching with a smirk. "I knew you'd bail. So I followed you."

"Well, thanks for the help, pal." I pushed passed him and he caught my arm.

"You know who's behind this. You need to tell me." He squeezed my arm tighter than was necessary and I looked up into his greedy little eyes.

"Demon. Been blocking our tracking spells. Don't know where he or Danny is. Good luck and Godspeed," I drawled. My body tensed the smallest amount, a spring coiling for action.

"Who's the corrupt witch?"

"Read the frigging case file." I ripped out of his hold and turned away. Anger roiled in my chest. My brother was in danger and the Council had handed the case over to this idiot masquerading as a deputy.

"You dumb bitch. You think you can get away with this because your daddy's a captain?" Masterson called, contempt bubbling from his voice. "Victor told me about your scan. We all knew it was going to happen sooner or later."

I froze, my teeth grinding so hard together that my jaw hurt. "Shut up."

"You know, I've watched you throw the goodwill of the Council in our faces for years," he said, and sauntered closer to me. "No one gets as much leniency as you. And why? What makes you so goddamned special, huh?"

I turned to look him dead in the eye. "Nothing. Except I

help people, instead of cheating on my wife and always being a day late and a couple million brain cells short."

He drew even with me, puffed up his lumpy shoulders. "Watch your mouth. You're nothing, and it's about time Victor saw it too. I hope I'm the one that gets to take you down."

A cold, vicious smile spread across my face. "Not even on your best day. Now go on, go see if you can pull your head out of your ass and find the demon."

"You're a real fucking cunt, you know that? What do you know? You're corrupted. Won't be too long before you're one of the Cursed."

Masterson was good enough to not die at the hands of some corrupt witch, but I was twenty years younger and in much better shape. He never saw the punch coming. My fist collided with his nose in a spurt of warm blood and a crunch of bone. He bellowed and staggered backward, eyes full of malevolence as he glared at me. I couldn't feel him drawing magic, not cut off the way I was, but I figured he would. Elemental witches never had to worry about their power supply and relied on their magic a lot more than I did.

He snapped his wrist and an unnatural wind slammed me back against the wall. Without my magical senses, the spell felt like an invisible dump truck crashing into me. Masterson closed the distance and backhanded me. My cheek burned and I tasted blood, but he was proving my point that he was a functioning moron—he should've stayed at range.

I ducked under his arm and darted around behind him, then dropped down to sweep out my leg. I caught him behind the knee. He crumpled to the ground and lashed out at me with a ham-handed punch as he fell, which I evaded almost effortlessly. I kicked him once in the ribs before straddling his chest, landing blow after blow on his doughy face. It was days of fear and powerlessness, years of anger and hurt, a lifetime of distrust boiling over. Right now, Masterson was everything

I hated about the Council, about myself, and I was just fucking done with all of it.

He gurgled pathetically and I stopped, one hand fisting his shirt and the other one drawn back behind my head. Blood slicked his face, matted his mustache, and his eyes were red and swollen.

"Oh my God," I breathed. Sick, hot threads knotted in my stomach. I hadn't meant to do this. "Masterson?"

He lie there, limp, sucking in choked little gasps. I pressed shaking fingers to his throat. Finding a pulse was only a mild relief. I'd attacked a fellow deputy. Coupled with the taint on my soul, I was well and truly fucked this time.

EIGHTEEN

I've faced down some pretty scary shit, but in that moment, I was a huge freaking coward. I dropped Masterson off at the nearest hospital, just leaving him in the waiting room of the ER, his head lolling and face turning a smear of purple and black. The moment he came to and told the Council what I'd done, the jig was up. I needed to stay off the radar until then.

My hands shook as I dug out my phone. I didn't even know why, but I tapped Sean's name.

"What's wrong?" he said as soon as I spoke, as if he could hear it in my voice. I stared down at my hand, knuckles cut and Masterson's dried blood caking my skin.

"I, um--I fucked up, Sean. In a big way. I don't know what to do. I can't go home." I was so stupid. Beating down Masterson just made me look like I had something to hide. All my clever plans for secretly defying the Council, for finding my brother--I'd blown them up in fit of rage.

"Come here," he said.

"No, I can't, you'll get in trouble too."

"Rachel," he said, a bit gentler. "Come here."

Twenty minutes later, I followed Sean's directions and

parked in a lot behind Holy Angels Catholic church, a sprawling mass of crenellations and flying buttresses and stained glass, and was totally confused. Sean was leaning against a backdoor to the church, legs crossed at the ankles and hands in his pockets.

"Sean, I'm really not in the mood for prayer," I said, gingerly climbing out of my Jeep. My hands and torso hurt, but more than that, I was just about to fall to pieces.

"I'm not trying to save your soul. I live here." He opened the door and I stared at him, frowning.

"What do you mean you live here?"

"I mean I sleep here, and my belongings are here, and I live here. There are apartments for church staff."

"Thought you worked for the FBI?" I asked as I walked past him into the church. It was cool inside and smelled like wood polish and incense.

"I do. I also work part-time at Hammond's Garage, and I do security for The Crimson Room downtown." He stepped in front of me and led me down a long hallway to a set of stairs.

"Jack of all trades. So what, the rent is cheap?" My utter bafflement over his home temporarily distracted me from the shitstorm I was in, and I looked around as we climbed the stairs. I didn't see any Jesus pictures or anything. In fact, it looked like a lot of Denver apartment buildings: brick and wood and colored by history.

"It's a long story." Sean opened a door and let me into a small studio apartment. Everything was precisely organized. Military discipline. I bet if I looked in his closet, his clothes would be color-coded.

Sean navigated me to a worn but comfortable couch and immediately examined me.

"I'm fine," I mumbled. Physically, anyway. I sank down onto the couch and buried my face in my hands while he filled a bowl with water and fetched a washcloth.

"What happened?" he asked, handing me the washcloth. I plunged it into the cool water and began scrubbing my hands. The pristine white cotton turned pink with Masterson's blood.

"Um, I, um, I sort of beat another witch unconscious. Where's Luke?"

Sean dragged a chair over to perch in front of me. "Apartment next door. Why'd you beat her?"

"Him." My hands were as clean as they were going to get and I wrung out the cloth as best I could before pressing it against my face. How the hell did I explain this without explaining the Council? I hid behind the washcloth for several minutes, letting the damp coolness soothe my stinging cheek and swollen lip. What if I did tell Sean? I was already screwed. What was the point of hiding it anymore?

Because if the Council found out he knew, they'd kill him. Secrecy was more important than one measly hunter's life.

I pulled the washcloth away and folded it over the edge of the bowl. Something wretched and nauseating twisted through me. I wondered if it was the corruption. I'd always had a temper, but what I'd done with Masterson went beyond that.

"I lost control," I said. "He was baiting me and I just--lost control."

"It happens, Rache. Been in a few fights myself."

"No, you don't get it. Not like this. I'm--something's wrong with me, Sean. Seriously wrong. I thought I had a handle on it, thought I could control it, but now " I shook my head. I shouldn't be here. Masterson was right. I wasn't special, wasn't important. I was just a junior deputy witch with an attitude problem. The corruption, this case, it was all eleven different kinds of fucked up.

I abruptly stood. "I've got to go."

"What?" He followed me as I almost ran toward the door, edging in front to block my retreat.

"Leave me alone, Sean. For your own good." I tried to squeeze past him but he leaned against the door and wedged it hopelessly shut.

"Hey, listen. It'll be alright." His eyes were soft and warm and they intensified my need to flee.

For some reason, that just pissed me off more. "Shut up! You don't know that!"

"Talk to me. Tell me what happened."

"Why do you care?" I snapped.

"What'd that witch say to you?"

"Just get away from me." I turned my back and stalked toward the window. The room felt too small, too vacant of air. Sean followed me. He grasped my arm, pulled me around to face him. I shoved him in the chest, yanking against his grip like a wild animal. I didn't want his fucking pity. I didn't want his concern or his questions. I didn't want to lose whatever fragile trust we'd built.

"I'm not going anywhere, sweetheart."

"You're a stubborn ass."

"Tell me what happened."

"I'm losing my shit, that's what happened." A bitter laugh escaped my throat. "You were right, Sean. I'm not human. I'm a monster waiting to happen."

"Rache, you're not. I was an asshole for what I said. And I was wrong." I stopped struggling for a minute and his grip loosened, becoming something kind. "What happened?"

"Victor said... it's supposed to be white..." I trailed off as panic seized me. I bolted for the door, but Sean grabbed me around the waist. I ripped free, stumbling back against the dresser.

"Rachel, c'mon. Just talk to me. I'm here." His voice was soft, caring. He tried to touch me and I exploded. I couldn't handle all this--my brother in danger, a psychotic bastard torturing people relying on me to save them, the doubt that threatened to strangle me, the Council, the conflict I felt about Sean.

"You're not a monster," he said. "I kill monsters. I don't invite them over half-crazy and try to talk sense to them."

"I don't belong anywhere," I whispered, my eyes still closed. I didn't want to look at him. "Why are you here? I'm a witch."

"Yeah, you're a witch. But you're also a good person." His leaned against me in an unsettlingly comfortable way and his voice, still rough and low, soothed me like a balm. "I've done a lot of terrible things in my life and I'm kind of a dick. But you... you care about those people. I saw it. And you saved me, knowing I might kill you. That kind of person is worth something."

I scoured his eyes for the truth, not wanting to fall into this trap again. Everything about him was warm and genuine, and that was almost worse than the cold bite of dishonesty. I could see the flecks of gold in his irises. The asshole had freckles across his nose and cheeks.

He folded me into a hug and I didn't resist. It was just like back at my cabin, when he'd drawn me in and let me cry. He didn't tell me to shape up. Didn't chastise me. Didn't call me hellbound, Cursed, broken.

"I don't know how to handle this," I mumbled, pulling back and wiping at my face.

Sean frowned. "Handle what?"

I shrugged and looked up at the ceiling. "I'm just... I'm so strung out right now. I feel like I'm going to fly apart. I don't know what to think, what to do. And it's just--it's too easy to think this is actually something between us."

He brushed the hair out of my face and tilted his head. "Rache, I know I gave you a hard time, but I'm not playing games with you. Do you know why I told you to come here?" I shook my head, and he continued, "'Cause you sounded real messed up and like you needed somewhere safe. I don't know what's going on with you. I don't know why you beat that dude. But I've been in war. I know what the good guys look like. And I know what it looks like when someone's lost."

"But... why? I'm a mess, Sean. And I'm dragging you into an even bigger mess. I just don't understand why you're helping me, much less why you care."

He chuckled and cupped my cheek. His fingers were rough, calloused--the mark of a man who worked with those hands--but also gentle. "For one, you don't take my crap. It's refreshing. For two, you're fierce. I mean, you could stand toe-to-toe with any Ranger. You don't give up. You're just someone I want to know. Is it so hard to believe that I actually like you?"

"Kind of, yeah." A half-starved smile lifted my mouth. "You've known me for, like, three days. This isn't some stupid Disney movie."

"And I'm not asking you for happily ever after. Intense combat--you learn stuff about people. More than you do over months of having coffee."

"Don't charm me with your Army logic."

"There she is," he said, smiling. "Feeling better?"

I leaned against him and sighed. It'd been years since I could let my guard down like this. I barely knew him, but maybe he was right. He'd put his life on the line to help me save my brother. He'd patched me up and taken care of me when it would've been easy to walk out. He did it all without asking for anything in return. Ryan had never loved me like I loved him. I think I'd always known that. He'd made me earn his affection. And here was Sean, giving it freely. Watching out for me when I couldn't watch out for myself.

I lifted my head and nuzzled against his cheek, our lips agonizingly close but not yet touching. It was stupid and bad timing and a regret in the making, but my head was a mess and I just wanted something good. Everything today was so fucked up, and that smell of gun oil and soap drifted over me, and suddenly I didn't care how bad of an idea it was to kiss him. Maybe it was the best bad idea I'd ever had.

My mouth crashed against his the way worlds collide. He tasted like candy and spearmint. His hand slid into my hair and I whimpered a little. When he'd kissed me at my parents' house, I'd thought he was restraining himself, like I was a frightened rabbit he didn't want to scare away. Now, though, that restraint broke. Sean fell upon me like a man dying of thirst, teeth and lips moving over my neck, hot breath against flushed skin.

Something broke in me, too. All the fear I'd been living under the last week evaporated, and the fear I'd carried inside of me for as long as I could remember quieted under his touch. It was like each brush of his fingers, each press of his mouth was trying to tell me that I was safe. I didn't know if I believed it, but I wanted to.

He'd stayed to help me save my brother. He'd patched me up and watched over me, like some kind of tireless guardian. He'd overridden his own prejudices to trust me. Maybe it was time I do the same.

Sean backed up, pulling me with him and guiding me toward the bed. My knees hit the edge and in the next moment I was on my back. "You sure?" he mumbled between kisses.

"Yes." I loved that he asked. I loved that I knew he'd back off if I said no.

Sean groaned and slipped a hand under my shirt, palm rubbing over stomach. "You don't like something, you tell me," he said, voice low and hoarse.

"Okay," I said, smiling and running my fingers through his hair.

He looked up as he laid heated kisses over my belly. I watched him methodically work his way up, pushing my shirt over my head. His hand slid beneath me, undoing the clasp on my bra with deft movements. He traced the ugly, puckered scar on my left ribcage, the one Ryan had given me, and those summer-grass eyes gave me a soft look. I shrugged a shoulder and heat flooded my cheeks.

Sean gingerly kissed the scar. He touched me in ways that made me understand what intimate meant. It wasn't about flesh and quivering and the flood of heat--although, don't get me wrong, I definitely enjoyed that too. It was being with someone who saw me.

His hands roamed up my sides, my arms, to find my own hands and twine his fingers with mine. My head fell back, eyes closed, and I sucked in a ragged gasp when he flicked his tongue over my nipple.

He kissed over the creamy swell of my breast, one hand working at the button on my jeans. I tugged at his shirt, and he broke away just long enough to pull it off. Flushed skin met flushed skin, and he mouthed at my neck with a primal need. My fingers dug into the broad expanse of his back, and when he murmured my name, rough fingers slipping into my panties, I let out a shameless moan. His hardness pressed against my thigh and he stroked my damp folds as if determined to make me moan like that again. I didn't let him down.

Sean rocked back on his knees, that sniper-stare pinning me in place as he pulled off my jeans and panties. I sat up and kissed him, our tongues rolling together, as I unfastened his belt. Sean pushed his jeans off, digging a condom out of a pocket before throwing them aside.

"Always prepared, huh?" I breathed, the corner of my lips lifting in a half smile.

"Army makes you that way." He flashed me a boyish grin. I lay back on the bed and he kissed his way up my chest and neck to my mouth. His lips covered mine when he slid into me. I whimpered again.

"Is your back okay?" he whispered.

"Yeah," I murmured. My hips rolled against his and I

wrapped my arms around him, dragging my fingers along his back. Sean wound his fingers in my hair and moved against me in a slow, steady rhythm.

"You're so beautiful." He sounded so real then, as if a weight had been lifted from him. He turned my face to his and kissed me hard, all tongue and teeth. I bucked and my back arched, like my body was crying out for more, *moremoremore*. His rhythm quickened, his urgency matching my own. I ran my fingers through his hair and he nipped at my neck again. Gun oil and soap surrounded me, mingling with my perfume and the smell of blood and grime.

We kissed again as he thrust harder, and little electric sparks that had nothing to do with magic swarmed over my skin. Heat coiled, tight and squirming in my belly, and I broke away from the kiss. The heat erupted and I cried out as waves of pleasure washed over me. Sean groaned and his body tensed, labored breathing in my ear. He groaned again and thrust deeply as his climax crested and waned. He collapsed against me, both of us panting, sweaty messes.

He rolled to the side and tugged me against him. We lay in silence for a long time, clinging to each other, his heartbeat rumbling against my ear as I traced idle designs on his chest.

"Let's get this sorted, get your brother back, and then I'm going to take you out. Be a gentleman. So you don't wig out again." I could hear the smile in his voice.

"I didn't wig," I grumbled.

"You completely wigged. But that's alright. Being all distressed isn't exactly the best time to be getting down."

"What did we just do, then?"

"That? That was sexual healing."

I laughed and playfully shoved him, then suddenly sobered. "Oh my God," I breathed. "We just had sex in a church."

Now it was Sean's turn to laugh. "The apartments aren't holy ground. We're safe. Getting a little worried?"

"No. It just seemed... I don't know, rude."

He laughed again and held me tight against him. Malevolent thoughts crowded at the corners of my mind but I shoved them back. Sean was the one good thing to come out of this mess. I wasn't going to let my bullshit issues ruin that.

A small metal charm hung on a cord around his neck. It was a horse, with the letter J engraved on it. "Talisman?" I asked, running my fingers over it.

"Something like that. It was my sister's."

"I'm sorry about what happened to her."

"Thanks. She--she loved horses. We had a neighbor with a couple and she'd be over there every day after school, working in the barn. What kind of twelve-year-old voluntarily works in a barn?" He was smiling, but his eyes were sad. "I just felt like I failed. My parents got divorced a few years before that and my mom was in Nevada with some deadbeat. I was the oldest. I should have taken care of her."

"It wasn't your fault, Sean."

"I know. But it still feels like it. She was a big reason I joined the Army, you know. I just thought--Luke told you about the hunter who helped us, Elliot. Knowing what happened to Julia didn't make it easier. It made it worse. The world didn't make sense, and I thought, I've got to get away from this. I couldn't protect Julia, but maybe I could protect other people."

"Is that why you became a hunter?" I asked. "To protect people?"

"Sort of. Figured I got this knowledge, might as well use it to make up for some stuff."

"What do you have to make up for?"

Sean grimaced and hugged me a little tighter. "I left my family, Rachel. They were falling apart and I just left. Luke, he was so angry. At the vamp, at me, at the world. He got caught up in the freaking Network because he was pissed off and lost and just wanted to keep anyone else's family being destroyed. And there I was, ten thousand miles away becoming some stupid war hero." The words were bitter and muscles worked along his jaw.

I didn't know what to say. I couldn't imagine what that had been like--for either of them. My hand slid over his shoulder, down to a tattoo encircling his bicep. "You get that in the Army, too?"

"Nah. Demon protection symbols. Keeps you hidden from them, usually, and stops them from possessing you."

"You're just full of surprises. Where'd you learn that?"

"The Internet."

"Does sex up your sarcasm?"

"Just trying to get on your level, sugar. Anyway, you should think about something like that, what with demons being hot for you. Add it to your chicken scratch."

"It's not chicken scratch, it's runes. Sigil magic for my shield." The blood-red eucalyptus blossoms and a tattered banner with three runes wrapped around my shoulder was the first magical tattoo I got.

"That must come in handy."

"It's saved my ass more than once. Only works against spells, though. Can't stop bullets."

He traced a seven-pointed star just below my collarbone, inked in a dark blue and set against a ring of fire. "What about this one?"

"That's my personal ward. Protects me against mind magic and other nasty shit."

"And this one?" His hand slid down my left arm, over a snowcapped mountain scene framed by a swirl of yellow aspen leaves.

"I just thought that was pretty."

He chuckled. I closed my eyes and sighed. A funny thing about pain: you never truly realize how much it's sucking out of you until it's gone. You feel the ache and the burn, but pain is exhausting on a psychological level. You carry around enough pain and fear and tension and your body ends up like the losing car at a monster truck rally. It amazed me how relaxed I was lying next to Sean. I felt like I could actually sleep.

"Who's Victor?" he asked a long while later.

"Hmm?" I blinked open drowsy eyes.

"Victor. Earlier you said something about some dude named Victor and something being white."

"He's one of the people I work for." My hand curled into a fist and I tried to cling to that peaceful state.

"He your commander?"

"Sean... I can't talk about it. I'm sorry." I sighed and blinked rapidly.

"Rache, you need to. I know what set you off was more than just a fight."

I mulled it over for a few minutes. "He's the boss of all us witches that deal with evil shit. He's known me a long time and he makes like he's watching out for me, but he's always made me feel like... like he wants to be the one to slip the noose over my head." I thought back to my oath. Victor had questioned me about why I delayed in joining the Council, why I'd gotten involved with a hunter, if I could live up to the responsibility of a deputy. He'd couched it all in concerned language, but his eyes had never lost that predatory gleam. It had all been very realpolitik but it had left me feeling cold. "What it boils down to is they think I'm dangerous, and I think Victor's just been waiting for me to go off the edge. A bomb about to go off."

"Why?" He frowned down at me.

"Because I used too much magic. The fight with the *bakemono*, breaking that hex on you... it was a lot." Fight with Masterson aside, I didn't feel evil. The soul analysis showed the early stages of corruption. Maybe it was too soon to tell. Maybe it was like that story about the frog in boiling water and I just didn't realize how much trouble I was actually in. I thought about what Victor said. Ley witches were at higher risk. I'd known that, but I'd never known why.

"I don't get it. Isn't that a good thing that you can kick ass and take names?"

"Kind of. It's a double-edged sword." I craned my neck to look at him. "You know the saying 'power corrupts'? Well, for witches it's not just a saying. The more magic we use, it changes us. Too much power and sooner or later you become a killer. It's what happens to deal witches--demon gives them power, they go off the rails."

"But... you're fine." The creases in his face deepened and he looked so perplexed that I laughed.

"That's what I keep saying. But the test says different." I held out my right wrist. "*Ostende veritatem*." Once again, the brand surfaced. For half a heartbeat, I hoped that maybe it would flare white. It didn't.

"They branded you," Sean said.

"You know about soul brands?" I asked, surprised. As far as I knew only witches used them--like this, anyway. Demons used a type of brand to mark their contracts. I'd seen it on perps we managed to bring in alive.

"I'm smarter than I look," Sean said, the corner of his mouth pulling into a grin. "So you're bound to someone? That's kind of fucked up."

"Well, not exactly. It's like..." Goddammit, how did I explain this without going into Council crap? "It's like your Ranger tattoo, except magic. It says I'm a kind of cop, and works like a witch Geiger counter. See how it's grey?" Anxiety twisted my stomach as I pointed at the brand. "It's supposed to be white. The more corrupted my soul is, the darker it gets."

"Who told you all that?" He spat the question as if I'd been fed a lie.

"It's sort of taught to us in basic training." Maybe I could just keep using these military metaphors. Sean accepted them and it was keeping me from exposing too much.

"Well, it's bullshit. You're not corrupted, and you're sure as hell not evil." The certainty in his voice took me aback and I shifted to face him.

"How do you know?"

"I just do." I gave him a look that said I wasn't buying it and for a moment, he hesitated. I caught the briefest flash of conflict, as if he was arguing with himself about something, and then his expression smoothed into a smirk. "Told you I'm smarter than I look."

He was hiding something, but my pot was in no position to criticize his kettle. "Well, anyway, it's their opinion that matters and they think I'm about to go all Darth Rachel. They want me to sit it out while they go after Wilkes."

"And are you?" He gave me a skeptical look and I snorted.

"They're sending in the witch equivalent of SEAL Team Six. Terminate with extreme prejudice. They'll say that they'll try to get Danny and Marcus back, but..."

"You don't believe them."

"I think when you're trying to stop a terrorist that's about to nuke your city, it's easier to just bomb the hell out of his compound than worry about the collateral damage." I tilted my head. "Am I wrong, Mr. Be-All-You-Can-Be?"

"Not entirely."

I buried my face against his chest. I didn't want Sean to see how much this whole thing was seriously fucking with me. If I went after my brother, I risked not only Council punishment but also further corruption. If I didn't go, he wouldn't survive the Genesis team attack. I knew how they operated. Their mission would be to stop the *bakemono* ritual at any cost, and Sean had just confirmed that the best way to do that was to level the place. Bury Wilkes with his victims. With the demon after me, it was far safer to just stay put, like

Victor told me. Let the Council hide me away. But would they, after what I'd done?

Memories played in my mind like a video tape--Danny reading to me when I had nightmares, playing games with me in the woods behind our house, tickling me, wrestling with me, making me laugh, holding me when I cried.

I saw his face as he used the last of his energy to save me from Finn. The love and devotion there as he shoved me toward Sean, his only concern getting me out alive. Tears rolled down my cheeks. What the hell was I supposed to do? Just let him die?

Danny would never give up on me. My big brother would tear apart the city with his bare hands to protect me. I could almost hear him now, telling me it was alright, that I shouldn't put myself in danger for him. That I should let the Council handle it, because it was the best way to keep me safe. It was easy to listen to that voice. I could go back to my parents' house, turn myself over to Victor, stand down. Put the responsibility on someone else. Save myself the pain and heartache and danger. It was very tempting, and also very cowardly.

I had no idea how I was supposed to save Danny. I didn't know where Wilkes was or how to find him. Even with Sean and Luke, Finn and one *bakemono* alone had kicked our asses. Factor in multiple shadow beasts and Wilkes slinging power around, we didn't have a prayer. I was a junior fucking deputy who'd already bailed on her family once and had five years of experience. I had no business going up against demons and crazy shadow monsters and lunatic deal witches with vendettas. Best I could hope for in that situation was to end up dead. The alternative was winding up in the demon's hands.

Sean hugged me tighter against him and I realized I was openly crying. "You must think I'm such a fucking basket case," I said shakily.

"I think you're hurt and exhausted and worried about your brother. I've been there. I was a wreck too."

"Did you cry?" I asked, looking up at him and roughly wiping at my eyes.

"Nah. Army beats the crying out of you." He smirked and I gave a watery laugh. "You know, Rangers excel at rescue missions. One of the things we do best."

"You saying I should defy orders?"

"I'm saying we should go in, get your brother and the other hostages, get out and let your spec-ops folks do their thing. We fail, they still nail Wilkes."

I chewed on that for a minute. It seemed a hell of a lot better than hiding in some hole. Danny would hate it, but it was my job to be the pain-in-the-ass little sister. No matter the risk, no matter the cost, I couldn't just leave him. He wouldn't leave me.

"First we have to find him," I said.

"No, first you sleep. Running on fumes is a good way to get yourself killed. Then you do your woogie-woo-whatever and Luke and me will see what we can do to help."

I smiled. We had a plan. I had back up. Sean was not only a hunter, but a freaking Army Ranger. That was a pretty damn good thing to have on your side. We could do this—I just had to stop wallowing in fucking self-pity and be smart about it. I took a deep breath, shoving panic and fear back into the lead-lined box in my head.

"You really worried that you're going evil?" he asked, backtracking to our earlier conversation.

"I don't know. I don't feel different, but you didn't see me with Masterson. I just couldn't stop. I was so angry. And I reveled in it," I said darkly. It wasn't just the rage and the loss of control. It was that I enjoyed feeling powerful. I enjoyed knowing that Masterson was at my mercy. It was an ugly side of me I tried to pretend didn't exist, one that I couldn't blame on the corruption. It'd always been there. The more my soul changed, the less I could control it.

"Look, Rache, people don't live in a world of good or evil. We're always a little of both. Maybe you got some bad parts to you, but so do I. So does everyone. At the end of the day, it's how you manage those bad parts that count. Trust me--it's my job to find true evil, and I'm good at it. You're not on the list."

NINETEEN

Late morning light danced across the carpet. I woke to the soft brush of lips against my cheek and smiled.

"What time is it?" I mumbled.

"Almost nine. I'd let you sleep longer, but Luke's on his way over with breakfast." Sean smiled down at me, his hair dark with moisture. I stretched, yawned, and bounded into the shower. Maybe he'd been right--all I needed was some sleep. For the first time in days, I totally felt like I could rock this bitch.

Luke showed up just as I was pulling on one of Sean's shirts. It was too big, but it wasn't covered in blood, which I thought was a fair trade-off. He sat a paper bag and a drink carrier down on Sean's desk. "Hey Rache," he said smugly.

"Oh shut up." I knotted the t-shirt on one side to keep myself from swimming in it. Luke dug a silvery package out of the bag and passed it to me, and I took a heavenly bite of a green chili breakfast burrito.

The brothers made sporadic comments while we ate, but I was deep in thought. Talking to Sean the night before made me replay Victor's comments. He said ley magic was the strongest thing out there. I couldn't break that demon's ward because I was only pulling a fraction of the line when I used a tracking spell, but if there was a way to reverse the equation, put the tracking spell inside the line, in theory the demon wouldn't stand a chance.

In theory.

The spelled iron bracelet rested cold and heavy on my wrist. I'd have to get rid of that thing if I was going to put my theory to the test.

"Hey Luke, you got that lock pick?" I asked, wadding up the burrito wrapper and tossing it into the trash bin.

"Yeah, in my room. Why, where're we breaking into?"

"Nowhere. I need this off." I extended my arm.

Sean frowned down at the bracelet. "What is that, anyway? I saw it earlier, but I was preoccupied."

Luke chuckled and I blushed, then said, "Spelled iron."

"The same thing the demon had your brother locked in—that stuff that cuts off magic?"

I nodded, my cheeks flaming. They couldn't know how embarrassing it was to be collared like this.

"Why are you wearing it?" Luke asked.

"Call it... probation." I tipped my head and grimaced. "That I'm about to break."

"Will that get you in trouble?" Sean's eyes flashed and a lopsided smile spread across my face.

"I'm already breaking curfew, might as well go for a joyride."

Luke retrieved his kit from his room, and with a little fiddling of the whosit and whatsit—I don't know what the tools are called, I use magic to pick locks—the bracelet fell onto the bed. Magic flooded back into me with such force that I staggered, and I rubbed at my now-free wrist as if the iron had wounded me. In a way, it had.

A jittery, almost feverish energy filled me. Not only was I about to try some seriously complicated magic, but I was pushing my boundaries with the Council further than I ever had. I was also taking a hell of a gamble that it wouldn't turn me full-on corrupted. If there was ever a reason to risk all that, though, it was my brother.

"So what's the plan?" Luke asked as I pulled out a stick of chalk from my backpack. I climbed on to the desk and started drawing sigils on the walls.

"First, I make this place invisible to all comers," I said, and then added with a grimace, "And myself." Just like my parents kept locks of Danny's and my hair, the Council kept the DNA of all its witches on file. Supposedly to protect us, but it was also a convenient targeting system if we stepped out of line. I could draw concealment wards on my body that should at least buy me some time, and add those same wards to Sean's apartment. That just meant I had to get to my cabin, collect my spell equipment, and turn all the magical locks before they got there first. Precious time ticked away until Masterson woke up, and at that point they'd know I'd gone rogue.

Yeah, should be super easy.

I scrawled every concealment charm I knew around the room until it looked like an artistic schizophrenia patient lived there. Then I went all *Memento* on my skin until I was covered with the same sigils.

"Well, guess we're cleaning this weekend," Sean said, looking around at my handiwork. "Now what?"

"Now I need you to give me a ride." I texted Ethan, telling him I was okay and asking him to make sure the coast was clear at my cabin. I needed to grab some supplies, both for the spell and for warding myself against the Council. Inside the room, I might be hidden, but once I stepped outside of those wards I was fair game.

I supposed I could have driven, but the Council knew my car, and I was afraid they'd know Sean's truck too. Discretion might be the better part of valor, but paranoia was the better part of not getting your ass set on fire. So I took the one way I knew the Council couldn't follow: ley lines.

The trunk of the main line cut right through Denver, following I-70 with little branches flowing off to the north and south. One of those branches would take me into the woods near my house. Besides the fact that I would miss traffic and get there within minutes, it also meant a silent, untraceable approach. I directed Sean to a stretch of unused warehouses near Stapleton. It was the closest thing to privacy in the middle of the city.

"So, um, this is going to look a little weird," I said, standing on the hot asphalt and twisting my fingers. "And by weird I mean I'm basically going to disappear into thin air."

"Come again?" Sean asked, raising an eyebrow.

"Remember how I said I could walk the lines? Well, this is how I do it. You guys just wait here, I shouldn't be long."

"Wait, shouldn't one of us go with you?"

I shook my head. "I can't take you with me." I could, technically, but I didn't want to risk it in case I got busted. "I'll be fine, promise."

Sean gave me a skeptical look and I flashed him my crazy smile. I turned around, exhaled a slow breath, and opened my second sight.

The palette of the city changed. Buildings were hulking, blocky voids, energetically empty. Trees exploded in a riot of greens and yellows, pulsing and throbbing like leafy disco balls. Little flickers of color dotted buildings, people going about their lives. I was tempted to look back at Sean and Luke, to spy on their true natures, but resisted. It's an intensely personal thing, looking at someone's aura.

A churning river of blue-white light cut through the middle of it all. I say river because there's no real word to describe it. Two-stories tall, crashing and churning and crackling like some physics-defying combination of water and electricity, its power drowning out everything else around it.

Rainbow colors chased across the surface. The whole thing was like a funhouse ride on acid.

I called up a circle around me, the thin, red-orange sphere glowing with the color of my own aura. Little streaks of grey chased through the fiery light, and I grimaced. The damage was already done. No use worrying about it now. I walked forward, the edge of my circle pushing into the line with a rubbery pressure, like holding a balloon under water. Another three steps and the line swallowed me completely.

I held my cabin firmly in my mind, piloting by feel as I hurtled across the city at unnatural speeds. The lines didn't care for such mundane things like distance and time, and I navigated them by focusing on my destination, making it real inside my mind. The bright, glowing colors swarmed around me, ever shifting, and a few minutes later something tugged at my gut. That was my cue.

I stepped to the side and popped out in the middle of a forest, sunlight filtering down through pine trees. Jogging over to a nearby trail, I made the quarter-mile trek to my cabin at an easy run. The place was deserted, as Ethan had said. So far so good.

I unlocked my door and dashed down to my workroom, shoving jars of herbs and my spare copper bowl into my backpack. The green spiral notebook where I kept my spell notes joined them, along with my hairbrush, some toiletries, some extra magazines for my Sig, and a change of clothes. One quick sweep around the place and I was sure I'd gotten what I needed.

I backed out of the door, my bag on my shoulder, and locked it. A swipe of my knife across my finger and I smeared blood on the sigil carved by the door. The blood dissolved under the pressure of magic, leaving nothing but the wood behind. My strongest wards hummed to life and sealed off my cabin. Just like mundane locks, they opened and closed from both sides.

All I had to do was hop the line back to Sean and Luke and we'd be set. The words *Well, that was easy* flashed through my brain, which should've been a warning that everything was about to go to hell.

I turned around to see two Council witches in their black tactical gear standing at the bottom of my steps.

"Rachel Collins, you're under arrest and hereby ordered to report for trial," one of them said. He was an Asian dude in sunglasses and barely looked old enough to be out of high school. He hadn't been on the job for long. Deputies never stayed that formal.

"On what charges?" I asked.

"Gross insubordination, assault of a Council deputy, and alleged illegal magic practice," the other witch said. I had trouble taking her seriously because she had her hair in frigging pigtails.

"Illegal magic? That's bullshit."

"You used forbidden magic to subdue a deputy."

I stared at them for a moment. What the hell were they talking about? Finally, it clicked into place.

"Oh Jesus Christ, Masterson's just pissed because he got his ass kicked by a girl half his age. There was no frigging forbidden magic," I snapped.

"Will you come peacefully?" Sunglasses asked.

I snorted. "They really didn't tell you who you were dealing with, did they?"

I was almost insulted. These deputies were fresh out of boot camp. I guess the Council wasn't expecting me to put up a fight.

Pigtails flinched first, a small twitch of her hand toward her gun. Poor kid. She wasn't used to the job, hesitated too much. It gave me the opening I needed.

I catapulted over the side of my small porch, drawing a veil around myself as I did. It didn't disguise sound, and if they popped open their second sight they'd find me, but I was banking on their inexperience.

Pigtails fired a shot that hit my wards on my cabin and ricocheted off, a deep reverberation like the muffled banging of a gong sending birds flying from the trees. I hit the ground and sprinted back toward the ley line.

Sunglasses was a little quicker on the uptake than his partner.

Do you know why people die in horror movies? Because they're always fucking looking behind them instead of where they're going. I'd been chased by real-world nightmares and wasn't that dumb, so I didn't see him actually cast the spell, but I felt the little prickle of magic a half-second before leaves stirred at my feet. An unnatural wind whipped across my veil, carrying the leaves with it, essentially creating a target with negative space where the leaves disappeared under my illusion.

Another gunshot and something hot sliced across my arm. I hissed and ducked behind a tree. Goddammit. Blood seeped between my fingers as I clutched the wound and silently cursed. I normally burned anything stained with my blood, but I just didn't have the time. I kept my hand clamped around the wound as best I could and scuffed my feet to obscure any stray drops. It'd have to do. I glanced around the tree. Sunglasses and Pigtails swept the area, guns raised and ready. The whirlwind of leaves probed the forest before them like magical sonar.

I had to keep moving. My only chance lay in reaching the line before they found me.

A few years ago, an outbreak of mountain pine beetle destroyed millions of acres of pine trees in Colorado. Bad for the national forests, but good for me in that moment—a towering lodgepole corpse careened drunkenly just ahead of the Dynamic Duo. They'd feel it the moment I tapped the line. I had to be fast, and accurate.

The ley energy rushed into me, hot and wild and tasting of the environment around me, and I flung out a hand toward the dead pine tree. A thread of ley magic shot outward, wrapping around the tree like a lasso. I jerked my hand toward my chest, commanding the energy back to me. A thunderous crack, some creaking like an old staircase, and then the tree toppled to the ground in a flurry of dirt and leaves and dried pine needles.

Sunglasses and Pigtails dove backward, dodging my impromptu lumberjack session.

My feet kicked up dust as I ran, the veil flickering under the strain of my injury. I may not have preternatural speed, but I'm a damn fast runner. I only needed minutes.

Which was about one hundred and ten seconds longer than it took to cast a spell.

Magic crawled along my skin again and the smell of chlorophyll invaded the air, and that was all the warning I got before something jerked my feet out from under me. I crashed like a puppet with the strings cut, taking a totally ungraceful mouthful of dirt. My injured arm screamed in protest and the impact launched a fresh wave of agony across my back.

Now I was acting like some idiot in a goddamn horror movie.

I thrashed, the bag on my back making it awkward to turn over. Something tight and unforgiving gripped my ankle and I looked down to see a vine that had no earthly business in a Colorado forest tying me down. More sprouted from the ground, twisting toward me like Attack of the Killer Goddamn Tomatoes. I looked up to see Pigtails leaning over the fallen tree trunk and rolling her wrist in an elegant little move. Fucking elemental witches.

I yanked on the line and threw my arm out. I couldn't summon fire the way they could, but that didn't mean I couldn't excite molecules in the air. They crashed into one another to create friction, and friction created heat.

Science, bitches. With magic.

The spell slammed into the tree trunk and shot up toward the sky, a blistering wall of exothermic energy so intense it distorted the air. It caught the edge of Pigtail's hand. She yelped and jerked back, and the vines slithering around me suddenly wilted and died. I ground my teeth, keeping the spell perfectly poised as a wall between them and me, and scrambled to my feet.

I swept my hand down in a semi-circle, transforming the energy as it soared back to me. I cut up trees, dirt, rock, probably a poor chipmunk or two. My superheated air crawled underneath the cooler air of the atmosphere, and the pressure differential did the rest to create a ley-magic fueled tornado in the middle of the woods. Debris flew everywhere, obscuring my vision. I dropped the spell and bolted. Without my magic fueling it, my dirt devil wouldn't survive more than a few seconds, but that was all I needed.

I sacrificed the veil for my shield and ran toward the ley line at top speed, zigzagging between trees to make myself harder to hit. A ball of fire smacked into a tree to my right. Everything slowed down, the world a surreal portrait of color. Adrenaline and shock.

I snapped open my second sight. The line surged just head, a brilliant ribbon of color in the dense crystalline forest. Another gunshot rang out, and I called up my circle.

I crashed into the line with little finesse, but I made it through without being shot again or set on fire. Fairy lights danced around me as I lay sprawled on my back, panting. I needed to focus or God only knew where the line would spit me out. My mind seized on Sean, on that abandoned parking lot, the buildings around it.

Several long minutes later, my gut clenched, and I was fairly certain it was the line and not me dry heaving. My entire arm was soaked with blood and my body ached from colliding with the forest floor, but I crawled out of the line. Hot asphalt greeted me, the world back in its normal colors. I collapsed and tried to catch my breath.

"Rachel!" Sean caught me under the arms and pulled me to my feet. "What the hell happened?"

"Got shot," I wheezed. Adrenaline faded, and with it came the surge of boiling pain that engulfed my arm.

"Yeah, I can see that. What I was asking was by who?" he demanded.

I shook my head. "I can't. Let's just get out of here."

Luke dug a towel that was more or less clean out of the toolbox bolted to the truck's bed and I used it to keep pressure on the wound until we got back to the church. The boys had stocked up since my tangle with the *bakemono*. They had an honest-to-God first aid kit now, complete with real anesthetic and disinfectant. They grow up so fast.

"You a magnet for dangerous shit," Sean said, stitching up my arm. "I'm going to have to start charging you."

"Do you have a frequent buyer program?"

He snorted. "Well, the good news is, it's mostly a really bad graze. Bullet passed through."

"Great," I grumbled. I didn't think the Council would spend hours prowling through woods just to find a couple drops of my blood, but it still made me nervous. Sean tied up the last suture and smoothed an extra-jumbo-size Band-Aid on top of it. I gathered up the bloody towel and gauze and took them along with my bag into the bathroom. Peeling off Sean's now-ruined shirt, I tossed it, the towel, and the gauze into the sink, then grabbed the extra shirt from my bag. With a tired sigh, I flipped on the ceiling fan, took out a small box of matches, and set the whole bundle of fabric on fire.

"What in the hell are you doing?" Sean asked. He came running to the doorway, Luke on his heels.

I gave them a level look. "Just call it a precaution."

"For what?" Luke asked, bewildered.

I weighed telling them the truth. It was about magic, not the Council. Should be safe. "You can use DNA to target a spell over long distance, or zero in on somebody with a tracking spell. It's better not to leave stuff like blood lying around."

Sean mulled that over. "Is that how Wilkes targeted me?"

"Probably. It's sort of like tracing a phone call using cell towers--you follow the signal to point of origin. Did you drink from a glass or anything?"

"Yeah. Dude gave me a glass of water."

"DNA," I said with a shrug. "He probably swabbed the glass, used that to target the hex."

Sean looked horrified. "Mother Mary. I'm never accepting anything from strangers again."

I chuckled and drowned my smoking embers in the sink. At the rate I was going, Sean was definitely going to lose his security deposit. We walked back out to the main room and sat down. I texted Ethan. If my plan to track my brother worked, I would need all the backup I could get to save him.

"So, what, you think the person who shot you was a witch?" Luke asked.

I mumbled something noncommittal.

"Rache?"

I looked up, distracted both by the texting and planning for the spell I needed to do. "What?"

"We were talking about who shot you," Luke said.

"Oh, right. I don't know. You just, you know, make enemies. I didn't exactly ask for a business card."

The brothers exchanged a look and Sean opened his mouth, but I was spared fabricating any more bullshit by my phone ringing. I didn't know the number and I frowned.

"Give me a sec," I said, stepping out into the hallway before answering the call.

"Rachel Collins?" A man's voice, rough and angry.

"Depends, who's this?"

"Detective Green, DPD."

I winced. I'd been so worried about magical cops, I forgot about the mundane ones. But if he were going to arrest me too, he wouldn't be calling. "It's not really a good time."

"Yeah, I fucking got that," he snapped. "Whatever you know, you need to tell me. Now. Forget whose case it is and all that bullshit about things you can't explain. I need to know."

Something in his voice sent tension thrumming through me. "What happened?"

"I got another goddamn body, that's what happened, and CBI's sent two new goddamn agents down here who clam up like the goddamn NSA when I mention your name. I don't know what kind of ship Denver runs, but this is a fucking nightmare."

My brain seized on only one word. "Male or female?"

"What?"

"The body!" My throat and lungs decided to go on strike and I had to call in a union negotiator just to get myself breathing again. Please don't be Danny, please don't be Danny.

"Female. Why?" He sounded even more suspicious, but I didn't care. I slumped back against the wall and rubbed my forehead.

"What makes you think it's the same guy?" He wouldn't be calling me otherwise.

"For the love of—are you allergic to giving a straight answer?"

I ground the heel of my palm against my eye. "Look, I'm—"

"Skip it. Right now you're keeping us from catching a serial killer. And I'm sick of it. I don't care what kind of higher-up protection you got, I'm going to file a grievance. Be lucky it's not a warrant."

I got the feeling he was about to hang up and I blurted out, "My brother's one of the victims. He's--he's missing. When you said body, I just... Who was she?"

He was silent for a long moment. "Her name was Yvette Burnham. Ran a local metaphysical store on Colfax, crystals and herbs and that kind of thing. That's where we found her."

I closed my eyes. I'd never met Yvette, but I knew her name. Like Kenny Godwin, she had been a low-level practitioner friendly with the Council. And now I'd gotten her killed.

"How do you know your brother's wrapped up in this?" Green asked.

I chewed on my lip. "Brad, you don't want to go down this hole. I promise you, you will not like what you find. My brother and the other vics--they all had something in common. I need to know how you connected this body."

Another pause. Sharp cop like that, he was evaluating my every word. "Mutilated like the others. Cause of death is more straightforward--gunshot to the head. But the body, it had a message. 'Tonight.' Now you tell me, why do I get the feeling that was meant for you?"

"Goddammit," I muttered, closing my eyes.

"You know who it is."

"Yes," I said quietly. "And I know how to find him."

"Great. Give me twenty minutes and I'll have SWAT wherever you want them."

"I can't. This is going to sound like a line from a frigging movie, but I honestly have to do this alone."

"What kind of police work is that?" He sounded thoroughly exasperated. "You want credit for the collar, I'll give it to you, I don't care."

"It's not about that."

"Then explain it to me."

"It's... complicated."

"You told me you were one of the good guys," he accused.

"I am."

"Give me one good reason to trust you."

"Because if I don't stop this guy, he's going to kill my brother. It ends tonight, Brad. I swear."

He sighed. "You have 'til morning to make the arrest. After that, I'm coming after him and you."

He hung up and I rocked my head back against the wall. The harsh fluorescent light hurt my eyes. At least I didn't have to worry about breaking my promise to Green, not technically anyway. Wilkes was going down one way or another.

TWENTY

Ethan arrived at Holy Angels a little while later, and the four of us sat in Sean's apartment while I explained my plan. No one liked it very much.

"This is stupid." Sean crossed his arms, giving me a look that said he thought I'd gone several flights over the cuckoo's nest.

"And dangerous. You don't even know if it's possible," Ethan said.

"Yeah, well, won't know until we try." I crossed my arms right back and gave all three of them a mulish look.

"Rachel, you're talking about holding yourself stable in a line, working a spell at the same time, assuming that you can pilot the line with your tracking spell, and then hoping that the concealment ward doesn't shut you down." Ethan shook his head. "There're so many unknowns in there, I don't even know where to start. Do you realize what could happen if the ward blocks you?"

I rubbed at my wrist, staring at the red marks I was leaving on my skin.

"What? What could happen to her?" Sean asked when I didn't answer. Ethan looked pointedly at me.

"If it blocks me, the line could dump me out anywhere," I mumbled.

"Best case scenario." Ethan gave me a hard look. "Worst case, it shatters her circle and she's lost to the line."

"What does that mean?" Sean's posture gained an aggressive edge.

"It means... I'd be stuck there, inside the line. Forever. Ley lines are powerful and caustic, and if my circle ruptures, it could just consume me."

Sean shook his head and planted his palms on the table, leaning toward me. "No. No way. You're not doing this. We'll find some other way."

"Sean, if you've got another idea I'm all ears, but the full moon crests in about two hours. There is no other way." He looked down, his fingers digging into the wood. My voice was quiet but firm when I said, "I can't let my brother die."

"And what if you die? How does that help him?" he spat.

"I'll be really, really careful." I swear to God, I wasn't trying to egg him on. Sometimes my mouth just says things.

Anger tightened his face. He looked at Ethan. "Is there a way to watch her? Pull her back before she gets lost?"

Ethan let out a puff of exasperated air and shrugged. "Not really."

Sean glared at me. "The instant it starts to go pear-shaped, you pull out and we find another way. Got it?"

"Yes, dear."

"Dammit, Rachel, this isn't a joke!"

"I'm not laughing." I stood up and faced him. "I know this plan has got too many holes and not enough safety nets. But Danny is out there." I took a breath, trying to convince my stomach not to crawl out through my throat. "And if this ritual goes down, a monster like we've never seen is going to be unleashed on the city and a whole lot of innocent people are going to die. I can do something about that. That's the only thing that matters. You guys have just got to trust me."

I didn't exactly get a resounding cheer of support.

While I was packing up my gear, my phone rang. I looked at the screen--my dad. I silenced the call.

It didn't deter him.

"You going to get that?" Sean asked after I silenced the phone for the third time.

I shot him a withering look and then typed out a text message.

Me: Can't talk

Dad: Rachel what happened? Masterson is in the hospital and he said you put him there.

Me: Long story. Don't wanna get you guys in trouble. I've got a plan, we're going for Danny. Call you later.

I put the phone on Do Not Disturb and shoved it in my pocket.

A little while later, we rolled up to an empty gravel parking lot inside the Rocky Mountain Arsenal National Wildlife Refuge. Just off of I-70, it was close enough to the line for me to access it, but more secluded than the parking lot I'd used earlier. I didn't exactly know what was going to happen, and I didn't want to risk prying eyes.

We walked into the trees and Sean caught my arm, pulling me back from the others.

"Tell me the truth. Will this work?" he asked.

"Honestly? I don't know. But I have to try." The more I used the lines, the more I risked further corruption. The power would scour my soul until nothing was left. I remembered how adamant Sean had been that I wasn't evil. I hoped he was right. I was banking an awful lot on that.

"Look, I have to say something. I was wrong--about witches, about you. But you're keeping secrets. I know it. You're not being honest like you promised, and all of this, walking through invisible lines, damn near teleportation... you're sort of wrecking my world view here."

I stared down at my boots. "Sorry."

He squeezed my shoulder and affection warmed his eyes. "I know you got your reasons. It goes against every instinct I have to trust you, but I'm doing it. It's just taking my brain a while to wrap around it all." He snorted. "Never thought I'd wish for just a good ol' regular demon hunt."

"Welcome to a brave new world, Horatio."

Sean huffed. "'A mote it is to trouble the mind's eye. In the most high and palmy state of Rome, a little ere the mightiest Julius fell, the graves stood tenantless and the sheeted dead did squeak and gibber in the Roman streets. Disasters in the sun; and the moist star, upon whose influence Neptune's empire stands, was sick almost to doomsday with eclipse.'"

I stared at him. "Uh, what?"

"It's Horatio's comment on the ghost. About how it nags at him, and it's like the omens before Caesar's death in Rome. Kind of how I feel right now." He noticed my shock and smirked. "You're not the only one with a book collection, sweetheart."

"It's not that. Just, um... I never actually read Hamlet," I admitted. "But don't worry, I don't intend to fall on my sword."

"You better not. I've got to have a chance to get you cultured."

I smiled and we caught up with the others. The line pulsed nearby, its energy brushing against my mind like a lover's touch. I took a deep breath and turned to face the guys. "Alright, let's do this."

Ethan handed me a copper bowl. "It's ready to go. Just needs your blood and fire." He looked deeply unhappy about this, and I couldn't say I blamed him.

"Remember, anything happens, you come out," Sean said.

I rolled my eyes and nodded.

Before I lost my courage, I turned my back on them and opened my second sight. A smaller branch of the line hummed and crackled in front of me, winding through the world in a rapid current. My red-orange circle snapped into place and I walked forward.

I sank into it with a little slurp of resistance, then the line surrounded me.

Blue-white light churned in eddies and swirls. I held that place in my mind--Rocky Mountain Arsenal, Ethan, Sean, Luke, the way the trees looked, the way the air smelled--and sat down cross-legged. It was sort of like sitting in a river. The line pulled at me, wanting to move. I pierced my finger and squeezed out a few drops of blood into the bowl, then set the spell on fire.

My tracking spell, using the last remnants of my brother's hair. If this didn't work, we were screwed.

Smoke wreathed my head and I inhaled deeply. I opened my circle a minuscule amount, creating a passageway between the spell and the line. My mind balanced on the knife's edge of following the spell and directing the line.

A force tugged at me, willing me to let go. I drifted for a minute, forgetting why I was here, not caring about anything except the incredible energy around me. This was life. The lines were the very heartbeat of the world, infusing all things. It begged me to become part of it, to disappear...

No. Focus.

I had a purpose here. I pulled my consciousness back together and built a barrier to separate my two locations. One side held the Callahans and Ethan there in that forest, and the other held Danny. He was my purpose. I had to find him. It was sort of like juggling torches in one hand and swords in the other. For a while, I groped about, unable to latch onto the spell. It slipped through my fingers like the finest sand.

Concentrate, Rachel.

My brother. His smell, sharp and pure, like saltwater. The time he'd taken the blame for a broken window because I was so scared of getting in trouble. His smile--that kind smile that put everyone at ease. The ley energy licked at the spell and suddenly I was flying forward.

Images spun in a dizzying array. Vertigo seized me, and my stomach roiled. The spell catapulted me toward a massive black wall--the demon's ward. I reeled, afraid of the impact, but the line took a dive and burrowed beneath it. The ward, the construct of a demon, meant nothing to the line. It was ancient, it was permanent, it was supreme.

The line careened to the right and streaked upward, and suddenly I was looking at Danny. He sat on a dirty floor, his back against a concrete wall and his knees pulled to his chest. His shirt was torn and blood stained his face. My heart lurched and I frantically looked around for Marcus, but I couldn't see him. Danny sat in an oval of crisp detail, but everything around him smeared into grey. It was as if the spell would only show me my brother and nothing else.

The line pulled, wanting to carry me on from this place. Cracks splintered across my circle, the line forcing its way in through the thin membrane that was the only thing separating me from disintegration. I screamed noiselessly, clawing against the line to stay with Danny.

My concentration slipped and the line invaded my mind. Scorching heat consumed my skull and for a second I forgot about everything but sheer blind panic. The images of Danny and the wildlife refuge disappeared. It felt like my head was being cleaved in two.

Focus, Rachel. Focus, focus, focus. Your life literally depends on it, you stubborn pain in the ass. Focus.

I was coming apart at a molecular level. The ley energy seeped into my circle, lassoing my cells. It wanted me to be a part of it forever, to become a part of everything and nothing, like freaking Brahman. I sort of liked being corporeal.

I strained against the pressure of the line, trying to pull myself back together. It was like trying to catch smoke--except the smoke was my goddamn consciousness and if I didn't get a hold of it I was going to be nothing more than stardust in a very literal sense. I flailed, and dimly registered my leg colliding with the copper bowl in front of me.

Fuck, this was a terrible idea. What the hell had I been thinking?

I squeezed my eyes shut and tried to steady my mind. The first image that surfaced in my struggling consciousness was Sean. Those summer-grass eyes. The way they crinkled at the corners when he smiled.

Suddenly, something gripped me and yanked me backward. Light spun around me and I had the distinct sensation of being sucked through a hose that was several sizes too small.

Burning pain, an intense *whoomp* against my entire body, and then I was laying flat on my stomach on the forest floor. My lungs made valiant efforts at gulping in air, but all the came out was a strangled cough. I wasn't entirely sure I remembered how to breathe.

"Rachel!" Strong hands lifted me upright and cradled me against someone's chest. The world spun around me like the devil's own carousel. I dry heaved and my vision greyed.

"Breathe, baby, just breathe," a voice whispered in my ear. I clung to the arms that held me, felt their warmth. They were real. The rock jamming into my left calf, that was real. My trembling body, that was real. I sucked in a deep breath and the scent of gun oil and soap greeted me. Sean.

"I know where they are," I panted.

It took me what felt like forever to recover. Sean half carried me back to the truck while I forced my autonomic nervous system to reboot.

"Don't ever do that again," he said. "I don't care what's at stake."

I gave him a lopsided, weary smile. "I don't plan on it." Everything felt hypersensitive--my skin, my eyes, my ears. Like my senses had been jacked up to eleven.

"What was it like?" he asked after a moment.

"Like the worst acid trip ever. Terrifying. Beautiful." I tipped my head toward Ethan. "Follow us. I don't know how many hostages Wilkes has, but we better be prepared."

He nodded. "Where're we going?"

"South."

TWENTY-ONE

Tracking spells gave me a location, not so much directions. This one in particular, I just sort of knew the way to go. The F350 snaked its way southeast, toward Aurora and into an area that was typically known for crack-heads and hookers.

"Right, here!" I cried. Sean whipped the big truck around a corner, swearing under his breath. I wasn't able to give a lot of notice for the turns. We would be travelling down a road and then a compulsion would strike, telling me where to go. Evidently, ley lines also cared little for logical directions, as we'd made several contradicting turns.

"This psychic GPS stuff sucks," Sean grumbled.

I looked at my watch for the seven thousandth time since leaving the wildlife refuge. Eight-ten. We were cutting this extremely close. Another feeling gripped my stomach and I ordered him to make a left. Ethan's headlights flashed as he followed us through the turn.

"Son of a bitch!" I doubled over and pain lanced through my head, flashing images of Danny, crouched on a cement floor and shouting.

"What? What's happening?" Sean demanded. He watched

me in the rearview mirror as Luke turned around and gripped my shoulder.

"We're close," I wheezed, pressing my hands to my face. This psychic GPS stuff definitely sucked. We rolled down a dimly lit street bordered by derelict buildings. "Stop here!"

The pain washed through me, leaving me reeling in its wake. We parked in front of an abandoned building somewhere between the size of a warehouse and a big damn store. Graffiti decorated cracked stucco walls and broken windows gaped overhead. A chain-link fence held back a courtyard that was two steps shy of a jungle. Faded letters proclaimed something about ladies' garments.

"This is it?" Luke asked, looking up at the building. Ethan pulled in behind us as Sean cut the engine.

"Yeah, they're here," I said. We exited the car and Ethan walked over to join us.

"Wards?" Luke asked, looking at me. I shook my head. The fence seemed to be the property's greatest defense.

Sean frowned. "This seem a little too easy to anyone else?"

"He wants me here," I said, checking my Sig's magazine and sliding it back into place.

"Great, and we're playing right into his hands." Luke shook his head.

"Okay, we go in, smoke Wilkes, get the supes, get out. Keep moving, don't get bogged down," Sean said as he chambered rounds into a tactical pump-action shotgun.

"I know," I said.

"Use rock salt rounds on the *bakemono* if all else fails, it might slow them down."

I tossed him a withering look. "I know. This is not my first rodeo, sweetheart."

Sean caught himself and cleared his throat sheepishly. "Right. Okay. Let's go."

The rusted hinge on the gate groaned as I pushed it open. We stole along the walk, Sean behind me, followed by Luke and Ethan. The door was barely shut, let alone locked. The son of a bitch was that arrogant.

I crept through the dim interior, moving as quickly as I dared. Dressmakers' dolls created unnerving silhouettes, and shadows warped and moved, shaped by the glow filtering in from streetlights outside. A cheaply made counter ran along one wall, its glass front busted out.

"Basement," I breathed, following a twinge in my gut. Sean nodded. We stole down the stairs, weapons ready. I also carried the iron spike and one *ofuda* in my pocket, courtesy of Ethan.

The unfinished basement ran the full length of the building. Studs marked the roughed-in walls and decades of detritus covered the concrete floor. Shelving, once likely used for inventory, ran along the wall opposite the stairs. Used needles and ratty blankets decorated a corner to my left. To my right, the room stretched into pits of deep black, punctuated by shafts of light filtered through small, dirty windows.

I moved toward the shadows.

We'd gone about ten feet when it all went to hell. I didn't even get a chance to call out before something seized me by the shoulder and flung me across the room. I collided hard with the floor, knocking the air from my lungs in an abrupt whoosh. My Sig bounced from my hand.

Snarls and yelps echoed around the room. Light suddenly flooded the basement, rendering me momentarily blind.

"Rachel!" Sean called. I whipped around. Shadowfang's twin brother launched at Sean, swiping sharp talons at his neck. He raised his shotgun and fired. The *bakemono* staggered, shaken by the purifying essence of the rock salt.

The effect didn't last long. The thing was up and snarling again before Sean had time to work the action on his shotgun. I saw three more of the damned things before my own personal *bakemono* ripped me away. Its slavering jaws shook me viciously, and I reacted the best way I knew how: I punched it square in the nose. I figured if it worked on Jaws, it'd work on Shadowfang.

It chuffed and jerked me around again. I heard the guys shouting, grunting, moaning. I couldn't separate their voices. I prayed I heard three of them.

I dug my heels into the floor, but my boots scraped uselessly along the cement. It whipped its head and slammed me into a wall. Several stitches burst along my back. I fell to trembling hands and knees. The world careened drunkenly around me. I shook my head and used the wall to claw my way upright. *Ofuda, ofuda, ofuda,* I needed the goddamn *ofuda.*

I jammed my hand in my pocket and my fingers closed around the smooth paper just as the *bakemono* launched toward me. I dove to the right. The monster folded in on itself in a way that nothing natural ever could. Its feet hit the wall and catapulted itself toward me.

Instinct took over and I hit the deck. I swear to God I could feel the breeze as the thing swiped at me with those goddamn claws. Shadowfang pivoted on its hind legs, snarling. I got a really good view of rows of serrated teeth and ropes of drool. Believe me, that kind of thing is best seen from a distance.

I sprang to my feet, snatching the iron spike out of my belt as it pounced. It happened so fast that if I'd actually tried to do it, I probably would have failed, but somehow I managed to swipe out with the *ofuda* just as Shadowfang leapt forward. The paper connected with the *bakemono's* head with a hiss.

The monster howled. I drove the iron spike between its ribs and it began to disintegrate.

I whipped around, panting. Sean, Luke, and Ethan each wrestled with a *bakemono* of their very own. A fourth creature flaked away into ash.

I bolted toward them. An arm wrapped around my neck, crushing my windpipe and lifting me off my feet. The iron spike clattered to the ground as survival instinct took over and I clawed at the arm. I couldn't get purchase with my feet for a hip throw. Supernatural strength slammed me face first against the wall. I was barely able to prevent my head from crashing into the cement blocks.

Cold steel pricked my side. That tends to make you stop struggling. "Hello, dollface," Finn purred in my ear.

"Look at you!" A dude in a t-shirt, hoodie, and jeans jogged over, his eyes alight with amusement, like he was watching a goddamn boxing match. His voice and body language were so different from the first time I'd seen him, it took me a full minute to recognize who he was.

Wilkes.

The demon turned me around to fully face him. Gone was the meek, cowering guy who stuttered and fidgeted and gave Hughes his own chair. The man in front of me now was confident, cool, almost casual. He looked more like the Jason Wilkes I remembered from Pueblo.

"Do you like my work?" Wilkes asked. He stepped aside and swept out his hand. At the far end of the basement, he'd erected a crude altar out of cinderblocks and a replacement door, the kind you buy at Home Depot. A young man, maybe twenty, lay in a boneless heap atop it, arms and legs tied to the cinderblocks. He made weak, pitiful noises, and dried blood and bruises mottled his face.

An iron cage sat against the wall near the altar, its bars glinting strangely in the light. Pieces slid into place in my brain. The cage must be coated in silver. Wilkes had made a custom prison for Jeff.

Next to the silver-and-steel box, a middle-aged man cowered on the floor, his hands and feet bound. Dirt smeared his face and a cut oozed from his head. Marcus Rodriguez. He was filthy, hair matted, skin decorated with marks running from deep purplish-black to a sickly yellow.

Beside him, his face so battered his eyes could barely

open, was Danny. He shifted against the iron cuffs locked around his wrists and feebly shook his head, as if to say I shouldn't be there.

Defiance reared inside me.

I swept my foot back, attempting to hook it around Finn's ankle. He moved with inhuman speed and sidestepped the attack.

I slammed an elbow back at him. He shoved the knife into my side--not deep enough to cause serious damage, but enough to get my attention. I groaned and the pressure on my neck increased. Warm liquid and burning pain spread across my ribs as I gasped for air.

Wilkes smiled. "Just look at you. You had to know you'd be outmatched but you still came. Your friends are caught, you're hurt, and you're still fighting. Freaking incredible."

The demon shoved me forward so that I stood perhaps five feet from Marcus and my brother. I wrenched at the arm around my neck, but it didn't budge.

"What, no clever reply?" Wilkes asked.

"Go fuck yourself," I snarled.

He clucked his tongue at me, apparently unappreciative of my dazzling wit. "But hey, Rachel, I got a question." Wilkes's expression turned violent and cold, all trace of amusement gone. "Did you fight this hard to save my wife?"

"Tried... too late," I gasped, the words difficult to get out around the chokehold on my throat.

"I know. That's what you said--did you remember, when I sent the flowers? 'You should know I did everything I could-- it was just too late.'" He pushed his hands into the pockets of his sweatshirt and walked closer. "But it wasn't too late. You let her be targeted."

"We...couldn't find..." Wilkes jerked his chin at my one-man iron maiden and sweet, rank-smelling air rushed into my lungs. I coughed and then continued, "We couldn't find the deal witch. We tried to save her, man."

"Bullshit!" His eyes blazed, but not with madness. It was hatred, and it was all for me. Awesome. "You used her as bait. You could have warned us."

"Would you have believed me?" I spat, but my gut squirmed. Wilkes wasn't wrong. We'd made the choice to try to snare the witch by using Bonnie. It was fucking shameful.

He dropped his head and chuckled. My insides turned to ice. Lesson I learned a long time ago--it's never good when they laugh really quiet like that. "You know, at first I blamed you. I'm good with computers, and after Bonnie died, when I saw her..." If I hadn't been pissed off and bleeding, I might have felt sorry for the guy. The spell that hit Bonnie Wilkes had been a nasty piece of work. Her skin had boiled from the inside out. Her eyes ruptured. Her organs were liquefied. The very best thing that could be said about it was that she'd died quickly. It's what happens when a jealous nutbag learns forbidden magic.

Wilkes looked up at me, his eyes hard. "I knew you weren't what you said. People don't just die like that. So I did research. I talked to every crackpot and conspiracy theorist on the Front Range. You know what I found?"

"A lot of bullshit about UFOs and haunted highways?"

"A shadow government. People with remarkable abilities. You know, I thought I was losing my mind at first. I mean, it was like the damn X-Men. But a few clever algorithms, a few programs looking for very specific criteria, and I hit the jack-pot. Secure server. High Council of Witches."

Son of a fucking bitch. He'd hacked our systems. That he'd even *found* our systems said a lot about his skill. Judging by the way he handled spells, I'd bet Wilkes had some degree of natural magic, and with his talent for computers, the Council could have used him. Too bad he'd gone all American Psycho.

"What do you want me to say? None of this brings Bonnie back."

"Don't say her name!" His eyes grew over-bright and his hands trembled. "She died because I didn't know what I know now. I didn't know about wards, or hexes, or concealing magic. That's when I realized, the problem wasn't you. The problem is that regular people like my wife have no protection from monsters like you."

"I'm not the one carving up innocent people, buddy."

"Innocent?" He gave a bark of bitter laughter. "They're not innocent. They're invaders. Sleeper cells. Bin Ladens with fairy dust."

"Jason, listen to me, you're wrong, man. Sadie was a good girl. She had a family. So did Jeff. What you're doing here, it's evil. And it's this fucking demon you're working with. He's twisted your mind." Finn chuckled, his lips brushing against my ear. I swallowed bile. "Did he promise you revenge?"

"Oh, this is so far beyond revenge, Rachel." Wilkes smiled. It would have been more comforting if he'd drawn a gun on me. "This is about justice. With my army, I'm going to make the world safe from your kind."

"Wow, okay. Guess it's good to have goals, even if they're fucking psychotic."

"I know. You're frustrated. You've worked so hard and I have to say, you came pretty close. But you never really stood a chance." Wilkes turned his back on me and walked toward the altar.

"You know, for someone who hates the supernatural so much, you've certainly been slinging a lot of magic," I said, playing for time. If he started that ritual while we were still monster bait, Danny and Marcus were dead and the entire city was screwed. "What's the matter—can't get it up without help from a demon?"

Wilkes looked down at the boy on the altar. A silver knife glinted in his hand. "I tried to do it by myself, but I wasn't strong enough. I needed Finn." He studied the kid like he was trying to decide where to cut. "You, all of you witches, werewolves, shapeshifters, vampires, and God knows what else. You pretend like you belong with us, but you don't. This isn't your world. It's ours."

I rolled my eyes. I fucking hate zealots. "Careful, slick. You're dealing with shit above your pay grade. This demon tell you the price for all this? That you'll go to hell?"

"It's worth it." Wilkes met my eyes and the look he gave me sent tremors of fear snaking up my spine. He was right-- he wasn't in this for simple revenge. He was a deadly combination of grief, conviction, and self-righteousness, and he was playing for keeps. "No one else will suffer what I did. And when I'm done, when we're safe, I'll bring Bonnie back."

"Wilkes, no!" I shouted, and thrashed against Finn. "What you bring back won't be her!" Necromancy, out of all forbidden magic, scared the ever-loving shit out of me. It was no joke to say it was the match on the kindling of the goddamn zombie apocalypse.

Wilkes smiled again, and this time it was actually kind of sad. "So now you care? Sorry, Rachel. Too late." He waved a hand and Finn swung me around. Ethan slumped against the base of the stairs, unmoving. Two *bakemono* remained, one each pinning Luke and Sean to the ground. Sean's shotgun lay a few feet beyond his grasp. My gun was off to my right. If I could get free, I could maybe reach it in one good dive.

Wilkes murmured something in another language and the *bakemono* holding Sean tore into his shoulder. Flesh shredded in a sickeningly wet rip and Sean bellowed.

"Stop it!" I screamed. Shadowfang raised its head, blood dripping from its jaws. They were only feet away and I was powerless to help them.

"You're wrong, you know," Wilkes said from behind me. "I traded my soul for the ability to bring Bonnie back. But for this, for my army? I got a hell of a deal. All Finn wanted was you."

"Really, I think I'm getting the deal here," Finn said. His

breath was hot on my face. "You have no idea the fun we're going to have with you."

"You want me, you got me. Just let these people go," I said, my heart hammering in my throat. Sean moved his head and groaned, and a wave of relief washed through me. He was alive, for the moment. "They're human, you dick!" I shouted at Wilkes.

"They made their choice when they sided with you," Wilkes said. I could hear him moving things around on the altar. We had to be close to the full moon. I needed to think of something fast.

"I've got an interest in these two choir boys too," Finn said. "They tell you about their secret churchy club, hmm? Maybe let it slip one night?" He released my throat and grabbed my hair, yanking my head backwards. The hand with the knife slid up my side, his thumb brushing over my breast. I jerked, and the knife bit into my skin.

"Leave her alone, you son of a bitch!" Sean yelled.

Finn laughed. "Man, if the good ol' Pope could see you now. One of his boys in blue--or white, I guess--defending a witch. What is the world coming to?"

Sean roared and fought savagely to free himself from the *bakemono*, but he may as well have been wrestling with a dump truck.

"Enough," Wilkes said. "We need to get on with it. Keep her under control until I finish the ritual." The demon turned me around again so that I could watch Wilkes work. The young man, who I guessed to be Thomas Springer, began to whimper and plead.

"Take a good look, witch," Finn whispered, malice dripping from his words. "This is just previews. We've got a whole host of party favors lined up for you." He bit my earlobe--and not a love tap, either. Jackass made me bleed. "Can't wait to hear you scream, Rachel. We're not really sure how it works, but we sure are going to have fun figuring it out."

"I love it when you talk dirty to me," I said, a few hairs ripping out of my scalp as I jerked against his hold. The deeper in it I was, the more my mouth ran. It's a gift.

Think, Rachel. You don't have to stop Wilkes completely, just disrupt the ritual. Maybe if you stare really hard, you'll develop the laser eyes. I huffed out a breath, trying to slow the jackhammering of my heart. Wilkes began to chant. He laid a hand on Thomas's head and the kid cried out in pain.

Fuck it.

I reached for the line, opening myself fully to it. I had no idea if the demon could feel me tapping it, so I drew in the ley energy as fast as I could. My skin burned and my lungs ached and my vision blurred, but the power invigorated me like a tonic. The demon tightened his grasp on me.

"What are you doing?" Alarm colored his voice. He felt the power, but he didn't know what it was. I smirked. Then I sank my hand into his abdomen.

"Foreplay." I unleashed the ley energy in one solid blast, driving it deep into his gut. He howled and flung me away. I hit the ground in an ungraceful heap, rolling over a couple times before skidding to a stop.

The iron spike was about six inches from my hand. Jenga.

I grabbed it and scrambled to my feet, looking back long enough to see Finn grabbing his head. Wilkes caught my eye but kept chanting. He was banking on finishing the ritual before I could reach him.

Sean's shotgun lay near my feet. I picked it up and emptied it into the *bakemono* holding him. The force drove it backwards and Sean wrenched free from its grasp. I tossed him the spike. He caught it and spun, slapping an *ofuda* onto the creature's head and ramming the spike into its chest. Movement caught my eye and I turned just as the *bakemono* holding Luke launched toward Sean. Its liquid shadow hide shimmered. Luke grabbed his own shotgun from the ground and fired.

The salt hit the creature's chest and rolled right off it.

Shit, it was transitioning into its permanent form.

"Go!" Sean yelled, backing up as he pulled out his Colt. "Stop the ritual!" He fired uselessly at the advancing monster. I didn't have time to think.

I pulled ley energy to me once more and flicked my wrist. The spell sailed across the room, a shock wave of concussive force. It hit Wilkes square in the chest.

He slammed into the wall behind him. Surprise lit up his face. He staggered for a moment, then skittered away from the altar, arms raised over his head. I flung another spell and his head snapped back as if punched.

"Please," he said. We locked eyes and for one instant, I saw the man behind the grief and rage, the one who had lost his wife in horrific fashion. But then I saw Jeff's body, and Sadie's, and Leon's. The cruelty inflicted upon them. The torment written across Marcus and my brother.

As a deputy, I was supposed to make my best effort to take criminals alive.

But tonight, I wasn't a deputy, and I wasn't here for justice. I was a sister, and I came for vengeance.

"No," I said. I made a complicated little motion with my hand and threw another spell at him. It left my fingers lethal and hot, backed by the power of the line surging through me. A snarl curled my lip.

If you've never smelled burning flesh, it sort of reminds you of meat cooking. It's a really weird association, because it almost makes you hungry, but then you remember what you're smelling is *human*. That mouth-watering, stomach-churning scent filled the air as my spell punched a hole clean through Wilkes, like I'd skewered him on an invisible beam. He didn't even bleed--the wound cauterized behind it, but I'd disintegrated his heart. His mouth dropped open and he scrabbled at his charred shirt, as if he could fix it, then he dropped to his knees. A cold, vicious smile spread across my face.

Little gurgling noises caught my attention and I looked back at the altar. The kid. He wasn't moving. I shook my head as if coming out of a daze and bolted toward him.

I'd taken four steps when a force knocked me into the wall. Lights popped in front of my eyes and I crumpled to the ground. Finn stood over me. His eyes burned with fury and blood dripped from his mouth. He reached down and grabbed my throat, choking me as he lifted me off my feet.

"Cute, witch. Let's see you do that now." Fetid, hot magic swarmed over me like horseflies and I frantically activated my shield. It was about as effective as defending myself with Saran wrap--Finn's power crashed against my shield and toppled it. I couldn't breathe. The demon's power smothered me, pressing me into the wall with agonizing force. One of my ribs cracked. I started to lose consciousness.

I glanced down just as Sean grabbed the demon from behind. The demon dropped me and I crashed unceremoniously to the ground. Sean swiped at Finn with a knife like the one I'd seen Luke use at the warehouse. The demon snarled and raised an arm.

The blade caught him just below the elbow. An angry hiss erupted from the wound. It glowed the color of molten steel and the flesh blackened and crumbled to ash.

Finn stared at Sean for one whole second before the hunter drove the knife toward his throat. I'll give the demon one thing--he had a keen sense of self-preservation. He vanished, leaving only the bitter smell of brimstone in his wake. Sean stared at the spot where the demon had been with disgust and more than a little disappointment. He bent down and slid an arm around me, lifting me to my feet.

"For once, I saved your ass," he said roughly, but I wasn't really listening. I pushed myself away from him and staggered toward the altar. Thomas wasn't moving.

"No, no, no," I moaned, and desperately pressed my fingers to his neck. Nothing. I began performing CPR, willing him to live. I pumped his chest. His body sagged beneath my hands, limp and broken.

"Rachel." Sean gently gripped my arms. "Rachel, stop. He's gone."

"That son of a bitch." My voice trembled as I let Sean pull me away from the boy. "He was just a kid."

"What happened?" Luke asked. His head sported a nasty gash and blood stained his left sleeve. He limped over to us and looked down at Thomas. "Didn't you kill Wilkes before he finished the ritual?"

"I did," I said. "He's just... dead."

Tears stung my eyes and it felt like my limbs weighed ten thousand pounds as I stumbled over to Danny. Luke picked the locks and I flung the cuffs away as if I thought they might come to life and magically close back around us.

Danny put a battered arm around my neck and pulled me to him in a surprisingly strong hug. "Stupid," he rasped. "Stupid for you to come."

"I know," I said. Tears leaking out onto his chest and I sniffed, clutching at his shoulders. "Never said I was smart."

He wheezed in what might have been a laugh, then Sean came over and helped lift my brother to his feet. The Callahans had freed Marcus and he shuffled over, grabbing my arm. Burns lined his wrists from the cold iron cuffs that had bound him.

"Thank you," he said hoarsely "Thank you I thought I was going to die. Thank you."

I just nodded.

We made our way out of the basement, Luke carrying a semi-conscious Ethan. Sean supported Danny and I kept a wary hand on Marcus's back. As soon as we were clear of the scene, I'd call Green to come collect Wilkes and Thomas. Sooner or later, I'd have to tell the Council, too.

"You need a ride to the hospital?" Sean asked Marcus as we hit the street.

"No. My kind--well, we tend to confuse doctors. I'll be fine." He looked at me and tipped his head toward Danny. "He's your brother, yes?"

I nodded.

"He was right--it was stupid, what you did. And brave. And right." Marcus put a hand on my shoulder and that wild magic, full of ocean and flowers, rolled over me. "*Beannaigh tú leanbh.*"

His eyes flared a totally unnatural electric blue. I felt the pulse of a spell, and with that, Marcus was simply gone.

We loaded Danny into the back of the F350 while Luke drove Ethan's truck. I texted my dad to say we were taking Danny to Swedish Medical Center and stayed silent for a long time, aside from giving directions. Sean didn't try to make conversation. The velvety night sped past my window. Beyond the few of us, no one would ever know what happened tonight. No one would ever know why a young man was killed long before his time, a victim of a war he never knew was raging. No one would know what I did to Wilkes.

I stole glances at Sean. He wasn't treating me any differently. I thought back to Andy Walker, the kid I'd killed in Fort Collins because he'd made a deal with a demon--Finn's first test for me. It seemed like a lifetime ago, back when things made sense and I knew right and wrong. Finn wanted to study my power, but I wondered if his true test were to see what choices I'd make. Demons tempt. They offer the things you don't want to admit you crave. Finn put that up against the lines I never thought I'd cross and I'd barreled right over them.

I let out a strangled bark of laughter.

"What?" Sean asked.

"Nothing." I stared out the window, but my eyes weren't

focused on anything. Minutes ticked by and the silence stretched between us. "I killed him, Sean," I murmured.

"You did what you had to. Trust me, sweetheart—I know it don't sit right, but you did your job."

Right. Because he still thought I was some kind of hunter. He didn't know about our system of justice, the way I'd violated the very laws I'd sworn to uphold. I'd felt vindicated in the moment I'd killed Wilkes. Righteous, even. But deep down I knew it wasn't right. His hands were raised. He was surrendering. If Sean knew that, he wouldn't be defending me.

I knew then what I had to do, and the thought of it made my stomach want to crawl up my throat. I looked at Sean.

I wanted to be saved. I wanted to prove I wasn't evil. There was only one way to do that.

I sent a message to Victor that I'd turn myself in by sundown tomorrow.

TWENTY-TWO

Swedish Medical Center took good care of my brother. Danny looked like nine kinds of shit, but he was awake and talking. At least, that's what my parents told me--I hadn't been back since dropping Danny off the night before. Luke and Ethan bore battle scars of their own, but nothing that would keep them down for long.

Sean and I spent the night at my cabin, where we patched each other up. He suffered some serious damage to his shoulder. I repaired it as best I could, although he still moved it stiffly. I had some gnarly gashes where the *bakemono* bit me, a torn ligament in my arm, and a new scar on my side. We both sported an assortment of other cuts and bruises.

At least my tattoos were undamaged.

The next morning, Sean made me tea and I cooked breakfast. He gave me a knowing look at the way I held my arm close to my body, and promptly took over the cooking.

"I know they're broken, but I'm not wearing a fucking splint," I grumbled.

Sean smirked. "What if I told you it was sexy?"

I rolled my eyes and stomped into the living room,

flopped down on the couch, then grimaced when my side hurt. I still wasn't going to wear a splint.

We lounged together in my living room and watched movies and talked about books. Hours flew like minutes, the sunlight marching across my floor betraying me with every second. No matter how I tried, I just couldn't figure out what to tell Sean. I hated myself for it, but my immediate future was uncertain at best, and I couldn't involve Sean any further. And the way I'd killed Wilkes gnawed at me. He was a murdering psychopath, but everyone deserved a trial. That was the basis of our whole system. It was the reason we looked down on hunters, who didn't give people a chance at redemption.

Redemption. I hoped that would hold true for me.

Sean sat beside me, his arm across the back of the couch. I snuggled against him while flipping through channels on the TV.

Another sincere-but-secretly-giddy reporter stood in front of the Denver Justice Center before the image cut away to footage of a rather familiar warehouse. I caught sight of Green, his hands on his hips and coffee stains on his tie. The reporter cited police sources that called the case some kind of satanic ritual gone wrong, the perpetrator killed by persons unknown. Officials consider the case still open, all information leading to the vigilante's arrest welcome.

I snorted. Maybe the Council hoped that by letting Green close this case, they could buy his complacency. Something told me that Green wasn't going to be that easy to shove in a drawer.

"There has to be something else on," Sean said, making a face.

"Don't you want to be an informed citizen?"

"Sugar, we lived it. I don't need no reporter telling me what happened. Besides, they got it all wrong anyway." He took the remote from my lap and clicked the TV off. "How're you feeling?"

"Peachy."

"No bullshit, Rachel. You doing okay?"

I took a pull from my beer. "I'm okay, Sean. I mean, I feel like a human chewtoy, but I'll live. Danny's okay and bad guy's down, so that's enough for me." I knew what he was really asking. From the moment we met, it'd been crisis after crisis. I'd only ever been real with him while I was half out of my mind with panic. I cleared my throat and stared down at my beer bottle. Awkward, awkward, awkward.

Sean shifted his legs back and forth, drumming his fingers against the back of the couch. I wished we'd left the TV on. "At least I scored one for my man card. Now we're even." He grinned slyly.

"Nope. Still two to one."

"What?"

"I shot the *bakemono* off you. That's two for me, one for you."

"I killed that beast. Call it one and a half."

I laughed, my eyes lingering a little too long on his. Don't torture yourself, Rachel. "What'd you do that demon anyway?"

"Trade secret," he said, winking.

I chuckled half-heartedly. It was getting close to sundown and I sat up, shifting back on the couch to put some distance between us. "Listen, Sean, things have been crazy this past week. And, um, give me a call if you ever need help on a case, or you want to grab a beer or something. But we, uh... we can't--can't do this."

He gave me an unreadable look. "Do what?"

"You know what I'm talking about. This--you and me--it doesn't work. Let's not make it any harder."

"Wow. First time I been shot down before taking off."

I picked at the seam of my jeans. "An ounce of prevention... okay, I don't actually know the rest of that saying, but the point is, I'm just being realistic."

He snorted. "No, you're not. You're deciding how this is going to end before it even starts."

I shot him a sharp look. "Listen, whatever happened between us--it's, like, the result of high stress, right? We don't have to read more into it. Instead of going through three months and then figuring out we don't work, I'm just cutting to the chase."

"What makes you think we don't work?"

"A million things, Sean," I said, sighing. "You don't even know me. I'm grateful for your help and I like you, but it just..." I floundered, waving my hand as I searched for words.

He gave me his sniper stare and I hated it. "Do you like being with me?"

"That doesn't--"

"Just answer the question."

"Yes, okay? But it doesn't matter."

"If I kissed you right now, would you deck me?"

"I--what?" My eyes narrowed like I suspected he was suffering the effects of head trauma. "Sean, come on. You can't honestly think this is not a giant freaking powder keg. You're a hunter. I'm a witch. We don't mix. And more than that, I'm fucked up."

"Everyone's fucked up, sugar." He sat his beer next to mine on the coffee table. "And those are your rules, not mine. I'm willing to try. That's all I'm asking of you."

I froze. A billion crazy, freaked-out thoughts exploded in my brain, and all of them said *run goddammit run*. But the smell of soap and gun oil rolled over me and calmed me down like a frigging sedative. Sean knew I was a witch--knew it, and was still here. Knew I was thirty-nine flavors of damaged, and was still here. Knew I wanted to bolt, and was still here.

But he didn't know what I'd done, or what I still had to do.

"Sean... I..." I dropped my head and tried to ignore the sting in my eyes.

He cupped my chin and lifted my face. "It's not a race, sweetheart. We'll slow down. Go out on that date like I promised."

Goddammit, I couldn't do this. I couldn't look him in the eye and lie, tell him I didn't want to be with him. He smiled at me and his eyes crinkled in the corners the way they did when he was genuinely happy and I was going to fuck it all up.

I swallowed hard against the lump in my throat. "Uh, I have to--there's something I have to do. It's going to take me a while."

"Need help?"

I forced a smile. "Oh, no, no, it's, uh, administrative stuff. CBI. They're, uh, they're sending me to an FBI-run forensics course." I'd attended one last fall, and it popped in my head like a ready-made excuse.

His face fell a little. "How long are you going to be gone?"

"About six weeks." These lies I could tell, because they weren't so opposite of the truth. It wasn't kinder for him. *Coward*, hissed a voice in my head.

"Not too bad. Maybe I'll come visit."

I nodded and smiled while my insides withered. The rotting, sour mess reminded me of what I was about to lose.

Everything had a price.

The sun had just started to touch the mountains when I walked Sean out to his truck.

"I'll call you tomorrow," he said, his hand resting on the door. Lingering. He didn't want to go, and I wanted to melt into the ground.

"Yeah, yeah that'd be good," I said. The words, like my smile, were mechanical.

He took my face in his hands and kissed me, slow, gentle, deep. I didn't hold back. I wanted to savor this.

"Talk to you soon, baby," he murmured. Then he kissed my forehead and climbed into his truck, grinning at me as he fired up the engine. He pulled out of my driveway and disappeared in a cloud of dust.

Goodbye, Sean. I'm sorry.

I closed my eyes and bit my lip, hard. The pain helped me focus. I texted my dad, telling him that it would all be okay. I should've told my family what I planned to do, but I was afraid they'd try to defend me. I remembered how they stood between Victor and me when he'd first revealed my corruption. I wouldn't allow them to go down with me.

My phone rang just as I climbed into my Jeep. My dad.

"Hey," I said.

"Rachel, what's going on? You just left Danny at the hospital, and haven't answ--"

"Dad, it's okay. I--" What could I say? That Victor was right, and I was turning evil? "I talked to Victor, I just have to go down and sort it out with him."

"The arrest warrant's still active."

"Yeah, he said he'd take it down after we talked." I was just lying to everyone today.

"You call me as soon as you're done, y'hear? We're worried about you."

I forced a smile into my voice, even if one wasn't on my face. "I know, Dad. I'll be okay. Tell Mom I love her."

A long moment stretched between us. "Love you too, girl."

I hung up, and all too soon, I was pulling up in front of the Council regional headquarters. Ice slid through my guts.

I sat in my Jeep for a long time, turning the spelled iron bracelet over and over in my hands. I hadn't said goodbye to Luke either. Maybe that was for the best.

Sighing, I walked into the building. Miss Manners wasn't at the desk. It didn't matter--I knew where to go. The small, dark blue-carpeted room with the rows of black metal chairs and two long tables. The one with the symbol of the High Council of Witches molded in silver hanging over the head of a captain.

The courtroom.

Victor, two witches in black tactical gear, and a woman in her fifties, steel-grey curls clinging tightly to her head, huddled around a dais at the end of the room. I recognized the matronly woman as Betsy Walden, another member of the Executive--head of the Research Branch.

They were talking in hushed voices that halted the moment they saw me. I calmly strode up to the long table on the left and laid the spelled iron bracelet on it. Next, I pulled out my Sig with two fingers on the grip, making it patently clear I was drawing to disarm, not to fight. I popped the magazine out and pulled back the slide, then laid the gun and magazine on the table. My CBI badge joined them.

I looked straight at Victor and said, "Let's get this over with."

Victor gave me a grim smile and nodded. "It's very reassuring that you turned yourself in. Betsy and I will take that under advisement."

"Sure you will."

One guard took up position beside the dais, while Betsy and Victor sat down behind it. Trials for Council witches were special. The punishments were worse.

The other guard approached me. "Please extend your right arm and state your true name for the record."

Her fingers curled around my wrist as I said, "Rachel Marie Collins." Magic swept through me and the brand swam to the surface of my skin, still tinted grey. The guard nodded at Victor and Betsy. I was me, free of any influence or spell.

"Rachel Collins, you are here to stand trial on the following charges: gross insubordination, three counts of aggravated assault of a Council deputy, evading arrest, and the practice of illegal magic. How do you plead?" Betsy read the words in a clinical tone that made me flinch.

"Guilty." The word made me feel sick, but I refused to bow my head. I'd acted just like the corrupt witches I took down, but that didn't mean I was going to put on a show for them. I don't do pity-parties.

"We know you bear the mark of corruption. By entering this plea, you are acknowledging that you willingly broke our laws and that, should you prove resistant to rehabilitation, your sentence will be death. Do you understand?"

"Yeah, I do."

Something flashed in those razor-blade eyes of Victor's. "Very well. Do you have anything to say before we pass judgment?"

"Yes, she does." Pasha marched into the courtroom as if she dared someone to tell her she didn't belong. Dark hair swept over her shoulder and a stylish sapphire blouse looked amazing against her rich brown skin.

My jaw dropped open. I was so grateful for her presence I wanted to hug her.

"I'll be speaking for the defense," she said, joining me behind my table.

"You're supposed to be in New Orleans. What are you doing here?" I whispered.

"Saving your ass."

"But—how?"

A small smile crossed her face and made her dark eyes glitter. "Daily briefings."

"Captain Devereaux, this is—well, you can't be here," Victor said.

Pasha looked back at him and raised an eyebrow. "Section 14, Article B of the Codex of Laws and Ordinances states that in the trial of a Council witch accused of forbidden magic, a deputy or captain may present evidence of extenuating circumstances."

"That—that's a technicality," Victor said. "That rule is there for cases where the nature of the magic in question isn't testable."

"That's not written anywhere. And I believe Rachel saving the city counts as extenuating circumstances," Pasha said coolly.

A near hysterical laugh bubbled up in the back of my throat. Victor, taking on Pasha? Oh, this was going to be good.

Victor opened and closed his mouth like a fish gulping for air and looked at Betsy. She shrugged. An ugly flush crept up his neck and he made a fuss of shuffling the papers in front of him. "Fine. Proceed."

"On the first charge, defendant maintains a guilty plea. She defied orders. But we ask for leniency, as she did so under extreme duress. Her brother was in danger," Pasha said.

"Deputy Collins defied orders by taking a case that the Council had denied," Betsy said.

"A minor infraction to save relations between the Platte River Pack and the Council, and one that could be argued falls into her role as pack liaison."

Betsy tipped her head. "But that still does not excuse her actions after not one, but two orders to stand down, going so far as to remove the spelled iron placed for her own safety."

Now it was Pasha's turn to incline her head. "Defense will stipulate, if the justices will agree that mortal danger to a loved one constitutes extreme duress."

Betsy opened her mouth, but Victor cut across her. "Deputy Collins has a record of defiance."

"We request evidence of that accusation if it is to be entered into these proceedings."

I almost choked. Pasha's tone was even and professional, but she'd just given Victor a giant fuck you.

The vice chair scowled. "No... formal disciplinary actions were ever taken."

"Then the Codex states that it cannot be considered in this trial."

Damn, Pash.

"Fine. Justices will grant leniency on the charge of gross insubordination," he said, and I was pretty sure he was grinding his teeth. Apply aloe to the burn, Vic.

"On the second charge, defense pleads guilty to the first count as it pertains to Deputy Brian Masterson."

"And the other two counts?" Betsy asked.

"Not guilty. Justices, we call Deputies Canh Ngyuen and Amanda Parker to present testimony on those charges."

I'll be damned. Sunglasses and Pigtails--or, I guess, Canh and Amanda--strolled up the aisle between the two sections of black metal chairs. They stopped behind the other table and the guard performed the same true name test on them as she'd done on me.

"Deputy Ngyuen, did you and Deputy Parker attempt to apprehend the defendant?" Pasha asked.

"We did," Canh said. He gave me a microscopic smile. "We failed."

"Can you please describe what happened that day?"

"We approached the defendant at her home and informed her of the charges. She declined to come peacefully. Deputy Parker drew her weapon and fired, but the defendant had veiled herself and began running into the woods."

"Did the defendant attack you in retaliation, Deputy Parker?"

"No."

I blinked. What the hell?

"She prevented us from arresting her, but the magic she used..." Amanda shook her head, her eyes on me. "I've never seen control like that. She dropped a tree in front of us and sent up an exothermic spell that could have boiled our skin off, but both my partner and I walked away without a scratch."

Pasha's eyes were on Victor as she asked the deputies, "And why do you think that is?"

"She didn't want to hurt us," Canh said. "She just wanted to get away."

"Captain Devereaux, are you honestly presenting evidence in defense of one charge that proves another charge?" Victor asked incredulously.

"Yes," Pasha said. "Deputy Collins pleads guilty to the charge of evading arrest. But as these deputies just testified, there was no intent to harm."

"Do you believe that?" Betsy asked. "That the defendant truly had no desire to hurt you?"

"Yes ma'am," Canh said, his dark brows disappearing under his bangs. "Her first move was a defensive one, and I think if she'd wanted to, she could've killed us. But she just ran. Trace magic came back clean--nothing illegal."

Amanda nodded and I gave them both a tight smile.

Betsy pursed her lips and looked sideways at Victor. "Agreed. Counts two and three on the indictment are dismissed."

I was breathing hard and my eyes bounced between the justices and Pasha like I was watching a tennis match. Leniency on one charge, and two dismissed. One more to go.

Canh and Amanda tipped their heads at me as they left, and Pasha turned to face the justices. The forbidden magic charge was the most ludicrous, but also the most serious. It was my word against Masterson's, since I highly doubted he took spell samples. They'd just show him to be a big fat liar.

"As to the last charge, the defense calls Reed Nazari, Master of the Denver Camarilla," Pasha said.

"What?" I blurted.

Reed lazily walked up the aisle, hands in his pockets and shirt collar unbuttoned. He wore no tie with his slate blue suit, and winked at me as he took his place at the witness table. Victor turned purple, and Betsy just looked shocked.

Guess they hadn't anticipated this one, but as a signatory to the Walsenburg Treaties, Reed had standing in Council courts. I just had no idea what the hell he was going to say.

"Mr. Nazari, please tell the justices what you know about the events that occurred on the night of July sixteenth," Pasha said.

Reed flashed a wicked smile. "Certainly. One of my subjects was attending to some business of mine in Five Points. As he came out onto Welton, he smelled fresh blood. This subject, he's young, and followed the scent on instinct. He observed Rachel and another witch in quite the brawl."

"Why are we not hearing from this subject, then?" Victor demanded.

"He had jury duty. Wouldn't want us to neglect our civic obligations, would you? It might draw attention," Reed drawled.

"Are you mocking this court?"

"Only mildly." He grinned but his eyes were cold and alien, and his incisors looked a bit too long. "I am Master. My subjects are blood of my blood. What they know, I know, and you will take it as truth."

Victor and Betsy both shrank back. Even my heart hammered a little harder than necessary. Reed knew exactly how disarming his genial attitude was, and how his charm made it all the more terrifying when he vamped out.

Pasha cleared her throat. "Did your subject witness the use of magic?"

Reed looked at her and his eyes were warm and playful again, the predator smile gone. "Yes, he did. By the other witch—I believe you called him Masterson. He was attacking Rachel."

"Did Rachel retaliate?"

He snorted. "She beat the hell out of him."

"Did she use magic?"

"No. As you know, my kind is very sensitive to your spells.

Rachel didn't cast a damn thing, and she certainly didn't use any forbidden magic."

I stared at the justices, my eyes wide, waiting to see if they believed him. Several long moments passed during which Pasha stood resolute, Reed yawned, and I tried not to fidget.

"The justices will accept this testimony. Charge dismissed," Victor finally said.

I exhaled a huge breath and rolled my head back to look at the ceiling. Thank fucking God. Reed gave me a sly smile as he left, which I returned. Cheeky bastard.

"Do you have any further evidence?" Betsy asked.

"No. But I ask the justices to please consider how many lives Rachel saved. Not just her brother's and Marcus Rodriguez's, but the lives of innocent people who would have died by Wilkes's hand. She provided justice for the Platte River Pack—justice that was required in order to maintain our treaty with them. She turned herself in. Corruption or not, she sought to do what was right, even at great risk to herself." Pasha paused and seemed to be choosing her words carefully. "I ask you to consider my personal recommendation as a captain of the High Council that she be granted rehabilitation."

"Thank you, Captain Devereaux," Betsy said. "We will need a moment to confer."

Pasha nodded, and Betsy and Victor left the room. I walked around and collapsed into one of the metal chairs.

"Jesus Christ, that was intense," I said.

"You're not out of the woods yet." She leaned against the table, her arms crossed. "You really got yourself in some shit this time, Rache."

"Yeah, I know. But, well, you know me and my life choices."

She chuckled. "Danny's okay?"

"He will be." I chewed on a hangnail for a minute.

"Where'd you learn all this crap anyway? Section blah blah, article whatever?"

Pasha threw me a withering look. "This is why I'm a captain and you're still getting your ass kicked around town. Did you even read the Codex?"

"Once. Mostly. Well, I intended to read it."

"Lord," she said and rolled her eyes, but a smile played around her mouth.

I toyed with my phone, typed out a few texts to Sean and then deleted them. I had no idea what to say. How could I tell him I was being sentenced by the same organization I couldn't tell him existed?

Texts to my brother met the same fate, but for a different reason. I was ashamed, and I didn't want to drag my family into this. I'd made these choices. Time to pay the piper.

"What happens after?" I asked quietly, and my foot bounced against the chair leg. "The deal witches I bring in alive. What happens after the trial?"

"We'll cross that bridge when we come to it."

"What happens after, Pash?" I needed to hear it. Needed to know.

"They are either deemed eligible for rehabilitation, or... they get put in a cell. To await execution."

Deputies generally didn't know the outcomes of trials. Our job was to bring the perps in. Captains and the Council dealt with the judgments. My chest felt too tight and I looked down at my hands. I worked my ass off to bring them in alive and for what? So the Council could kill them.

Like they could kill me.

"How bad is it?" she asked, and I knew she meant the corruption.

I shrugged. "I don't feel different. I mean, I know what I did to Masterson was wrong. And there's... Pash, I did something, and it—it's not good." I spoke to my hands.

"Rache," she said tiredly, "let's get through this giant crap-heap before you go building a new one, okay?"

"No, I need to say this. I need someone to hear it, and you're the only person I can tell." I stood up and paced, suddenly agitated. I needed to get Wilkes's murder off my conscience.

"Rachel--don't." Her tone drew me up short. Pasha was pleading with me. "I can't know incriminating information about you, not right now. Tell me later, okay?"

I picked at my cuticles. "Even if it might change your recommendation?"

"It won't. Whatever it is, it wasn't because you're evil. It was because you were pissed off and being dumb. Like how you are ninety-eight percent of the time."

My mouth twitched. "Only ninety-eight?"

"Well, you have to sleep sometime."

I grinned and sat back down in my chair. "That was a lie, you know. With Reed. None of his vamps were there."

"Was it?" Pasha raised an eyebrow. "I only know what Reed told me and I can't prove otherwise."

I snorted. "Thanks, Pash. Even if, you know, it doesn't work out. Thanks."

"Yeah, yeah. Don't get all maudlin on me."

The doors swung open and Victor and Betsy walked back up the dais. I scrambled to my feet and stood behind the table. My fingers tapped against my thighs in a frantic, staccato rhythm.

"In light of the evidence presented," Victor said, "we have decided to accept the pleas of the defendant and recommend that she be brought to main headquarters for rehabilitation."

TWENTY-THREE

The hour-and-change trip down to Council HQ outside of Colorado Springs sped by. The building hunkered against the side of a mountain at the end of a winding gravel drive, surrounded by thick pine trees. No matter how terrified I was, I kept my head up. Even when we bypassed the assembly hall--where Council meetings were usually held--and my guards walked me along cold marble hallways to an elevator. One pushed the button for Sub-basement 1. Holding cells.

They showed me to a room that, for a prison cell, was relatively comfortable. A bed was bolted against one wall, a desk against the other. A privacy screen concealed a toilet and a tiny sink. There was a potted geranium on the desk.

The guards ordered me to change into a pair of black scrubs. They took my clothes, my phone, my keys, even my damn ChapStick. I paced the cell and waited. I actually had no idea what went into rehabilitation. All I knew was that the witches who came through it never said anything about it, except that they were grateful for the Council's help. A claim I found dubious to say the least.

Footsteps in the corridor, and I instinctually put my back to the wall. A man melted out of the shadows. Intense blue eyes, khakis and a polo. He looked like a high school gym coach. Whoever he was, I didn't like the way he looked at me, like I was a bug about to be squashed.

"Rachel Collins," he said. "I am here to run a series of tests on you to determine the extent of your corruption. Should you pass, we will begin the rehabilitation process."

"Swell. Can I get a name, Coach?"

He frowned. "You may call me Camael. I am in charge of the Genesis teams."

Holy shit.

"Fantastic." I sniffed and straightened up, cracked my neck side-to-side. "Where do we start?"

DANNY, bloody and lifeless at my feet.

I collapsed to my knees and fought for air. "Danny? Danny, no, no, wake up!"

Camael stood in front of me, his hands clasped behind his back. Danny's blood was all over his shirt and he stood there looking at me like a bored fucking tourist.

My chest heaved. Magic whispered at me to make him pay, to avenge my brother. I squeezed my eyes shut and shook my head.

"Stop," I begged. Pressure squeezed my head, pushed at me to release it with a spell, and I doubled over. "Stop!"

The pressure lifted and I slowly opened my eyes. I was strapped into that goddamned chair. Metal and adorned with restraints, it occupied a windowless grey room. This was where Camael performed his tests.

"Again," he said, and before I had a chance to catch my breath, he plunged me back into that dream-like darkness.

Everything around me seemed real, like the knowledge of where I actually was had somehow been obliterated. I'd never seen magic like this and I had no idea how he was doing it. My personal ward would stand up to the hypnotic voice of a Master but crumbled before the Genesis team leader.

All I knew was that I hated it.

This went on for hours every day. Each time, he dropped me into the middle of a scenario that pushed all of my weak spots.

Pasha, her eyes burned into nothing but gaping black holes. My parents, their ribs protruding from decayed flesh and faces locked in silent screams. Sean, a hole burned into his chest and his summer-grass eyes filmy and vacant.

The worst was when he showed me Wilkes. He made me relive that moment a thousand times, until I finally reigned in my temper enough to let Wilkes live. Of course it was a lie, a fantasy. But I guess it was the conditioning that mattered.

Sometimes he'd flood me with so much power that I thought I was going to explode. He whispered in my ear about how good it must feel, to know I was invincible, that I could strike down all my enemies. He never told me what I was supposed to do, so I was left fumbling for the right answer. Nine times out of ten, I failed. My temper got the better of me and I lashed out, at which point Camael would bring me out of the dream world, tell me I had failed, and start again.

The tests put me through so many magical ringers, I didn't know half of them existed. I felt dismantled, scrubbed raw, eviscerated. Camael was relentless and didn't say more than three words the entire time. After a while, I figured out what was happening. The tests stripped away all my mortal trappings and laid bare my soul. It was an exposed nerve subjected to the equivalent of chemical tests to see where it stopped responding. Where the dead cells were hidden. Then

Camael cut away those necrotic pieces like a surgeon debriding a wound.

Soul magic is serious shit. To handle it that way, pushing and prodding, and to excise only the corrupted pieces--I understood now why Camael ran the Genesis teams. The guy could murder me with his pinky.

The tests left me crying and vomiting in my cell. Fever burned me up and sweat slicked my skin. My heart hurt, and I don't mean the organ.

The tests were nothing compared to the rehabilitation.

For weeks, Camael invaded my head and hammered on every trigger I had. I guess the point was to show me when to stop, that I had limits, but it just felt like torture to me.

"You must have faith," was all he ever said.

I told him what he wanted to hear and kept my magic in check. I learned not to react.

Or maybe I just quit caring.

I earned rewards for good behavior. Cooperating in a session got me a book to read. Five sessions in a row without fighting back got me a phone call with my family. Fifteen sessions and they let them visit. They held them out like a damn carrot dangling from a stick.

I shuffled into a grey windowless room. Everything down here was grey. The upper floors of the Council HQ were flush with comforts and modern technology, rich wood tones and framed photographs of famous places around the world. Here in rehab, they didn't even make an effort. One way or another, witches never stayed here long enough to bother.

It shocked me to see that Danny was fully healed. How long had I been here?

My brother looked just as shocked at the state I was in. He leapt up from his seat at a metal table and wrapped his arms around me. I buried my face in his chest, hardly daring to believe this was real.

"What've they done to you?" he breathed in my ear.

I just clung to him harder.

Swiping at my cheeks, my brother released me to the bone-crushing embrace of my mother. My dad hugged me and kissed my head.

We sat at that little table and I tried to smile, tried to show them I was okay.

"How much longer do you have to be here?" my mom asked.

I shrugged. "Don't know. They didn't tell me."

"This is bullshit," my dad barked. "You more'n proved that you're not corrupted."

"Dad, no. Just—just let it go." I forced a smirk. "You know me. Takes a while for a lesson to sink in."

I guess they didn't buy it, because I learned later that Danny had nearly landed himself in a cell beside me for clocking Victor on their way out. My goody-two-shoes brother. It made me proud.

I thought about Sean a lot. I wondered if he thought about me. Pangs shot through my chest every time I remembered I hadn't called him. I should've texted him when I had the chance, at least to say goodbye.

I sat in the corner of my cell wearing those black scrubs, my hair in a messy ponytail. A spelled iron bracelet hung from my wrist. I never got used to it, always feeling sick and empty. Metal squealed and the door swung open. Victor stood there with Camael at his back.

"I have good news, Rachel," Victor said, favoring me with a genuine smile that still looked rather shark-like. "Double good news, in fact. Your treatment is done. I know it hasn't been easy, but it was worth it—you passed."

"What does that mean?" I asked. My voice sounded empty and flat against the concrete walls.

"It means you get out of here, go back to your home, to your family. You may even go back to work."

"Work?" A harsh, bitter laugh echoed around the cell and

it took me a moment to realize it was coming from me. "Are you fucking kidding? After all this shit, I'm done, Vic. I'm not working for you anymore."

"Rachel." He frowned and looked disappointed. "You know that's not an option."

Right. Lifetime of service or death. That was the oath I'd taken, and I didn't have the skills to transfer to another branch. I was made for only one thing, and we both knew it. I sighed and shoved myself to my feet. At least I'd get to sleep in my own bed tonight. "So now what?"

Camael stepped forward, his hands in the pockets of his Dockers, a bland smile on his face. "Now, Deputy Collins, the hard part begins. You remain on the right side of the law or I will find you."

I snorted. He took my wrist in a surprisingly gentle grip and unlocked the spelled iron bracelet. Magic flooded back into me with a force so strong I saw double, and sagged against the wall.

"Bring her things," Victor said, speaking to someone I couldn't see.

A couple hours later, two witches in black tactical gear dropped me off at my cabin. I wore the same clothes as the day of my trial. My keys, my ChapStick, my phone—I had everything back. The witches said nothing as I climbed out of the blue Expedition. Guess they weren't big on long goodbyes.

I shuffled up my steps, pausing to look over my Jeep. It was clean and looking like the day I left. Danny. I smiled.

Being back home felt surreal. It was like having nothing to look at but grey walls, black scrubs, grey blankets, and my lone pink geranium had made my eyes oversensitive to colors. Everything looked too bright, too sharp. I ran my fingers over the pass-through between my living room and kitchen. No dust. My family had kept my cabin in pristine condition, ready for me to return. It made my chest feel too tight and my eyes burn, and I realized I was smiling.

I took a long shower and crawled into bed. I wasn't tired. I just wanted something that was mine. I opened my laptop and for a minute thought something was wrong with it. The date read October. I knew it had felt cool when we left the HQ, but it was hard to swallow I'd been locked in that goddamned cell for three months.

Eventually, I worked up the courage to charge my phone.

SC: Hey sugar

SC: Tried calling but you didn't answer

SC: Rache you okay?

SC: It's been days Rachel I'm worried about you

SC: CBI says you're on leave what the fuck is going on

On and on the texts went, dozens of them. Multiple voice mails that I couldn't bring myself to listen to. I curled in on myself, too broken down to even cry. What must he think of me? I should've known that he'd come looking when I didn't answer his calls, but if I was honest, I'd never expected to survive my trial. Pasha's intervention had saved my life, but now I had to face what I'd done to Sean.

He knew where I lived, where I worked. How long before I had to face him?

This was stupid. I knew how to avoid hunters, and I'd treat him the same way. There was no reason to find him. There was no explanation I could give that would make up for what I'd done to protect him. I tried telling myself it was better this way, but it didn't cure the emptiness in my chest.

I slept late and went through the motions of getting dressed the next morning. My clothes hung from my body and it was only then that I realized how thin I'd become. My skin was wan and my hair brittle. Good thing I wasn't vain. I made the best of it and drove out to CBI. Work at least gave me something else to think about besides how miserable I was.

"Hey, Rachel, welcome back!" Troy Medina, a vanilla CBI agent, grinned toothily and clapped me on the back. "Good to see you up and walking around."

I smiled and nodded. The Council had given some bull-shit reason for my absence, I was sure. They were thorough that way.

I found my CBI boss, Jamie Wallace, in his office, like no time had passed at all. I knocked on his open door and said, "Um, I'm back." God, that sounded lame.

He looked up and smiled. "I was expecting you tomorrow."

"I been gone long enough, don't you think?"

"Tell me about it. We missed you, Rache. How'd the surgery go?"

I blinked, but quickly recovered. Rehab had improved my ability to lie, at least. "It was surgery--as well as can be expected, I guess."

"Well, we're glad you're back. I'm sure you know about Ethan."

I frowned. I hadn't been allowed contact with anyone except immediate family while in detention, and the Council hadn't exactly debriefed me when I got out. "What about him?"

Jamie looked mildly uncomfortable. "Well, uh, that he got reassigned. To another partner."

"Oh. Yeah, of course." What had I expected? That he would just sit around waiting for me?

Jamie smiled again. "Don't worry, I put in a request for you. Should have your new partner tomorrow at the latest."

Fan-freaking-tastic. That was exactly what I wanted to deal with. I nodded and left his office, wandering across the bullpen to my desk. It was pretty much as I left it--giant stack of unfiled paperwork, some Post-Its, my pictures in their frames. A few get-well cards littered the surface. I shrugged off my jacket and hung it over the back of my chair.

It was like moving through a dream. I didn't know what to do next.

"Well, you survived."

I looked up to see Pasha standing beside me. "Yeah," I said hoarsely. "Why aren't you home in NOLA?" Showing up for my trial was one thing, but I couldn't fathom why she was still here.

"Well, they want a captain to watch you, so I applied for a transfer back to Denver. I figured I'd save everyone else the trauma of working with you, seeing as how I'm used to it." She smiled faintly. Her tone was joking, our usual banter, but she looked at me like she expected me to fall apart any second.

I mustered up a grin. "Oh, get down off the cross. Somebody needs the wood."

A flicker of relief crossed her face. "Welcome back, Rache." She held up a file. "We've got a case in Wheat Ridge. You got all your marbles back together?"

"You say that like they ever were together in the first place." I took the folder and flipped it open. Autopsy reports showed three victims drained of blood. All three had their throats ripped open wide, like some massive animal had mistaken them for a snack.

"You call Reed?" I asked.

"Yeah. Not one of his. And he can't find it."

"Feral then. Should be fun."

"Fun?" Pasha stared at me. "Do you remember what it's like to hunt a feral vamp?"

"Yeah. Ethan and I took one down in June." Holy hell, that was only four months ago, but it felt like eons. I made myself smirk. "Some of us work for a living. Are you going to whine the whole time?"

"Lord," she said, shaking her head. "I knew I was crazy to volunteer for this assignment. You better buy me a lot of alcohol."

I pulled out the incident reports and started to read. Maybe if I kept going through the motions, it would get easier and I'd feel better.

We hung around the office until late that night, easing me back into the swing of things. Mostly, I think she was just keeping me company. I didn't complain.

"Rachel?"

I turned around in shock. Sean stood in the doorway. His mouth was hanging open and his eyebrows drew tightly together over his eyes.

"Sean. How did you--"

"I drive by sometimes. See if your Jeep is here." He shook his head and his chest heaved with labored breaths. "Where the hell were you?"

I got up from my desk and scurried over to him, ushering him out into the hallway for a modicum of privacy. "I'm--I'm so sorry."

"Sorry?" He barked the word at me and I jumped. "Months, Rachel. Months. I was worried sick. I thought you were dead."

"I know, I know, I should've called, I just... I didn't know what to say."

"How about the damn truth! That would've been a good start." He shouted at me, eyes dark with anger and his face sharp and cold. I struggled to breathe. It was like Camael all over again, and for one, horrible second, I thought I was back in that godforsaken chair. I squeezed my eyes shut and bowed my head.

"I'm sorry, I'm sorry, you're right--I lied. I was..." What could I say? "I was--I was in rehab."

Sean scowled. "Right, rehab. Do me a favor, don't treat me like an idiot."

"Magical rehab."

That drew him up short. "What the hell does that mean?"

I shot a glance back toward the unit office and lowered my voice. "For the, uh, corruption. On my soul."

His scowl deepened, but at least he wasn't yelling anymore. "That guy--what was his name? Victor?--he the one who put you there? I told you, Rachel. You're not evil."

I huddled my arms over my chest. The hallway seemed too small, and ringing filled my ears. I shook my head and Sean must've noticed me losing it, because he put a hand on my shoulder.

"What'd they do to you?" he asked softly.

"Nothing. I'm fine. It's okay. Everything's okay now. I'm fine, honestly."

"Sugar..." He pressed his mouth into a thin line. "I know what torture looks like."

"Sean, I'm sorry, I just--I can't do this right now," I said, and my voice shook. The tremors spread to the rest of my body and I tore away from him, backing down the hallway toward the unit office. "I'll call you when I get home, okay? I swear. I just--I can't."

I stumbled back to my desk and panted while I dug my nails into my palms. I wasn't there anymore. They'd let me go. I was okay. I was good. I'd passed.

"Rache? Here," Pasha said gently, and pressed a cool bottle of water into my hand. I drank from it greedily, draining the whole bottle, and rocked my head back. The water helped, and I forced myself to take slow, measured breaths.

"He say something to you?" she asked, and there was a hint of violence in her voice.

"No. No, it--it wasn't him." I exhaled a long breath and finally looked at her. "Have you seen this before?"

She frowned and shook her head. "Witches I sentenced, I didn't know them. Didn't see them after. You want to talk about it?"

"Not right now. I just... I just want to go home."

She followed me to my cabin, I guess to make sure I didn't careen off the side of the road in a fit of vapors, then left me alone. That was the thing about Pasha: she knew when to talk, and when to be quiet.

It was late when I curled up in bed, but I wasn't going to break another promise. I hit Sean's name on my phone and twisted the sheet round and around my finger while I waited for him to answer.

"Hey," he said. "You okay?"

"Yeah, I'm okay. I'm in bed."

"Rache, I'm sorry about earlier. I should have known, the way you looked--I was just so shocked, and then pissed, and I--"

"It's okay, Sean. I deserved it."

"No, you damn well didn't," he snarled, and I didn't think that venom was directed at me.

I smiled a little. "I couldn't call you. They took my phone. And I shouldn't have lied to you about the forensics academy. I wished to God I hadn't."

"Secrets are one thing, Rachel. But you lied to my face. How many times are you going to do that?"

"I know. It was stupid. I just--I didn't expect to make it out."

"What do you mean?"

Dammit. I wished I could tell him. "The corruption. I thought it was going to destroy me." Not a lie, at least.

"You're not corrupted. Whoever did this to you, you need to report their asses. It's wrong, sweetheart."

"Can we talk about something else?" The more he pressed on the rehab, the more my skin crawled and my limbs shook. I wanted to shut those memories away and never think about them again.

"'Course." I heard shuffling, like he was adjusting the phone. "How's your brother?"

"Fine. He healed up fine." I chewed on my lip. Conversation had come so easily before. Why was it so awkward now? "You still working on that Gran Torino?"

"Yeah, just got some parts in actually. Maybe you could come by and work on it with me."

I smiled. "Maybe."

"Maybe I could also take you out to dinner. Would you be okay with that?"

I lay back against my pillows and sighed. "Sean... I don't think I can. I don't want you to take that the wrong way--I thought about you all the time while I was gone." Emotion choked my voice. Camael's images flashed through my mind. "And I think... maybe at another time, it could be really great. But I just can't be with you like that right now. I'm under a microscope at work and I need to get myself put back together first."

"Sugar," he said, and his voice was so warm I wanted to wrap myself in it forever, "that all makes sense. I told you it's not a race. I'll back off and you tell me when you're ready."

"What if I'm never ready?" I asked as a tear slipped down my cheek.

"Then that's okay too."

"You're still my friend?"

"Absolutely. I care about you. That doesn't stop just because we're not dating."

I let out a strangled laugh of relief that mixed with tears and wiped my cheeks. "You are infinitely patient and I have no idea what I did to earn that, but thank you. I could really use a friend right now."

"Whatever you need, I'm there." He sounded so gentle, like he would be happy to stick around and glue my pieces back together. For the first time in months, I felt like I might be okay.

"Okay. Okay," I said, sniffing and blowing out a breath. "Then I want to ask your help with something."

"Name it."

"The demon that got away, Finn. He set this whole thing in motion, and he said they had plans for me." I licked my lips and something surged inside me--resolute, immovable, strong. "I want to track him. I want to know what he was planning."

I could hear the smile in his voice. "When do we start?"

Rachel Collins will return in DON'T FEAR THE DEMON

ACKNOWLEDGMENTS

It took nine years to bring this book from concept to publication, and I received help from an innumerable amount of people along the way. I would be remiss if I didn't send an incredible thank you to Pherin Bailey, who has ridden the Rachel Collins train from the very beginning. She's been my cheerleader, my editor, my beta reader (of all seven million versions), my sounding board, my therapist, my number one fan, and most importantly, my friend. This book simply would not be here without her. In that vein, I'd also like to thank Phoe Boudreau, who read scenes out of sequence to calm my nervous writer brain, who has fiercely supported me and believed in me even when I didn't, who has championed my work to anyone who would listen. (I also owe a shout-out to her mom, Kathy Hamelin, for being my second mom and lifting me up whenever I needed it.) Likewise, Amanda Barrentine and Steph Snow have listened to m talk out plot points, proofread for me, gave me ideas, supported me, and generally made me believe that this book could find success. My critique group, Highlands Ranch Fiction Writers, also deserves my thanks as a whole, with some members in particular: Claire Fishback and Michael Haspil. Both have given me invaluable feedback and Mike was kind enough to give me a blurb. To the entire Pikes Peak Writers community— y'all are the best, and I've never met a more wonderful and supportive group of people. Last but not least, I would be lost without the support of my dad, John Hopkins, and my brother, Joe Hopkins. I'm sure I have left out someone, so please forgive this beleaguered writer brain of mine, and to all the friends and fellow writers who helped me with every part of this project— thank you so much! Rachel thanks you for her existences as well.